Toward the Sunrise

Books by Judith Pella

Beloved Stranger
*The Stonewycke Trilogy**
*The Stonewycke Legacy**
Texas Angel / Heaven's Road

DAUGHTERS OF FORTUNE
Written on the Wind
Somewhere a Song
Toward the Sunrise

RIBBONS OF STEEL†
Distant Dreams
A Hope Beyond
A Promise for Tomorrow

RIBBONS WEST†
Westward the Dream
Separate Roads
Ties That Bind

THE RUSSIANS
*The Crown and the Crucible**
*A House Divided**
*Travail and Triumph**
Heirs of the Motherland
Dawning of Deliverance
White Nights, Red Morning
Passage Into Light

*with Michael Phillips   †with Tracie Peterson

JUDITH PELLA

Toward the Sunrise

BETHANYHOUSE
PUBLISHERS
MINNEAPOLIS, MINNESOTA

Toward the Sunrise
Copyright © 2003
Judith Pella

Cover design by Dan Thornberg
Photos of the soldier of Japanese descent (item number 210-G-151-868) and the
Manzanar Relocation Center (item number WWII #30) are courtesy of the National
Archives.

Published by Bethany House Publishers
11400 Hampshire Avenue South
Bloomington, Minnesota 55438
www.bethanyhouse.com

Bethany House Publishers is a Division of
Baker Book House Company, Grand Rapids, Michigan.

Printed in the United States of America

ISBN 0-7642-2423-9 (Trade Paper)
ISBN 0-7642-2846-3 (Hardcover)
ISBN 0-7642-2845-5 (Large Print)

Library of Congress Cataloging-in-Publication Data

Pella, Judith.
    Toward the sunrise / by Judith Pella.
       p. cm. — (Daughters of fortune ; 3)
    ISBN 0-7642-2423-9 (pbk.)
    ISBN 0-7642-2846-3 (hardcover)
    ISBN 0-7642-2845-5 (large print pbk.)
    1. World War, 1939–1945—Fiction. 2. Americans—Foreign countries—Fiction.
3. Japanese Americans—Evacuation and relocation, 1942–1945—Fiction.
4. Newspaper publishing—Fiction. 5. California—Fiction. 6. Sisters—Fiction.
I. Title II. Series: Pella, Judith. Daughters of fortune ; 3.
    PS3566.E415T69   2003
    813'.54—dc22   2003014253

About the Author

Judith Pella is the author of several historical fiction series, both on her own and in collaboration with Michael Phillips and Tracie Peterson. The extraordinary seven-book series THE RUSSIANS, the first three written with Phillips, showcases her creativity and skill as a historian as well as a fiction writer. A Bachelor of Arts degree in social studies, along with a career in nursing and teaching, lends depth to her storytelling abilities, providing readers with memorable novels in a variety of genres. She and her husband make their home in Oregon.

Visit Judith's Web site:
www.judithpella.com

PART I

"But that's what men are for, isn't it?
To go out and do things while you womenfolk
look after the house."

WALTER PIDGEON
(*Mrs. Miniver*, 1942)

1

Los Angeles, California
June 1942

CECILIA HAYES glanced wistfully at the coupon book in her hand. She knew the rationing of sugar wouldn't hit her home too hard. Even with Jacqueline back with them, they would not be consuming a great deal. Keagan did have a bit of a sweet tooth, but the doctor had instructed him to keep his weight down after his heart attack, so this would be further motivation to help him in that goal.

But talk of rationing other items was growing. Coffee, for example, was soon to be placed on that list. Already, Cecilia, along with their new gardener, Manuel, had planted a "victory garden," clearing away a patch of flowers for the space. She'd never grown vegetables before. It should be fun. And truly, she could hardly complain about the so-called sacrifices of war. She and her family had plenty. She seriously doubted that any Americans were hurting from privation, at least not from want of physical goods.

The hurt was present, though, from the parting of loved ones, the fear, the worry. Even the Hayeses, with their wealth, had not escaped it. And having three daughters hadn't spared them, either.

Cecilia glanced out the French doors of her study, where she sat at the small Chippendale desk. The peaceful beauty of her gardens, with the fragrance of roses drifting in through an open window on a warm June breeze, could not dispel the constant knot in the pit of her stomach. For a mother with only daughters, she had as much to worry her as those with sons in battle. And perhaps she had a son in battle, as well. But she could not think of that. It turned the knot into a quivering mess.

It was bad enough to have one daughter in Russia with Hitler rampaging on all sides. Cameron might not be in the military, but she was a newspaper correspondent, and Cecilia feared her audacious eldest daughter would sniff out all the trouble she could find. She had always been so fearless and assertive that she seldom considered caution, especially if it prevented her from seeking the news. Yet Cameron's most recent letter had indicated she was changing, if not in her essential personality, in ways certainly as vital. Foremost, she said she had made a commitment of faith in God. This thrilled Cecilia to no end, though she knew few details of what had led up to this astounding change in her daughter. The letter had come via the diplomatic pouch, as it was called, and through a friend in the State Department, not by the slower and less reliable regular mail. It appeared to have been written quickly. Well, the how of Cameron's new faith didn't really matter. Cecilia was simply comforted in the fact that Cameron was no longer alone in her life's walk. And it seemed she would need that spiritual presence more than ever, for there were struggles in that walk. She had written of the death of her friend and *Journal* reporter John Shanahan. Her words, though brief, had indicated a deep grief. She had gone on to express hope and joy in her relationship with that Russian doctor, whom she didn't dare name even in a communication sent via the embassy. But Cecilia knew better than anyone that such an entanglement with a Russian could bring little but more grief.

At least communication with Cameron was possible, and Cecilia had some assurance that she was well. There had been no word from Blair since the Japanese had invaded the Philippines. Of course, Blair had always caused fear and worry in Cecilia, so the tense knot that represented her middle daughter was only a bit larger than before. Blair's rebellious past life had carried her to the brink of disaster, but the last place Cecilia would have imagined this daughter to be was in the middle of a war. Blair had always been far more concerned with clothes and hair-dos and such. Cecilia had received only a trickle of news out of the islands, but whatever was happening over there, it had to be a drastic lifestyle change for Blair. If only there was one tiny shred of hope that she was all right, but Keagan said not to expect anything. Since Corregidor fell in May, a mere month after the fall of Bataan, the enemy's hold on the islands was complete, and it would be a miracle for anything more than a bit of news to get past the Japanese blockade. Cecilia certainly believed in miracles, but she also must be pragmatic—or else go crazy. She would not cease in her prayers, but she must prepare herself for a negative answer to those prayers. It might be some time before she would see Blair again, though even with her pragmatism, she would not believe her daughter dead. Most likely she was now a prisoner of the Japanese and would have to sit out the rest of the war in a prison camp. That couldn't be too terrible, could it? At least she would be safe from battles.

Cecilia put away the ration book, rose, and patted the wrinkles from her suit. The clock in the parlor sounded noon with its lovely lilting chimes. Jacqueline would be home from her doctor's appointment soon. There was just time for Cecilia to speak with the cook for a few minutes about dinner. Keagan had called to let her know that Harry Landis, who had recently been promoted to managing editor of the paper, and his wife would be coming to dinner tonight. She hadn't entertained much lately, so she wanted to make it special. The Landises were nice people. She didn't want to think they were the first guests to come to her home since Jacqueline's marriage. She didn't want to think her friends were snubbing her because of that. She didn't *want* to think of many things. Yet it all pressed upon her constantly.

As Cecilia finished conferring with Cook in the kitchen and was heading back toward the front of the house, she heard the front door open and close. She came into the entryway in time to greet Jacqueline.

"Right on time, dear," she said with a smile. But her smile slipped as she realized it might appear as if she had been impatient. "It's just a coincidence I'm meeting you at the door. I don't expect us to run right out." They had plans for lunch and shopping.

"I don't mind if we do," said Jacqueline, laying her pocketbook on the entry table. "I'm starved."

"I should have met you downtown and saved you time."

"I know how you hate to drive, Mom, and it's really not much out of the way. I just can't make it as long between meals as I used to." She grinned, and even if it was a cliché, she really did glow, to Cecilia's eyes at least.

Jacqueline didn't even "show" yet, but there was a vital and joyous demeanor about her that could not be crushed by war or separation or worry. She knew she carried more within her than a child. She carried hope, the kind that would help this country survive anything leveled at it. And maybe the fact that her child was of two races made it an even greater beacon of promise. At least that was what gave Cecilia the courage to accept what was still just a little difficult to imagine. Her daughter was married to a Jap—that is, a Japanese young man. Her first grandchild would probably have slanted eyes, black hair, and a yellow tinge to its skin. But it would be Jacqueline's child, and that's all that mattered.

"Nevertheless," Cecilia said, "feel free to take a few minutes to freshen up. There are a couple of things I need to do in my sitting room. Come there when you are ready." She tried to sound casual, not wishing to pressure her daughter with how much she had been looking forward to this outing. But the truth was she had been anticipating it since they had planned it two days ago. They were going to shop for maternity clothes and a layette. What mother, and soon-to-be grandmother, wouldn't be excited over such an excursion?

"Perhaps while you are waiting you'd like to take a few moments and read the letter from Cameron that came today," Jacqueline said. Cecilia noted there was mail lying with Jacqueline's purse, two letters to be exact. Jacqueline took one of the letters and held it out.

"Why don't we save it and read it together over lunch?" suggested Cecilia.

"A wonderful idea!" Jacqueline tucked Cameron's letter into her handbag. "All right, then. I'll just be a couple of minutes." She took her purse once more from the table, along with the remaining letter, and went upstairs.

Cecilia didn't inquire about that second letter. No doubt it was from Sam. He wrote her nearly every day, and the envelopes were usually quite thick, as was the one in question. Cecilia recalled the letters she used to get from Keagan when he was off in Russia. They were few, very far between, and never more than a few lines each. Apparently Sam had a lot more to say, or perhaps he just had lots of time on his hands there at the internment camp. But Cecilia didn't want to think of where Jacqueline's husband was. She didn't want to visualize the father of Jacqueline's child, Cecilia's grandchild, walled behind barbwire, shuffling idly about with masses of other internees cut off from the flow of their lives for no other reason than the slant of their eyes. She certainly didn't want to picture her daughter in that same place, as she surely would be quite soon now that she had graduated from college. Some couched the necessity of the camps in terms of national security, but Cecilia had met Sam, and he was an upright, honorable man, as American as any white boy lining up at the military induction offices all over the country.

Cecilia gave a frustrated shrug. She was thinking of it in spite of herself. She went to her sitting room to await her daughter.

The temptation to read the letter from Sam the moment she reached her room overwhelmed Jackie. She knew her mother was waiting, but she couldn't help herself. She'd just skim it as quickly as possible, then read it again later more carefully. It wasn't as if she didn't read each of Sam's letters many times anyway. Laying aside her things, she plopped on her bed and quickly tore open the envelope.

June 20, 1942

Hi from Manzanar resort and health spa! Wish you were here—oh boy, do I wish you were here!!! I know I say that with each letter, but you are part of me now, and I am just not complete without you. Yes, it is me, the same guy who tried to talk you out of coming here at all. I've changed my tune a little, I guess. I do keep hoping this war will end soon and there will be no need for you to come at all. Each day this place gets a little more civilized, and I am beginning to think we will make out okay here. It's not as lavish as our first apartment, I am sorry to say. Remember how decadent we were with one whole room to ourselves? And that nice soft bed that only gave me a backache every other night? The beds here at Manzanar are . . . well, at least they are beds. What more can I say? Papa and I just finished putting up a plywood wall to divide the little room we have here for the family into two rooms. The word rooms *you must understand is a euphemism for cubbyholes. He and Mama now have their own space. It doesn't block off sound, but it gives the illusion of privacy. I don't know what you and I will do. I have been hinting that the little partitioned space might be better used for a newlywed couple. Perhaps we can switch off with my parents. See what fun you'll have to look forward to?*

Are you sure you really want to come?

Well, enough of that. How is Sam Jr. doing? Tell him hi for me and that I love him—okay, or her! I was so proud to hear of your graduating near the top of your class, but I knew you would do well, for you were always conscientious about grades. I hope you didn't lose too much sleep during finals, because you are sleeping for two now and eating for two, also. Are you getting fat yet? Speaking of getting fat, Mama has gained ten pounds since coming here. She is furious. There's lots of rice and starchy foods—I'm in heaven, as you can guess! But Mama says she will sue the government if she can't lose that weight when she gets out. Papa has lost weight. No justice, I guess.

Oh, Jackie, I love you so much! It just hit me again as it does about every ten minutes. You are my wife! Wow! I hope you don't get any flack about coming to live here, but I expect your father can use his influence to smooth the way. That's an irony, isn't it? Someone trying to get into this place! And your father helping. But we live in a crazy world.

Tears welled up in Jackie's eyes. Every letter from Sam evoked a gamut of emotions in her. Tears, laughter, anger. His letters ran the same gamut, at least as much as they could while trying to be careful of the censorship he knew each letter must face. They both made a conscious effort to curb their anger, which was focused mostly at the government. The last thing they wanted, should their letters be read by others, was to be labeled as malcontents. Generally, however, Sam tried to be upbeat, telling one amusing story after another. Sometimes you'd think he really was at a resort. But then pathos would slip in, right in the midst of a joke, and her tears would flow.

Well, it would not do to meet her mother with puffy red eyes. She would save the rest of the letter for later. There were nearly ten handwritten pages. How did Sam think of so much to write? And it was all interesting, hardly ever forced. Guess he really was a writer at heart.

Jackie laid aside the letter as she eased herself from the bed, pausing at her dressing table a moment to freshen up her lipstick and straighten her hair. She noted the waistband of her linen skirt was much snugger than the last time she had worn it. This shopping trip was coming none too soon. She knew her mother was looking forward to it, but that thought caused some of Jackie's melancholy to return. When she went to Manzanar, it was going to be hard for both mother and daughter to be parted during this exciting time. Her father had even upbraided her for this very thing.

"Heaven knows, Jackie, we aren't thrilled over having a little Nip grandchild, but you are still our daughter. And your mother is heartbroken that she can't share this special time with you."

Leave it to her father to take a well-meant remark and twist it into a reproach. Jackie had had to bite back an angry retort even as her own heart quailed. And that convinced her more than anything of the wisdom of leaving, for though she would miss having her mother close during her pregnancy, she would in no way miss attitudes such as her father's. She had no idea of what to expect at Manzanar, but at least there Sam would be at her side.

Shaking this mood, she took up her handbag. "Let me be good company for my mother, Lord," she murmured as she left her room.

2

Moscow, Soviet Union

THEY WERE ALL gathered in Carl Levinson's room at the Metropole. It was the first time since the news of Johnny Shanahan's death a few days ago that all the correspondents had been able to get together for a wake. Cameron wasn't certain if Johnny would have wanted all this fuss. One thing she did know: he wouldn't have wanted tears and long faces. She had shed her share of tears despite that, but at least this room of mostly men resembled more drunken bash than wake.

Johnny would certainly have approved of that! The men had been consuming vodka like water, as if not only drinking many toasts in Johnny's honor but also drinking his share.

"Here's to the best poker player I've ever seen!" slurred Donovan of the *New York Tribune* as he raised his umpteenth glass of clear liquid.

"And to the fastest typist!" cheered Ed Reed of the *Chicago Daily News*.

Everyone laughed. After a couple of hours of this, they were finally reaching the bottom of the barrel of accolades for their departed colleague.

Cameron lifted her glass of club soda. She never could keep up with Johnny or the others when they were drinking, and she had no intention of trying. She didn't need to get drunk to honor her friend. She would just keep writing dispatches and trying to get some semblance of the truth out of Russia. That would be the best tribute to him.

The knock at the door could barely be heard over the raucous laughter. But when the sound finally penetrated, everyone stopped and tried to look concerned. It could be a police raid. The NKVD was notorious for curbing any fun the journalists wished to have.

Finally Levinson wobbled his way to the door and flung it open defiantly, as if he were Shanahan himself. "Yeah?" challenged Levinson.

"I heard there was a party going on here." It was Alex Rostov.

Levinson blinked. He had never been too certain of what to make of the Russian doctor who had been raised in America, left that country under a shadow of scandal, and entered Russia as a member of the Communist Party. Cameron knew Levinson was decidedly anti-Red in his personal philosophy, so in case he might try to slam the door in the face of the intruder, she hurried forward.

"I thought you'd never get here," she said. "I invited him, Lev. You don't mind, do you?"

"Any friend of Shanahan's is welcome here," Levinson said with a cryptically arched brow.

"I was definitely that," said Alex with conviction.

Levinson shrugged and stepped aside. "Okay, then."

Cameron had the feeling he was welcoming Alex as much for her sake as for Shanahan's. They all knew she and Alex were in love. Some, like Lev, didn't understand it, but they respected her enough to look the other way. She appreciated that respect. She had been working all her life to attain it. But she knew now there was more to life—to her life. There was Alex, and there was this new faith in God she was just beginning to experience. Total self-reliance was no longer her ultimate goal. She wasn't sure what her goals were now or what they should be. There was a lot yet to figure out. But since that evening, a few days ago, when she had finally surrendered to God, she had felt an almost overwhelming sense of freedom. She'd always feared faith was a prison—and maybe it was the way some practiced it—but she knew that for her, surrender was being set free. *Everything* now did not depend solely on her own strength. What a burden that had been, carrying all on her own shoulders, though she hadn't even realized it until now.

But Cameron's pessimistic nature also made her aware that she was still floating somewhat on the initial euphoria of her new faith. There would surely be some spiritual hurdles ahead to face. The greatest one certainly was standing at her side. She didn't want to think of Alex as a hurdle. Goodness, he was heart and soul to her! Yet loving him was going to present difficulties and might even challenge her commitment to God.

But if this war was teaching her nothing else, the lesson of living day by day was at least sinking in. She wasn't going to worry about all the ways life could wrench this man she loved from her. He was here now, and that was enough.

Donovan placed a glass of club soda in Alex's hand. They had seen enough of him by now to know he didn't touch alcohol. They only guessed it had something to do with the scandal in the States. In fact, Alex had once been seriously addicted to drugs and for that reason now touched nothing that might invite another addiction.

Alex joined the group in making toasts to Johnny. Some given previously in the evening were repeated, but no one cared. The party went on for another half hour or so before everyone began to disperse. It had actually begun to wind down long before Alex's arrival. The evening communiqué by Soviet Press Department Chief Nikolai Palgunov would be given soon, and drunk or not, these journalists were not about to miss their deadlines.

As Cameron and Alex turned to leave, Lev placed an arm around Cameron in a most uncharacteristically warm gesture. "I'll never forget you and Shanahan and me chasing through Yugoslavia and Greece together with the Nazis nipping at our heels. That bonded us, ya know, and now that Shanahan is gone, I'll try to do my part to be the friend to you that he was. Ya know, look out for you and all." His voice was slurred but no less sincere. Cameron didn't even rankle at the suggestion that she needed to be taken care of.

"Thanks, Lev." She twisted around and gave him a fond hug.

"But I know how mad you get at being nursemaided," he added with a lopsided grin, "so just so you know, I need taking care of, too."

"Why, Lev, I'm speechless!"

He grinned even wider. "I better enjoy that while I can!"

They all walked to the elevator together, but Cameron got off on her floor to get her coat and purse. Since there was an hour until Palgunov's communiqué, she and Alex had made plans to meet at a small park near the Kremlin. She had to shake her NKVD tail first, a chore at which she was becoming quite adept. Alex no longer had a police shadow. Along with his induction into the Red Army, he had been given the trust of the authorities—a trust he was pushing to its limits. Then again, the Soviets also had limits to their trust, so they were fairly even. It irked Cameron that he had given so much to this country, even been wounded in battle, and still he was not afforded even elemental freedoms. But why should he be treated differently from any other Soviet citizen? The police certainly weren't going to allow any latitude for a couple in love. If they knew about their relationship, Alex might be tossed in a gulag and Cameron deported.

All of winter's snow had finally melted, though there remained a chill to the air even in June. Evening was coming on, emphasizing the chill, and Cameron groused inwardly at the inconvenience of having to meet Alex outside. But two days ago a new "key lady" had been assigned to her floor in the hotel, and she sensed this woman took her side avocation as NKVD informer far more seriously than had the former woman. Best not to push the "system" too far.

At frequent intervals Cameron passed signs of Moscow's recent struggle against the enemy. Sandbags, often made of an array of colorful fabrics from women's cast-off clothing, were piled against buildings, while rubble also dotted the streets where bombs had fallen in the constant shelling. There were still air raids but nothing like what had occurred six months before. Cameron had been in Kuibyshev, five hundred miles to the southeast, for most of it, but she had experienced a small taste of the Battle of Moscow, and she gave a shiver now at the memory.

The Battle of Moscow had been won, but the Germans were still a viable enemy. Only a month ago they had routed the Russians in Kharkov, where Alex had been wounded. He had told her of the horrors there, where tens of thousands of Russians had been trapped in an enemy encirclement and been killed or captured. Though tempted, Cameron couldn't print any of what Alex shared, for the events at Kharkov had been kept strictly hush-hush by Soviet officials.

Now the Germans had launched an offensive against Sevastopol, but little news was coming from that Front of the war. A few local reporters were sending dispatches out of the area, but no foreign correspondents were allowed close enough to learn anything. With the fall of Kerch, the eastern gateway to the Crimea, it would be only a matter of time before the Soviet naval port on the Black Sea would fall, as well. The port city had been under siege for months already, and despite its illustrious military history, even Sevastopol would be hard-pressed against a full-out German push.

Thoughts of war quickly fled Cameron's mind as she reached the city park and glimpsed Alex. He was seated on a bench partly obscured by large bushes that were just getting their summer foliage. Before approaching, Cameron gave a quick glance around to make sure she indeed was not followed, and despite the chill she was thankful for the cover of encroaching shadows. But she was certain she had given the police the slip on the crowded metro.

Alex laid aside the newspaper he had been reading when she sat down beside him. His eyes roved over her as if they could never get enough of seeing her, as if the yearning to hold her was almost more than he could bear. She felt the same way, but they both restrained the urge to touch more than their hands together. Police scrutiny might not be a fear, but there were other eyes around, and one could never be too careful in Russia.

"Are you okay?" he asked with intensity in his blue eyes and his voice, both of which she loved so dearly.

"As okay as I can be when all I want to do is kiss you . . . and I can't!" She squeezed his hand.

He smiled. "Patience builds character," he murmured in a droll tone. "I was worried that the wake for Johnny might be hard for you."

"My dear love," she cooed, still gripping his hand, wanting so much more. "It is always hard when I think of him. The waste of his death, the sense that he had so much more to give, but mostly that I have too few friends to lose even one. It doesn't bother you, does it, that I loved Johnny the way I did? Not like I love you, but—"

He held a finger gently to her lips. "I understand. Besides, you've risked too much to love me for me to ever be threatened by another, even a ghost. I suppose there was a time when Johnny and I were rivals of sorts, but even he realized he was not the man for you."

"Only you, Alex." An ironic smile slipped across her lips. "I once thought of myself as such a woman of the world, far too sophisticated for the sentimentality of love. But you changed all that. I used to say with great conviction that I wasn't the 'marrying kind.' But, Alex, I'd marry you in a minute if I could."

With a roguish grin, equal to any of Johnny Shanahan's, Alex said, "But I haven't asked you yet."

"Well, I am still worldly enough not to believe the man has to do the asking!"

He laughed, a sound that rang clear and uncluttered. How she loved that about him—his openness, his almost total lack of guile. Once he'd had an air of mystery, secrets untold, which perhaps he still maintained with others, but with her he was as crystalline as the summer pool his eyes now so resembled.

"Perhaps neither of us need to ask," he said. Then he turned intense. "But we will marry someday."

"I spoke with Bob Wood, my friend at the embassy. I am afraid they won't intercede for us. They don't want to risk sabotaging the delicate balance of U.S.-Soviet relations that a marriage between an American and Soviet citizen might cause."

"I would have been surprised if they had, but I guess you had to ask. And certainly the Soviet government won't give their approval. Oh, there might be a slim chance if you agreed to become a Soviet citizen and renounce your American ties, but I won't ask that of you."

She sighed. "No more than I'd ask you to escape Russia and return to the States, where you'd have to give up medicine. We seem to have a regular impasse before us."

Silence fell between them. How quickly bliss degraded into a thick morass. What was to become of them?

Cameron stared distractedly at a young woman tossing a ball to a child. The little boy with blond curls giggled as he caught the ball rolling on the grass and raised it over his head to return to the woman. Not every child had been evacuated from the city, though perhaps this one had recently returned, his parents deeming Moscow safe again. For the first time in a long while Cameron thought about the child, Sasha, who had innocently brought her and Alex together nearly a year ago during Cameron's first air raid in Moscow. Alex had said the boy's baby sister had recovered from her illness, which had kept the family in Moscow for a time, and that the family had finally moved east. Cameron supposed they were well and safe.

She remembered thinking at first that Alex might be Sasha's father. He would make a good father and with his golden hair and strong Nordic features would produce beautiful offspring. Cameron felt a thrill of excitement at the thought of giving Alex children. She had never considered having children in the past and certainly had never pictured herself as a mother. But she did not cringe at the idea now but rather anticipated it. Love did funny things to people.

Would love surmount all the obstacles set in Cameron and Alex's way? She didn't see how, but it suddenly occurred to her that she had recently bound herself to "the giver of miracles." She hadn't done it for the benefit of such things, but there could surely be no harm in taking advantage of this particular boon. Somewhere in her past church attendance—all a bit fuzzy because she had paid so little attention—she recalled hearing the saying, no doubt from the Bible, "Ask and you shall receive."

She turned to Alex, her heart fluttering just a little. She was nervous about *asking*—it didn't come easily to her nature.

"Alex, can we pray together about our future?" A wan smile twitched upon her lips as she realized she still hadn't been able to say the word, so she made herself add, "Can we *ask* God to make a way for us?"

Alex bit his lip as sudden emotion invaded his features. "Ah, Cameron . . . hearing that . . . it touches me so! Of course we can pray together. I've wanted to for so long now."

They didn't bow their heads or close their eyes, so as not to draw undue attention, but they clasped hands, and when they each uttered their prayer, it seemed they were simply conversing. Cameron felt most comfortable with that approach. She liked *talking* to God far more than reciting some liturgical expression.

They had no sooner finished when the little boy's ball rolled toward them and bounced on the toes of Cameron's shoes. Cameron scooped it up, and a moment later the boy himself toddled up.

"Mine!" he said in Russian.

"Yes, it is," Cameron replied, also in Russian, and with a friendly smile gave him the ball.

"*Spasiba*," he said.

"*Pazhalusta*," she answered in the standard response.

Watching the child return to his mother, Alex commented, "Your Russian is improving."

"Sophia has been a good teacher. But I've decided not to make my progress generally known. I think it could come in handy to know more than the Soviet authorities think I know."

"The war can't go on forever," he said.

She thought he was speaking more of their future rather than of cat-and-mouse games with the Soviets. "Now that America is in it, we are sure to whip the Germans just like we did in the Great War, and we'll throw in the Japanese for good measure. Alex, this war is going to change the world, not all for good perhaps, but some good will come of it. And now that America and Russia have been allies in the greatest endeavor in this century, I am sure there will be new openness between the two countries. That can only benefit us."

"Yes . . . it is possible."

"I do hate it that when I am finally optimistic about something, your Russian pessimism kicks in."

"I'm sorry. But I do think we'd be better off to put our faith in God rather than in governments, especially Stalin's government. I know Molotov just signed the Soviet-British Treaty with Anthony Eden, affirming their wartime alliance and their cooperation after the war, but you and I both know Stalin will agree to anything in order to win. Logically, the reward for the people's incredible war effort should be new freedom, but do you really see Stalin—the man who so ruthlessly purged Russia of even the slightest opposition less than ten years ago—relinquishing one iota of his power after the war?"

"Yet knowing that, you came here at the tail end of those purges in '39." She didn't know why the bitterness crept into her tone. Had he not come to Russia, she might never have met him. Yet had he stayed in America, there might have been a chance of their meeting and being free, as well.

"I was crazy with bitterness and self-hatred back then. But you know my main reason was to have a chance to practice medicine. Still, regret sometimes eats at me. But . . . then I remember that Russia gave me you."

She took his hands again and gave him a fervent appraisal. "Alex, we best not try to second-guess fate, or God's will. I realize God put us here and now. There can be no what-might-have-been."

"God put us here, and He will see us through . . . somehow." Suddenly Alex jumped up. Still grasping her hand, he said, "Come with me."

She didn't question but rose and hurried along at his side. He drew her out of the park and across the street and down a deserted alley.

"Reduced to meeting in alleys," he said. "But I must kiss you. I must hold you!" Not waiting for a response, he wrapped his arms around her and drew her close. Their lips touched, and she surrendered to his tender passion with her own, holding him as tightly as he held her, letting their kiss deepen until it encompassed all the frustration they felt in their situation. Moments passed, and minutes. Cameron wondered if she would ever be able to let go.

All at once she sensed a different sort of intensity from Alex, and she knew there would be more adversity to face before God was ready to answer their prayers.

"You're leaving, aren't you, Alex?" she murmured, her lips brushing his ear as she spoke.

"I didn't know how I would tell you."

"When?"

"In two days."

"Oh . . ." She could think of nothing more to say. She gripped him tighter.

She should have been expecting this. He was in the Army, after all, and the only reason he'd been here as long as he had was because of his wounded leg. She should have noticed at Johnny's party that Alex was no longer using his cane. He'd be going back to the war now, to danger. And if that were not bad enough, they were doomed to be separated again. She didn't even bother asking where he was going. She would never be able to go there or even write him letters. All that they had must be held in their hearts.

"The war can't last forever," he repeated like the litany of some tired chant.

"Yes it can." Tears spilled from her eyes.

He brushed his fingers over the moisture on her cheek. "I didn't want to make you cry. I know how you hate to cry."

"I'm n-not c-crying!" she wept.

"I love you, Cameron, so very much. I will take you with me in my heart. You know that."

Nodding, she noisily tried to sniff back her emotion. "Curse this war!" For the moment she didn't care about accepting God's will. She knew she would later, but now she could do nothing more than ache inside. "Just remember, doctor, we have plans, so don't you dare get yourself killed!"

"I wouldn't dream of it, not when I've got you waiting for me."

"I will always wait, Alex. I love you so."

3

Luzon Island, Philippines

RAIN BATTERED the thatched-roofed hut, and it felt to Blair as if she were sitting under a waterfall, except she was fairly dry. Only a few drops of water penetrated the hut, and none where she was seated on a wooden stool stirring a pot bubbling atop a small woodstove.

The door of the hut creaked open, and a woman quickly slipped in, dripping a puddle of water onto the dirt at her feet.

"I have found wild onions for the soup," she said in Tagalog.

"Wonderful, Rosita," said Blair, also in Tagalog, though a broken, accented variety. "It needs something." At the moment the steaming mixture contained only meat and some roots. Blair did not know exactly what the meat was and hadn't asked when Rosita's husband, Fidel, had brought it in. It had already been cleaned and dressed, ready for the pot. There wasn't much normal meat left on the island, at least not for those in hiding, so she had suspicions the critter in the pot was a rat. But she tried not to think of that. If the others in the compound were willing to eat the stuff, then certainly it wouldn't harm her. Nevertheless, the boiling meat did not smell entirely appetizing, so onions were a boon not to be refused.

"Thank you, Rosita," Blair added with a grateful smile. "Shall I cut them up?"

"No, you rest. I can do it."

Rosita Vargas, who was about thirty-five or forty—she was as secretive about her age as a Hollywood star—went to a table that held many cooking implements and began the task of peeling and

27

cutting the onions. She hummed a soft tune while she worked but was otherwise quiet. She was a plain-looking Filipina with black hair, which she pulled back into a long ponytail. Her face was round but proportional to her slightly plump figure, and her dark eyes were small and shrewd. Yet there was a warmth about her, in her smile, in the soft tone of her voice.

It had been her voice that Blair had heard nearly two months ago when she had been half conscious and probably more than half dead in the jungle from an attack of malaria. The tender hands that had reached out to her had also been Rosita's. But it had been her husband, Fidel, who had lifted Blair with strong arms and carried her to this place, this island of refuge in the midst of the war-torn Philippines. Yes, the war seemed far away here, though the compound was still on the Bataan Peninsula, the caretakers' huts of an abandoned banana plantation. They were deep in the jungle, and so far the Japanese had not taken an interest in the area.

Why should they? They had control of all of the Philippines now, and though they would want to wipe out pockets of resistance and hunt fugitives, they had their hands full with these tasks closer to civilization. Of course, there was always the worry that as things stabilized in the more populated areas, the Japanese would go farther afield to secure their position on the islands. And Fidel had brought word back from his hunting expeditions that there were bands of guerrillas operating in the jungle, which could bring enemy patrols down on them.

In the last weeks Blair had expended little energy worrying about such things. Truth was, she'd had little energy left in her to spend. She wondered if she would ever feel strong again. Days of real health seemed as far away as a frivolous life in Hollywood, surely not merely since the beginning of the war. But she reminded herself she was looking for strength in the wrong place if she was expecting it from her body. She had a new source of strength she was drawing from now—the God she'd found only a couple of days before Bataan fell to the enemy.

She found it easy to fall back into old habits and thought patterns without anyone around to remind her of the changes in her life. But, conversely, it was also at times difficult to remember why she had come to the Philippines in the first place. She had been seeking Gary and hoping to repair the damage she had done to their marriage by her lies. And right along with that she had been seeking God, believing Gary would be instrumental in her success in this endeavor, as well. But she had found God without finding Gary. At least she would never wonder if her faith was because of Gary, nor would he have cause to doubt that, either. All that had happened after the start of the war now appeared to be some sort of divine plan, as Meg Doyle had spoken of back at the mission. It helped to think of it in those terms, anyway. It helped, when weakened both physically and spiritually, to know all the seeming chaos, the danger, the heartache were meant for a purpose.

Nevertheless, as her physical stamina began to increase, so also did an inkling of worry that the outside world could intrude upon her recent peace. She sensed, though, that a bit of inner tension might be a good thing. She could not let herself get too comfortable with this external peace. God had given her weeks of it because she had needed it, but she reminded herself that there was still a war on. The Japanese had won here in the Philippines and perhaps, as reports indicated, in most of East Asia, but she knew the United States wasn't going to sit back and accept that. She quashed back a seed of resentment that her government had let the Philippines go, telling herself they had probably had no choice. But Fidel said MacArthur had promised the people of his beloved Philippines that he would return. So the people clung to that, as must Blair.

But more than the promise of a general she did not know, Blair had other reasons to keep fighting. Gary might well be in a Japanese prison camp, as no doubt also were Meg and Conway Doyle. Their daughters, Patience and Hope, were probably also in a camp, and very likely so was her dear friend Claudette. Even if Claudette had made it to Corregidor, that island fortress had fallen to the Japanese in May, so all who had taken refuge there would now be in POW camps, as well. She thought of others she cared about. Mateo Sanchez, the minister's son. Was he a POW? And Silvia Wang, Blair's nightclub employer in Manila. Was she still safe in her mountain villa? Blair remembered how she had so desired to join Silvia there but had finally gone to Bataan in hopes of finding Gary. Would things have gone differently had she not changed her route so long ago?

That hardly mattered now. And to be honest, Blair was glad she had gone the way she had. Oh, the path had been hard and miserable at times, but if she had not come this way, she would never have met the Doyles or her newer friends Rosita and Fidel. And she might not even have met the one who was becoming her best friend—her Lord Jesus.

However, she couldn't lie to herself; her fleshly self was still miserable most of the time. She would never grow accustomed to the filth, the mud, the jungle teeming with slithery creatures, and the horrible food that she dared not look at too closely. But Meg Doyle had once told her God accepted you even if you hated bugs and filth.

Blair set aside the stirring spoon and went to her mat to lie down. She was stronger now, but the simple act of stirring a pot could still exhaust her. She was glad her mat was in the cooking hut so she could help out a little yet still be near her bed. There were four huts in the compound. Rosita and Fidel and their family, which had included four children and Rosita's aged mother, occupied the other huts. Rosita's father had died of heart failure a few months ago, and her two oldest sons were in the Army. That left Grandma Maria, whom Blair did not see much because she was bedridden in one of the other huts, and the two youngest children: Ernesta, twelve, and Pepillo, who was fourteen.

Rosita brought the bowl of cut onions to the cooking pot and dumped them in. As she stirred, she said, "I forgot to tell you, Pepillo just returned from the valley."

The boy had gone yesterday to see if he could gather some food, which was in ever short supply at the compound.

"Did he have any luck?" asked Blair. She was doing quite well with Tagalog now after two months of nearly constant lessons from the Vargas family, though her speech was still accented and a bit broken. Unlike her sister Cameron, Blair had a head for languages. Now that she thought of it, French and Latin had been the only classes in which she'd made good grades. She enjoyed mimicking the accents, and she had an excellent memory. She supposed those were the only worthwhile talents she'd brought to the Philippines, besides her music, and they were coming in quite handy.

"Pepillo got some salt, but that is all. I think there will be more in the markets soon because the Japs are adopting a more friendly line with the Filipinos. They want us to feel safe and free to return to our farms so that crops can be grown."

"That means you would be safe if—"

"Hush, Blair. Say no more."

"But it is true. If you weren't harboring me, you would be safe." Blair felt her weakness clinging to her like old skin. She was placing these good people in great danger, but she could no more be left on her own than she could hike a mile. She still needed the Vargases.

"We are safe here—all of us."

"Promise me, Rosita, that if the Japs come, you will turn me over to them and save yourselves."

Rosita just shook her head and said nothing. Blair should know better herself, for if the Japanese came, the Vargases wouldn't be spared so easily. It was death for harboring fugitives, and turning her over probably wouldn't help. Rosita and her family already stood condemned if they were caught.

"Was there any other news?" Blair asked to distract herself from those grim thoughts.

"Yes, there was," said Rosita, who also seemed relieved for the distraction. "Rumors say an important battle was fought out in the ocean near an island called Midway. They say the Americans won a great victory over the Japs."

Blair had learned to put little stock in rumors. In the last weeks she'd heard stories that ranged from Allied troops landing in France to Hitler being on the run to Germany's outright defeat. Then there were the rumors spread by the Japanese—she hoped they were only rumors—of the total destruction of the United States Navy and of successful Japanese landings in Alaska.

"I hope the American victory is true." Blair sighed. She'd believe none of the rumors until she was on an American ship headed for home.

"Pepillo also got some quinine." Rosita patted the pocket of her cotton housedress.

"How did he ever get that?"

"My boy has become very . . . resourceful since the war started." The woman smiled wryly. "That is a better word—resourceful—than thief, yes? He is not really a thief, not in his heart."

"I know that, Rosita. The war is forcing all of us to do things we might never have done otherwise. Anyway, you keep the quinine for reserve. Those herbs you gave me have helped for now." Blair hadn't had an attack of malaria for days.

31

"I think you should take it for prevention."

"Your family may need it."

"We have not had malaria. We are immune. Please, Blair, take it. If we need more my ... resourceful son will get more." She paused, then added with a slight touch of defensiveness in her tone, "He assures me he got it from the Japs, not from innocents."

Blair couldn't argue further. It did seem as if the Vargases were immune, and she really wanted to get strong and stay strong. Something deep inside her seemed to be telling her that she was not destined to sit out the war in the safety of this banana plantation. She'd been given the gift of several weeks to recover and gain strength, but she could not shake the sense that God had other plans for her. Oh, that did seem rather presumptuous of her. To think God intended to use her! But her small knowledge of the Bible did tell her that God had used people even less deserving than she in mighty ways. Prostitutes, thieves, tax collectors, to name a few.

It was possible. And she had one thing many Americans on the island didn't have—she was free. How might she use that freedom? How might *God* use it? Maybe she couldn't be a guerrilla. She'd heard there were bands of them roaming the jungle and harrying the Japs at every chance. And many of these were Americans. Well, she couldn't blow up bridges, rail lines, or ammo dumps—she couldn't tell one end of a bomb from the other! But there must be some productive part for her to play.

As her health returned, she began thinking more and more of how she could help the war effort. Her music skills were probably useless now, but she did have an aptitude for languages. Could she learn Japanese? What else? She had gained some nursing skills while working at the Army hospital just before the fall of Bataan. She didn't get sick at the sight of blood anymore.

Dear God, please find a way to use me! I know I used to be quite oblivious as far as this war was concerned, but I'm not anymore. I can't be. I am in the middle of it, and I want to do my part, not sit here in safety while others fight. They are my battles now, too, and I want to fight them even if it means getting dirty and eating awful things. I am beyond that, too.

She smiled at that all too true reality. Not a soul who had known her in Hollywood, except maybe her family, would recognize her now by her appearance or her manners. She was wearing

Rosita's castoffs, old cotton dungarees and a cotton blouse, faded but whole. Her own clothes had all but fallen off her weeks ago. The tropics were murder on clothing. She still had the same shoes, sneakers, now practically sandals for all the holes in them, but Fidel had found a way to tie them on her feet that was quite utilitarian if not attractive. The condition of the rest of her body was not much better. The last time her lips had been touched with lipstick had been long ago in Manila. The polish on her nails had chipped off completely, which was just as well since her nails were mere stumps now. And her hair! The last decent cut had been given her by Meg Doyle a good three months ago. Rosita had hacked it off again with blunt scissors a couple of weeks ago because it was easier to keep clean that way. And it had been nearly six months since any peroxide had touched it. Luckily, her natural color was only a few shades darker than the platinum she'd used for years. Still, her roots stood out darkly against the lighter ends. And all that only seemed to emphasize her sickly, gaunt appearance, which was helped only a little by her tropical tan. Though she had no scale to weigh herself, she guessed she'd lost twenty pounds since leaving Manila, and Rosita's too-large clothes made the loss appear even greater.

Well, if God had thought to cure her of vanity, He'd been successful. Still, she would love to look halfway decent, and the first time she laid her hands on some lipstick, she was going to use it gleefully. But that was no longer of prime importance to her. Her priorities had changed drastically in the last six months, and for that she was thankful.

But there was more in store for her, she was certain. More changes. It scared her and excited her all at once. First, though, she had to get well, put some flesh on her bones and a spring to her step.

———

Over the next months Blair worked toward gaining back her health. In August, however, the supply of quinine ran out, and she had a serious relapse of malaria. She remembered that Alice Wharton, the Navy nurse she had met before the fall of Bataan, had told her that malaria stays in one's system and the symptoms can resurface even years after exposure. Of course, this attack could be an entirely new bout because, as always, Bataan was infested with mosquitoes. She wondered if she would ever get well. Was she doomed to be a helpless woman always at the mercy of others? Blair tried not to dwell on that possibility, but with so much idle time on her hands, there wasn't much else to do.

Desperate for some distraction, she put Fidel and Pepillo on the lookout for a Japanese language book when they went to market. Maybe she could make herself useful even if her body was too weak for much. But Fidel and Pepillo were not successful in their search.

4

SOMETIMES GARY thought restlessness was his worst enemy. It had been nearly four months since the fall of Bataan, and he had spent every day of that time in hiding. After a couple of grueling weeks of hiding in the jungle with his fellow fugitive, Ralph Senger, he had learned of a camp run by an American civilian named Albert Johnson, who had owned a mine before the war. Nearly half dead with starvation and disease and knowing they couldn't keep running as they had been and survive, they found the American's camp. The ex-miner had made a pretty nice camp, well hidden in the foothills of the Zambales Mountains, that offered sanctuary to escapees from the Death March, as they had come to label that fiasco in which the Japanese had transported their captives in Bataan north to POW camps.

Many of these men were so sick that even after several months of doing no more than sleeping and eating, they had barely been able to function. Not a few died in Johnson's camp. There were times when Gary wanted only to die, as well. Besides malaria and dysentery and general malnutrition, Gary had been hit with beri-beri. His feet had been hideously swollen before coming to the camp, and while on the run, he had taken some bad cuts that had ulcerated. His feet throbbed so painfully at times he wondered if amputation would soon be necessary. His cure had come in an odd and disgusting way. One of the men in Gary's hut had brought a stray dog into the camp, and the animal had discovered Gary's feet and begun licking them. Gary had tried to fight the animal off but had simply been too weak to do so effectively. Ralph had suggested that Gary let the dog have his way. At first the idea of it had made Gary almost physically sick, but after a few of the dog's repugnant "treatments," all of the purulent dead skin on Gary's feet was cleaned up, and in a couple of weeks his feet were actually healing.

Near the end of summer the Japanese had discovered the camp and raided it. Gary's good fortune, or as Ralph liked to call it, "divine luck," held. He happened to be using the latrines about twenty yards from the camp when he heard the commotion of the raid. Knowing there was no sense in attempting to make a stand against the enemy, he lit out for the jungle. Fighting would have been hopeless, for there were few weapons and very little ammunition in the camp. He did regret leaving Ralph behind, but he knew the worst that could happen to any of the men would be their recapture. He did hide out in the vicinity for a couple of days in the hope that his friend would come along.

Then he headed for the lowlands. He was ready for some action. His health wasn't perfect and probably would never be again, at least not until he could get back home to California. But his feet were almost like new, and they had troubled him the most. Now he felt fit enough to seek out one of the guerrilla bands he'd been hearing about in the camp. Maybe he could get one of them to help him rescue Ralph.

Almost immediately after making this decision, he stumbled into a Jap patrol. Again he had no weapon, but some streak of stubbornness made him determined to fight. He had come to enjoy his freedom.

There were only three soldiers in the patrol. Only? He didn't know why he felt so cocky except that he'd been so sick before that it was easy to overestimate his current health. As Gary blundered into the clearing where the men were taking a break, leaning against some trees and smoking cigarettes, they were just as startled as Gary at the sudden encounter. The soldiers had been fairly quiet before discovery, so Gary hadn't heard them, but he should have smelled the cigarette smoke before coming upon their place of respite. After months of sedentary life, his instincts apparently were shot.

One of the Japs grabbed his rifle—nothing wrong with *his* instincts!

The Jap fired but did it quickly without taking aim. Thus,

despite Gary's sluggish responses, he managed to dodge the shot. But as he ducked and feinted to the right, he tripped over a hidden root, and that sent him sprawling toward another Jap who had just laid hands on his rifle. Gary crashed into him, and the force of the blow ejected the weapon from the man's hand and dropped it to the ground an inch from Gary's hand. All his past training suddenly coalesced, the sluggishness falling away in that single instant when his survival depended on it. Wrapping his hand around the rifle, he found the trigger and squeezed, firing wildly, hoping the third man was somewhere in the line of fire. A scream a moment later sounded promising.

But the first man was now ready to fire again. Gary rolled out of harm's way a moment before the weapon blasted, and as he rolled, he fired at the second Jap, who was struggling to draw his side arm from the holster. One quick look confirmed that Gary had hit him. The first man had by this time taken cover behind one of the trees, and Gary prudently did the same. But he knew this battle couldn't end in a standoff. He would have to kill the remaining man to prevent him from warning other Japs in the area. Likely the shots had already given a warning, so he didn't have much time to do what needed to be done.

A shot grazed the side of the tree behind which Gary was hiding, sending bits of bark spraying into his face. He wasn't about to waste precious ammo with the same kind of futile shot. He had to get his enemy out into the open. He grabbed a rock and tossed it, rustling some brush about a dozen feet from the man. It was a poor ruse and wouldn't fool a child, but Gary could think of no other way. Another shot blasted in at Gary's hiding place.

He felt precious seconds tick by, knowing that at any moment other enemy soldiers could swoop down on him. Three had been more than enough for him to handle. Any more would be impossible.

Gary heard another faint rustle. Had the Jap soldier tried the same ruse of tossing a rock? But the sound was almost immediately followed by a sharp grunt.

Gary waited for something—another shot, the arrival of other Japs . . . something. Several seconds passed though it seemed like an hour, and then a voice spoke.

"If you're a friend, show yourself, 'cause I sure don't want to wait here all day till more Japs come." The cursing that peppered the statement was as recognizable as Ralph Senger's rumble of a voice.

"Stay under cover, Sarge," Gary said. "There's still a third man who may just be wounded."

"He's dead."

Only then did Gary rise from where he had been hunched behind the tree, but he did so cautiously until he saw his friend. "We better hightail it outta here!" he said with a barely restrained grin.

Gary never thought he'd appreciate a sight more. Perhaps if it had been Blair to step out into the open, but as it was, he was ecstatic to see the gaunt, grizzled face of his friend squatting there as he wiped the bloody blade of a knife on the grass. Gary only vaguely wondered where Ralph had purloined the knife, but the man was ever resourceful.

"I'm with ya, Hopalong! Let's go," Ralph replied with a grin spread across his rough features.

They gathered up all the weapons and ammo they could find, then took off. They ran three miles without encountering any more of the enemy, then resting in the cover of thick jungle growth, they caught their breath and talked.

Ralph told how he and about half the men in Johnson's camp had been captured. The others he guessed had scattered through the jungle. Only he and three others in captivity had the heart to attempt another escape. After getting safely away, the other two wanted to go deeper into the mountains and hide there to wait out the war. Ralph figured Gary would try to get to a guerrilla outfit, for they had already talked about this at Johnson's camp, so he wanted to go toward the lowlands in hopes of running into his friend. So he and the other two split up. And, of course, Ralph did run into Gary, and at the perfect moment.

"Hey," Ralph said, "I've escaped capture twice now. I wonder what the record is?"

"Well, don't try to break it. Twice is enough, isn't it?"

But Ralph had a thoughtful look. The man was crazy enough to try for it if indeed there was some kind of record.

"Where to next, partner?" Ralph said. "We're dressed to kill now," he added, patting one of the Japanese rifles.

"You know as well as I that we can't use this gear unless we absolutely have to. Any American or Filipino soldier knows the distinctive sound of Jap rifles, and if we use them, they might just shoot us before asking questions."

"So why'd we take them?"

"Better us to have them than the enemy."

Ralph smiled and nodded. It was the kind of logic a seasoned warrior would use.

Finding guerrillas was no easy undertaking. For one thing, they didn't want to be found, and if you did find some, then came the even stickier problem. Guerrillas came in all sizes, shapes, and characters. There were many unsavory types who were taking advantage of the disorder in the country to roam about using the guise of "guerrilla" to rob and terrorize not only Japanese but civilian locals, as well. There was also a faction of Communist partisans who spent as much energy fighting the Japanese as they did the Americans, who they felt were every bit as much oppressors of the Philippines as were the Japanese, in a way even more so because the Americans had been around a lot longer.

So Gary and Ralph spent much more time on the run, hiding and dodging the Japanese. More often than not they survived merely by the good graces of the Filipino people who, for the most part, were sympathetic to the Americans. These Filipinos risked their lives in order to give the fugitives shelter and food, and they did so generously. Gary would forever be in their debt.

One family, the Albans, gave Gary and Ralph shelter for two weeks. Then a Japanese patrol came near the village and they were forced to flee before the family was compromised. Their departure had been especially hard on Ralph, who had begun to grow fond of Filipa, Mr. Alban's twenty-two-year-old daughter. Gary had been surprised and even at times amused at how the tough veteran had softened, to the point of mush, around the pretty young woman. When they were forced to run, Ralph promised Filipa he would find a way to come back for her. Gary thought it might just be the lonesomeness of a fugitive talking, yet he was understanding. He, too, yearned for the touch of the woman he loved.

"We gotta do something to end this war!" Ralph declared as they hid in a culvert that night. They both felt more lonely than ever after the warmth and friendliness they had so recently experienced with the Albans. The rain poured down on them, and they were soaked with no hope of finding shelter any time soon or food or even an affectionate look. But it was none of these things that had motivated Ralph's words at that moment. "The sooner the war ends, the sooner I can marry Filipa!"

"I didn't realize you were that serious about her" was all Gary could think to respond. He was shivering with cold.

"You don't have the corner on love, Gary."

"Love?"

"Yeah! You got a problem with that?" barked Ralph defensively. Then he shook his head, sending a spray of water into Gary's face. "Aw, don't mind me. I know I've been acting like a fool these last couple of weeks. But that gal got to me. I think I love her . . . I'm pretty sure I do . . . but maybe it's just this stinking war. A man gets lonely, you know."

"I know. . . ." Gary replied thoughtfully. He shivered again, and he didn't think it was from the cold rain beating on his body.

"I guess you do. You and your wife never could get a break, either."

In the months of their sojourn Gary had told his companion much about his relationship with Blair. Sometimes he'd said more than he planned when he was out of his head with fever.

"That's why we gotta get out of this mess we're in, so we can get back our lives," Gary said, feeling a pang of despair. "Sometimes I think running and hiding and starving *is* what our lives are going to be from here on out." He couldn't shake the sense that he would die a fugitive. By rights he should have died already. He didn't know why he had cheated death so often. "I've almost forgotten what a normal life is. I can hardly even envision what it was like in the States. Driving a car, going to a restaurant, eating my mom's pot roast, holding hands with my gal under the moonlight. It's like a dream I'm waking up from that's fading quickly." Only as he said the words did he realize the truth of them, how the reality was this moment, wet, starved, and shivering in a ditch. The rest was maybe just his imagination. Blair might even be just a figment of his imagination.

"At least you got your faith, Gary."

"Yeah . . . th-that . . ." Gary's teeth were chattering—he couldn't stop them.

"You gotta hang on to it," Ralph said. "I need you to. It helps me. I never thought much about God till I met you."

"Get your own faith, Ralph," he said sharply. Then feeling bad for his tone, he added softly, though more dismally than with any encouragement, "I c-can't carry you. I can b-barely carry myself. Sometimes I don't f-feel God at all." All of a sudden he realized he was trembling all over, not merely his teeth chattering.

"You okay, Gary?"

Gary nodded. Or was that just his head shaking? "J-just l-life." Before he knew it, he was lying in the mud at the bottom of the culvert, curled up and still shaking.

"We have to get shelter," Ralph said. "Maybe the Albans—"

"N-no. T-too dangerous for th-them."

"We gotta do something. Sure, the shakes are just part of life, but they can still kill."

"Guerrillas. . . ?"

"How can you think of guerrillas now?"

"Our only way out . . ." Gary hardly knew what he was saying, yet it was the only way he could express what he was feeling. "L-like you said, Ralph . . . end the war . . . we gotta . . . only thing . . ."

The rest of the night was a blur to Gary. The dreams were nightmares. His father's '39 Ford, driverless, ran Gary down, then he vomited his mother's pot roast. And Blair . . . she was a ghoulish vamp in a sequined dress, screaming songs at him like a banshee.

A voice said, "I'll be right back . . . I'm gonna find help. . . ."

Later he sensed the coming of daylight, and some rational part of him knew he was a dead man if a patrol discovered him where he was, but he had not one ounce of will within him to do anything about it. On one level he knew Ralph had gone for help; on another he felt abandoned, alone with his despair. It stopped raining for a short time and the sun warmed him, and he thought it was almost as good as a friend. Then came another downpour, like buckets of water being dumped on him, so when he heard voices again, they were muffled and distorted.

"Well, I'll be a pie-eyed toad. It's really him!" A Texas drawl. A cowboy wandering by mistake into his dreams?

"Well, did ya think I was lying?" A gruff, foul mouth, so sweet to Gary's ears.

"Pedro, Mario, give a hand here."

Slipping and sliding in the mud, several men jostled Gary's body, lifting it with some difficulty from the ditch. They lost Gary once, and he bounced back down to the bottom. He heard cursing and apologies. Finally he was at the top. Maybe it was the jostling about, but his head cleared a bit.

"Ralph, that you?"

"'Course it is. And I found us some guerrillas, for what rotten good they are at the moment."

"Aw . . . don't you go talkin' thataway, Sarge," said the Texas drawl. "We've come to the rescue."

"Sorry, I forgot myself," Ralph replied with just a hint of sincerity in his tone.

"Do I recognize that voice?" Gary asked. His mind was clearer, but his vision was blurred by fever and rain.

"Why, it's your old pal Woody!"

Gary tried to smile but wasn't sure if he succeeded. "You really a guerrilla now?"

"Sure 'nuff, partner. Now, let's get you outta here, then we can all have a nice long talk where it's warm and dry and even have a bite to eat."

Gary said no more. The words *warm, dry,* and *eat* were enough of a tonic to give him a boost of energy. He made sure that his rescuers didn't have to carry him. Braced between Ralph and Woody, he walked most of the way and was dragged the rest. He had a feeling they didn't have the strength to carry him anyway.

They had finally found some guerrillas. Maybe the war wouldn't last forever after all.

5

ROSITA VARGAS was usually a calm, fairly imperturbable person, so when she burst into Blair's hut, there was no doubt something terrible was wrong.

"Blair! There are Japanese about a mile away," she said breathlessly. "I think they are only looking for workers for the rice harvest. But if they have come this far inland, I doubt they will pass us by. What do you want to do?"

Blair had hoped her safe haven in the Vargases' compound would have lasted forever, but she had lived each day prepared to vacate on a moment's notice. She had few belongings, but they were all together, ready to be stuffed into the knapsack Pepillo had bought for her in the market. There was also a few days' supply of food in the knapsack. Surprisingly, she was also emotionally prepared to flee. She felt no panic. Why should she? Living as a fugitive for many months now, she had learned to expect her world to change in the mere beat of a heart.

"I must go," she said calmly. She had always known that she would not unduly endanger the Vargases.

"They may just talk to Fidel and move on," Rosita said. "What reason would they have to search the huts?"

"And if they do take it into their heads to search? They might ransack the huts just for the fun of it. I won't take that risk." Blair immediately grabbed the knapsack and began to pack.

"There are some caves in the hills," Rosita said in a resigned tone as she turned toward a cupboard and took out a few items of food. "They are well hidden, but Pepillo knows where they are. He used to play there. He can take you." She handed Blair a few tins of tomatoes and a packet of dried fish. "I wish I could spare more."

"I feel bad taking even this, but I can't see how I will get any food in hiding."

"We will bring you supplies when we can. And who knows, it may just be for the night." Rosita bent down by Blair's sleeping mat and began rolling it up.

When the packing was done, Rosita left to get her son. Blair surveyed the hut that had been her home for so many months. It was pathetic as living quarters, but she was going to miss it, and even more she would miss the company that came with it. Perhaps she would only have to leave for a night or two. Yet the plantation and the caretaker's compound were fairly isolated. It was a good three-hour trek on foot to the nearest village. Why would the Japanese come this far on the off chance of finding one or two workers? Had someone in the village learned there was an American hiding at the plantation and informed? She had tried to be careful, staying indoors most of the time. But someone could have observed her from a distance when she came out occasionally for some air and sun. Even with the deep tan she had developed after months in the tropical sun, and wearing a scarf to cover her hair, she still hardly looked like a native.

Her musings were interrupted by Rosita's return. Blair gathered up her things, then suddenly feeling emotional about leaving, she set everything down and gave her friend and rescuer a hug.

"Thank you so much, Rosita! I can never begin to repay you."

Rosita gave Blair a warm squeeze in return, then patted her shoulder. "You repay me by staying safe and alive, eh? So my effort won't be in vain."

"I will try my hardest." Blair smiled, then left the hut.

It started to rain as she and Pepillo hiked away from the compound. With the rain as emphasis, the two-mile trek was as miserable as any journey through the jungle had ever been for Blair. Slipping and sliding in mud, getting slapped in the face by thick foliage—some things she just never got used to! But she endured it with better grace than she had in the past, though she was certain it wasn't exactly "grace" that made her endure but rather a dogged resignation to her fate.

The hike was mostly uphill, and though Blair was healthier now than she had been in a long time, she was still exhausted when they came to the hideaway. It was indeed a cave, though more like a crevice in the rocky hillside, but well hidden. A plane flying at just the right angle and altitude might chance to see it, but certainly no one on land could unless they came right into the clearing surrounding the cave, and Pepillo assured her no one ever came around this area. Yet he did caution her not to build a fire or go too far afield looking for food and water. He showed her a small waterfall several yards from the cave that, because it was the rainy season, was gushing with water. He said it would be safe to drink.

She thanked him effusively, then he left her alone to settle into her new "home." The cave was dry—perhaps even dryer than the hut had been in a downpour, but that was all that could be said for the place. It was about five feet wide at its opening and about ten feet at its widest point inside, while it went back into the hill perhaps a dozen feet, narrowing considerably the farther back it went. She could barely stand upright at the highest point. She spread out her mat near the back, then realizing there was little else to do, she lay on the mat and promptly fell asleep.

Boredom was perhaps her worst enemy during those long, lonely days in the cave. After two days of exile Pepillo managed to bring, along with a bit more food, a couple of books—one a Philippine guidebook and the other a child's reading primer. Blair had never much enjoyed reading, but the pure mind-numbing tedium of her days impelled her to read both books several times even though they were written in dry, uninteresting styles.

Two days after Pepillo's visit, Rosita came to the cave, but Blair's joy at seeing her good friend was dulled because she brought bad news.

"The Japanese soldiers are not leaving right away. They have heard of guerrillas operating near here and are setting up headquarters in the big house of the plantation so as to keep close patrol over the area." She gave a shudder. "Imagine! Japs less than a quarter of a mile from us! I have never been so frightened."

"Have they ... done anything?" Blair asked, restraining her own shudder, yet not able to keep all misgiving from her tone. She'd heard many rumors of the brutality of the Japanese.

"No, but they have come to our compound, and they strut

around—and I don't like the way they look at my Ernesta." She looked away but not before Blair caught a look of shame in the woman's eyes. "I do not know if it will be safe to come up here very often. I am so sorry!"

"Don't you dare come up again," Blair said as firmly as her sinking stomach would allow. "I don't eat much, and there is enough food here for several days."

"I feel so terrible about this, but it is as much for your protection as ours. They are watching us closely. Perhaps in a few days, when they lose interest, we can come back with food."

"I understand, Rosita." Blair patted the woman's shoulder. "Don't worry. Why, this place is heaven compared to some places I've been in since this war started."

Rosita gave Blair a tearful hug before departing. She left a small cache of food, as well. Blair worried that this would deplete the Vargases' own stores, since the nearest village didn't have market for two more days and one could never tell if there would be enough on sale for everyone. Yet she couldn't refuse it, not that Rosita would have heard refusals anyway. The truth was, Blair had no other resources. She couldn't hunt, and there was nothing in the way of fruit near the cave that she could gather. And with the Japanese patrolling the area, she could not risk going more than a few feet from the cave. She tried not to think of one of the enemy soldiers stumbling upon her hideout by accident. She just had to be careful, do nothing to draw attention to that part of the hills.

Another thought struck her. Were guerrillas in the region? If so, maybe some of them were Americans. Oh, to see a fellow countryman! She loved Rosita and her family, and there would always be a tender place in her heart for the Filipino people as a whole because of all they had done for her, yet how she missed the sound of an American voice, someone she could talk to about familiar places and things. Of course, not many soldiers would be familiar with her old haunts in Los Angeles—the Coconut Grove, Sardi's, Sunset Avenue. But it would be heavenly to talk to someone about hamburgers and hot dogs, even if she probably wasn't going to taste any for a very long time.

She didn't even want to hope that Gary might be free and in the jungle somewhere. But if he was . . .

No. Thoughts of Gary just made her present plight too hard to bear. She had to put him into God's hands and hope that God intended them to be together one day, and then she had to put her mind on other things. And doing just that, she looked through the sack of supplies Rosita brought. Oh, bless her! Besides food there was another book. *Huckleberry Finn*. It was a boy's book, she knew, but she didn't care. She would read anything that would offer her distraction, and this book had to be more interesting than a child's schoolbook.

She tried to read the book slowly, but even at that, in the next five days she read it through twice. For an old book, it was actually quite readable, not wordy and dry like some of the old literature she'd been forced to read in school. Maybe if they had assigned books like this one, she might have tolerated her courses better.

Despite this, she was still nearly dying of boredom. In all her adventures in the Philippines, she had seldom been completely alone. She thanked God for that now, realizing what a gift it had been. She also asked for fortitude to bear this experience.

One day as she doggedly began reading *Huckleberry Finn* for the third time, she got the idea to hone her acting skills by reading the book out loud with appropriate accents for all the characters. It turned out to be a fun and engrossing exercise. If anyone did pass by, they might think she had finally cracked up, but she no longer cared. It was a great distraction.

As the second week of her exile ended, her voice was getting raw so she had to rest from her oral reading. No one had come to visit her, but though she longed for a friendly face and conversation with a real person, she was relieved her friends were not taking that risk. She just hoped no ill had befallen them. When the rain let up, she went to the opening of the cave and sat in the sun for a while. As her strength was returning, she found herself wanting some exercise. Perhaps it wouldn't hurt to hike around a bit in the vicinity of the cave. She hadn't seen a living soul since Rosita had been there a week ago. Maybe she could find some fresh fruit. There were banana trees in abundance not too far away and even some mango and papaya, though it was a bit early for them to ripen.

She rose, just to stretch. She hadn't really convinced herself of the wisdom of a hike. Vaguely she thought she heard the sound of rustling, like feet treading through the brush but some distance away. She stood very still and listened. Yes, someone was coming.

Probably just Rosita or Pepillo. Yet she scurried back inside the cave nonetheless. Her heart was pounding and a sense of dread was settling over her. In a moment she realized the reason. The Vargases had always approached the cave from a different direction than the one from where she heard the sounds.

Could they have taken a circuitous route for security? Oh, please let it be so. She had been thinking a lot of learning Japanese, but she didn't want to take lessons from a real Jap! Just in case, she made sure all her belongings were out of sight of the cave opening, and she also scooted up close to the wall at the back. Then she listened for a familiar, friendly voice.

The sounds of approaching feet came closer and still no friendly greeting. She began to mentally brace herself for capture. She'd had a good run. Maybe it was for the best that it was finally ending. She had always been conflicted about putting those who helped her in danger. Moreover, in a prison camp she might see some of her old friends and know they were all right. Perhaps she would even see Gary, though of course the military prisons were probably kept separate from the civilian. Nevertheless, there was something inviting in the thought of capture and being relieved of the constant fear of capture that had clung to her these last months. Then a voice broke into her thoughts.

"I think we lost 'em."

"I c-can't go on no more, Tony."

"We can hide in that cave, at least until tonight when we can try to get away under cover of dark."

"M-maybe by th-then . . ." The voice deteriorated into a shuddering groan.

Blair didn't need to hear more. The voices were speaking English with American accents. American soldiers!

Still, she was cautious as she crept to the cave opening and peered out. They were about twenty feet away, but she recognized U.S. Army uniforms, though the khaki was faded and the cloth was ragged. One of the men was lying on the ground, curled into a ball and trembling—she knew that position well. He had to be suffering from an attack of malaria. The other man squatted down beside him.

"I have some medicine," Blair said, stepping completely out of the cave.

The man who was squatting jerked around, almost tumbling over with the force of his action. An instant after he got his balance, he leaped to his feet. He blinked several times and even rubbed his fists over his eyes.

"Am I dreaming or something?" he finally asked with such bewilderment, it was possible he really did think he was delirious. No doubt he'd had his share of bouts with malaria.

"No, but why don't you get your friend into the cave and get both of you out of sight. Then we can make introductions."

He quickly complied. Blair recalled the conversation she had heard. They had spoken of "losing them," so it was likely there were Japanese nearby.

The two men were filthy, obviously malnourished, and completely bedraggled. Yet Blair did not hesitate to give the sick man her mat. Then she rummaged through her things and found the few quinine tablets Rosita had recently brought her. She gave the man one with a drink of water from his canteen. Then she and the other man went a little distance from him—indeed, there was only a *little* distance to be had in the cave, which had shrunk considerably with the arrival of two guests.

"I'm Lieutenant Tony Hillerman," said the soldier. "My buddy is Corporal George Dinsmore." Then he added, "What in the world are you doing out here?"

"I'm a fugitive from the Japs, just as you appear to be," she said with a smile. Because she thought her own appearance to be only slightly less bedraggled than his, she had no concept of the effect that smile might have.

Apparently she had overestimated the decline of her looks, for the fellow just gaped at her, his mouth hanging open.

"Do you want something to eat?" she asked, realizing after a few moments of silence that he must be shy and needed encouragement to talk.

He swallowed and licked his dry lips. "Yeah . . . I mean, yes, miss, I am mighty hungry."

She gave him what she could, knowing she still had to ration her supplies and also cognizant that if he was starving, he should eat only a small amount. He must have been familiar with the backlash of eating too much and too quickly on an empty belly, because he was careful to take it slowly. A bite of food, then a bit of conversation.

"What's your name?" he asked as he chewed the dry fish.

"Blair Hayes." She hardly even hesitated over her last name. Gary and their marriage seemed so far in the past that she often wondered if it had ever even existed. So as not to think about that and because she needed to know, she asked, "Are there Japs after you?"

"We encountered some four or five miles from here, but I think we shook 'em off long before we got here."

"Then they haven't left," she mused. "They came here nearly two weeks ago looking for guerrillas. Are they looking for you?"

"I doubt it. We aren't really guerrillas; in fact, we've been looking for a band to join up with. We've been holed up in the mountains. George is pretty sick, and we decided to come out of hiding hoping to find help for him. Each time his attacks get worse. I've been wondering if we just ought to give up. At least the Japs have quinine."

"So do I. A little at least."

"George wouldn't want to take more of your medicine. Do you have malaria, too?"

"I haven't had any problem with it for weeks now. I think I'm over it."

"You don't ever get over it, they say."

"Well, anyway, there is no need for you to surrender, at least for the present. This is a good hiding place, unless—" She stopped herself. No sense in making the fellow feel worse than he already did.

But it was too late. He took up her unfinished thought. "Unless we've brought the enemy down on you." He shook his head. "I don't think we did. I'm sure we lost them miles from here."

"It's no good to worry about that anyway. I have learned to live from day to day. No place is safe forever."

Tony shook his head again, this time with a touch of admiration in his eyes. "You sound like a seasoned veteran, miss, or Blair. May I call you Blair?"

"You better call me Blair!" Then she laughed. "Forgive me. I'm a little touchy about names."

"Why is that?"

"It's a long story. But I do feel as though I've been dodging the

Japs forever, at least since I evacuated from Manila in December. That's less than a year ago, but it feels like . . . eons. Do you know the date? I've lost track."

"I know the feeling. It's October, but I can't tell you the exact day. What brought you to the Philippines?"

"My husband is stationed here. I came to be with him, but that hasn't worked out too well. The war got in the way."

"Who is he? Maybe I know him."

Blair had long ago quit asking every soldier she saw about Gary. It had never helped in the past, and as it turned out, it did no good now. Tony didn't know Gary, but he was also in an infantry regiment, and as she questioned him about his experiences and told him about some of the things Gary had shared with her on the few occasions they had been together, she somehow felt a little closer to Gary. It surprised her how good that felt, since she had been trying hard to push away thoughts of him. She didn't know why being reminded of him now made her feel better rather than worse.

Blair learned that Tony was from California, the San Francisco Bay area, specifically Oakland. He had been to Los Angeles, and she had been to San Francisco, so they both enjoyed talking about, and hearing of, familiar places. Blair's wish had come true. It wasn't a big thing, yet connecting in this way with home and with Gary bolstered her and gave her renewed fortitude to go on and to keep fighting for her freedom.

6

THREE DAYS LATER George Dinsmore was back on his feet, and both men were ready to move on.

"I want to go with you," Blair told them at breakfast. They were eating the last of the tinned tomatoes. Her supplies had dwindled considerably with two more mouths to feed, but that wasn't the reason for her desire to leave. She'd been thinking a lot about her situation since the soldiers' arrival. Encountering these two Americans had filled her thoughts with Gary. What if he was free out there somewhere and she was able to find him? And beyond that, she was feeling more strongly than ever the sense that she needed to somehow help with the war effort. She still had no idea what she could do, but hiding in a cave wasn't accomplishing anything.

"Why do you want to do that?" Tony asked. "You got it pretty good here. You been here a couple weeks undetected. It might be possible for you to wait out the war here."

"I'm tired of waiting, Tony. I'm dying of boredom. Imagine sitting alone in this place for months, even years! I might see the Vargases once in a while, but I hate putting them in jeopardy. I just can't stand the thought of being alone again." She knew she wasn't truly alone, that God was with her, but she was certain He wouldn't be offended by her statement. He understood the basic human need for companionship.

"I can see what she means, Tony," offered George. "I don't want to be alone, either. You ain't gonna leave me alone, are you, Tony? Please take me, too."

"'Course I'm taking you!" Tony glanced at his friend and rolled his eyes.

Blair had thought George's somewhat off-kilter behavior had been due to delirium from his bout of malaria, but as the symptoms of the illness diminished, Blair noticed his mind was . . . well, she thought of it as quirky at first but now wondered if he was simply mentally unbalanced. When she had worked at the hospital just before the fall of Bataan, she had seen some cases of battle fatigue. Some of the men snapped out of it after a few days in the hospital, away from the pressures of battle, but not all. After the hardships of battle, the stress of escaping and running for one's life, along with extreme physical abuse, it was a wonder more men hadn't fallen victim to mental collapse. And she still wasn't certain why she, of all people, hadn't. She wondered what her father would think of *that*! Perhaps his spineless good-for-nothing daughter wasn't so worthless after all.

She felt sorry for George, but she hoped his problems didn't make Tony reluctant to take on another helpless companion.

"What about me?" she asked in a tremulous tone. How she hated the weak sound of her voice when she wanted him to think her independent and strong.

"I think you are crazy for leaving this place," Tony replied noncommittally.

"I'm not crazy yet, Tony." She smiled. "A fool probably, but a desperate fool."

"Well, I can't tell you no, not when you took us in and gave us your food. But you can see for yourself that George and I haven't been making out very well. Our luck has been rotten, and I can't guarantee it'll improve. You might be better off waiting for someone else to care for you."

"I'll take my chances. Besides, I'm not entirely helpless." This last she added with just a touch of defiance.

"Okay, then, pack up your stuff."

It took Blair only a few minutes to gather her things, but when she was ready to leave the cave, she found herself stalling despite her pleading with Tony to take her. She hated to go without first seeing Rosita. Yet the risk of going to the compound was too great, and she didn't want to risk leaving a note in the cave, either. In fact, she tried to leave the cave as if it had never been inhabited in case the Japanese did come upon it. If they thought someone had been hiding here, they might connect it to the Vargases and take out reprisals on them. There was no choice but to leave and pray that someday, somehow, she would encounter her friends again.

Tony decided to head toward the lowlands, where he and George had been heading before ending up in Blair's cave. That would be their best chance of running into partisan groups. Of course, it also afforded a likely opportunity of encountering Japanese. But Tony and Blair had a similar attitude about capture. Though they would like to avoid it, they did not think it would be the worst thing to happen to them. And when the last of the food ran out, a POW camp looked even better. Only when they were pressed did they realize just how desperate they were to remain free.

It happened on the fifth day of their journey. Their last meal had been the previous day. George especially was hit hard, not so much by his malaria but by his mental condition, which seemed to deteriorate with the food supply.

"I want some apple pie, that's what," George said as they plowed their way through a particularly thick growth of vines and brush.

"Keep your voice down," admonished Tony.

They had avoided the established trails by keeping to the thickest part of the jungle, but one could never tell where the enemy might pop up. Blair shuddered at the shrill whine of George's voice.

"Ma put some on the windowsill to cool," George persisted. "Come on, let's get it."

"Please, be quiet," begged Blair softly but with desperate firmness. She gently patted his shoulder to soothe him.

He wrenched away from her touch. "No! You ain't gonna keep me from it!"

"Calm down," ordered Tony.

Just then they broke out of the thick growth, and to their shock they stumbled upon a road, something they had been avoiding for days.

"There's my house!" yelled George. "I'm gonna get me some pie."

They could just see the thatched roof of a hut perhaps a hundred yards away on the other side of the road. George broke into a run.

"Come back here, you fool!" called Tony.

He took off after George, and Blair was about to follow when the sound of an engine broke upon them. George was across the road now, and Tony in the middle. Blair froze more in panic than anything else. A second later the vehicles came into view—military vehicles, for few others besides the Japanese could procure gasoline.

There was no question as to whether her companions had been spotted. The vehicles screeched to a stop, and the occupants bounded out, shouting. Blair gave her next action no thought except that she would not be left to run alone through the jungle again. And perhaps that gnawing sense that a POW camp might not be so bad also made her more willing to take some risks. Nevertheless, she raced across the road to join up with her companions. Neither of them stopped to admonish her for her stupidity. They were running for their lives with a half dozen enemy soldiers hot on their tails. The fugitives' only salvation was that the enemy vehicles could not negotiate the thick foliage on the opposite side of the road into which Blair, Tony, and George had plunged. It would be a foot chase even for the enemy. But the Japanese did have weapons, and they fired a few times on the run but missed their targets.

Blair and Tony caught up to George, who was oblivious to what was happening.

"Pie!" he cried and turned toward the hut, which was now out of sight but still the focus of George's thoughts.

Tony grabbed his arm. "No, this way."

"Ma's house. Gotta get to Ma's house." Unaware of the enemy pursuers, he headed in the direction they were coming from.

Tony tugged at his friend's arm again, but George broke away. Tony started after him, then stopped and shook his head. They would all be dead if they went that way.

"I tried to stop him," Tony said miserably.

Blair knew that he and George had been friends since before the war, but there was no time now for her to comfort him.

Tony and Blair started running again, but a moment later rifle shots split though the air once more. The fugitives paused for an instant and looked at each other, then Tony shook his head and they took off again. After a few minutes Blair no longer heard the sounds of pursuit. Had the effort of killing George—if indeed he was dead—slowed the soldiers? She tried to convince herself he had only been captured and that for him it might be the best thing.

Five minutes later the sounds of pursuit began again, but this time Blair and Tony had more of a lead. They came upon another hut. It was obviously abandoned, but Blair still thought it odd when

Tony ran to the door and yanked it open.

"They'll find us if we try to hide in there," said Blair breathlessly. Had poor Tony gone over the edge, as well?

But he was inside, so Blair followed. As soon as she was in, he slammed the door shut and threw closed the latch. The latch, a metal bar, was rusty with disuse, so it took a bit of effort, but it did finally lock. Blair was contemplating their sure doom when Tony headed toward a window across from the door.

"Come here. Let me give you a boost," he said.

Still perplexed, she nevertheless obeyed. With pursuing Japs within earshot, it was no time for debate. He gave her a boost up and out the window, which had no glass in it. He followed her a moment later, and with hardly a pause for breath, they sprinted away once more.

Once more the sounds of pursuit grew distant. She suspected that Tony hoped the enemy would waste a few minutes trying to break into the hut, thinking the fugitives were still in it. Whatever the case, they got a fair distance away, and Blair was just beginning to think they might be safe enough to stop for a breath. She didn't think she could run another minute and wasn't certain how she had come this far without collapsing.

Her sense of security lasted only a moment, however, before something suddenly slammed into her. She could only manage a muffled cry as she was wrestled to the ground. She could hear Tony's shocked yells, as well. They must be surrounded by enemy patrols. But she couldn't think of that at the moment. All she could think of was getting away. Logic said it was over. She was finally captured. But she couldn't make her body obey logic. She fought and struggled mightily. She heard a sharp yell from her assailant as her knee connected with a tender area of his body.

"Blair! It's okay." That was Tony's voice. Why was everything suddenly silent except for her struggles and her captor's groans?

Other hands grabbed her from behind. She knew it was over now. She made herself relax and only then realized she'd had her eyes shut through most of the few moments of struggle. When she opened her eyes, she saw a man doubled over in front of her. His light brown head of hair couldn't possibly be Japanese. She turned and saw the man holding her from behind had dark skin and black hair, but he wasn't Japanese. He was Filipino. Another white man with pale hair was standing by Tony. They were both panting from their struggle.

"What? Who?" They had clearly found more Americans, though it seemed impossible.

"I was wondering the same. Who y'all are," said the man standing by Tony. "You okay, Sarge?" His question was apparently directed at the man doubled over, since he grunted a rough "Yeah."

"Listen, there's Japs not far away," Tony put in.

"It do look thataway," said the pale-haired man almost as if the situation amused him.

"We better scrap the mission then," the Filipino man said.

"I reckon so. But the captain ain't gonna be happy 'bout that. He near broke his neck to get this dynamite."

Blair noticed packs on the men's backs and shuddered at the thought that she had been fighting with men carrying dynamite.

"We can use it another day," said the Filipino.

"But when is another convoy gonna pass this way?" The blond man paused, then added with resolve, "We still have a half hour before the convoy passes this way. I could get to the bridge and set the fuses—"

"Not on your life," said the man Blair had injured. He was upright again and seemed all right. "The enemy is alerted now. I like to take risks as much as the next man, but this is just stupid. Besides, we got to do something about this gal, so we're getting out of here."

"Who put you in charge?" demanded the blond man. "You're only a sergeant. I'm a lieutenant."

"I'm a lieutenant, too. And I don't care who's in charge. We got a woman to think of."

"'Pears to me she can take care of herself—leastways she took pretty good care of you, Sarge."

The fellow they called Sarge just grunted. "Let's move while we got a choice."

"Where are we going?" Blair asked. She wasn't all that sure she could take care of herself—lucky blow notwithstanding—but she still didn't like the idea of being pushed around by strangers, even if they did appear to be friends.

"Guess we'll take you back to camp with us," said the one called Sarge. "Unless you want to keep running away from the Japs."

"It's all right, Blair," said Tony. "I think we've found us some guerrillas."

Blair had never intended on arguing. She followed quite willingly, though it meant another jungle trek before reaching their destination and the hope of a bed and food. Blair groaned inwardly. She was so exhausted, and there was no time for even a brief rest or proper introductions. The sarge took the lead and kept a grueling pace. Of course, it made sense that he wanted to put as many miles as possible between them and the Jap patrol. He didn't stop for three hours and then only for a few minutes during which a morsel of food, barely enough to take the merest edge off Blair's hunger, was doled out. But she was grateful they shared their scant supply.

Sometime after dark they stopped for the night. Blair was anticipating the chance to talk to these Americans after a bit more food was doled out. Maybe they had heard of Gary. But after the small meal she was so exhausted that she lay down and immediately fell asleep. She was awakened before dawn by the sarge, and they started their unrelenting trek again. She still knew nothing about these men, but she had the impression they wouldn't have given her much information had she had a chance to ask. Secrecy was certainly a matter of survival for them.

Just before sunset they passed through several checkpoints—in reality some rather ragged-looking sentries—at which appropriate passwords were given. Then they came to the headquarters of the partisans. Blair was a little surprised at what greeted her. It seemed more civilized than she had expected. Civilized, of course, was a relative term in the Philippines. For a partisan hideout in the middle of the jungle, it was every bit as nice as the Vargases' compound. There were two huts and a couple of lean-tos that were probably for supplies but contained only a couple of crates. There were half a dozen men in the compound engaged in various activities. One man was stirring a pot over a campfire. Hot food! Blair could have nearly wept at the idea of that alone. She noted little smoke rose from the fire, indicating they had to be careful of the enemy even though the camp had appeared quite secluded when they had approached.

"Hey, Jack!" Sarge called to one of the men. "Is the captain in his hut?"

"Yeah, but he's sleeping. He was out all night trying to work a deal with the Commies."

"Well, I think he'll want to see our visitors."

The fellow named Jack took a closer look, his gaze resting

particularly on Blair. Blair used to get that kind of look all the time from men—pleased and slightly wolfish. She had gotten a few such looks from the sarge's men on their journey. Still, it surprised her. She knew she looked a sight. These men had obviously been deprived of female company far too long.

Jack went to one of the huts, knocked on the door, and after a muffled reply, went inside. In a few moments Jack emerged. He was followed by a tall figure who had to stoop a bit to clear the door lintel. He was rubbing his hands over his face, having apparently been wakened from sleep. Blair did not get a good look at the man for a full minute except for his ragged clothes, a mix of uniform and native garb. Then he straightened and dropped his hands as he ambled toward the newcomers.

Blair gasped at the same moment the tall man stopped dead in his tracks.

"You okay, Captain?" Jack asked.

" 'Fraid we picked up a couple of strays," said the sarge.

"You look like you seen a ghost, Gary," the blond man said.

At that moment exhaustion, hunger, and shock closed in on Blair. She felt herself sway. Don't faint now, she admonished herself. But the sarge's hand shot out quickly to steady her. Then Gary rushed forward and put his arms around her. She didn't know if it was an embrace or just an attempt to keep her from falling. She didn't care.

"Gary, is it really you?"

"Guess I've changed a lot."

"Me too. It's been so long."

"Like a lifetime."

She nodded.

"Thank God, we're finally together."

"Yes," she said, and the smile that bent her lips was weak only because of her exhaustion. "Thank God."

Before she realized what was happening, she was swept off her feet as Gary lifted her up into his arms. He was still as strong as ever, even though he looked forty pounds thinner. He carried her as if she were a feather and took her into one of the huts.

7

THERE WAS LITTLE of redeeming value in the Owens Valley, at least that Jackie could readily see. This was the California desert. The more famous Death Valley was less than a hundred miles to the southeast. After three months of residence here, Jackie had tried her best to find some good in the place. She'd had the misfortune of arriving in the heat of summer, such incredible heat that she still wondered how humans could survive it.

The extreme weather—blasting hot in summer, bone-chilling cold in the winter—was only part of it. For here was located one of the concentration camps into which the Japanese had been herded last spring. Manzanar. The name sounded to Jackie like the idyllic title of a romantic novel. It was hardly that. Manzanar was a dreary, dust-ridden expanse of ugly barracks surrounded by barbed wire, complete with armed-guard towers. She found it quite fitting that the government, which had imprisoned its citizens and loyal residents simply by nature of their race, would choose this particular setting for a camp. In fact, she'd heard that all the other camps were in similar environments, stretching across the most barren areas of the western states.

She found it especially ironic that she'd had to fight to get here. Most of the ten thousand residents would have given anything to get out. After her graduation from UCLA she had counted on her father's influence to smooth the way for her to join her husband in the camp. But when it came down to actually watching his daughter go to a Japanese concentration camp, he'd had a drastic change of heart. He regretted even giving his blessing to her marriage. And he refused to help her in this insanity of going to the camp.

The WRA, War Relocation Authority, also was reluctant. She tried to get an assignment to teach at the camp, for she knew from Sam that they were in desperate need of teachers and only Caucasians were given these jobs. But her marriage to a Japanese man made her risky material for such a position. She tried to point out the inconsistency of their subsequently deeming her "unfit" to reside at a camp as an internee. But in many cases the WRA was making up the rules as they went because there was simply no precedent for this mass imprisonment of Americans. Even more so, there was no precedent for the treatment of a white wife of a Japanese man.

Totally frustrated, Jackie decided to do what Cameron always did, rather successfully, to get her way. She tried the bullying tactic.

"Listen here," she finally told the clerk, "I am going to Manzanar. You are not going to stop me. I am going to have my baby with his father there. And that is that!"

"Your baby?" queried the man, peering up at her over the top of his horned-rimmed glasses. He was seated at a desk, and she was standing because no chair had been offered her.

"Yes," she said sharply. At that time she wasn't showing much, so it was understandable that the man hadn't concluded she was expecting, but regardless, she was too riled up now to be polite. "Yoshito Samuel Okuda is the father. I have been trying for the last week to get permission to be with him."

"No one told me about a child. He is half Japanese?"

She rolled her eyes. "Yes."

"Well, the child will have to go to the camp. There is no question about that. Any person who is more than one-sixteenth Japanese cannot avoid it. There are nurseries at the camp run by nuns, and children without their parents are well cared for—"

"You nincompoop!" Jackie burst.

The clerk sputtered and gave her a sharp look. She knew she was making it worse for herself, but this was the last straw. She didn't care if the man didn't realize the child wasn't born yet. The whole process was so ridiculous, she was too appalled to be logical or polite.

But she did take a breath and modified her tone as she realized she had hit upon a sure way into the camp. Obviously there would be no precedent for this, either. But she sensed they would want to confine a "dangerous" half-Japanese child enough to also accept the mother.

"My child isn't born yet, sir," she said evenly. "I am afraid if you want to put him in a concentration camp, I will have to go along." She gave a thin smile.

The clerk sputtered again, then shuffled some papers, stamped a couple, and finally handed her one. "Here is a pass into Manzanar. Take it with my blessing!" His voice was filled with far more sarcasm than blessing of any kind.

Her mother had tearfully seen her off at the train station. She had promised to come visit her and to be there when the baby was born. Now, three months later, Jackie longed to see her mother, missing her terribly. Yet on the other hand, she did not want her mother to come here, to see this place where her first grandchild would be born. It would break Cecilia's heart. It nearly broke Jackie's when she thought of her baby being born behind barbed wire.

And that was only the half of it. The barracks themselves were shabby, shoddily built structures with cracks in the siding that let in the copious desert dust and protected little against the extremes of temperature. There were no private baths, only latrines, and until recently the women's latrines had not even had separate stalls. This was changed only after an uproar from the female residents.

She'd heard one woman say of her tiny apartment, "I would not even keep my animals in such a place!"

Jackie tried to adopt Sam's imperturbable attitude. He was positive about everything, or tried to be. When the other internees complained about the Caucasian proclivity toward using rice as a dessert with a sweet fruit topping, he just shrugged and said at least it wasn't green. And he meant that in two ways—at least it wasn't a vegetable, and at least it wasn't moldy, as so much of the food often was. This insensitivity on the part of the white cooks infuriated Jackie. No Japanese ate rice in this way. It was meant to be eaten as a main dish, not sweetened.

She tried to have a good attitude, but so much about this place made her angry. Sam hinted it might be her pregnancy that made her so much more emotional than usual. She knew better. It was the crass injustice of it all. And she wasn't the only one to be angry.

Many of the residents of Manzanar were angry, and she knew even Sam was churning inside with ire. Perhaps for her sake he quashed it down, to set a good example, but she knew he was on edge. He might not be willing to consider doing what some were thinking of doing—renouncing their American citizenship and returning to Japan—but she knew his smile, his patient shrug, his sardonic jokes, were merely a façade. She prayed that all that simmered inside him did not explode one day.

Despite the WRA's decision that she was not fit to teach at a camp, those who actually did get the jobs were far more reasonable and accepting. The white teachers, most of whom were women, did not commit to teaching Japanese children in a concentration camp, with low pay and scanty supplies, unless they felt a deep concern for these particular children. So for the most part the teachers employed here were loving, giving people who welcomed Jackie for who she was and did not look down upon her for whom she was married to. And when she inquired about helping in the elementary school, she was eagerly accepted. Because she did not yet have her teaching credentials, she acted as an assistant in two classrooms. She was even paid for her labor—$14 per month, the average wage for internees who worked at various jobs in the camp.

She would have worked for free because she loved teaching and because she was often bored to distraction. Sam encouraged her but reminded her that in a couple of months she'd be far from bored. How she longed for the birth of their child, barbed wire notwithstanding! And perhaps the new baby would help bring the Okuda family back together.

Oh, they were quite together in a physical sense! Eight of them crammed into a unit in Barrack #18 that was approximately sixteen feet by twenty feet. There was the partitioned-off area made by Sam and his father last spring that was large enough for two of the army cots and some standing room. This was where Mr. and Mrs. Okuda slept, and Sam had never been able to convince them to take turns with him and Jackie for the use of it. Other parts of the room were curtained off with blankets: an area for Sam's sisters, Kimi, Miya, and Mika—Kimi complained constantly about the injustice of having to share a "room" with her baby sisters; another area for T.C., Sam's brother, just large enough for his cot; and finally an area for Sam and Jackie. Privacy was a forgotten commodity. Often Sam and

Jackie would miss meals—all served community style in a mess hall—just for the chance to be completely alone in the apartment.

The close quarters induced tension, but there were enough other reasons for short tempers in the family. For one thing, Kimi was miserable and made sure everyone knew it. She missed her boyfriend, who had gone to a different camp. She never missed an opportunity to say that she wished they had gotten married before the evacuation, as many young people had done in order to stay together. But her parents had felt she was too young, and before their minds could be changed, Susumu, Kimi's young man, had been sent to a camp called Heart Mountain. So Kimi blamed her parents and lost no opportunity to tell them.

Then there was sixteen-year-old T.C., the nickname he had adopted to honor his favorite baseball player, Ty Cobb. He was quiet and morose most of the time and very bitter about the evacuation, though he refused to talk to anyone about it. He spent as much time as he could away from the apartment. Jackie feared he was getting in with a bad crowd. She had once seen him and a few other boys smoking behind a latrine. This had nothing to do with why he resented Jackie, but he did seem to, and though he was quiet about it, his hostility was clear to everyone. His reason appeared to be simply because she was white—at least that's what Sam said he had gotten out of his brother during a confrontation.

Miya and Mika, who'd had birthdays in the summer and were now twelve and eleven, were, for the most part, adopting Sam's patient attitude. They played with their friends, enjoyed school, and generally tried to make the best of their situation. Mika was sick a lot, though. The terrible scourge of dust in the valley had caused an allergic reaction, and she had developed a form of asthma. They all suffered from nearly constant diarrhea because the food was so different from what they were accustomed to and was of poor quality. Everyone in the camp was affected, but children were hit the hardest.

Finally, there were Mr. and Mrs. Okuda. Jackie's first day in Manzanar best illustrated the situation with them. Sam hadn't been able to meet her at the gate because he hadn't known the exact time of her arrival, so she found the apartment on her own. He was there waiting and greeted her with all the exuberance of a young husband who had been separated from his wife for several months. The whole family was there, as well, and observing the scene, but Sam was not in the least reserved in displaying his ardor. Jackie tried not to be self-conscious. She was just as eager to embrace and kiss her husband, but the others in the room were nearly strangers to her. The couple of days she had stayed with them when she and Sam were first married had done nothing to bond them to her. In fact, she'd been in school most of the time and had seen little of them.

Eventually Sam let go of her, except for keeping one arm around her and staying close by her side. Jackie gave a greeting to each member of the family.

When she came to Mrs. Okuda, she smiled as broadly and warmly as she could. "Thank you so much for having me here," Jackie said and reached out a hand to her mother-in-law.

Mrs. Okuda smiled and started to reach for Jackie's hand, but from the corner of the room, where two mismatched chairs made a little sitting area, there came a distinct snapping sound.

Mr. Okuda was seated in one of the chairs, his eyes focused on the newspaper he was holding and which he had apparently given a sharp snap at the appropriate moment. He did not look up, and the whole time he never looked at Jackie or acknowledged her presence. Jackie glanced at the man and smiled but received no response. Mrs. Okuda looked at her husband and the smile of greeting she had begun to offer Jackie twitched and faded. Her hand dropped.

But in a somber tone she did say, "Welcome to our home, such as it is." Then Mrs. Okuda's eyes skittered toward her husband again.

Sam leaped into the awkward pause, asking Jackie about her trip and other news. The other young people, apparently feeling excused from the formal welcome ceremony, went about their own business, chattering among themselves. Sam showed Jackie where to put her suitcase and assured her that after lunch they would fetch her other cases, which had been too much for her to carry from the office.

Jackie hadn't noticed when Mr. and Mrs. Okuda left the room, but soon their voices could be heard behind the plywood partition that was their bedroom. The plywood, as Sam had once told her, indeed gave only the illusion of privacy. The voices of the couple, which had begun quietly, soon rose so that even neighbors could hear. Jackie had not a clue of what they were saying because it was all in Japanese, but she was sure she was at the center of the conversation.

Sam had often assured Jackie that his mother liked her, so now she tried to imagine that Mrs. Okuda was upbraiding Mr. Okuda for his rude behavior. Jackie had hoped for a better reception from the man but had not expected one, since Sam had hinted the man regretted giving his blessing to the marriage. Ironically, Jackie thought that Keagan Hayes and Hiroshi Okuda could probably be great friends if they ever met. They certainly had much in common with their stubborn intractable attitudes.

Still, it did not really please her that Mrs. Okuda was taking her side. She did not want to be the cause of a rift between her in-laws. She hoped that if Mrs. Okuda was forced to choose between her daughter-in-law and her husband, she would choose her husband. And as time passed, that's what appeared to happen. Oh, she was civil, speaking to Jackie when necessary, but avoided her whenever possible. Mr. Okuda, on the other hand, continued to act as if Jackie did not exist, quite an impressive feat with eight people crowded into 320 square feet of living space.

At least tensions eased a bit outside the apartment. Sam still experienced some alienation from his friends, but many of them had begun to warm up to him again. Unfortunately, his two best friends did not, which proved difficult for Sam.

Both Sam and Jackie agreed that her position in the school was helping, for as she started to endear herself to the children, the parents also began to accept her. Jackie found that she was happiest at school, where her students did indeed quickly grow to love her and look up to her. Except when she was alone with Sam, this was the only place in Manzanar where she felt truly welcome.

8

Mrs. Okuda tried gallantly to keep her family together despite all the tensions. But even without tensions, barracks living and mess-hall dining were enough in themselves to tatter the fabric of the family.

One Sunday in October the stressful situation reached a climax of sorts. Sam, Jackie, Kimi, and the "little sisses," as the family referred to the younger girls, were in the habit of attending the Protestant church together. T.C. refused to go to church, and Mr. and Mrs. Okuda attended Buddhist services. Because this had been the general way of things before the evacuation, it caused little stir. The problem was Sunday dinner following church. This meal had always been an important event in the Okuda home, though in fact nearly all meals had been family events. At Manzanar all meals, including Sunday dinner, were taken in one of the mess halls with crowds of other internees. Mrs. Okuda hated this aspect of camp life more than any other. She hated not being able to cook, an activity she had especially enjoyed. She hated it when her children would go off and join friends at other tables. But the one thing she had managed to hold together was Sunday dinner, insisting that everyone eat together for that one meal.

On this particular Sunday, Sam and Jackie realized they'd had absolutely no time alone all the previous week, and they were desperate for just a few minutes to themselves. After church Sam told his mother they would be late for lunch, which on Sunday was the main meal.

"Now, don't say you will be late and then not show up at all," Mrs. Okuda admonished.

Guiltily, Jackie realized they had done this on more than one occasion. But could she and Sam really be blamed for stealing a half hour alone?

"No, Mama," Sam assured, "we will be there."

"Mama," put in Kimi, "George Tsuyoshi wants me to have dinner with him today."

"No," Mrs. Okuda said firmly. "We have dinner together."

"But, Mama, just this once. Please . . ."

"George can eat with us," conceded the woman.

"We like to be alone once in a while, too," pouted Kimi. She apparently had lost interest in her former boyfriend, her supposed fiancé. But Susumu was far away, and who knew when they would be together, if ever. Kimi was young, and with the uncertainties of life, her fickle nature was not too surprising.

At that point, probably afraid of becoming embroiled somehow in Kimi's dilemma, Sam grabbed Jackie's hand and tugged her back to the apartment, where they did have some time alone.

But true to Sam's word, they returned to the mess hall twenty minutes later, where there was still a long line of people waiting to be served. When they finally got their food, they began threading their way around the tables full of diners, looking for the Okuda table. Jackie began to think the family had finished and left, though they never finished a meal that quickly. Then she saw why it had been hard to find them. Mr. and Mrs. Okuda were seated alone at a table. Not literally alone, for the long table was full of other diners, but they were the only Okudas at the table.

Sam nudged Jackie and nodded toward the far side of the room. Miya and Mika were seated at a table with about a dozen other kids their age. In another part of the hall, Kimi was seated with her friend George. T.C. was nowhere to be seen and very likely was at another mess hall entirely. How had that happened? But it was easy for Jackie to imagine the way of it. Probably Mrs. Okuda had given in to Kimi's insistence, and that had opened the floodgates for the other children. In all likelihood T.C. probably hadn't asked to eat elsewhere but had just escaped in the general exodus. Had Mrs. Okuda had more support from her husband, she might have prevailed, but lately Mr. Okuda had given up all semblance of being in authority.

Jackie and Sam joined his parents and tried to keep up a lively conversation. But the two elders said nothing. Mrs. Okuda's food was hardly touched, and Jackie was almost certain the woman was on the verge of tears. Her lower lip trembled, and Jackie understood her silence, for certainly if she spoke, the tears would flow.

Politely waiting until Jackie and Sam finished their food, Mr. and Mrs. Okuda lingered not a moment longer before rising and leaving the mess hall. Jackie's heart quaked for the woman, and she wanted so to reach out and give her a comforting hug, but she feared not only being rejected but also upsetting the woman even more. So she and Sam followed them back to the apartment, where the elders went to their room, Mrs. Okuda explaining they wanted a little nap.

"Shouldn't we talk to them?" Jackie asked Sam in a whisper.

"What can we say? What can we do?"

"I feel so bad that we contributed to the situation by being late."

"What do you want to do, Jackie, give up the little time we have alone together? I don't think I can do that, even if it does hurt my parents a little."

"I just can't stand to see your mother so hurt and upset." Jackie's lips trembled as she felt emotion rise. Maybe she *was* more sensitive now because of her pregnancy, but it was no less real.

"It's not entirely our responsibility—"

"Sam, why are you being so unfeeling about this?"

"What? Is it all my fault suddenly?" he said shortly, his voice rising.

"Keep your voice down, Sam—"

"I've got to whisper now, in my own home? It's bad enough I have to kiss you with a dozen eyes around and eat with a thousand people! I'm sick of it. None of this is my fault!" He jumped up from the cot where he'd been sitting. Jackie feared his emotional volcano might finally erupt. "I'm sorry, Jackie," he added tightly, his anger barely controlled. "I just can't stand it. I can't stand that my mother hurts and that I can't be a real husband to you. I can't stand seeing my family fall apart. I can't—" He bit off the rest of what he meant to say and shook his head dismally. "I've got to be alone for a while."

He spun around and left the apartment. Jackie stared after him, for a moment in complete shock, and then the tears started pouring from her eyes. Sobs quickly followed. She tried to be quiet. She heard soft snores from the Okudas' room and didn't want to wake them, nor did she want them to know she was crying. She thought about leaving, but what if she ran into Sam? If he needed to be alone, she wanted to respect that. She prayed none of the rest of the family would come in just then.

She tried to dry her eyes with the corner of her sweater. She didn't feel like getting up and rummaging through her things for a hankie. But new tears came as quickly as she dashed away the old ones. She couldn't help it. She kept thinking of Mrs. Okuda's hurt and Sam's confusion and even poor Mr. Okuda's coldness, which she was certain was more a result of this horrible situation than the fact that his son had married a white woman. She thought of the injustice of the evacuation. Even Kimi's botched love life made Jackie cry. And poor T.C., who was cutting himself off from everyone who loved him.

And finally she thought of her mother. Thinking of the Okudas losing their family just made her think of losing her own family. Her sisters, her father—but mostly her mother.

Oh, Mama! I need you.

Only then did she realize how difficult these last few months had been. Living under these appalling physical conditions was only half of it. Mostly it was that sometimes, even with Sam, her best friend, at her side, she was so lonely. And she often felt out of place. She was not a racist, yet she often felt her differentness acutely. No matter how American many of the younger people here were, she still did not really fit in.

She sniffed and sobbed and hiccuped. She didn't hear the floorboards creak as they usually did with the lightest step, and when she glanced up, there was Mrs. Okuda looking in through a crack in the blanket curtains.

"May I sit with you?" the woman asked quietly.

Jackie saw her mother-in-law's eyes were as red as Jackie's must be. "Yes, please do." She scooted over to make room on the cot, which wobbled with the weight of them both.

"Did my Yoshito make you cry?" Mrs. Okuda asked.

Jackie could only shake her head as new sobs momentarily

controlled her. Finally she managed to say, "It's . . . just everything . . . so heartbreaking."

Mrs. Okuda nodded with sympathy. Tears filled the older woman's eyes.

Jackie didn't know if she found the courage to speak her next words because of her own need or because she was fairly certain her mother-in-law's obvious need would keep her from rejecting Jackie. But she said, "C-could you hold me? I so miss my mother. . . ."

Mrs. Okuda did not hesitate. Her arms went around Jackie as if it was the most natural thing in the world to do—a mother comforting a weeping child. Between her own sobs, the older woman uttered comforting murmurs. "There . . . there . . . we will get through this. . . ."

Jackie nodded. She really did believe it now. The woman's arms helped bolster her faith.

They held each other until all of their tears subsided. Then Jackie became sensitive to their close environment and started to ease away.

"I don't want to upset Mr. Okuda should he come out," she said to explain her actions.

Mrs. Okuda kept one arm tightly around Jackie. "He is sound asleep. Don't you hear his snores?"

Now that it had been brought to her attention, she did hear them, soft and steady behind the partition.

"I'm so sorry for the tension I'm causing," Jackie said.

"You have no reason to be sorry. My husband is a stubborn man." Then a tender smile bent the corners of her lips. "But he is a good man, Jackie. You must understand that."

"I know. Sam respects him greatly and strives to be like him. In fact, I think Sam is a lot like him, and that is why Sam is such a fine man, too."

"Yes, they are both fine . . . but they are men." Mrs. Okuda chuckled softly. "Not as strong and sensible as women, and it is nearly impossible for them to accept change. At least Sam is young, and that helps. But my husband . . . this is so hard for him. He knows nothing but to be the head of his family. Now that has been taken from him, and he has nothing."

"But he is very much respected still."

"He makes no important decisions anymore. And even the small decisions, like Kimi wanting to eat with her boyfriend, he has given over to me. I fear he has given up."

"Does he blame me, Mrs. Okuda?"

"I don't know. He will not speak of you. But I think his heart will change when you give him a grandchild. A grandson especially would be nice."

"I'll try my hardest."

Mrs. Okuda squeezed Jackie's shoulder. "I wouldn't mind a granddaughter myself. When Mr. Okuda awakes, I will show you something I have put away in my wicker chest. Now, my daughter, I will tell you something else. You and I need each other. Kimi and the little sisses are growing away from me, and though I don't much like it, that is natural for them to do. So I need you even more and the little one you carry, too. And I sense you need a mama, especially while you are here. I would like to be a mama to you, not to replace your mother but just as a substitute while she is gone, if that is okay."

"What about Mr. Okuda? I don't want to come between you." Though she was trying to be sensitive, she was also nearly breathless with excitement. Nothing in a long while had felt better than Mrs. Okuda's arms holding her and comforting her. There was simply nothing like a mother's touch.

"I have let him have his way because this move was so hard on him," Mrs. Okuda replied. "Now I realize it is also hard on me, and I must care for my own well-being if I hope to help my family. Being a part of your and Yoshito's life is my one way of doing this. I don't know how I will bear losing my children as they grow, but I think it will help if I am not alienated from Yoshito and if I have you for a friend. Is that selfish? I don't know."

"I don't know, either, Mrs. Okuda. I am so happy right now that I don't care. We need each other, and that's enough."

Sam returned in an hour and apologized to Jackie for his outburst. She accepted his apology, though she really held nothing against him. It had all worked for good. He was thrilled to hear about her talk with his mother.

Later that evening Mrs. Okuda invited Jackie into her room. Mr. Okuda had wakened from his nap hours ago and was out visiting with some other men. Before Jackie ducked around the plywood wall, she caught a glimpse of Sam sitting in one of the chairs, a book in hand. But he wasn't looking at the pages; instead his gaze was on the two women. He was smiling.

Mrs. Okuda and Jackie knelt in front of the wicker chest as the older woman opened it and took out several items.

"Baby things I have been making," she said.

Jackie gasped with pleasure. Even when Mrs. Okuda hadn't been speaking to Jackie, she had been sewing things for the baby!

There were two baby kimonos unlike anything Jackie had ever seen. They were made of plain white muslin and stitched all over with colored thread. It wasn't embroidery but rather a plain running stitch in intricate patterns like scallops, diamonds, and hexagons. There was also a receiving blanket done the same way and a large cloth bag made of navy blue fabric with a striking pattern stitched in white thread. Finally, there was a pink cotton bonnet embroidered in traditional fashion with little flowers and yellow ducks.

"It's all so beautiful!" Jackie exclaimed. "When did you have a chance to do this?"

"I have nothing but time on my hands here. And you are gone teaching, so I can do it in secret. I don't want it to be secret anymore. I want you to know how I love you and my grandchild. Do you mind that it is pink?"

"No. I think a little girl would be nice, too. Sam leans toward a boy, of course."

"I will make a blue bonnet, too. And booties, as well. I will love Baby Okuda the same if it is a boy or a girl."

Jackie felt ready to cry again, so she turned her attention to the baby things. She fingered the fabric and admired the perfect stitching.

"I have never seen anything like this," she said. "Is it a Japanese craft?"

"It is called *sashiko*."

"Your stitches are so even and small. It looks simple, but I suppose it was very hard to do."

"It is easier with practice. I have been doing it for many years."

A brief pause followed, and then Jackie had an inspiration.

"Mrs. Okuda, could you teach me to do this?"

"Oh yes, I would love to."

"I've done a little embroidery, but I'm not very good at it."

"I'll have you making stitches like mine in no time," Jackie's mother-in-law said enthusiastically.

The time they spent with these lessons, usually an hour or so in the evening, became Jackie's most treasured memories of her time at Manzanar. And it had less to do with learning a fine Japanese craft than it did with the company of Sam's mother, the friendship formed, and the pleasant conversation that went with the lessons. They talked about a wide range of things. Jackie loved learning about Japanese culture, about Mr. and Mrs. Okuda's youth in Japan, and about their experiences as immigrants. But mostly Jackie appreciated talking about raising a family, motherhood, and especially giving birth. Jackie was nervous about these things, but Mrs. Okuda's frank comments and honesty did much to prepare Jackie for what was soon to come.

Many of the tensions remained in the family's life at Manzanar, but Jackie could not believe how having one more ally, one more friend, helped her over many rough spots.

PART II

*"Then you know you are expendable.
In a war anything can be
expendable—money or
gasoline or equipment or most usually men.
They are expending you and
that machine gun to get time."*

W. L. WHITE
They Were Expendable, 1942

Moscow, Soviet Union
Fall 1942

AFTER ALEX's departure to the Russian Front, Cameron's life fell into its accustomed routine. Her transfer to the Pacific Theater of the war never transpired. Max Arnett had suggested it before he learned of Johnny's death, and Cameron had considered it once, thinking her relationship with Alex had ended. But all had changed drastically. There was no point now to the game of "catch me if you can" with Johnny that Max had initiated at the beginning of Cameron's foreign assignment. And Max must also realize Cameron no longer needed the challenge of beating Johnny to prove herself. The game had been fun, but her success was her own now. And all things being equal, Max preferred his best correspondent, his most experienced in Russian affairs, remain in Moscow. Cameron had ensured her position by wiring her publisher and informing him of her desire to stay.

She now had every reason to remain in Russia. Here there might be a slim chance of seeing Alex again. Until then, she had a job to do.

And that job became eminently more interesting one morning when she received a telephone call that an interview with a high Soviet official had been arranged by her friend Boris Tiulenev. "Uncle Boris" was a friend of Nikita Khrushchev, a senior Party leader who had pretty much controlled the Ukrainian Party apparatus before the war and now was in the South-Western Region of the State Defense Committee, directly under its chief, Budenny.

Cameron had high hopes for the interview because Khrushchev, as a Ukrainian official, must have some firsthand knowledge of the disastrous battle of Kharkov and the current struggle in Sevastopol. But Uncle Boris crushed those expectations when he instructed her about off-limit topics, including Kharkov and any ongoing battles. For all practical purposes, then, the Party leader didn't plan to talk about the war at all. Still, no journalist would turn down any such interview even if it promised to be just the usual Party drivel. If she was truly worth her stuff as a journalist, she ought to be able to wring something significant from the man.

She met Khrushchev in his flat in one of the drab apartment buildings erected near the Kremlin in the thirties. The apartment itself was a modestly appointed place and had the look of temporary usage, probably used by Khrushchev only during his official visits to Moscow. She was welcomed into the living room by a tall, solidly built man who appeared to be about fifty, with black hair peppered with gray and combed severely away from his face. His dark eyes were sharp behind the lenses of horn-rimmed glasses.

"I am Stanislav Tveritinov, Comrade Khrushchev's assistant, and I will act as interpreter." His soft tone contrasted with his commanding features. His English was heavily accented but adequate.

"Thank you, Comrade Tveritinov. As you know, I am Cameron Hayes of the *Los Angeles Globe*."

While Tveritinov made formal introductions, Cameron quickly assessed her subject. Uncle Boris had mentioned that Khrushchev was of peasant stock and had spent his younger years working in the mines of the Donblass region. He did indeed look like a man who had toiled long with the weight of the world over him. Somewhat squat, he had thick, powerful shoulders, no neck to speak of, and a heavily jawed face. His eyes were narrow, seeming to be perpetually squinted, making it difficult to tell the color, but Cameron thought those eyes could be equally jovial or as incisive as a blade. Two or three moles dotted the rugged surface of his broad face. His thinning pale hair was marked by a significantly receding hairline, which made judging his age difficult. Cameron thought he was the sort of person who had probably always looked old, even as a young man. She knew, however, that he was forty-eight.

"I shall have to thank my friend Boris for sending me such a pretty journalist to speak with," Khrushchev said through his interpreter.

"I am most appreciative of your willingness to be interviewed. My readers back in the States will be fascinated, I am sure," she said in English, which Tveritinov translated.

Cameron knew enough Russian to pick out words here and there and glean the general meaning of many phrases, but she couldn't have managed without the interpreter, though she had decided to keep to her ruse of not revealing her knowledge of the language. Nevertheless, she did know enough of the language to realize Khrushchev and Tveritinov each spoke Russian with a different accent. She assumed Khrushchev's denoted his Ukrainian roots, but she couldn't decipher Tveritinov's. She thought she detected a similarity to Marfa Elichin's accent, her half-brother Semyon's cousin, to whom she had spoken in Vdovin, near Sverdlovsk in the Urals. She also noted that Khrushchev's speech was coarser, earthier, than his assistant's more refined usage, but the interpreter "cleaned up" Khrushchev's cruder phrases in his translation.

"Come, sit down and let's talk," said Khrushchev.

They moved to the seats in the room, a drab brown sofa and matching chair. Cameron sat in the chair while the two men settled on the sofa. She took out her pad and pencil. There were already some notes on the pad, questions she wanted to cover, but Khrushchev took the lead.

"In America I see they have finally brought you women into equal standing with men," he said. "In Russia, of course, women have always worked side by side with men, at least since the Revolution. Only the socialized state has been able, in the words of Lenin himself, to complete the emancipation of women and bring them to occupy the same position as men."

"And this is so even in the mines where you labored, Comrade Khrushchev?"

"There are some jobs, admittedly, that men are better suited for. But I have seen women work machinery in the mines. And now with our men at the Front, women are even filling positions thought only fit for men. Russian women are strong, even those not born of peasant stock. Of course, the peasants are strongest. I know that for a fact because I am of peasant stock. In Russia, you see, where all are equal, peasants can rise to positions of authority." He smiled, bringing out deep crow's-feet around the corners of his eyes and revealing poor dental work and crooked teeth.

"My father was born a peasant in Ireland," Cameron couldn't resist saying. "He is now a powerful newspaper publisher."

He laughed. "Ah, you Americans!" he said and without missing a beat adroitly changed the subject. "Have you been on the Moscow metro, Miss Hayes? A structural marvel, a wonder of the world, no less! By sheltering the citizens of Moscow during the air raids, it has played a huge part in sparing the people from the Nazi dogs who tried to invade this city. It is very deep, you see, the deepest underground railroad in the world."

"Yes, I have traveled on it. It is impressive."

"I was instrumental in its building. I was second-in-command of the project. Me, a poor man from the Ukraine who toiled with his hands most of his life."

Cameron knew the metro was indeed a marvel, but she had also heard rumors of the high loss of life due to the deplorable working conditions during its construction. Khrushchev failed to mention that when he continued, and Cameron had enough sense not to press the point.

"The job was completed miraculously in a year," he went on. "Even *Pravda* praised my work on the project. I received the Order of Lenin for outstanding achievement, but I mention it only so you will know of the incredible fortitude of the Russian people." There was not even a hint of modesty in his tone. He appeared to greatly enjoy singing his praises right along with those of the Russian people.

"Oh yes, Comrade Khrushchev, I have witnessed firsthand how incredible you Russians are," she said. "When this war is over, the world will owe a huge debt to you."

"Not many in the West give us such credit."

"Perhaps you'd be surprised at the extent of support you have in the West."

"Well, now America is in the war. Together we will smash the German barbarians!" His jowls shook a bit with his enthusiasm.

"I see you are in uniform, Comrade Khrushchev," she commented. "What exactly is your role in the war?"

He grinned. "Yes, yes, this is what interests you. The war—Russia's Great Patriotic War. I am of the rank of major general, by the way. But I thought you understood that I cannot speak of the war in detail nor of any current actions."

"Of course, but surely there is something you can impart to my readers about the war. Most of the recent action has been in your specific region, has it not?"

All humor drained from his face, leaving a cold, hard visage. She saw now that, though he liked to play the rough-hewn, somewhat jovial man of the people, there was a layer to Nikita Khrushchev that spoke of a ruthless nature. Cameron reminded herself that this man had survived the great purges of the thirties—not merely survived but *advanced* in his political position, as well. In Russia such a feat took cunning as well as ruthlessness. And she suspected even more than that. She wondered how many of his dear "people" *he* had helped Stalin send to the gallows.

"You know, Miss Hayes, I was growing to like you very much." The icy aspect did not leave his face. "I would not want to change my good opinion."

"I am sorry, Comrade Khrushchev. I have overstepped propriety." She hated the taste of crow but knew better than to antagonize someone who could potentially be of great use to her. Goodness, she told herself ruefully, but that sounds as cold as Khrushchev himself. Yet in Russia such an attitude was not only useful, it might also be the difference between life and death. And someday, when she and Alex were able to be together, it might mean *their* life or death to have the good graces of a man like this.

"I have heard of the brashness of Americans," he said, his tone lightening slightly, "and I can forgive your misstep. But in Russia it is best to use discretion."

"Perhaps I can take another direction, then?" she asked and he nodded. "I have found it impossible to obtain an interview with Comrade Stalin. Perhaps you can share something about him for my readers. Do you know him personally?"

"Yes, I do." He glanced at Tveritinov, the first time anything passed between the two men beyond what interpretation entailed. Cameron couldn't define that brief look, but if she was forced to make a guess, she might almost think the two men shared a secret that Stalin might not appreciate.

"What is he really like?" she encouraged.

"He is a great man, the greatest genius of humanity. Our friend and father. The greatest man of our time." Again there was an undertone and a sense that Khrushchev was reciting his words of praise by mere rote. Could it be that he blamed Stalin for the debacle in Kharkov? There were rumors that Stalin had forbidden retreat even when the situation had been at its worst. Of course that disaster must have touched Khrushchev personally, since this was his home region. There might well be some bitterness in him over this issue.

"Do you work directly with him in regard to military matters?" she asked, hoping to somehow dig beneath the façade.

"I have, of course, though my immediate superior, Comrade Budenny, is next in the chain of command. But my Little Father Comrade Stalin has sought my advice . . . even if he does not always take it." He stopped and cocked a brow suspiciously, as if he suddenly realized he was being sucked into saying more than he had intended. "Now, now, Miss Hayes, let's not get off on the wrong foot again. Do you expect me to criticize my illustrious leader?"

"Criticism is often healthy for a government to hear."

"Not in Russia, if indeed I had any criticism, which, of course, I don't." His lips quirked slightly, ruefully. "Our great leader is the greatest military commander of all time. He will lead us to victory!"

The firm set of the man's jaw clearly indicated to Cameron that there would be no more lapses.

She endured another half hour of Party propaganda and blatant Stalinist bootlicking from the man before he lapsed in his rhetoric. Finally he rose and abruptly ended the interview. She was relieved. She figured she had only enough material from the interview to tack a paragraph onto another story.

"I am at your service, Miss Hayes, should you wish another interview."

"*Spasiba*, Comrade Khrushchev."

On her way back to the Metropole, she berated herself for her inept handling of the interview. She was certain Johnny Shanahan would have wheedled the truth from the man. There had been moments when it had appeared as if Khrushchev had *wanted* to say more, to reveal the truth behind all the secrets. Johnny would have found it all out. He would have been relentless. Cameron wondered how much her own sense of self-preservation had controlled her actions. Was she too concerned about staying in Russia because of

Alex? Was that preventing her from taking chances?

The very fact that she was asking herself such questions was probably answer enough. It all made her stomach churn. And only as an afterthought did she think she might pray about the matter.

10

SOPHIA WAS waiting for Cameron back in her room. She had finished reading the daily newspapers and was typing up correspondence for Cameron. The *clackity-clack* of the Underwood typewriter greeted Cameron as she opened the door.

"Oh, Sophia, you are a wonder!" Cameron said as she laid aside her handbag and hung up her coat. "You have made yourself indispensable to me, you know."

"I am glad to hear that, Cameron, because this is the best job I have ever had." She paused only a moment before continuing her work.

Cameron smiled at the young woman's informal tone. It had taken months, but Cameron had finally gotten Sophia to consider her more as a friend than a boss. Yet the girl, now only twenty, had matured so much in the last year that she was more often than not the mentor of the relationship. Cameron remembered the child-woman who had come to work for her last year, her innocent doe-like features, her delicate fragility that had often made Cameron feel like a horse around the girl. But Sophia, more than anyone, proved Khrushchev's praise of the incredible strength of the people of Russia. She had survived the calamity involving her husband, his horrific experience of witnessing the massacre of hundreds of Jews by the Germans, the bungled attempt to help him escape Russia, followed by his arrest by the NKVD and then his being sent away to a gulag. And now Sophia might never see him again. Beyond that, Sophia had toiled in the Women's Brigade during the Battle of

Moscow, digging ditches under enemy fire to shore up the city's defenses.

Of course Russians were hardy, but Cameron knew that was not the only source of Sophia's ability to endure. Cameron now knew it was the woman's faith in God that was her foremost sustenance. And it had been more than mere coincidence that here in atheistic Russia Cameron had fallen in with this woman of faith and her family, the Fedorcenko clan, who had proved to have such a profound influence over Cameron.

"How did your interview go?" Sophia asked, her fingers still flying over the typewriter keys.

"Pure dental work."

"Pardon?" Sophia paused, a perplexed crease to her brow.

Cameron laughed. "You know, like pulling teeth to get any useful information from the man."

Sophia giggled. "I will remember that phrase and use it sometime. I bet even my grandmother has not heard of that Americanism."

"You are welcome to it." Cameron sat at her desk, where the dailies were stacked neatly, and picked up *Pravda*. Sophia had circled in red, with a brief description in English in the margin, any items that might be of interest for an article. Cameron often thought that Sophia could probably write the articles herself, for they were mere regurgitations of the Soviet-controlled press.

Quickly distracted, she lowered the newspaper and turned to her friend. "Sophia, what do you know of this Khrushchev fellow?"

"I am sorry, I know little more than that he is very big in the Ukraine. Perhaps my father knows more."

"Ask him the next time you see him, won't you? I doubt there is anything of interest to my readers, but he seemed a fascinating character, and I'll want to include a bit about him in my journal. For posterity's sake if nothing else."

"I am sorry your interview was not as successful as you hoped."

"I suppose it was my fault."

"How is that, Cameron?" Sophia stopped her work and turned her attention completely on Cameron. "Do you think it has to do with your new faith?"

"I don't think so, but I know now that I must make some changes in my methods. In the past I didn't much care what civil or moral laws I broke in order to get a story. I skewered some good people to get the truth. I'm on uncertain ground now, feeling my way, hoping God will check me if I go too far. But, Sophia, seeking the truth is at the core of Christianity. And seeking it is still a noble cause, though my approach might have to be more circumspect." She leaned back, forgetting the newspaper in her hand altogether. "Thus far, I haven't been tested much in this area. I hope it doesn't make me soft. I don't think it has to. The problem is, I don't feel Christianity is what's keeping me from taking the risks I used to relish. It's fear, Sophia, fear that if I push too hard, if I step out of line, I will be deported and never see Alex again."

Sophia reached out to Cameron, her large eyes filled with compassion. "Yes, I see how fearsome that can be." The glint of sadness in her eyes no doubt indicated she was also thinking of her husband, Oleg. When her own cautious nature had slipped and she had let herself be talked into the escape plan, mostly by Cameron, she had lost her husband. If Cameron had felt then what she was experiencing now she would never have encouraged such a risk.

"My father used to say, 'Nothing ventured, nothing gained,'" Cameron said. "I don't want to be paralyzed by my fears. I am still a journalist and must do my job competently. But I have always strived to be more than competent. I've had to be better than my colleagues. That's my edge."

"Cameron, you must not expect so much of yourself. Right now you are in a certain stage of your life, a stage that includes the love of a man. There is nothing wrong with your feeling the need to protect that relationship. But believe me, I have followed your work more than anyone, and it is not slipping. Yes, perhaps you might have been able to push Mr. Khrushchev harder, but no one is harmed that you didn't. I think when it is truly important, you will not fail."

"I hope so. I still have a commitment to my mother to keep, and I think my reticence has held me back from that, as well." In the last few months the search for her mother's son, her own half brother, had not only waned, it had come to a grinding halt. After speaking with Semyon's cousin Marfa in Vdovin and learning little more than the name of the official who might have arranged for the child's adoption, Cameron had done little. She had intended to make inquiries about the official in Sverdlovsk, but the risks in doing so had been too great. Sophia, with a greater ability to broach Soviet bureaucracy, had tried and had merely learned that a man by that name had left the area several years before. What more could Cameron do? As Sophia's father had once told Cameron, finding a missing person in Russia, especially for a foreigner, was all but impossible.

Sophia confirmed this with her next words. "There is not much more you can do, whether you are afraid to take risks or not. I could do some checking—"

"Not on your life! I'll not let others take my risks for me."

An affectionate smile played upon Sophia's lips. "But I already told you I was willing, so the risk is mine, not yours!"

"In any case, that doesn't mean we have to throw out practicality entirely," Cameron replied. "You are certainly under close police scrutiny. It is not only dangerous, it is foolish."

"What if I ask my father to look into it? He has no more than the usual police attention upon him, and he keeps far too busy for even that to be effective. He could quite easily track someone under the guise of his job."

"That is a tempting suggestion."

"He would be happy to do it, I am sure."

For all her recent maturity, Sophia could be quite guileless at times. Dr. Yuri Fedorcenko was a good, decent man, but even he would never be "happy" to place himself in such a position. Still, he might be willing. And it was possible the danger to him would indeed be minimal.

"I would have to share your family secret with him," Sophia added.

Thus far only three people besides Cecilia Hayes knew of her illegitimate son. Cameron, of course, Sophia, and Alex. Cameron had imparted the story to Alex before he left on this most recent assignment to the Front. She still didn't know why she'd told him, except that she did not like having such a big secret between them.

"I don't have a problem with that," Cameron said. "I am sure he can be discreet. I would agree to him doing this only if he didn't take any undue chances."

"My father has survived his whole life in a police state," assured Sophia. "He knows how to take care."

"I wish I could ask him myself, but it is probably best if you do it."

"I only pray something comes of it. Ah, Cameron, it will be so wonderful for you to be reunited with your brother."

Again Cameron noted a bit of naïveté in her friend. If anything scared Cameron at all, it was the anticipation of that moment when she and her older brother would meet eye to eye. And she wasn't certain such a meeting would be for the best. Wouldn't it just deepen her mother's torment, knowing he was alive yet never having a hope of meeting him herself? And what of Semyon? Who was to say he'd be thrilled to learn of a family in distant America? Even more fearsome was the prospect of her father's reaction. Keagan Hayes was likely to explode with the force of a ton of TNT upon hearing of his wife's unfaithfulness and the fact that it had produced a son—the one thing he had failed to do himself. *If* he found out, of course. But how much longer could Cecilia keep such a secret from him?

Cameron had made a promise to her mother, a promise she would try to keep. And she would pray that God somehow would keep it from hurting too many people.

"Cameron, before we return to work, there is something I have wanted to mention to you. . . ." Sophia paused with uncertainty. "I am not sure if this is the best or the worst time to bring it up, after what you have shared about taking risks."

"Go on, Sophia. It will eat at you otherwise."

"You and I have had some wonderful talks about faith in God."

"We have," Cameron interjected. "You have taught me so much."

"I am young, Cameron, and though I have been raised in a Christian household and know much, I am still lacking in much wisdom about faith. I think it would be good for you to talk with others more mature in the faith."

"I don't have many options here."

"Alex told you about the underground church he had attended—"

"Oh yes, and it nearly destroyed us."

"Do you still feel antagonism toward it?"

"Of course not. At least I now understand his need. But I guess

I still wonder if it is a necessary risk. Do you think I should go to one of these churches?"

"I wanted at least to suggest it to you."

"Well . . ." A small panic gripped Cameron. Perhaps it was just a residual from before her change of spiritual perspective, when any mention of attending church would ignite her fleeing instinct. Yet her reluctance toward taking risks was also fresh within her, and a part of her asked why she should take this particular risk. What was the point? Just to mingle with others who shared her new faith? Certainly Sophia was enough contact, and Alex, when he was around.

"I understand your reluctance," offered Sophia.

"I only wonder, you know . . . if it's worth it." She would never stop hating herself for fearing, and it might never become easy for her to accept that weakness in herself no matter how mature her faith.

"I cannot answer that. But consider the value of other points of view. There are many facets to Christianity, and you may be cheated if you have only my perspective or Alex's."

"I have my mother's, as well."

"Yes."

Cameron sucked in a breath. "I don't know why it scares me. It's not just the risk. It would be entirely different if I were going to the group for research. But this is personal. That's it. I have never been good at exposing myself on that level."

"All you can do is think about it."

———

The evening was chilly and dark with the blackout still in force in Moscow. A light drizzle fell, hardly making a sound as it splashed on Cameron's umbrella. The streets were quiet, too. Less and less civilian traffic traversed the roads now that nearly all gasoline was diverted to war use. And in this residential area, not even military vehicles were present.

Cameron tried to decide if the silence of the night was good or bad. It made her footfalls seem to echo even against the wet pavement, and she certainly stood out more noticeably on the deserted street. On the other hand, it was easier for her to detect whether she was being followed. As usual in these situations she had made a great effort to ensure she was not. She was also careful not to make it appear as if she was *trying* to lose her tail. That was the trick, to make the police merely think they had fouled up when they lost track of her. She didn't want to return to the Metropole and be arrested on mere suspicion. She had tried to appear as though she were on a meandering shopping excursion.

So now she was alone.

She hoped.

Sophia had promised to meet her at the home of Vassily and Marie Turkin. There was no way they could go to the church meeting together, but Cameron regretted that restriction for more reasons than companionship. For one thing, she was not at all certain that she wasn't lost. Some street signs on main thoroughfares were gone because of the war, which made it difficult for her to get her bearings. On top of that she had the problem of matching the Cyrillic letters on the signs that remained with those that Sophia had written, which were also Cyrillic, but they still had to be carefully scrutinized—in the dark no less—because of Cameron's unfamiliarity with the Russian alphabet. And she couldn't risk asking directions, for she'd be immediately pegged a foreigner, and the chance of being reported was too great.

When she felt she had found the right place, she entered the apartment building, thankful there was no doorman present to question her. This was an upscale neighborhood, but wartime demands overrode the luxury of a doorman. She climbed the inside stairs—the elevator wasn't operating—to the third floor and found what she hoped was the right apartment. Goodness, she was going to feel foolish if she was wrong, but more than that she'd have a lot of explaining to do as to why a foreigner was roaming about here.

As she raised her hand to knock on the door, she was suddenly flooded with all the uncertainties she'd expressed earlier about the necessity of doing this. It wasn't too late to turn around. She'd have plenty of time to attend church, safely, when she returned to the States. However, that particular thought finally made up her mind. When did she plan to return home? Any return, even for a visit, might mean losing Alex, so she could be in Russia a very long time. She needed to be exposed to other believers. Sophia was right about that.

She rapped lightly on the door, then sucked in a breath and

made herself face this new challenge as she had always faced things—with pluck, if not courage; with stubborn determination, if not resolve.

A tall, rather attractive woman opened the door.

"Good evening, I'm . . ." Cameron began in her best Russian but hesitated over giving her name. What if this was the wrong house? But she had gone too far now for hesitation. "I'm Cameron Hayes."

"Welcome to my home," the woman said in refined English.

There was no further scrutiny as the woman stepped back and ushered Cameron into the apartment. Cameron supposed Sophia had given a clear description of her so that no further questioning was necessary.

"I am Marie Turkin," the woman said.

She appeared to be about forty years old, an inch or two taller than Cameron, with blond hair, stylishly coifed. She was the picture of refined elegance. She led Cameron down a short entry corridor, pausing at a doorway on the right. It led to a room where about a dozen people were gathered. Cameron immediately recognized Sophia and, seated beside her, her grandmother Anna Yevnovona. Cameron smiled at them, glad to see familiar faces.

Before fully entering the room, Marie Turkin said, "I will not try to introduce everyone, Miss Hayes—"

"Please, do call me Cameron."

"All right, and I would be pleased if you would call me Marie. As I was saying, many of our guests may not wish their names known, and you also may not wish your name told. So do not think it rude if we dispense with introductions. Each person will give their names as they choose."

"Yes, that sounds reasonable."

"I will introduce you to my husband, though. He already knows your name. Vassily," she said, leading Cameron into the room.

It was a finely appointed parlor furnished in well-kept antiques. Cameron hadn't been in many Russian homes, but this was easily the finest. Somehow the Turkins had managed to hang on to their nice things through war, revolution, more war, and more upheaval. But Cameron's attention was drawn from the surroundings to the approaching man.

"My husband, Vassily," Marie said.

He smiled warmly, crow's-feet crinkling around the corners of pale but expressive eyes. "A pleasure to meet you, my dear!" He took her offered hand and shook it firmly. His hand was soft, obviously not having been exposed to much manual labor. He was balding, and what hair he had was streaked liberally with gray. He appeared several years older than Marie. He was also several inches shorter. In appearance they seemed a mismatched pair. She was stately, almost regal, elegant and gracious in a reserved manner. Even her attire was fashionable, especially by Russian standards. He, on the other hand, was dumpy, artless, seeming almost bemused. His clothing, a gray pinstriped suit, was rumpled and several years out of date. Yet Cameron could see compatibility in them, as well. Their differences balanced each other out. Together, they immediately made her feel comfortable.

"You have a lovely home," Cameron said.

"We are happy to be back in Moscow," Vassily replied. "I suppose our life here has made us soft. But Kuibyshev was rather roughhewn."

"So you evacuated there?"

"For a short time, yes."

Now that Cameron thought about it, the underground church Alex had attended had been in Kuibyshev. "Did you happen to know my . . . friend, Alex Rostov?"

"Ah yes, a fine man."

"We have not seen him in some time," Marie said.

"He is at the Front."

"Oh! May God bless him!" Marie said with such intense sincerity it surprised Cameron. "Now, come and join us."

Cameron was seated in a chair next to Sophia, who would act as interpreter. Though the Turkins spoke good English, others in the group did not, so the meeting would be conducted in Russian. For about an hour, everyone in turn shared a little, mostly in the way of requests for prayer. There were medical problems that needed prayer, some financial problems, but by and large the requests were for loved ones at the Front. When it was Cameron's turn, it would have been easy for her to decline to speak—two others had also remained silent and no one seemed bothered by this. But she found it just as easy to put forth her own prayer requests, for Alex especially, and for her sister Blair. She felt reluctant to ask for anything specifically for herself, but since she knew this was a problem of hers she must confront, she made herself ask for the courage to do her job to the best of her ability and in such a way that God would be pleased with her.

When it seemed everyone was finished, Vassily spoke. "I've always felt offering such requests as we just have is in its own way a prayer. So now let's just spend some time talking to our God. If you care to pray out loud, that is welcome, for it will bless everyone. But feel free to pray silently if you wish."

Cameron had the feeling his direction was spoken for her benefit. She certainly didn't feel ready to pray out loud in front of others, especially strangers, so she was relieved at the man's words.

Cameron did not pray aloud, and she wasn't certain if she ever really prayed silently, either. But she did listen. And she was touched in a way she had not expected. She thought she would hear people merely asking God for things, such as solutions to the problems that had been mentioned earlier. There was a little of that. For the most part those who spoke told God how special He was to them, thanking Him for helping them, guiding them, loving them. Cameron was amazed at the gratitude expressed. These were people in the middle of a terrible war, in which everyone in the room had no doubt experienced the injury or death of a friend or loved one. These people were suffering from privations no one in America could imagine. On top of that, they were forced to meet in secret, with the threat of exposure, even in the more liberal wartime atmosphere, a clear danger.

Yet they found things—many things!—to give thanks to God for!

"Thank you, Father, for giving me the courage to come here tonight."

"Thank you, God, for the chance to see my son on his short leave."

"Thank you, Jesus, that the butcher's shop actually had some meat today!"

"I give thanks, my Lord, for your care."

"Thank you, Lord God, for the peace you've given me in my heart."

On and on . . . until Cameron was certain she must be wrapped in the sweetest world possible. A world without care or hurt or confusion. This, she knew, was what faith was all about. God was strength and stability, though the world was in chaos. She remembered the song her mother used to quote often. "O God, our help in ages past, our hope for years to come, our shelter from the stormy blast, and our eternal home." Why that had stayed in her mind all these years, she did not know, but she did now see what it meant for God to be "our eternal home." In the past she'd always thought it must mean when you died and went to heaven. But these people were experiencing that "eternal home" now, wrapped in their faith. This was the real world to them. Not that they were oblivious to the strife buffeting them, but it wasn't nearly as real as the home they had in God.

Later, when the group had dispersed, some going home, some remaining to share tea together, Cameron spoke to Marie Turkin. "Have you ever heard the song 'O God, our help in ages past'? That's the first line if not the title."

"Yes, I have. It is a beautiful song."

"My faith is very new, Marie, though you probably already guessed that. But I remember my mother singing that song. I thought of it while listening to everyone give such wonderful thanks to God. It is really what you all have, isn't it? That peace in the middle of a storm?"

"Yes, I believe it is." She smiled thoughtfully. "We do not often sing in this meeting. We have no musical instruments. We had to sell our piano some years back, and few of us have talent singing a cappella. We used to have a member with an autoharp, but she can no longer attend. I will try to find the words to this song and translate them into Russian. If we can't sing them, at least everyone would be blessed just to hear them."

"Maybe I can find a copy in the American or British embassy. Surely someone there has a hymnal."

"We will try to have it next time we meet."

In that moment Cameron knew she'd find a way to meet with these people as often as she could. Whether they sang the hymn or not. She wanted to be around these folks. She had no doubt she'd learn much from them.

"How often do you meet, Marie?"

"Once a week if we can. But not on a regular schedule. We change frequently to avoid detection. The time and place of our meeting is usually passed on by word of mouth to our group. Sophia will tell you. We will be most pleased to have you come again."

"I want to, but I don't want to place you in jeopardy."

"We all have to take care, of course, but in the end we will leave that in God's hands. I feel He wants you to come, so He will make a way."

Cameron smiled. She was coming to like her new faith more than she expected. She'd known of her need before, and she'd realized it was the way she must follow. She hadn't always been certain she'd *like* it, though. But these people . . . and this God who gave so much . . . what else was there but to like it . . . to love it?

11

THE AIR RAID began when the ship was two hundred yards from
the dock. Bombs struck the water, their detonation forcing geysers
of water to rise, spraying the ship and the surrounding dock as if it
were just another autumn storm. There had been so many of those
storms over the last days that as Alex's ship had made its way down
the Volga, he barely noticed he was soggy. Except, of course, this
"rain" was not limited to water, and it was far more lethal. One
bomb struck the stern of the ship. The men manning the antiaircraft
guns there were thrown into the air, some landing in the water—
perhaps they were the lucky ones. Others hit the deck of the ship,
and when Alex reached them to render aid, most were dead or
beyond help.

The bombardment kept up relentlessly, delaying their docking.
The Germans were determined to keep these troop ships from rein-
forcing Russian lines. There were three ships in the convoy, with
thousands of soldiers on them. They were all but sitting ducks, even
with their guns blasting down an occasional enemy plane.

"Medic!" someone screamed.

Trying to keep low, Alex crawled toward the sound, over the
bodies of those whom he had been unable to get to in time. A
German Messerschmitt winged low, strafing the deck inches from
him and tearing up a corpse that had shielded Alex, sparing him
from becoming a corpse himself. As bits of flesh flew in his face, he
turned aside and vomited. He'd seen so much blood and so many
mangled bodies in the last year that getting sick now seemed

ridiculous. The heaving of the boat certainly didn't help matters. He'd only discovered recently that his stomach was not well suited to the water.

Reaching his destination and finding the man who had cried out earlier still alive, Alex felt like laughing—not from joy or even relief, for such feelings had been dulled in him for some time now. No, it was probably from simple hysteria, laughter that tottered on the edge of tears.

"Where are you hit?" Alex asked, scrutinizing the man and seeing nothing immediately apparent.

"It hurts, doc! Please help me!"

"Yes, I will, but where?"

The man's legs were intact, his arms both whole. Alex gently rolled the man toward him and surveyed his back side. Then Alex's insides heaved again. The back of the man's head was missing.

"God . . . the pain!" moaned the soldier.

Alex gave the man a shot of morphine, then left him to die, hoping to find another patient he might have a small hope of saving. But much too quickly he used up his supply of morphine and bandages. He and a couple of corpsmen tried to get some of the wounded belowdecks, where a makeshift surgical theater had been set up. With rudimentary surgery some of these men might be repaired enough to be evacuated to the hospital several miles away.

The ship rocked with the impact of another bomb. It threw Alex against a bulkhead. His head cracked hard against the metal, but he clawed desperately at consciousness. There was too much work yet to be done to allow the luxury of blacking out.

"Dr. Rostovscikov!" yelled one of the sailors. "The ship is going down. We must abandon ship."

Alex shook his head to clear it, then struggled to his feet and hurried with the sailor back up a companionway to the deck. Lifeboats were being lowered, but many men were simply diving into the water. They had just as good a chance of surviving. In any case, the lifeboats were needed for the wounded.

When Alex finally reached the shore in a boat loaded with wounded, he had no way of knowing how many men had been lost on the sinking ship. Hundreds of wounded were lying on the ground surrounding the docks. A Red Cross flag had been unfurled over the area designated for the wounded. But bombs still came so close that the ground shook constantly. At least there was less danger of strafing here, which in a way, Alex considered more terrifying than the bombs. Those low-flying planes, so close you could sometimes catch a glimpse of the pilots, were somehow more personal.

Stalingrad. It used to be one of the great industrial cities of the Soviet Union. Sprawling along the banks of the Volga, covering a good twenty-five miles. A half million inhabitants.

It used to be.

Then in August the Wehrmacht, commanded by General Friedrich Paulus, set its sights on the city. The fall of Kerch, Kharkov, and Sebastopol had paved the way, allowing the enemy enough of an inroad to hit Stalingrad with one of the most astounding bombardments in history. On a single day in August there had been an air raid involving six hundred German bombers. Nearly forty thousand people had been killed. That had been at the height of the German offensive. Now, two months later, little of the city was left unscathed. If it were not for the constant explosions, bombs from the air, antiaircraft fire and gunfire, and soldiers and equipment on the move, it would look more like an ancient ruin than a once thriving modern city.

But the desolation definitely was not ancient. The stench of smoke and the acrid odor of explosives were fresh. The blood was still moist and new.

Alex bent over a patient in the surgical tent that had just been raised. The man's chest was shattered, but the insertion of two chest tubes to drain the blood offered hope. At least Alex could patch him up enough for him to make it as far as the battalion hospital twenty miles from the Front. After debriding the wound and draining it, Alex began repairing tears in the lung. The overhead lighting was poor and flickered with every explosion. When he finally closed the chest two hours later, he knew he had missed many tiny tears but hoped the chest tubes would keep the man from drowning in continued seepage of blood until he could be operated on under better conditions. Alex could afford to spend no more time with the patient, for there were a dozen others waiting. He could do little, it seemed, to help any of them, but he must hope the little he could do was enough.

Hope was often all he had, and he clung to it as tenaciously as some of these wounded were clinging to life. He silently prayed over each man as his hands worked furiously to heal. He must never think he was working alone. He must never let that sense of help-lessness overwhelm him. He knew God did not intend to save every man who passed under his scalpel, yet that did not mean God was not with him. Just knowing God was present sustained him.

———

A shell burst not ten feet away. He dropped and rolled, protect-ing his camera at all costs. Lieutenant Semyon Tveritinov reminded himself once more that this is what he had sought, what he had begged his father for—to be in the Red Army, to be in the midst of the action, shooting photographs if not Germans.

However, debarking his troop ship an hour ago, he had been so terrified he'd nearly wept. He'd certainly almost forgotten the cam-era gripped in his hand, because in the last hour he had taken no photographs at all. Every thought and action had been concentrated upon staying alive. Now lifting his head from the dirt, he saw a group of newly arrived troops lining up at a supply truck receiving their weapons. One weapon issued per two men so that when the man with the rifle fell, the other would be there to pick up the fire-arm and continue the fight. Semyon had known of shortages, but this made him physically sick. Or was that still fear roiling in his gut?

Finally making himself remember the camera in his hand, he lifted it to record the scene of a pair of soldiers jogging away from the truck with one rifle between them.

A hand grasped his arm. "Save your film, boy."

Semyon wrenched his arm away as he spoke. "That's *lieuten-ant*!" he snapped defensively. But as he turned his head toward the other man, he saw the insignia of a captain on the man's shoulder. "I'm sorry, sir," he added quickly.

"It's easy to be confused in this mayhem," the captain said, though his gruff tone somewhat disguised the sympathy in his words. "Where are you assigned?"

"I am Lieutenant Tveritinov, propaganda officer. I am assigned to Colonel Nuraliev's department."

"Come with me."

"Where?"

The man's brow arched as if he didn't appreciate being questioned by a man of lower rank, then he shrugged. "You haven't reported in yet, have you?"

"No, sir. I just got off the troop ship."

"Then you should report in before you use your camera. There are rules, you know."

Yes, of course . . . rules. Any propaganda officer worth his salt ought to know a photo of the blatant shortages at the Front would not be in the best interests of the war cause. Though an inner creative drive had told him that particular shot was artistically profound, Semyon must remember who he was and what, above all else, was most important.

He followed the captain, dodging gunfire and explosions until they were well back from the battle zone. But even out of the hot zone they had to be cautious because there might well be snipers hiding anywhere. The captain explained all this as they moved, mentioning that now with the fighting in the streets of the city itself, it was quite a different game from what Semyon might be accustomed to. Semyon did not inform the man that he wasn't accustomed to *any* kind of battles. This was his first. If that wasn't obvious to the fellow, why enlighten him?

Pausing before a burned-out building, the captain motioned Semyon around a heap of rubble to a basement door. Here was a sentry who, after clearing their credentials, admitted them. They negotiated a rickety stairway that led them into a dimly lit cellar. Only a single overhead bulb provided light for an area that covered about a thousand square feet, but there was a thin strip of natural light coming in through a couple of narrow windows at ceiling level. The blackout shades were raised since it was daytime. The room itself was a hive of activity, typewriters clacking, conversations buzzing, men coming and going, several passing them on the stair even as they descended.

The captain brought Semyon to one of the desks. "This is your new man," he said to the clerk seated there.

"Lieutenant Semyon Tveritinov reporting for duty," Semyon said crisply. He did not salute, noting the clerk was only a corporal.

"The colonel will want to see you, Lieutenant, but he is busy now. Have a seat. It shouldn't be too long."

Semyon was too keyed up to sit. After the captain departed— Semyon never did learn the man's name—he wandered about the room trying to get a feel of the place. His first impression was that no one had bothered to clean here before it was commandeered as press headquarters. It still smelled like a disused basement, dank and dusty. The floor was hard-packed dirt, and the ceiling, low and dingy, was strung with cobwebs. The colonel's clerk may have had a desk, old and marred as it was, but for the most part crates served many as desks and chairs. Yet no one was idle here. The feeling of urgency permeated the room almost more than the musty odors. Almost as important as the battle raging above was the task of disseminating information about it. Much of Semyon's earlier terror dissipated as this feeling of importance caught hold of him.

He was filled with an intense sense of purpose. His mother had tried to convince him that drawing propaganda posters in a sterile office in Moscow was vital. She had wept that he was about to waste his talents. She had begged him to reconsider this lunacy. It hadn't fooled her at all that he was still in the same department. She had guessed that he had wanted a frontline position, and she knew what his leaving Moscow must mean. There had been a moment or two when Semyon had almost let himself believe her, that he was doing an important job in Moscow. Why change? Why break her heart in the process?

Did he need guns pointed at him to think he was a good Russian?

Yes.

And that was what his mother would never understand. How he wanted her to understand! And how he hated hurting her and giving her cause to worry. But being a good and loyal Russian superseded even her feelings. It was everything! She should have realized that, for she and his father had raised him to be that way. Country, Party, then family. It was his father's credo and now his own.

As he absorbed the urgent vibrations in this basement, Semyon now knew beyond all lingering doubts that he had done the right thing.

Within an hour of his briefing with Colonel Nuraliev, Semyon was back above ground and making use of his camera. Armed with the rules of conduct for propaganda officers, his assignment was to photograph various sites in the city that had recently been retaken from the Germans. Corporal Svejkin was to be his guide. It wasn't that the colonel didn't trust him to be on his own, but he was new, and even Semyon realized the expediency of a breaking-in period.

Several days after that first assignment, those areas photographed by Semyon were back in German hands as the enemy began an all-out push to take the northern industrial sectors of the city. Now he knew why no one had bothered to clean the cellar headquarters of the Press Department for it was moved twice in nearly as many weeks. The following weeks, into October, proved to be the worst for the Russians. Getting reinforcements was becoming more and more difficult, and transporting supplies across the Volga became next to impossible. The priority for all propaganda officers was to lift the morale of the soldiers who must fight the enemy on empty stomachs and nearly empty guns. Heroes had to be found and exploited. And if there were none to be found, they were made.

Semyon encountered a sixteen-year-old boy who had gone behind the lines and slit the throats of half a dozen German sentries. At least he had German uniform insignias to prove his feat, and they were tinged with fresh blood. Semyon paraded the lad before the troops to remind the men what Russians were made of. The soldiers were bolstered by the lad's grizzly accomplishment, and as a direct result one platoon charged an enemy machine-gun nest, captured it, and paved the way for an important Russian advance.

Semyon photographed the boy with his bloody trophies, and *Red Star* ran the story. The boy was given a uniform and the rank of private—he hadn't even been in the Army before that! Later, when the boy confessed the whole story had been a lie, Semyon threatened the boy with arrest if he ever told anyone the truth. The boy slunk away, back into obscurity, and Semyon felt only a little ashamed because of what he himself had done. Good had come of it. Wasn't that all that mattered?

After that Semyon found himself in the midst of the battle for the Stalingrad tractor works, which had been converted to making tanks. Incredibly, the Russians held the factory for days, though pushed mightily on all sides by the enemy. It was said that during the battle, tanks actually rolled off the assembly lines firing their guns. Semyon thought if this were true, it would make a marvelous photograph. He enlisted the aid of several soldiers who provided cover so he could get close enough for a good shot.

They attempted to cut through an alley that led to one of the loading docks, but when they reached the end, enemy fire was so thick, they were forced back.

"We cannot get to the tanks." The intensity of the blasts all around forced Corporal Svejkin to yell, though he was inches from Semyon's ear.

"Let's try the north end of the building. There's not as much fighting there," Semyon insisted.

A shell exploded fifty feet away, spraying Semyon and his companions with dirt and debris as they dropped and rolled to safety. An instant later they were back on their feet and racing north. But there seemed to be no sheltered place. Still, Semyon was determined and pushed on to another place until finally his tenacity was rewarded. Here, Russian tanks were rumbling out of the factory. Semyon had no way of knowing for sure if these were in fact fresh off the conveyor belt, but they were firing, and it made a stirring picture.

Of course, the enemy was firing back, on the ground and from the air. But Semyon was so intent now on aiming his camera that he hardly noticed anything but the focus of the lens and the composition of the picture.

In the same instant that Semyon snapped his shutter, an explosion shook the earth, knocking him off his feet. As he bounced and rolled, he only vaguely felt something sharp impale him in the back. He reacted with far more emotion upon hearing his camera crash to the ground than to the piercing pain in his body. Even as he tumbled forward into the dirt, he grasped futilely for his fallen camera.

12

Leninsk was about thirty miles from Stalingrad, on the other side of the Volga. The Leninsk Hospital, where most of the wounded from Stalingrad were evacuated, was by no means fancy, but it was cleaner than the field hospital where Semyon had first been treated for his wound. It was, however, no less crowded and teeming with activity. He woke feeling woozy from morphine, but the pain in his back was nicely dulled by the drug. The faces bent over him came slowly into focus.

"Ah, are you finally coming around?"

"Father?"

"Yes, of course it is me. And Comrade Khrushchev, as well."

Semyon saw the faces more clearly now. He hadn't realized his father was in the area. He was happy to see him yet at the same time felt bad for pulling him away from his important work. And his boss, as well! Maybe his wounds were worse than he thought. In the field hospital he'd been given to believe the wound was minor and he'd be back on duty in a couple of days. Now here he was in the battalion hospital, where surely only the most desperate cases were brought.

"I am happy to see you, Father, I truly am. And Comrade Khrushchev, I am honored that you came to visit me. I know you are both busy men."

"We are never too busy to visit a hero of the Soviet Union!" exclaimed Khrushchev.

"I am no hero—"

"You have been wounded for your country and Party," corrected Semyon's father in that tone of his that broached no argument.

Semyon chose a new tactic. "Father, you won't tell Mother about this, will you?"

"If the doctor says it isn't serious, I suppose we can keep it quiet, for a time, at least. We don't want to upset her, of course."

"I don't feel it is serious, Father. I don't know why I was brought here."

Semyon's father cleared his throat and directed a sly glance toward Khrushchev. "You are getting the best care possible, and that is what matters, son."

"How did the battle go?" Semyon asked, changing the subject once more, not wanting to think what that sly look between the two men meant. He knew he was the son of an important man, but he was never completely comfortable with it.

"The battle continues, lad. But the German butchers are weakening." Stanislav Tveritinov glanced again at Khrushchev, who gave a minute shake of his head.

Semyon supposed that silent communication was not meant to be seen by him, so he pretended to straighten his pillow. Of course they wouldn't want to upset him with the gory details of battle, but his father had said quite enough with the simple statement that the Germans were weakening. Only weakening, not defeated.

"Enemy losses are high," said Khrushchev in that tone meant to bowl over simpletons. "Three thousand Germans dead on the day you were wounded alone. We were able to evacuate thirty-five hundred of our wounded across the Volga to receive medical aid. This is a record. It means, as you must know, the enemy's hold is failing."

"That is good." Semyon tried to sound enthusiastic. But he'd heard reports from others that were not as encouraging. He'd heard the Russian forces at the tractor plant had been cut in two, and only a small area to the north of the plant, near where he had been wounded, was now in Russian hands. He'd heard that in one day thousands of bombs had been dropped on the Russian forces. There would be no more tanks blasting their way off the assembly lines. That made him remember something else, and he gladly turned to yet another subject. "Father, they told me my camera was recovered. I took some excellent photos if they turn out."

"You did indeed," Khrushchev answered. "*Pravda* will carry them in the next couple of days."

Semyon was thrilled to learn this yet at the same time a bit miffed that his film had been developed by others, who'd had the audacity to judge which were fit for publication. As quickly as that thought invaded, however, he berated himself as he had done frequently of late. He was no artist, no photographic prima donna, and even if he were, he had no ownership of his work. All was for the Party and was the property of the Party. He was only a tool of the Party.

"I am honored," he forced. He was, of course, but the artist in him still felt slightly affronted. "And it is time I returned to my work."

"I believe a short leave can be arranged for you, son. Your wounds certainly warrant one. What do you think, Nikita Sergeiovich?"

"I see no reason why not."

"But I don't want a leave," Semyon protested. He feared above all else that if he let himself be removed from the Front, something, or someone, might keep him from ever returning.

"Perhaps I should be the judge of that," interjected a new voice. A white-coated man approached Semyon's bed. He was tall, fair-haired, a bit gaunt in the face but had an air of authority about him. He was obviously a doctor.

"Are you my doctor?" asked Semyon.

"Yes. I am Dr. Rostovscikov." He moved to the side of the bed where Khrushchev stood and very smoothly, without saying a word, nudged the man aside. Khrushchev scowled at this effrontery, but apparently even he knew that in a hospital a doctor held some small authority over even the great viceroy of the Ukraine.

"You'll release me back to my unit soon?" persisted Semyon.

Dr. Rostovscikov grasped Semyon's wrist, feeling for his pulse. In a half minute he dropped the wrist and referred to the chart in his hand. "You've a slightly elevated temperature."

"I feel fine. The room is just exceptionally warm."

"Um-hum . . ." murmured the doctor. "Please turn a bit and face your father so I can check your wound."

Semyon complied and could feel Rostovscikov lift the dressing, then press it back over the wound several inches below the right shoulder.

"The wound is inflamed."

"Certainly I have seen men with far worse wounds still fighting on the front lines," argued Semyon as he returned to his back.

"None of them are my son," said Tveritinov.

"I will not have special favors because of that, Father."

"Of course not, my boy!" boomed Khrushchev, elbowing his way closer. "Why don't we let the doctor be the judge, yes?" He glanced at the doctor with a rather piercing look in his small dark eyes. This was the look that had always bent others to this powerful man's will. It very clearly told the doctor that he would be the judge as long as he judged in Khrushchev's favor.

Semyon worried that the doctor would be cowed by this powerful and influential man, even if he was a good six inches taller than Khrushchev. But the doctor returned Khrushchev's gaze steadily.

"He will be on a three-day program of sulfanilamide for infection. After that, he should be well enough to return to his unit."

"Three days!" groaned Semyon.

"A leave still isn't out of the question," persisted Semyon's father.

"I have no authority in the issuing of leaves," said the doctor. "My authority does prevail while he is under my care, and he will remain here for the next three days. After that"—he gave an apologetic shrug to Semyon—"I can only hope good sense will prevail." He then crisply snapped shut the chart, but before turning, he added, "A nurse will be here in a few minutes to administer your first dose of medication. After that I want you to rest." To the visitors he said, "Comrade Tveritinov, Comrade Khrushchev, I would suggest you take only a few more moments to say your good-byes."

Semyon did not think he much liked seeing these two great men being so summarily dismissed by a mere doctor who, by the insignia on his laboratory coat, was only a captain. Yet he could not deny a certain satisfaction, as well. There would be no leave, he was sure of that. This doctor was not about to let one of his patients receive favor over another if he could help it.

Five minutes later, after Semyon's visitors had departed, the doctor returned holding a glass of water and a small tray with a medicine cup on it. "Here is your first dose of medication."

"I thought a nurse would bring it."

"I could find no nurse who wasn't busy, and I didn't want you to wait any longer than necessary for the medicine."

"All the sooner to leave this place and return to the Front."

"All the sooner to heal your infection."

"Why was I brought here to this hospital?" Semyon asked as he took the glass and pill. "I'm no doctor, but I don't think I was wounded that badly."

"Only a bit of shrapnel in your back, which required a couple dozen stitches. But when your father learned you were wounded, he insisted you receive extended care here. He wants the best for you."

"Just tell me no one died because I took the bed of someone more needy."

"Don't fret over it, Lieutenant Tveritinov," the doctor replied with a touch of sympathy in his voice. "It was beyond your control." He turned to go but again paused before adding, "No one died because of you."

"Thank you, Doctor."

But Semyon knew that wasn't entirely true. He thought of the men who had been covering him as he took his photographs. He'd learned in the field hospital that two of those men had been killed in the same blast that had injured him. He also thought of the soldiers who perished while taking the machine-gun nest—men who had acted because of lies he had perpetuated. He wished his wound hurt more. He didn't want to be protected—not by medicine, not by his father. That was why he was so eager to return to battle, though his desire to serve the Party still came first. He'd lived a life of such ease that he did not know what substance there was in him, who he was and what strengths he had. He had a vague memory of a pain long ago in his life—a deep, heartrending pain. But even his memory was serving to protect him, because he had no idea what had been the cause of that distant pain or if perhaps it was only something from his nightmares, but he knew that since then he had been protected far too much.

————

Alex left the ward not certain why he had gone back. The medication could have waited for a nurse. Yet he'd felt the lieutenant had wanted to talk. He supposed it was enough to reassure the fellow, who despite his father and his father's friend had enough of a conscience to chafe at unwarranted privileges.

Imagine, of all things, to have Stalin's top watchdogs visit his ward. Cameron would be impressed if he ever had the chance to tell her. Yet the last thing in the world he wanted was to come under the scrutiny of such men. He probably should have been more humble in their presence. But, considering, he'd been as humble as humanly possible. For despite his assurances to the young lieutenant, there was little Alex hated more than men throwing around their power in order to get favors for family and friends, especially when others might suffer in the process. A more seriously wounded man *should* have been in Semyon Tveritinov's bed. Doubtless no great harm was done this time, but it still irked Alex.

Perhaps that was because he himself felt a slight guilt over the fact that he was in this nice hospital, safe from bombs and strafing planes and all the other horrors he'd witnessed on the front lines of Stalingrad during his first weeks at that assignment. But when the chief of staff here realized Alex was in a field hospital, he immediately had Alex transferred. Dr. Citovic had known Alex in Moscow, and he apparently had a great regard for his skills and felt they would be put to better use here. Alex had to obey orders and, like Semyon, he had no control over his situation. Yet he hated being safe when he knew others every bit as skilled as he were in danger.

He thought of Lieutenant Tveritinov's turning down an opportunity for a leave. Would Alex's sense of nobility extend that far? He decided he would probably jump at any opportunity to return to Moscow. He missed Cameron desperately, far more than when they had been parted a few months ago, when they had been parted emotionally as well as physically. Now that they were united in heart and spirit, he felt her absence more keenly than could be imagined. When there was time to think, he could only think of what it would be like to be with her all the time, without having to look over their shoulders.

That would be heaven! To have a life with her, to be married. And, if he should be fortunate above all men, to have children to share with her! He prayed daily for that dream to somehow become reality. He saw no way it could at the moment, but he knew God saw things differently. *With God all things are possible.* That was more than a fine Scripture he'd memorized. It was a lifeline.

He'd had a letter from Yuri recently. His friend couldn't say anything directly about Cameron, or little else of import for that matter, because of sure censorship, but the wise doctor had managed a few cryptic words. "Do you remember the bird we found before you left, the one with the broken wing? Well, her wing is healed, and you will be happy to know she has joined other birds of her kind and seems very content."

The "bird" must be Cameron. And the "other birds" Alex had decided must be other believers. It was the only thing that made sense. Cameron was attending a church, no doubt the secret church Yuri attended. This both warmed Alex's heart and caused a small twinge of jealousy. How he wanted to share such experiences with her! Yet he also found it wondrous to think of her worshiping God with other Christians and enjoying it, as Yuri's words about contentment must indicate. Yes, all things were indeed possible with God.

"Dr. Rostovscikov," came a tinny voice over the loudspeaker, "wanted in Ward C. Stat!"

It was even possible that this war might end someday.

13

Luzon, Philippines

FOR THE FIRST time since coming to the Philippines, Blair thought of this place as a true tropical paradise. It had nothing to do with the balmy tropical breezes or the sweet fragrance of orchids and hibiscus and ginger in the air, nor with the thick green canopy of palms and other verdant foliage overhead. Even those few days she'd had with Gary before the war began, when she had not yet learned to hate the jungle, did not compare with the present. Then both she and Gary had been struggling with confusion and with the shadow of the past, of her past mistakes. Every moment they'd had together then had been tainted by those things, like an inescapable pall hanging over them.

Now, for the first time in months—no, for the first time in her life—she was content. She was with Gary, but her contentment was not derived entirely from that. It was simply that everything was finally right, as it was meant to be. She laid her head back in the jungle grass, gazing up at the waterfall Gary had brought her to see, and marveled at the miracle God had wrought.

"I told you it was spectacular," Gary said. He was sitting beside her, but his eyes weren't on the waterfall at all—they were gazing down at her.

Blair had seen many impressive sights since her jungle wanderings had begun. The waterfall by the cave where she had most recently sojourned had been nearly as big and vivid as this one. But only now, it seemed, could she truly appreciate the sights surrounding her.

"It's marvelous," Blair said. "Will it dry up when the rains stop?"

"Some, I suppose. That's why I wanted to bring you here now. The dry season will be upon us soon."

"I look forward to it. I feel so soggy."

"But that's not the only reason," he added, a mysterious smile twitching his lips.

"Hmm, ulterior motives?"

"It's hard for us to be alone in a camp with a dozen men roaming about."

She nodded. They had been able to talk a couple of times in the week since her arrival, but privacy was limited, and Gary had also been forced to be away for a couple of days. Mostly they had talked about their experiences in the last months. She had told him about her new relationship with God, and he'd said he had guessed there was something different about her at that first meeting. Yet there hadn't been time to go into much depth, and certainly there had been no talk of the future. Maybe they were both just a little afraid to broach that subject. Yes, Blair was content now, but she knew God did not intend for her to wallow in her contentment. Eventually He would shake things up a bit.

"I guess there's still a lot for us to talk about," she said finally. "But we don't have to rush things. Just being together is sweet enough to last me for a while."

"It's the sweetest thing I've tasted in a long time." He reached out and took her hand. "But it's not enough for me, Blair. I don't want to rush things, either, but we both know our world can go up in a puff of smoke in an instant—" He broke off and chuckled. "Wow, that sounds like the line soldiers going off to war have used on women since the beginning of time. But you know it's not just a line in this case, don't you? We must be honest with ourselves. We cheat death every day we're alive here. Grim reality, but true." Pausing, his dark eyes momentarily seemed to turn inward.

Blair could almost see death and danger clinging to him. Her experiences of the last months must certainly pale compared to his. He was not merely playing hide-and-seek with the enemy but was actively thwarting the Japanese. Her heart ached for him.

He went on fervently, "We've waited long enough. I want to be married, truly married. I'm ready."

No longer able to lie back lazy and relaxed, she wiggled to a sitting position, tilting her head to face him. "I've waited months to hear that, Gary." But she sighed, some of her contentment slipping. "Yet for so long I've been afraid of making the wrong move, with the wrong motives . . . I just want us to be certain."

"I couldn't be more certain. You're not, then? Is that what you're saying?" His tone was patient, even gentle, but it held an edge, as well.

"I have wanted you from that first day," she said tenderly. "When you crashed my father's birthday party, you in your new, crisp uniform and your incredibly handsome face that stood out in a sea of fine-looking men, I was instantly drawn to you. Then I got to know the wonderful man that lay beneath the surface, and my heart was yours. I haven't changed one iota from that."

"Then what? What holds you back, Blair?"

"When I last saw you, things were still rocky between us. I could tell you were still hurt by what I had done. Now we are back together for only a few days, and you're ready to put it all behind us."

"Don't you trust my feelings?" Now the edge of his tone was distinctly wounded. "Don't you believe my words?"

"You have been suffering terribly for months, starving, sick—"

"And that makes me desperate for a woman? Maybe even any woman?" His eyes were suddenly as hard as his voice, like a soldier, not a husband, like the toughened guerrilla warrior he had become. He jumped up and walked to the edge of the grass clearing, facing the waterfall.

"I'm sorry," she breathed. "I've always only wanted you to be as sure as I am."

A couple minutes of silence followed her words, and then he turned, came back, and sat beside her again. All the hard edges were now softened as he gazed at her.

"Blair, I could have had other women. You should see what goes on in a camp of lonely men when a few women show up. There have been women around quite willing to offer comfort to men defending their country." He took her hands again, stroking their thin bony surface with his thumb. "But I was married to you, and that commitment meant even more to me as time passed. You kept me going when I could have died a hundred times. I always had

117

assurance that what we had was worth waiting for, worth bearing intense loneliness. I have been ready for our marriage to be real for months now—in fact, it has felt very real, even though we weren't together. Only one obstacle stood in the way, and that was your faith, but I had little doubt God would deal with that. And He did! So don't you see? I have been ready. This isn't a sudden thing. Can you believe that? I am really not as complex as you seem to think I am."

"I believe you!" She brought his hands to her lips and kissed his rough, coarse fingers. "Your inability to lie is one of the things I love best about you."

"I wouldn't lie to you." He added with a wry grin, "I might lie to the Japs but never to you!" There was the merest of pauses, and then with a slight crease in his brow he said, "There's still hesitation in you, isn't there?"

"I don't know why," she said with a grimace. "I must be nuts!"

"I think you just need time for it to sink in," he said. "Our path has never been smooth."

"Maybe that's it. My entire *life* has never been smooth, so for something to work out so perfectly . . . it just makes me nervous."

He burst out laughing. "Honey, you can't call this perfect! We are fugitives in the jungle, enemies are all around us, capture is easily a heartbeat away. We are starved, dirty, disease-ridden—"

"And for me it is perfect, because it is with you!"

Still laughing, and she was chuckling, too, he caught her in his arms, his lips brushing her cheek. He held her firmly, and amusement quickly turned to fervency.

"I love you so, Blair!"

"Gary . . ." was all she could say as tears sprang to her eyes.

"I've got to go on a mission tonight," he said after a while. "We'll talk more when I get back." When she nodded against his shoulder, he added, "But I won't pressure you. This will happen when we both feel right."

"Thank you! Believe me, I won't make us wait forever."

"Hey, Gary." A voice came from the jungle on the other side of the clearing. In a couple of moments the owner of the voice appeared. "I know you didn't want to be disturbed," said the fellow everyone called Sarge, though he was actually a lieutenant and his given name was really Ralph Senger. Blair had caused him some discomfort upon their first meeting, but since then they had become friends. He wouldn't even listen to her apology for what she had done, insisting it had been self-defense on her part. And he never mentioned it himself except to sometimes make a wry reference to her as Gary's "Amazon Woman."

"What's wrong?" asked Gary. He obviously knew, as Blair was quickly learning, that Ralph was not a frivolous man and would not have interrupted if it hadn't been important.

"Woody and Fernando brought in a prisoner I think you should see. Says he's been looking for you and won't believe he's found friends until he sees you."

"Did he give his name?"

"Won't say a thing except that he will talk only to you. He's wounded, too, so I don't blame him for not being cooperative."

Gary rose and gave Blair a hand up. "Time we got back anyway."

As they walked, Gary asked, "How'd he get wounded? What happened?"

"He was prowling around on the far perimeter of the camp. Fernando shot him. You know how jumpy Fernando has been lately."

"Everyone's jumpy, but I don't want us shooting first and asking questions later. That's not how I want this band to operate. I didn't hear any gunfire, so it couldn't have been too close." Shaking his head with dismay, he added, "Is the man going to live?"

"I think so."

When they reached the camp a few hundred yards from the waterfall, Blair was about to go off on her own to give the cook a hand with the evening meal. Food was in short supply, but Blair had become quite adept at making do with very little. She remembered when Meg Doyle had to teach her how to cut a carrot. Now she could make a pretty tasty stew out of the most bizarre ingredients.

She gave Gary a parting smile as he followed Ralph to one of the two huts. She tried not to give what was behind the hut door another thought. Thus far Gary seemed to want to keep his Army business separate from their relationship. For the present she was content with that but felt she needed to become more involved eventually if she was to have a part in the war effort. For now, though, there were too many other things to work out between them without making that an issue, as well.

She went to the lean-to where the meager cooking supplies were kept and where Tom Morris, the resident cook of the partisans, was at the laborious task of cracking apart a coconut. These were a lot of work, but if they could be found, and if a man had the energy to climb one of the tall palms to get some, Blair was able to make a fairly decent soup out of the coconut meat. It was especially nice if there was some wild chicken and hot peppers to go with it. But she barely had a chance to greet Tom when Gary poked his head out of the hut and called her.

"I think you better come, Blair."

She hurried to the hut, supposing Gary wanted to make use of her meager nursing skills. Inside, besides Gary and Ralph, there was the fellow named Fernando, a squat, muscular middle-aged Filipino whom Blair had seen only one other time. Gary motioned to her to come to the mat on which a figure lay, and when she was close enough to get a good look at the prisoner, she gasped.

"Mateo! It that really you?" She quickly knelt down beside the mat.

"I get two for the price of one," Mateo said with a weak smile. "Friends at last!"

"Goodness! I have wondered so many times what became of you. Let me see where you are hurt." Her insides quaked.

How many times indeed had she fretted over him, wondering where he was or if he was okay? She'd felt like a worried mother or a sister. That special bond with him had greatly deepened since that day in Manila at the start of the war when his father, Reverend Sanchez, had asked her to take Mateo with her when she evacuated the city. She hadn't wanted the responsibility of this young man added to her burdens then, but she had grown to love him as a brother and a friend. Now her friend was suddenly returned to her. *Dear God, please let him not be hurt badly.*

"My leg," he said. "I wish it was anywhere but my leg. I got to work, to fight. . . ."

"I'm going to have to rip your pant leg," she said, seeing the circle of blood on the fabric around his upper thigh.

"No, Blair, you can't. I . . . well, it's all I got to wear."

"It'll be too painful if we try to take them off—"

"You can't do that!" With beseeching eyes on Gary he added desperately, "Don't let her do that, Captain Hobart. I don't have—"

120

He tugged Gary close and whispered something in his ear.

Gary then turned to Blair and, obviously trying to restrain amusement, said in as somber a tone as his dancing eyes would permit, "Blair, the boy wants to guard his modesty."

"Oh, Mateo!" she said tenderly without even a hint of making light of his feelings. They had been through a lot together, often sleeping in the same room or camping together under the jungle canopy. Yet through all that they had always managed to maintain their modesty. He was still only seventeen years old and had a right to be shy. She brushed back a lock of his dark hair that had grown into a scraggly mess of waves. She realized she did love this boy, like the little brother she'd never had. "I won't look at anything but the wound, I promise."

Gingerly she tore apart the coarse cotton fabric of his blood-soaked pant leg. The trousers were already quite worn and didn't need much effort to pull apart. Blair had thought her time of working in the field hospital had cured her of any queasiness at the sight of blood, but her stomach churned when she saw the wound. Her closeness to this particular patient was probably the reason.

The injured upper thigh was saturated with blood, making inspection difficult. However, she could see the bullet hole, and since there was no exit wound, she was certain the bullet was still lodged inside. She needed medical supplies but feared all she'd be able to find was a knife and boiling water.

"Gary, can you have one of the men boil—"

Her words were cut off by shouts, gunfire, and other sounds of mayhem.

"Stay put!" Gary told her as he jumped up, strode to the window, and lifted a corner of the cloth covering it. Ralph drew the pistol he had strapped to his side in a holster while Fernando drew the lethal-looking curved knife he wore in a bamboo sheath. "Bandits!" Gary said. He seemed very calm, as if this was a normal occurrence.

Ralph took up a position on the other side of the window. He and Gary, who also drew the pistol he wore in a holster, fired a few times from the window. Fernando was helpless with only a knife if the hut was invaded, but Blair didn't want to consider that possibility. She kept her attention on Mateo, who had begun to wiggle around as if he intended to join the fight. She leaned over him protectively, holding him down.

"Let me go!" he said. "It's my fault!"

"Hush, now, and lie still," Blair told him. "You don't want to make that wound bleed any more."

"But—"

"Hush!" Blair's tone was harsher than she had intended because at that same moment something knocked against the hut door.

Fernando rushed to the door and threw closed the latch just as the single knock became several hard pounds. Blair's heart raced as she looked wildly around for a weapon, but there was nothing within reach, and under no circumstances would she leave Mateo's side. He continued to squirm, and she had to nudge him back to the floor a couple of times.

The battle outside lasted only fifteen minutes, but they were terrifying minutes, perhaps even more so because she could see nothing and had no idea if at any moment they would find themselves at the mercy of their attackers. Silence fell, and she would have feared the worst except that when she looked toward the window, Gary and Ralph had holstered their pistols and in no way appeared about to surrender. The pounding on the door had ceased, as well, but when Fernando tried to open it, something blocked it. He had to give it a hard shove, and when it was finally open, Blair could see two feet sticking out from the other side. She also caught a whiff of smoke.

Again instructing her not to leave the hut, Gary exited with the other two men. Whoever it was that had attacked the camp had been repelled, but there was no guarantee they would not return with reinforcements. Gary had said bandits. Not Japanese. Blair knew the roaming bands of bandits could be worse than the Japs. Most were just out for themselves, bullying and terrorizing the local population. But there was always the chance some were collaborating with the Japanese and might well give away a partisan hiding place. With an awful sinking in her stomach, Blair feared they would soon be forced to pack up and leave. Another jungle trek might be a little different now that she was with Gary, but still, it seemed that just when she was feeling secure some upheaval would come and spoil it.

To keep her mind from such thoughts and because Mateo was

growing quite agitated, Blair turned her full attention to him. She could do nothing more than murmur words of comfort and wipe the sweat from his brow, but that did seem to help. His previous struggle had made the wound bleed again and must have moved the bullet into a more precarious position, because he seemed in far greater pain now. The bullet had to be removed.

"Mateo, promise me you will keep still. Any movement is going to cause you greater pain."

He nodded, having experienced firsthand what his struggles had done.

"I have to get some supplies," she said. "I'll be right back."

Blair stepped from the hut, and one look at the camp told her that finding anything was going to be a chore. It appeared as if a typhoon had passed through. The bandits had made the most of the short attack. The other hut had its door hanging off its hinges, a corner of it was on fire, and several men were furiously beating out the flames with blankets. Blair, seasoned fugitive that she was, instinctively noted the smoke and prayed other enemies did not see it.

The two lean-tos were demolished, and the few supplies they held were under rubble. The cook fire was also stamped out, and she despaired of getting boiling water to clean Mateo's wound. There would be others needing care, as well. She saw two bodies lying on the ground that appeared beyond any help, but other men hurrying about the camp were bruised and bleeding noticeably.

Gary came up to her. "I thought I told you to stay inside," he said shortly.

"Mateo needs help," she said.

"I don't think we could have done much for him even before this," he said grimly. "We have only a few bandages and a little iodine."

"That bullet has to be removed," she said. "I think it moved and is up against a nerve. He's in a lot of pain. I'm sure you have other men who need help, too."

"It's all got to wait." He glanced toward the burning hut. The blaze was getting away from the men with the blankets. "If there are Japs near, they won't miss this smoke. We have to get out of here."

"Mateo can't be moved."

"I'm sorry. We have no choice. I'll talk to him." He headed toward the hut.

Blair followed, though she really didn't see how Gary's talking to the boy would help. She had hoped that Mateo might have fallen asleep, but he was wide awake when they entered the hut and was shuddering with pain. That he was not screaming or yelling, she could tell, was only by great force of will, but she could also see he was in enough pain to do both.

Gary squatted down beside the mat. "Mateo, the bandits set one of the huts on fire, and we have to evacuate before the Japs locate us. You understand, don't you?"

"I'm sorry, Captain Hobart."

"Hey, you have no reason to be sorry. We shot you—"

"No . . . it was me . . . I led the bandits here . . . I . . ."

"What are you saying?"

Blair wondered the same thing. Surely he couldn't have done it on purpose. But would it matter, especially to the other men? She knew how brutal some guerrillas could be because of their desperate situation. She knew that even if a man was suspected of collaborating with the enemy, be that enemy Japanese or bandit, he often wasn't allowed to live very long. But Gary was in command, so nothing like that could happen here. Could it?

"They captured me a few days ago," Mateo replied, his words broken and halting with his pain. "I escaped yesterday. I tried to be so careful, and I was sure no one was following me. But . . ."

"They let you escape." Gary's words were statement not question. His tone was harsh.

"At first when they captured me, I thought they were guerrillas. . . . I wanted to join up with the partisans. I was looking for you, Captain Hobart. I'd heard you were leading a band and had a camp somewhere around here."

"So you asked them about me?"

"I know it was stupid—"

"Yeah . . . yeah, it was stupid."

"Gary," Blair said, "you know it's sometimes impossible to tell friend from foe."

"That's why you keep your mouth shut until you know. I lost two men—"

Blair laid a hand on Gary's shoulder, and whether it was her touch or that just then Mateo squeezed shut his eyes and clenched his teeth as a fresh wave of pain coursed through him, Gary paused and sucked in a steadying breath. He seemed to reconsider his initial instinct to reprimand the boy. With forced evenness in his tone he added, "Don't worry about it, Mateo. We were in this camp longer than was safe anyway. But tell me one thing—were any of those bandits named Dizon?"

"I d-don't know. They didn't g-give out names."

"Okay, Mateo, you rest. We'll be moving in a little while. We'll try to make it easy on you." He started to rise, then stopped. "I'm glad you found me, Mateo. I'm gonna take care of you now, and so is Blair."

"I don't want to be taken care of. I want to fight—"

"Then work on getting better," he ordered sternly. "You can't fight with a bum leg."

"Okay, Captain," Mateo conceded, his voice momentarily steady as a rock.

Blair walked with Gary to the door of the hut. "Can the men rig up some kind of litter for him?" she asked.

"I'll get them working on it. We'll leave within the hour. I'm sorry, Blair."

"Like you told Mateo, there is nothing to be sorry about."

"But he did have something after all." He smiled grimly. "And I fear I do, as well. Mateo may have brought Dizon here, but the attack wasn't random. He was after me."

"Why? Who is Dizon?"

"Not all the enemies you make in this business are Japs," Gary said with a ragged sigh. "Dizon is a Communist partisan. I think he hates Americans worse than Japs. I was trying to parlay with him a while back. Instead, a fight broke out, and one of my men killed his brother. He's been after me ever since."

"But you didn't kill his brother."

"It was my man and my responsibility. Anyway, I know you were feeling content here. I wish it could have lasted longer."

"I don't care how long it lasts as long as we continue to be together."

"I can make no promises, Blair. But you know that's what I want, too, more than anything." He gave her a quick hug, then left.

Blair knew contentment was a fleeting thing. That's why, she was certain, the Source of contentment must be within, not dependent on circumstances.

"God, I won't count on having Gary forever, yet if it could be for just a little while longer..."

She must learn to appreciate the gifts as they came, not that she had much choice in the matter.

14

THEY TRUDGED through the jungle until a couple of hours before nightfall. Three hours had passed since the attack. From his makeshift litter Mateo groaned with pain, though the men carrying him took great care to hold him steady. Gary had said nothing to the men about what Mateo had told him. Blair suspected they would not have been so careful with him had they known. Two of their number were dead because of what Mateo had done. They would not be forgiving of that.

A secluded place was found to camp for the night. One of the men knew of a location several miles away that would make a good permanent camp, but they couldn't reach it until tomorrow. Blair was relieved they could not travel at night, because she wasn't certain Mateo could take much more. If only there was some pain medication for him, even some whiskey, but there was nothing of the kind. Gary had told her his mission that night would have been to raid a Japanese truck convoy they'd heard would pass by on the main road ten miles from the old camp. They had hoped that besides destroying the convoy, they might raid some of the supplies it carried. That plan was scrapped now because of concern that the gunfire from the bandit attack and the smoke from the burning hut might have alerted the Japanese.

"Gary, is there a village nearby?" she asked. "Maybe there would be a doctor."

"The nearest village is ten miles from here. I could send one of the men, but I doubt he could be back here before tomorrow."

Blair glanced over at Mateo. He'd passed out from the pain, but that wasn't her greatest concern. If the bullet remained in him, it would cause infection, which, left untreated, could lead to gangrene and even the need for amputation.

"Gary, I have to remove that bullet." The confidence of her tone surprised her. *She* had to remove it? What was she saying? But who else if not her? None of the men knew any more than she about such things.

"You are quite incredible!" said Gary, his voice full of admiration. That tone warmed her. When had anyone ever admired *her*?

"I just have to do what has to be done." She was a bit defensive. The admiration of others was nice, but she wasn't entirely comfortable with the sense of responsibility that went with it. "It's what I have always done."

"True, but there's more to it. You are changing."

"I suppose I am. Who wouldn't after all that has happened to me?" Then she added with a wry grin, though the hint of defiance in her tone was real, "But as soon as I get back to the States, I just might go back to being pampered and spoiled."

"And you'd deserve it." He was smiling, too.

"That wouldn't bother you?" Some of her amusement faded as she realized that was another valid worry.

"Back home when you were acting like the girl next door, I knew you were pampered and spoiled. I still loved you. And I will continue to love you. In fact, if we ever do get home, I hope to do some of the pampering and spoiling myself! Don't you understand? I can see the whole picture now, and I love you even more than before."

"Amazing!" she breathed.

He nodded. "You are amazing."

"Enough!" She laughed. "I can take only so much fawning at a time."

"Get used to it, honey. You're gonna get a lifetime of it."

Her head was nearly spinning but returning to the beginning of their conversation steadied her. "We were talking about Mateo. What medical supplies do you have?"

"We've got some iodine and bandages, maybe a couple of other things in the first aid kit. Not near what you need."

"Gather what you can, and let's get this done while there's still some daylight."

Gary had not underestimated the supplies. Yet Blair thought she had what was necessary for the job, except for some kind of pain-killer. She could only pray Mateo would pass out before she got too far. Then she cleaned her hands and Gary's knife with iodine and saturated the wound with most of what remained. There was just enough left for cleansing the wound later. Finally, she kneeled over her patient. Her mind spun. What did she think she was doing? She might have assisted at a few surgeries, but she'd never held a scalpel. How was she ever going to find the courage, or sheer audacity, to actually cut into this poor boy's skin?

Gary had the answer to that. "Go ahead, Blair. I'm praying for you."

She smiled her thanks.

Besides his prayers, Gary held down Mateo's shoulders while Ralph grasped his legs. Fernando, feeling responsible for this needing to be done at all, stood at Blair's shoulder should she need an extra hand. With no reason for delay, she lowered the knife over the exposed wound. She glanced at Gary again. He nodded with assurance.

"Okay, Mateo," she said, "I'm going to cut you now. It's going to hurt."

He mumbled something that wasn't clear because Gary had put a knotted rag between his teeth.

Then she cut. In her intense concentration, she forgot to be sick as the skin spread open around the blade. Once the skin was cut, she carefully eased away tissue and fat. Mateo would surely die if she inadvertently cut a blood vessel. So she worked slowly, by mere fractions, millimeters, probing with the point of the knife, wishing she'd thought to look for something more blunt for this particular job. She could feel Mateo's shudders, then they stopped.

"Is he still breathing?" she asked. Her voice was shakier than her hands—thank God for that!

"He just passed out," Gary said.

"Well, that's a blessing."

If she had hoped to find the bullet directly in line with the gun-shot hole in his leg, she would have been disappointed. But she knew it had moved, and she hoped as she moved to the right of the wound that the bullet had gone in that direction. It seemed a logical guess since that was toward the knee, and most likely the bullet would have moved down not up. But as she probed and prodded deeper into the wound, she despaired that she'd made the wrong choice. Sweat beaded on her forehead in the unrelenting heat and humidity. At least it wasn't raining.

As if he'd read her mind, Fernando swabbed a cloth across her forehead.

"Thank you," she murmured. Just like a real doctor . . . no, she had absolutely no delusions about that. She hadn't a clue what she was doing. She could kill this boy. Then she thought of dear Claudette, who was hopelessly in love with Mateo. She couldn't botch this. Someday this nightmare would be over and they would have their lives back—and she wanted to be an auntie to Mateo and Claudette's children.

Tap! Not a sound but a feel that was different from the soft tissue she was probing. She'd found the bullet! Gently she pushed aside more fatty tissue until she saw the metallic base. And suddenly she realized the great flaw in her surgical procedure. She had nothing to grip the bullet with. She had been so worried about cutting the skin, she hadn't considered the rest of it.

Dumb, flighty Blair—again. Just when she thought the story of what she was doing might one day truly make her father proud, she had bungled the task. No sense disappointing Dad, she thought bitterly.

Then she gave her head a shake. She wasn't doing this for her father. She didn't care what he thought, but she wasn't about to disappoint him or anyone.

"I need some tweezers to remove the bullet," she said, looking at her helpers for ideas. "I know there aren't any in the kit."

"Fernando," Gary said, "go ask and look around. See if you can come up with something."

Gingerly, Blair continued to probe around the bullet with the knife point, hoping she might catch some grooved spot and lift it out, but it was too slippery for the blade to grip anything. She tried with her fingers, as well, but they were too blunt to get a good hold, and her fingernails, what with her poor diet, were simply too flimsy to help. In a couple of minutes Fernando returned.

"This isn't exactly what you are looking for," he said, "but maybe it will work."

He held up a pair of bamboo "tweezers." Blair had seen some of the Filipino men use these to pluck out stray facial hair in lieu of shaving, since they usually didn't have heavy beards. It was a process no different from plucking her own eyebrows, yet there was no comparison between her fine tweezers and these bulky, clumsy-looking things. She gave both the bamboo tweezers and Fernando a dubious look, but since she had no better solution, she took them and lowered them into the wound. Too late she realized she hadn't disinfected them with iodine. *Oh, God, please don't let that matter!*

With the point of the knife, she cleared away tissue that had spread once more over the bullet. Then, with the tweezers in her other hand, she tried to wedge the tip of them around the bullet. She tried several times to grasp the bullet, but seeping blood made visibility poor, and she could not be too forceful with the knife in trying to keep the area clear for fear of cutting something vital. When she thought she had a good grip and attempted to tug, the tweezers slipped off. They simply did not have the needed traction.

The earlier phase of the operation had been slow and tedious, but this was nearly torture. The tweezers kept slipping off, and her prodding had the effect of pushing the bullet back in, undoing any progress she made. She was surprised at how firmly the bullet was wedged and would have feared it might have penetrated a bone except that its previous movement indicated otherwise. Blair's back ached, and her arms started to tremble from the physical effort. A bead of sweat traveled to the end of her nose, but Gary had taken up Fernando's previous job and quickly wiped it away. She smiled her gratitude but could say no more for fear of losing her concentration.

She despaired of ever being successful. She should have waited and found a doctor. This was the most harebrained thing she'd ever done! Worse still, the sun was starting to set, and the light was failing.

"You've got it!" said Fernando, standing near and ready to help if needed.

Yes, the bullet had moved significantly with that last tug. Finally she felt she had a good grip. A couple more tugs, and at last she whipped the horrible thing out. She started to toss it to the ground.

"Wait," said Ralph, "I'll wager the boy will want that as a souvenir."

Fernando grimaced. No doubt he wanted no such reminder around of the fact that he had shot Mateo.

Blair had been miffed at him for what he'd done to her friend, even though she knew he hadn't done it intentionally. Now, though, she knew he had helped save Mateo, and she felt sympathy for him.

"Never mind that!" she said and gave the bullet a hard toss into the bushes. "I never want to see that ugly thing again!"

Fernando, who hardly ever smiled, let his lips twitch in a look of gratitude only Blair could see.

With a needle and the last bit of catgut in the first aid kit, she stitched together the incision, finally dousing the area with the last bit of iodine before applying a bandage. There weren't many of those left, either. Fleetingly she wondered what the men wounded in the fight had done about their wounds. She felt bad she had forgotten all about them in her concern for Mateo.

Mateo wasn't out of the woods yet. There was still the possibility of infection. She thought of those dirty bamboo tweezers and gave a little shudder. And how good was that iodine? It might have been sitting in the kit for years. She was somewhat comforted when, an hour or so later, Mateo woke and said his leg felt a little better and he could wiggle his toes, which meant she hadn't sliced a major nerve.

———

The next day they reached the new camp. It was a little higher in the foothills than before, and the men did not seem happy about this. She asked Gary why they were so disgruntled. In her mind the lowlands were Jap country and the farther away from them the better. Gary only shrugged and told her not to worry about the men. But she did worry, especially when some of them gave her covertly sour looks.

She finally cornered Ralph on the edge of the camp, where he was cleaning his pistol.

"Have I done something to make the men mad at me?" she demanded.

"Okay, I'll tell you as long as you don't hurt me!" he said with mock fear.

"I want to know why the men look at me as if I've done something wrong, something to offend them. Gary won't talk about it."

"That's 'cause he doesn't want you to know he's protecting you." There wasn't a single curse word in his statement. He'd been trying especially hard to clean up his speech around her.

"Me? I should think it would just be smart to stay away from the Japs."

"We can't fight them if we're hiding in the mountains. Besides, it's harder to find food the higher up we get, and the mosquitoes are worse up here, too. We're farther away from our civilian contacts here, and another problem is the mountain people. If the Japs know we're operating here, their reprisals against the locals are pretty harsh."

"Won't they be just as harsh toward the folks in the lowlands?"

"No. They are coming to depend on the rice farmers for their food to be too hard on them." Ralph scratched his head, seeming to silently debate something. Finally he said, "A couple of our boys are from the mountains, so they, especially, don't like having to endanger their people."

"Because of me."

He shrugged. "They are going to have to live with it," he said firmly. "Gary is right to protect you."

"But I don't want special favors. I don't want to get in the way of the fighting. I want to help."

"Well, get that out of your mind right now," interjected a new voice. Gary's. He had come out of the jungle with an armload of firewood.

"I thought you, of all people, would be above eavesdropping," said Blair, affronted.

"I just happened along," he replied defensively. "Regardless, you're talking crazy."

"This is my war, too, Gary!"

"Time was you didn't give a hang about the war."

"You must know that has changed. You even noted it just the other day."

He sucked in a frustrated breath. "Yes, I realize that, but you don't need to be involved."

"There you are wrong, Gary. I do need to be involved! I have scores to settle with the Japs, too. And I have friends who are probably POWs, and I want to help free them."

"I don't mean to preach at you, Blair, but settling scores doesn't seem to be the kind of thing that God would want of you."

"And what are you doing?" she shot back accusingly. She was mostly angry because he was right. Vengeance wasn't a very godly pursuit.

"I like to think I'm just fighting the war that's been given me." His tone held a touch of defensiveness. "I'm paving the way for MacArthur's return, helping to liberate these islands—"

"Come on, Gary," put in Ralph. "You have to admit that your motives aren't all that pure, either. None of ours are. We all want to get even—for Bataan, for the Death March—if only just a little."

Gary shook the wood he'd been carrying to the ground and absently brushed away bits of bark and dirt from his shabby khaki shirt. He sat down in the grass next to Blair and Ralph.

"I don't want to be that way," he said dismally. "Maybe it is true, but it's against all that I know to be right."

Blair patted his arm. "The reasons you gave before are true, as well, and they are the most important ones. The revenge . . . it's just an insidious worm of human nature that we all have to battle and keep praying that it doesn't consume us. That's all we can do. God knows we are human. We just have to trust He will help us keep that worm in check so we aren't taken over by the desire for revenge."

"You got yourself a good woman here, Gary," Ralph said.

"And I'd like to keep her."

"Gary, I stopped being a hothouse flower the day Bataan fell, maybe a little before. Though you might try to do so with your very life, you can't shelter me. I am in this battle."

"There are several other women who work for us," Ralph said. "They can get to places a man often can't."

"Thanks, Ralph," Gary said sourly, then shrugged with resignation. "If a need arises, I'll use you, Blair, but I can't just throw you to the wolves."

"What about the location of the camp?"

"You're not the only reason we're here," he said, still a touch defensive. "We have to lie low for a few days, let Dizon cool down, and let our trail cool off. But if it makes you happy, we'll be here only a few days because we have to get supplies somehow."

"Gary, Mateo said he's been to Manila recently," Blair offered. "He saw his father, who is very active in the underground in the city."

"I'm not surprised," said Gary. "I've thought of contacting Reverend Sanchez, but there hasn't been time or the means."

"Mateo is sure his father can get us supplies. He's done so for other partisans. The only problem is that Mateo will be off his feet for a good while and thus unable to contact his father." Blair paused in an attempt to give Gary the chance to suggest what she was hoping for and thus spare further conflict. When he didn't speak, she went on, "It has to be someone he trusts." She thought it was obvious she was referring to herself.

"I'll do it, then." Gary's statement wasn't what Blair wanted to hear.

"You can't go into Manila, Gary!" Ralph quickly interjected. "Are you nuts?" He added a few other choice words before he realized what he was saying. With a reddened face he looked at Blair. "Excuse me, Blair. I . . . uh . . . forgot myself. But can you blame me? That's the most foolish suggestion I've ever heard. A white man roaming the streets of Manila would be arrested immediately and would have to go to great lengths to prove he wasn't an enemy alien."

"Do you think it would be less foolish for Blair to go?" Gary jerked his steely gaze toward Blair. "Yes, Blair, I knew exactly what you were getting at."

"I could do it, Gary. I've been thinking about this. There are other whites, especially women, in Manila who aren't American and are either neutral or Japanese allies. I met an Italian gal when I lived there. But I think with my coloring, I'd do better to pass as a German national. I know a little German. I'm quite good with languages—"

"Hold it!" Gary's voice rose ominously. He'd been willing to accede in *theory* to Blair's desire to help in the war, but when it came to an actual plan, apparently that was more than he could handle. "You are not going to Manila. At least not until we think this through."

Blair thought he might as well have added, "And probably never." But she kept silent. She didn't want to botch her chances by saying something stupid. And it was probably better to let Gary give the idea some thought. He was the leader of this group and for good reason. He knew what he was doing.

"Okay," she said in a conciliatory tone, "but I'm willing to go, and I'm sure I can do it."

Gary rolled his eyes and shook his head.

Ralph muttered with just a hint of pride, "Amazon woman!"

15

GARY HAD SENT out one of his men to gather information to see just how much the attack by Dizon had stirred up the Japanese. That fellow returned two days later with some good news. The enemy had only tightened their security a little more than usual. And they certainly had not sniffed out the new camp; neither had Dizon. But the best news was that the convoy Gary had planned to raid before the attack had been delayed and now was expected to pass on the same road in two days.

So another mission was quickly planned. An hour before Gary and a small contingent of his men departed on this new objective, Gary took Blair aside and explained why he must go. She didn't see the need for the explanation, but it seemed to make him feel better.

"I don't want to leave you now with everything so unsettled in the camp," he said. "But we've been having such sour luck lately that I feel we have to put our best men on this. I guess I'm beyond false modesty. For some cockeyed reason, I have a talent at this. Anyway, both Ralph and I are going."

"You mustn't worry about me, Gary," she assured. "I'll be fine. Just get some morphine and some sulfa if you can."

"If the convoy hasn't any medical supplies, I'll scour the villages." Then, still seeming to need to reassure himself of her safety, he added, "Tony Hillerman, who came with you when you first found us, seems to be a good man. He said he'd stay and look out for you. Three others will remain here, as well. But I need every other man for the mission."

"I'll pray for your success."

"I really hate to leave you—" He stopped abruptly when she opened her mouth to protest, then added quickly, "Not just because I worry about you. I've enjoyed being with you. The talks we've had. We haven't had much time to enjoy each other, but what we've had only makes me want more."

"We'll have more, Gary. I know it!"

"I'll see you in four or five days."

His kiss was fervent, and his arms were reluctant to let go when Ralph called that they were ready to depart. Blair watched him go and kept telling herself that she truly was sure this would not be the last good-bye. Yet she berated herself for continued hesitancy in dropping all barriers between them. Suddenly she knew her fears were foolish. Gary had spoken of their talks, and indeed they had not merely talked but had opened their hearts to each other. In these last few days they had become closer than ever. There was no reason not to have a true marriage. In fact, in this uncertain world, there was every reason for it.

She wanted to call after him, but he and the other men had already hiked out of sight. So she comforted herself with the determination that when he returned, she would give herself completely to him.

There was much to keep her mind occupied in the meantime. Caring for Mateo consumed her emotionally and physically. He took a turn for the worse as his wound turned red and began to fester. There was nothing to do but try to keep his fever down, a full-time task with the oppressive temperatures in the jungle. All she could do was fret and pray and apply wet cloths to his face and chest.

The men who remained in the camp were busy building a hut, keeping guard, and hunting for food. They were successful in only the first two endeavors. The camp remained safe and the hut went up quickly, though not in time to avoid a few good rainfalls. Mateo had been kept fairly dry in a natural cove that was covered thickly with palms and vines. But it was still miserable, and even the hut, when they were finally able to move into it, was unable to keep away the mosquitoes that seemed particularly pesky in this new location. In a way Blair was glad the hut was rather flimsy, with its barely covered sides and a nipa roof that would not withstand a strong wind. She didn't think they would be in this location for long. All the other reasons for moving to the lowlands aside, the mosquitoes alone should convince Gary of the impossibility of remaining here for long.

Tony and a Filipino named Albert both were hit with malaria attacks. Blair prayed more fervently than ever for medical supplies. Some food wouldn't hurt, either. Game was scarce and there was little ripe fruit—they had all suffered the ill effects of eating green fruit and desired to avoid that at all costs. With two men ill, only two others were left to hunt and stand guard. So they subsisted on their stores of rice. There was not even salt to season it with.

During the next days when Blair wasn't busy with Mateo and the other two sick men, she would walk to the edge of the camp and listen for the arrival of Gary and his men. She knew all about "watched" pots never boiling, but she couldn't help herself. Too much depended on Gary. Besides the group's survival, her own emotional survival was tightly woven with him.

Woody developed a bad case of the shakes, and the other men were starving. Gary had hoped to find some food along the way but found only enough to take the barest edge off their hunger. From the beginning the mission seemed doomed.

Shading his eyes from the glare of the lowering sun, Gary peered through jungle brush at the road below to the west. If his information was correct, the convoy should pass this part of the road just before sunset. Could he take it with only four men? Not only would Woody not be able to go, but someone would have to stay behind to watch him. And it was Woody who was the most knowledgeable about explosives and knew best how to set the dynamite charges.

"You thinking about scrubbing the mission?" Ralph asked as he crawled, almost soundlessly, up next to Gary.

"Our information says these will be troop trucks," said Gary. "We could cripple them badly if we took them out. And there's bound to be supplies, even if we could get only the first aid kits each truck is sure to have."

"I don't see how we can proceed with only four men. Woody definitely can't come, and someone will have to stay behind with him. Our explosives will disrupt the trucks and do a lot of damage if they work, but there will still be some Japs left to fight."

Gary didn't like it when Senger turned cautious. He was usually the risk taker of the outfit, so when he was skeptical, it worried Gary. Yet he thought of Mateo and his great need and of Blair, who was starving with the rest of them.

"Ralph, you know how important this is."

"We could scour the nearby villages. There ought to be some stuff to scrounge."

"That won't damage the trucks and eliminate the Japs."

"You're not talking revenge, are you, Gary?" Ralph's brow quirked. He was never a man to be judgmental, so his words stung all the more. That conversation earlier with Blair was still fresh in their minds, so perhaps Ralph thought that particular argument might swing him away from going on with the raid.

"I'm just thinking about doing what we committed to when we started this guerrilla fighting. Don't you go soft on me, Ralph."

"You are in charge," Ralph said with more confidence than Gary thought he deserved. "I'll do what you say. Let's take Marcos and Costas. Roxas can stay with Woody—he's also barely on his feet and would slow us down."

"All right. You and Marcos handle the explosives. Costas and I will cover you."

"I need to talk to Woody one more time to get a couple details straight, then I'll be ready to go."

They returned to where they had left the others, and Gary explained the plan. Woody tried to argue, but it was a pretty weak attempt since he couldn't even sit up. Roxas wasn't happy with the arrangement, either, but he knew how to take orders. While Ralph conferred one more time with Woody, Gary took stock of their weapons and ammo. There were three M–1 rifles and a tommy gun, which he gave to Costas mostly because he himself didn't particularly like using that weapon and the other two men would be too busy with the explosives. But Ralph and Marcos did each take an M–1, and they all had side arms. Ammo for these weapons was, as always, at a premium, but there should be enough.

When they were finally ready, there was about an hour left to dig trenches in the road for the dynamite and set the fuses. They hoped the Japs didn't show up early. There were enough explosives to set charges at about thirty-foot intervals in four places. They had chosen a section of road that was dirt and gravel, but the surface was still hard even with recent rains, and it took more time than expected to bury the dynamite and hide the holes and fuses, which were long enough to stretch from the side of the road into the jungle a few feet.

Gary's heart raced as he watched the men work, fearing the convoy would come along at any moment. This was taking much longer than planned. He finally sent Costas to help as he scanned the length of the road. They finished at a frantic pace. Then nothing happened for some time. Had their information been wrong after all? All that rushing and now there was time for Ralph to double-check all the fuses. Gary began to assess in his mind the locales of the most friendly villages in the area in case the convoy didn't come. He hated to depend on the villagers for help because their supplies were not that abundant, either. Yet there would be no other option if this mission should fail.

Despite his dismal thoughts, his senses were alert, and he noted the sound of approaching trucks long before they came into view. He signaled Ralph and Marcos to get into position to light the fuses.

The first truck rumbled around a curve in the road. Because Gary had the best viewpoint, the others were watching for his signal. It was torture to wait until that first truck passed the first three bombs so that it would come into line with the last bomb. Allowing time for the fuse to be consumed, Gary gave the signal when the truck was an appropriate distance from the explosive, and Ralph lit it.

In a matter of a few seconds the guerrillas went from an excruciatingly long and silent wait to seeing complete mayhem as the first bomb ignited right on target and blasted apart that first truck. The troops inside that truck flew through the air with bits and pieces of vehicle, much of it landing on the staff car directly behind the truck. The car veered off the road into a ditch to avoid debris and hit the ground with such an impact it sparked the gas tank, sending the vehicle up in a blaze.

The other explosives were set to go off at five-second intervals. Two of them were timed perfectly, but one must have been a dud because it did nothing. Those that exploded, though, did a significant amount of damage. Four trucks in the six-truck convoy were destroyed, along with a good percentage of the men they carried. Another staff car also went up in flames. They had succeeded in doing some damage, but there were still thirty or forty of the enemy in the undamaged vehicles that the dud had missed. The Japs were quick to recover from the shock of the attack and began hitting hard at the guerrillas. Although Gary had expected some resistance from the Japs in the convoy, he had thought the odds would be better. He'd also expected to have more men and to easily eliminate the remaining Japanese. Now he would be thankful if they got away with their lives.

Ralph managed to get his hands on a Jap tommy gun, and between him and Costas, they made some headway. Gary tried to fire at the unexploded dynamite, hoping to ignite it, but after missing several times, he finally gave the order to retreat. Knowing there were at least a couple dozen Japs left to give pursuit, Gary and his men tore through the jungle, pausing only to gather up Woody and Roxas. They were slowed down considerably with the new additions.

"We better split up," Gary panted. Woody had stumbled and fallen. "I'll take Woody. The rest of you know your way back to camp, so take care and get there in one piece."

"I'll stick with you, Gary," Ralph said as the others ran off in several different directions.

"I gave an order, Lieutenant," Gary said. "Don't waste time arguing." He didn't like giving his friend orders, so he added, "Look, Ralph, I'd like one of us to get back and take care of Blair."

Ralph knew it was a sound argument and protested no further. Still, Gary despaired at seeing his friend jog away. Then he turned his attention to Woody, who was too senseless by now to argue strenuously about being the one to hold Gary back. Gary didn't expect they would get far but hoped, if nothing else, that perhaps he could waylay the Japs and give the rest of his men a chance to get away. He still had a rifle and ammo, so he looked around for a good defensible spot and found it at the thick base of a banyan tree. He knew the enemy would pass that way, for he could already hear them clamoring toward the place. He put Woody under cover, then loaded his rifle and waited.

When the enemy arrived, Gary fired until his gun jammed, then was forced to surrender. At least maybe Woody could get some quinine from the Japs. Gary's only regret was in not getting those supplies so desperately needed. No, his truest regret was having to leave Blair once again.

16

TWO DAYS LATER Blair was walking on the edge of camp before sunset, as was becoming her habit. She no longer expected to hear the return of the men. Why would they happen to show up just when she was taking her walk? No doubt they would come when she least expected them. However, Gary had said they should be returning about now, so she walked and listened but heard only the chattering of a family of monkeys that lived nearby.

Yet there seemed to be tension in the air, or was that just her own rising tension and desperation? Every man in camp was now sick to some degree. Tony had recovered a little and was out trying to forage for food. Albert was very sick, and Blair feared he had contracted something besides malaria. Fernando looked as if he could barely stand, but he was making an attempt to guard the perimeter of the camp. Tom Morris was down with malaria. And Mateo . . . Blair wondered how much longer he could last without medication of some sort.

Oddly enough, she, who had been sick so much since leaving Manila, was the most healthy one, but that was only relative to the condition of the others. Just walking the short distance to the edge of camp exhausted her, and she knew another malaria attack could strike at any time. Thus she began to think more and more of going into Manila and trying to make contact with Reverend Sanchez.

Because she expected to hear the men clamor through the jungle and announce their triumphant return, she was taken by surprise when a figure sprang up silently out of the jungle foliage only ten feet away. But as quickly as she controlled her surprised gasp, she also controlled a twinge of disappointment that the figure was not Gary. Yet, Ralph Senger was surely the next best thing. Could Gary be far behind?

"Oh, Ralph, you are finally back." She peered over his shoulder. "How far away are the others?"

"Didn't anyone think to set a guard?" Ralph growled, seeming not to have heard her question. "My approach wasn't challenged even once."

"Everyone is sick," Blair replied. "I wouldn't have been much good myself as a guard, but Fernando is somewhere trying to do the job."

He shrugged and sighed. "Anyone else come back yet?"

"What do you mean? Aren't they with you?" Blair's stomach tightened. "Where's Gary?"

"Everything went sour," he said as he came nearer. "I'm starved. You got something cooking?"

"We're down to eating just rice. No one was up to looking for food."

Ralph started treading toward the camp, and Blair hurried after him, feeling fear clutch her throat even as she fought back frustration at Ralph's ignoring her questions.

Finally she grabbed his arm and spun him around to face her. "Ralph, tell me what happened."

He closed his eyes and let out a shuddering breath. "I gotta rest, Blair. I gotta at least have some of that rice. I'm so tired, so . . . shaky." He ran a hand through his hair.

She saw then that his hand trembled, and she feared it wasn't just from hunger and fatigue.

"Come on," she said as gently as her inner torment would let her. "I'll find you something to eat."

The pot of leftover rice from breakfast was cold, but there were still a few spoonfuls left, and that much only because everyone had been too sick to eat it all. Ralph plopped down on the ground and began scraping the inside of the pot with a wooden spoon. Though it wasn't enough food to fill a bird, it did seem to steady him a little. His hands still trembled, but he was now more inclined to talk.

"We blew up part of the convoy but not enough," he said wearily. "Woody was sick, and there just weren't enough of us. The Japs

146

got us on the run, and we had to split up. Gary took charge of Woody."

"Ralph, please don't tell me . . ." but she couldn't finish the sentence, much less the thought. Oh, Gary, what has become of you?

"He told me to make sure I got back to take care of you," Ralph went on dismally.

"No . . ." Blair could say no more as words were consumed with sobs.

She crumbled into Ralph's arms, which she could feel shake even as they held her. She wanted to feel sorry for him, to help him, yet she could think of nothing but her own misery. Had she given her heart to a cruel God, then? A God who would taunt her by bringing her and Gary together for only a few days and then take him from her again? Was she expected to hang on to her faith anyway? Oh yes, the purpose of faith was just for times like these—hard times, desperate times, she thought bitterly.

But a person could take only so many hard times! Hadn't she had her limit? What did God think she was made of? Not steel—that was her sister Cameron, not her.

"I just can't take any more!" she cried and did not realize she'd said the words aloud until Ralph replied.

"He'll show up, Blair. He's tough and he's smart."

"Ralph, sometimes it all seems so futile. Why don't we just surrender? It can't be that much worse being POWs. Maybe Gary would be better off if he's captured." But her voice trembled over the words. She knew what capture would mean for Gary. He would be tortured. They would know he was a guerrilla leader and would expect him to have valuable information. But of course Gary would die before revealing anything.

She cried for some time, and Ralph awkwardly, though faithfully, comforted her with tender pats on her head and back. Then she felt his hold on her weakening and his voice getting soft. It made her force down her own grief and focus attention on him.

She helped him into the hut and down onto one of the mats spread out on the dirt floor. She feared he'd be hit with a full-blown malaria attack at any time.

Blair scanned the makeshift infirmary and knew something had to be done. Further, she knew that she was the only one left to do it. She must swallow her own bitter despair and do what had to be done. She found Fernando, who was seated by a tree some fifty feet from the camp with a rifle propped in his hands, but he was sound asleep. When she gave him a nudge, he came awake sharply with a glare on his face made fiercer by being startled awake and by disgruntlement at himself for falling asleep on duty.

"Fernando, come back to camp," she said. "We need to talk."

Seeming to realize the futility of his guarding, he obeyed without argument. She woke up Tony Hillerman, as well. He'd been sleeping in the hut, but the others were too sick to notice the disturbance of his exiting. They were also too sick to be part of the task that must be done. She and the other two men sat outside around the fire pit, which had no fire burning now. The only light was provided by a half-moon.

"I am going to go into Manila and try to make contact with Mateo's father." She braced herself for argument and was a little surprised when none came.

"We're with you, Blair," said Tony.

"Tony, you can't come—"

Just then the flimsy bamboo door of the hut banged open, and Ralph Senger appeared.

"What are you doing out of bed?" Blair said in a scolding tone.

"Well, do you mind if I take care of a little business in the jungle?" he said, scowling back at her.

"Of course not," she said with a hint of apology.

He looked at each of them in turn. "What's going on?"

"Nothing. We're just talking." Blair knew too late that her tone was defensive. She had realized Ralph would never let her go to Manila without Gary's approval, even if he had defended her before. It was more because of that than his illness that she hadn't called him to the meeting, despite the fact that he was the recognized second-in-command of the group.

Ralph strode closer to them and spoke as he stood towering over them, as if to emphasize his command. "You're not a very good liar, Blair."

She laughed. If he only knew! "Go back to bed. You shouldn't have to worry about anything but getting better."

He dropped down on the ground next to her. "I'm not that sick now that I've had some rest. And I am in command until Gary returns—or am I mistaken, Blair? Did Gary make you commander of this outfit without telling me?"

"I recall your telling Gary that I should be able to help in the work of the outfit," she replied defiantly.

"Is this about going to Manila?"

"It has to be done, and you know it. You also know I am the only one to go, because I am the only one Sanchez will trust. You can't possibly stand in the way."

"Don't tell me what I can or can't do!" he retorted, not bothering to alter his salty language for her sake. But her offended grimace made him add quickly, "Sorry for my language, but—" He paused, catching himself before he cursed again. "It's different now. I'm responsible for you!"

"That's the silliest thing I ever heard!"

"What if Gary comes back and you are off to who knows where, or worse, you get caught? He'll kill me."

"He will not," she countered. "He will understand the absolute need. Anyway, I am not in the Army, and I am not under your command. I can do what I want." She knew the moment the words were uttered how foolish they were. She was expecting Fernando to accompany her, and he *was* under Ralph's command.

"Gary never told me how ornery you were."

"I can be when it's important."

He nodded thoughtfully, either just agreeing with her on that point or giving his assent to the mission. She couldn't tell which it was.

"So is this important?" she prompted.

"You know very well it is. But I'm going with you—"

"You can't go for the same reason Gary couldn't. I might as well carry a red flag—or a white one—with you along. With just Fernando, I might pass as a local if no one looks too closely."

"I can take you to my girlfriend's village," offered Fernando. "It's on the way, and she can give you some clothes that would help."

Because Ralph was a pragmatic man, he argued no further. They made a few plans, though for the most part there were few other arrangements to be made. Fernando had to be convinced, however, not to take along any weapons, and they discussed ways Blair might dye her hair, but in the end they decided to see what Fernando's girlfriend might have to offer. They agreed she and Fernando would leave at first light. Ralph insisted on standing guard the rest of the night so that Fernando could get some sleep. As for Blair, she lay on a mat in the hut near Mateo, as had become her habit so she could be near if he should need her. His presence this night, his moans of pain, his fevered thrashing, reminded her of how vital this trip was. But it didn't help her to sleep. When the first light of morning pinked the sky, she was wide awake, if not rested, and ready to go.

———

It would have taken longer to get to Manila on foot, but halfway to their destination they were fortunate enough to catch a ride in the hay cart of a sympathetic farmer. But because the man snickered at the idea of Blair trying to pass as a Filipina, she had to ride in the back covered by the hay while Fernando rode up front with the farmer. She thought her country garb was quite authentic—a dark blue cotton skirt and a peasant blouse with colorful embroidery around the hem and sleeves. The outfit was well worn and faded but the nicest clothing she'd had in months, at least since she'd left the Doyles' mission. Fernando's girlfriend had given the outfit to Blair, not that there would have been a chance to give the things back, but it was nice to know she had something of her own. Two whole outfits, including the clothing given her by Rosita that she had been wearing, now belonged to her! She would never take her wardrobe for granted again. As for her hair, nothing had been found for a dye so she merely tied a scarf around her head.

About five miles outside of Manila they reached their first serious checkpoint. Until then they had met Japanese on the road, and some had even stopped the cart and questioned the driver, but none had made any attempt to search the load of hay. Fernando had warned her that closer to the city they might not get off so easily.

"Papers," the Japanese guard said through a Filipino interpreter.

The farmer handed his documents over to be scrutinized, but then the guard must have looked at Fernando, because Blair heard him shift around on the seat and say, "I got 'em somewhere."

Did he have papers? She hadn't thought of that, and he hadn't mentioned anything about taking his papers. Maybe he was just being coy, because to be too eager with a guard often made him even more suspicious.

"Ah, here," Fernando said.

There was some shuffling of feet, then the interpreter asked, "Your business in Manila?"

"Gotta sell this hay," the farmer said.

"It is just hay back there?"

"I wish I had more. A little too early for harvest."

Blair heard boots scraping in the dirt, and her heart skipped a couple of beats. Though she was practically suffocating under the load of hay, she knew it wasn't a thick enough covering to withstand prodding hands.

Fernando spoke. "Sir, can you tell us if the hay market has moved? It has been a while since we have been in Manila."

The boots stopped. There was a flurry of conversation in Japanese as she supposed the interpreter and the guard conversed. Then the interpreter said. "Same place as always. I asked the guard to hurry along. It is getting close to lunchtime, and I'm hungry. So is he."

"Then we can move along?"

"Yes, get going. Can't you see the line growing behind you?"

The cart lurched into movement, and Blair let out her breath. No one had touched the hay. Later Fernando told Blair the interpreter had given him a covert wink when he had mentioned wanting a lunch break. Obviously the man was a sympathizer. He must have also noted something that Blair found out about when Fernando came to help her out of the cart—part of her skirt had been sticking out of the hay during the entire time at the checkpoint. The guard had missed it, but the interpreter no doubt hadn't. Blair remembered her bitter thoughts back at camp when she learned Gary had not returned with Ralph. She had doubted God and the validity of her faith, yet despite that He had taken care of her by putting an interpreter at that checkpoint who was sympathetic and a guard who didn't pay attention to details.

God must have known she really hadn't meant those harsh thoughts about Him. But just in case, she offered a brief prayer asking His forgiveness.

"I'm still so weak," she prayed silently. "But, dear God, you are so patient with me, I can hardly believe it. Thank you. I'll try to do better next time you throw me a curve."

Manila hadn't changed much in nearly a year except there were many more Japanese faces on the crowded streets. Blair and Fernando were on foot now, the farmer having gone his own way. The sight of the enemy so nonchalantly bustling by was, to say the least, unnerving to Blair, who had spent so many terrifying months attempting to avoid them. Even if they noted she was white, they must have assumed that anyone walking so boldly down the city street must be there legally, because no one stopped her. Still, she never let down her guard. No telling when someone would harass a person just for the fun of it. She conjured in her mind a story of her being a German and she had left her papers back at her apartment. She wondered if Japanese men were as susceptible to a pretty smile as all the other men she had encountered.

An hour after passing that checkpoint, they reached the Sanchez home. The reverend was there and quite shocked to open his door and find Blair standing before him.

"Praise be to God!" he exclaimed. "I thought I'd never see you again." Then he hustled Blair and Fernando quickly into the house and shut the door. "You can't be too careful these days. Most of my neighbors are safe, but one can't always be certain."

As Blair entered his home, she felt an immediate sense of being enveloped in warmth and homeliness. Though the pastor had been widowed for years and had kept house himself, the front room was neat and cozy, if not richly appointed. He offered Blair and Fernando chairs, which they gratefully took. Blair ran her hand along the upholstery of her chair, amazed that something so simple could feel so incredible. When had she last sat in a real chair? And bless the man's dear heart! Though she could tell he was bursting with questions, he didn't begin asking them until he fixed a tray of food and brought it to them. He hadn't even asked them if they wanted refreshments, since it was clear on mere sight that they were both half starved.

Only then did they talk. Since he had seen his son Mateo a month ago, he knew most of Blair's story up to the fall of Bataan. As for himself, he was still caring for his flock, but he was also involved in an underground endeavor to smuggle food, money, and other goods into the various POW camps near the city.

Finally Blair knew she had put off long enough telling him about Mateo.

"I am so sorry, Reverend," Blair said after she told him. "We haven't been able to give him the care he needs. That's why I have come to Manila."

She heard Fernando shift in his seat. She wasn't about to mention his involvement and hoped he wasn't worried. Then he spoke.

"You are a man of the cloth, Reverend Sanchez," Fernando said, "and I cannot deceive you."

Sanchez's eyebrows knitted with confusion.

"It was I who shot your son. I do not deserve it, but I beg your forgiveness."

"Why would you. . . ? I don't understand. . . ." said Sanchez, still perplexed.

"Reverend," Blair interceded, "Mateo came to the camp unannounced, and Fernando thought he was the enemy. The wound itself wouldn't have been that serious if he'd had proper treatment. I am afraid his present condition is as much my fault. I—"

"Please stop, both of you!" said Sanchez. "I will forgive because that is what will make you feel better, and because God would want me to, but in my heart I can see you both are not truly to blame. And I can see you both took a great risk in coming to Manila in order to help Mateo. That is what I see most clearly."

"Can you help us, Reverend?" asked Blair.

"I am willing to help, of course. Food I can get readily, but medical supplies are more difficult."

———

Blair had to remain in Manila four days while Reverend Sanchez made his contacts and set up arrangements. But the wait was well worth it. Once one of Sanchez's allies who worked in a hospital learned of Mateo's condition, she spared no risk to relieve her Japanese overlords of a fine cache of medications—several doses of morphine with syringes; enough quinine to stave off malaria in the guerrilla band for three or four months; bottles of vitamins, aspirin, iodine, and peroxide. But the most precious item was sulfa powder and a few pills, at least enough to wipe out Mateo's infection—if Blair got to him in time.

Sanchez understood the need for speed, as well. It was his son, after all. So the moment his friend dropped off the medical supplies, he made arrangements to get Blair and Fernando out of town. He wished he had another car to give her, but any non-Japanese behind the wheel of a motorcar would be under immediate scrutiny. He did, however, produce another farmer with a wagon who was returning to his village. This farmer, unlike the one who had brought Blair into the city, was accustomed to carrying "special" cargo. He had a secret compartment built into the wagon, which Blair and the cache of medical supplies fit into nicely. It wasn't the most comfortable ride Blair ever took, but that pack of medicine lying beside her made it tolerable. Fernando again could ride up front with the farmer.

Sanchez had also made arrangements for supplying the guerrillas with food. This would take a few days, since the foodstuffs were transported by a more circuitous route from contact to contact until they reached a specified rendezvous point where someone from Blair's camp would meet the contact and receive the food after the exchange of prearranged passwords. Sanchez had done this before and had a good system in place already. So far, at least, it had been successful in eluding the Japanese.

Sanchez also came up with another item Blair had requested— forged papers designating her a German national. The papers would be ready in a few days and would be sent later along with the food.

As Blair hugged Mateo's father and bid him good-bye, she felt as if Christmas had truly come early. She needed only one more gift—no, two. For Mateo to still be alive when she returned to the camp and for Gary to have returned.

17

GARY AND WOODY trudged into camp two days after Blair's departure for Manila. They had spent a couple of days as prisoners, but because the Japanese had taken time to question them while still in the jungle in hopes of finding the rest of the partisans, an opportunity for escape had more readily presented itself than if they would have been transported to a POW camp. This opportunity had come none too soon, since another day of questioning, with the beatings that went with it, would have left them both far too incapacitated to mount any escape. Also, they had learned that the Japanese planned to execute them if they did not talk soon.

But no one in the guerrilla camp was inclined to celebrate their return. Besides most of the men being too sick to gather enthusiasm, there was also the demoralizing fact that the rest of the men who had gone on the mission were still unaccounted for. But Gary was even less inclined to celebrate when he heard what Blair had done. He couldn't be angry with her even if he'd had the energy for anger. He knew she had acted out of need not whimsy, and he had known from the first time she had mentioned going to Manila that she would be the one to go if anyone went.

Still, he agonized over their seemingly ill-fated relationship. What was God doing? Or could He truly be blamed? This was not a war God had caused, and surely He hadn't caused any of the bad things that had happened to Gary and Blair. Yet, didn't He have *some* responsibility toward them? Of course He did, but it was beyond Gary to understand God's intent in all this. Logic and years of faith told Gary it wasn't right to lay blame on God, but that didn't soothe the pain in him now. It did help a little when he realized he had returned to camp when surely Blair had despaired he wouldn't. It gave him hope that she also would return.

Yet he knew how much could go wrong and how little prepared Blair was for this kind of work. She couldn't fight the Japanese. He wasn't even certain she knew how to use a gun. If she was captured, how could she escape?

I am with her.

The words washed over Gary that first night of his return as he lay under the stars unable to sleep because of his torment. The words were silent yet as distinct in his mind as if Ralph had stepped from the hut and spoken them. They gave him comfort and assurance, as they were meant to, yet they also had another effect on him. For the first time since learning Blair had given her heart to God, he realized her faith was *hers*. It truly existed apart from him. She had often said how she felt her finding God was somehow wrapped up in him, and he had worried, as she had, that it would be *because* of him, and if he was not in the picture, her faith would die. This had eaten at him over the last days when he'd been a prisoner and facing execution. He didn't want to be the cause of her faith because that would also make him the cause of her loss of faith.

Now God assured him otherwise. If he should die, a possibility he faced every day, her faith would not. God was with her.

Gary realized something else. There was no more reason for them not to be truly married. He saw now that Blair's hesitancy had been valid, though she had noted other reasons for it. He saw that the question of individual faith was the most important piece of the puzzle in their relationship, a piece that finally fit into place.

When she returned—yes, *when*!—he would convince her that the time was right, if for no other reason than they walked a tightrope between life and death. She must, like him, desire to spend what life they had left united in heart and soul.

———

Blair didn't know what she would do if Gary had not returned to camp. Yet everything had gone so well with her trip to Manila that she wondered if it was expecting too much to have one more gift.

Why not?

Hiking through the jungle, now on foot, with Fernando at her side and the precious pack of medicine hitched to her back, she questioned this silly inclination of hers to fear too many gifts. It wasn't really fearing the gifts as much as it was waiting for the other shoe to drop. The cause of this ridiculous attitude wasn't hard to ferret out, either. She'd never truly believed she deserved anything good. She had felt so worthless all her life that when something good did happen, she just naturally expected it to somehow blow apart.

But things were different now. Maybe she still didn't deserve good things, but in the last year God had proven over and over that He didn't give because His children deserved. He gave because He loved. That was a lesson she had never learned from her own father.

The success of the Manila trip was further proof that God had continued to care for her. He had given her an abundance, far more than she had expected. She thought of an item stowed with the medicine, a gift from Reverend Sanchez. He'd given her a Bible, and while they had waited for the supplies to come, they'd had several wonderful talks. She had shared with him her moments of despair and her anger toward God.

He had responded, "I think if we can't get angry at God once in a while, we probably don't have an honest relationship with Him. But as we ought to do with any friend with whom we have a rift, we should seek forgiveness the moment we realize we misspoke."

"I did that, Reverend Sanchez."

"Then accept the fact that He understands and forgives you."

"Yes, but I am afraid it could happen again. Life here challenges my faith at every turn. There are so many hardships, I fear they could overwhelm me." Tears welled up in her eyes, for she knew uncertainties still faced her back at camp.

"Blair, God will forgive you as often as you ask. And He will never desert you, no matter what struggles you face. He will be there to help you bear them." Then Reverend Sanchez had gone to find the Bible, and when he returned, he opened it. "Here is something that has given me great comfort since the war began, since I have not heard from my older son in months, and when I did not know if my Mateo was alive. Listen to this, Blair. 'If I take the wings of the morning, and dwell in the uttermost parts of the sea; even there shall thy hand lead me, and thy right hand shall hold me.' This is from Psalm 139. The entire chapter is a great comfort. I will give you this Bible, and when you have a chance, you can read it all."

"Thank you so much!" Blair clasped her hands gratefully around the plain black book. "It does seem as if we are in the 'uttermost part of the sea,' doesn't it? Stranded there in the jungle with no civilization around at all, I wonder sometimes if God could be there. No churches, no buildings . . ."

"But He is there."

"I will remember that."

She now told herself that if God could be with her in the farthest reaches of the Philippine jungle, she could count on His faithfulness in other things, as well. She need not fear that if things were good between her and Gary, they would soon deteriorate. And even if something bad did happen, that was life. The road was not always smooth. Yet God was there. And if this ordeal in the Philippines didn't teach her anything else, she had to learn to appreciate the blessings when they came and to accept the hardships when they came, too.

So she wondered again what she would do if Gary had not returned.

She did not wonder at all what she would do if by some miracle he was waiting for her in camp. It was time they were married. It was time they were one.

By the time they reached camp, it was almost anticlimactic when she saw Gary seated on the ground in the clearing in front of the hut.

Almost.

In fact, though, it was perhaps the most climactic moment in Blair's life. In that single instant of time, everything made sense. For once in her life, all was crystal clear. Her past, her future, her present had all converged on this moment. And the best part was she did not worry if a shadow would darken the scene.

Gary set aside the rifle he had been cleaning, rose, and reached her in two strides. As his arms went around her, she sensed he knew all her hesitation was gone. She thought he would take her that minute into the jungle to be alone. And she would have gone had she not felt the weight of the pack she wore and the urgent need of the medications it held.

All indeed was right with the world just then, for Gary seemed to read her mind. "Mateo is still alive," he said. "Do you have something for him?"

"Yes! Oh, Gary, God provided all that we needed and more to come later." Now for the first time she hesitated, a little shy. "Do you mind if I see him first?"

"Of course not. Then . . ." He suddenly got that schoolboy look she remembered from when they had first met, a guileless young man, not a seasoned warrior. "It's true, then? You have had a change of heart?"

"My heart is the same, full of love for you," she replied with a grin. "But my silly mind is changed, or at least it has come into proper focus. It's time we were truly man and wife."

"Come on, then. Let's take care of Mateo, then . . ." He paused. Much was clear between them, but she could tell he was uncertain how to proceed. She also had questions about that. He voiced his first as they walked to the hut. "Do you want a minister to repeat our vows?"

"I don't know. I haven't given that part any thought." They reached the hut. "Let's think about it while I work."

First she gave Mateo a shot of morphine to ease the pain while she worked on him. Then she got him to swallow one of the sulfa pills, and finally she packed his wound with sulfa powder and put on a clean bandage. After that she gave all the men a dose of quinine while Fernando handed out some food he'd been carrying in a small sack, a bit to tide them over until Reverend Sanchez's contact could be made. It was only some cheese and biscuits. There was also some tinned meat that they would make into a soup for later. Blair thought it would make a nice wedding feast.

While she finished making her rounds among the men, it became clear to her how she and Gary should handle their "coming together."

Later they sat by a small fire Gary had built. They were munching cheese and biscuits as Blair stirred the pot of soup she had just made. "Gary," she said, "I think I know what we should do."

"Good, because I haven't a clue."

"It makes sense, in a way, that we haven't been sure about our first wedding. On the surface it might appear as if you married me because of the lies I told you." She flashed back to that awful day when her husband of two days had learned that she was a nightclub singer and she had lied to him about being a Christian.

"We both know that's not entirely true," he interjected. "I saw more than the lies about the Christian girl next door who could cook. I didn't love only the lies."

She smiled, a thrill tingling through her as she realized anew the depth of his love. "Yes . . ." she said, a little uncertain, yet her confidence built as she spoke. "And despite my deceit, my heart was true in its love for you. We can't deny we both loved each other then, and regardless of what has come between us, there is something in me that still looks upon the wedding we had in California as very real. How do you feel about it?"

"It was the happiest day of my life." He paused, taking a thoughtful bite of cheese. "Even if two days afterward was the worst day of my life."

"It was the happiest day of my life, too. My father walked me down the aisle! That alone made it a wondrous day. My family was there, loving me, supporting me. I don't think they had ever supported me in anything before that."

"It's a day we should always remember as our wedding day, then," he said. "And as I said before, I have always felt married after *that* day."

"That's why I don't think we need a minister now."

"Not that we could find one easily anyway."

"It is enough for this to be between you, me, and our God."

"There is a place not far from here where we can be alone and safe," he suggested. "I'll tell Ralph we'll be gone for a while and ask him to save us some soup for later."

———

They stood beneath the boughs of a banyan tree that was draped with vines of orchids. Gary plucked a white one and tucked it into Blair's hair.

"It is just as well this isn't our real wedding day," Blair said. "We look a sight."

"You are a wonderful sight!"

She smiled her pleasure at that dear lie. She was wearing the faded blue dress borrowed from a stranger. He was in his ragged Army khaki shirt and borrowed trousers. Both of them were in bare feet. She only hoped that one or the other of them didn't get a malaria attack just then.

They had both agreed that though their wedding in California would stand always as their wedding day, this day also needed some bit of ceremony to mark it. Gary suggested reading something. He said hunger and illness was making it hard for him to remember Scripture he'd once memorized. Then she triumphantly produced the Bible Reverend Sanchez had given to her.

They held hands under the banyan tree, and Blair opened the Bible to the place they had chosen. Gary had helped her find the verses she thought most appropriate to read. She had heard them read in church and also remembered when Gary had once quoted them to her.

"'Though I speak with the tongues of men and of angels, and have not charity, I am become as sounding brass, or a tinkling cymbal. And though I have the gift of prophecy, and understand all mysteries, and all knowledge; and though I have all faith, so that I could remove mountains, and have not charity, I am nothing. And though I bestow all my goods to feed the poor, and though I give my body to be burned, and have not charity, it profiteth me nothing. . . .'"

Blair looked at Gary and knew the truth of those words. Without her love for Gary, she would truly have been nothing. That love had changed everything for her and had pointed her toward the greatest love of all—the love of Christ.

Then Gary took up the reading because this was the promise he'd made to her on their honeymoon in California and he'd kept through all the storms of their relationship.

"'Charity suffereth long, and is kind; charity envieth not; charity vaunteth not itself, is not puffed up, doth not behave itself unseemly, seeketh not her own, is not easily provoked, thinketh no evil; rejoiceth not in iniquity, but rejoiceth in the truth; beareth all things, believeth all things, hopeth all things, endureth all things.'"

He smiled as he read the words, and she knew he wasn't holding them over her but offering them as a gift of his trust and his hope.

They read the last verses together with one voice. "'For now we see through a glass, darkly; but then face to face: now I know in part; but then shall I know even as also I am known. And now abideth faith, hope, charity, these three; but the greatest of these is charity.'"

Later when Gary embraced Blair and they were truly one, she glimpsed a little of what those verses meant. Of course there was a higher, far more spiritual level to them, but for her and Gary she saw that though their world at this moment was dark with war and privations, their love gave them clarity, perhaps a small hint of what it meant to see face-to-face. Their life had become sharp and clear and focused. They had no idea what the future held. Tomorrow might find their newfound union literally blown apart by death or separation. Yet what truly mattered was love. For Blair, and surely for Gary, also, that meant more than anything.

PART III

"The watch-tower

Stands where

Escape is impossible."

<small>TULE LAKE INMATE</small>
Years of Infamy by Michi Weglyn

18

Manzanar, California
December 1942

ICY WIND GUSTED through the grounds of Manzanar as Sam made his way home from his job at the camp factory that made camouflage netting. He was startled at first when he heard someone jogging up behind him. When he turned and saw his old friend Charlie Tetsuya come toward him, he didn't know how to feel. Charlie had not spoken to him more than twice since they had come to the camp.

"Don't you know better than to run up behind someone like that, and at night, too?" Sam said. He was tired and not in a mood to be friendly, especially not to this man whose few words to Sam had been less than civil.

"Sorry, Sam. I didn't want to call out your name." He stopped and looked around.

Of course he wouldn't want to be seen in public talking to a supposed *collaborator*. In Japanese the word for such a person was *inu,* loosely translated as "dog." Sam knew many of his neighbors called him that behind his back because of his marriage to Jackie. It sickened him and confused him. He didn't like the implication nor to be associated with such types, yet neither did he want to be associated with the opposite ilk, those who were bitter and rebellious toward America. Nevertheless, he didn't wish to be the kind of man who sat on the fence. Consequently, he felt that he fit in nowhere.

"Sam, do you know where your brother is?"

"T.C.? I have no idea."

"I didn't think so." Charlie put a hand on Sam's shoulder and drew him into an alley between two barracks. "Look, I know we have sort of drifted apart since coming here—"

"Sort of?" Sam said harshly. "You've hardly spoken to me, Charlie."

"I still consider you a friend."

"You have a funny way of showing it."

"Surely you've got to understand the pressures I'm under—all of us, for that matter. There have been threats made against some who appear to have associated a little too closely with the white administration or with the JACL. I have to look out for my family."

Sam shrugged but supposed he could not hold too much against his childhood friend, who was obviously as torn as he. The politics of the camp left everyone in a quagmire of emotion. No wonder the tensions in Manzanar were mounting as dangerously as they were in his own home. Everyone was being pulled in so many different directions that no matter where one landed, he was liable to be hurt. The JACL, or Japanese American Citizens League, was the group most often referred to as *inu* by the opposing faction because of their stalwart support of the American government. Also, they had assisted the WRA in ensuring that the evacuation was orderly and peaceful. To add to the quagmire, a Manzanar Citizens Federation had recently been formed. It supported volunteering for military service and had stirred a debate a few weeks previously when an Army recruiter had come to Manzanar.

At the other end of the spectrum were the Black Dragons. Their intent was to obstruct, by harassment and violence if necessary, any who supported the JACL or the Citizens Federation. These groups stirred the pot of confusion and unrest among the internees, which wasn't difficult to do at Manzanar because many of the residents had come from Terminal Island, near Los Angeles. They had been given a mere forty-eight hours notice to evacuate their homes and had suffered great financial, not to mention emotional, upheaval.

"I don't know what you're getting at, Charlie," Sam finally responded. "I try not to get involved in politics."

"And you have never been threatened?"

"No, I haven't."

"Did you never wonder why, when you are so obviously a likely candidate for being a WRA stooge?"

Sam rankled at the accusation but managed to keep his mouth shut and shake his head.

Charlie continued. "Someone has made sure your name stays off the Dragons' black list."

"Why would anyone do that?" Now Sam was just bewildered. "I can't even believe we are having this conversation. Not too long ago, Charlie, all you wanted to talk about was baseball and movies and girls."

"That was before we were shafted by our own country. Now I'm angry."

"So you are one of those Black Dragons?"

"No, but I attended some meetings of various groups. Mostly those planning to form a Kitchen Workers Union. The Black Dragons are instigators there, I'm sure, and they were at the meetings. I don't want to see anyone hurt, and I don't want to go to Japan like some of them advocate. But I want to see justice done. I don't think we Japanese should sit silently by and watch our rights as American citizens be destroyed."

"I don't, either. I've considered getting involved with some of the less radical groups, but I doubt even they would trust a man married to a white woman."

"They seem to trust your brother."

"What does that mean?"

"That's what I wanted to tell you—well, part at least. I saw T.C. at one of the Kitchen Union meetings. He was very chummy with some fellows who I know are Black Dragons. That's probably why you have never been harassed."

"No . . . not T.C. He—" Sam broke off sharply as he saw how lame his denials were. He could not say his brother would never do that. T.C. had just turned seventeen. He had never been interested in politics. But if Charlie could change, so could anyone. And T.C. had already changed much. He was moody and quiet and had closed himself off from his family. Sam thought his brother was very angry, as well. He remembered a brief encounter with T.C. a few days ago that should have been revealing to Sam, but he'd been too dense to put deeper significance to it—until now.

"T.C., it would be nice if you had dinner with us tonight," Sam had suggested. His brother was spending less and less time with the family.

"I have other plans."

"Look, T.C.—"

"Don't lecture me!" he had retorted. "And don't call me T.C. anymore. I'm Toshio. Got it? I don't need any white baseball player's name."

He'd stormed off after that, and every night since he had not come home until everyone was asleep. Sam only knew this because he himself slept so poorly and was usually awake to hear his brother creep into his bed. So Sam couldn't really deny Charlie's words. There was no reason for him to lie about it, anyway.

"This whole situation stinks," Sam said miserably to his friend.

"I'm sorry everything has happened as it has," said Charlie. "I miss your friendship."

"I miss yours, too, and YoYo's. What's he been up to?"

"He is trying to stay out of the middle of things. His mother is sick, and he takes care of her much of the time."

"I didn't know that. I'll go see him. And my mother will want to visit Mrs. Inoki. They were friends once."

Someone walked by the end of the alley, and Charlie ducked deeper into the shadows.

Instinctively Sam lowered his voice. "I feel like we're spies or something. What else is going on?"

"You better keep your family inside for the next couple of nights," Charlie replied. "I think there's gonna be trouble. Did you hear about Fred Tayama getting assaulted?"

"Yeah. It's terrible. I suppose he was on the Dragons' black list. He's a JACL leader."

"I think he took personally some accusations the leader of the Kitchen Workers Union was making about the assistant project director stealing sugar and meat to sell on the black market. The anti-administration bunch also thinks Tayama is an informer."

"So the union guy beat him up?"

"They have always had it in for each other. Anyway, the union fellow—his name is Ueno—was arrested with a couple of others for the assault. The thing is, Ueno was taken to the county jail in Independence rather than to the camp jail. Everyone is up in arms over that. They're organizing a protest, and there is already so much anger and resentment, anything could happen."

"I appreciate the warning."

"The Black Dragons want to clean out all stool pigeons and traitors. I'm afraid your brother may not be able to protect you anymore."

"I'm not a stool pigeon," protested Sam. "You know that, don't you?"

"I wouldn't be telling you this now if I didn't. But you've got to know that it won't matter much to the Dragons if you aren't. Your marriage alone condemns you."

"Jackie is due to have our baby any day."

"If you go to the administrators, they might offer you protection."

"That's all I need, isn't it? If I run to them, I'll be labeled a collaborator that much more." His mind spun with alternatives. Maybe he could make them let Jackie leave the camp. Perhaps she could have the baby in Independence, though that would mean he wouldn't be there. She wouldn't leave, anyway.

"I have to get home, Sam," Charlie said. "Maybe when everything settles down we can get together, play some cards or something, like old times."

"Sure, Charlie." Sam's response was no doubt as lame as Charlie's suggestion. If life did settle down . . . but how could it in a concentration camp? Nor would it ever be like old times again.

That night Sam made sure he was awake when his brother crept into their room at two o'clock. He didn't know what good confronting T.C. would do, but he'd felt so helpless since talking to Charlie that this was at least something he could do.

When the door opened, Sam rose from his father's chair where he had been waiting and strode forward. T.C. gasped in surprise.

"What in the world!" T.C. said in a whisper.

"Come with me," Sam intoned quietly as he grasped his brother's arm and propelled him back out the door onto the dirt street that fronted the barracks.

"Are you nuts?" T.C. kept his voice low, but it still registered his ire as he wrenched his arm from Sam's grasp.

"Funny," Sam said, "I was going to ask you the same question."

"What are you talking about?"

"I'm talking about your late nights, your avoiding the family—"

"What's it to you, anyway? You're not my father!"

"Someone's got to take you in hand, T.C., and since Papa can't—"

"I told you I'm Toshio!"

"Well, *Toshio,* you need to answer for your behavior. What have you been up to?" Sam demanded. He had wanted to talk calmly and reasonably to his brother, but unexpectedly his own anger rose up. Anger that he was forced to have this conversation, anger that his father had given up, anger that he was only trying to help and T.C. was glaring at him like he was the enemy.

"I don't have to tell you anything," T.C. retorted. "I'm going to bed." He turned away from Sam.

Sam was not a violent man. The last and probably only other time he had ever laid a harsh hand on anyone was when he'd hit Jackie's ex-boyfriend for speaking ill of her. His brother's surly attitude now roused him once again. He stepped into Toshio's path, flung up his hand, and shoved him up against the wall of the barracks. T.C. hit the siding with a hard thud.

"Why, you . . ." T.C. sputtered and could get out no more as he tried to strike back.

The brothers were fairly evenly matched. Sam was taller and probably stronger, but T.C.'s anger equalized the odds, certainly giving the younger, smaller man strength beyond normal. He lurched at Sam with his fist. Sam ducked, his reflexes quick despite the fact that he'd never expected this to become a physical confrontation.

"*Inu!*" T.C. spit as he flexed his arm for another strike.

"Stop it, Toshio!" Sam grabbed his brother's fist. "I just want to talk."

"I don't talk to traitors!" The younger brother struggled to free his hand even as he brought his opposite fist up for a sharp uppercut into Sam's ribs.

Sam let out a gasp as his brother's punch landed right on target. His breath was knocked from him, and he loosened his grip in reaction to the blow. T.C. was stronger than Sam had judged him to be, and before Sam had a chance to regain his balance, T.C. directed another blow, this time hard into Sam's jaw. Sam stumbled back. Both were now panting like dogs.

For a few moments they merely circled each other while they caught their breath. Sam knew at that point he should just walk away, yet that wasn't going to help T.C. It would only make him think he'd won. But beating his little brother to a pulp wasn't going to help him, either. Sam opened his mouth to try reasoning once more, but at that moment T.C. flew at him, wrestled him to the ground, and began pummeling him with his fists. Sam fought back until he felt the awful rage in his brother's blows. It so shocked him that he could not make himself respond except to raise his arms to deflect the blows as best he could. A few hit their mark, and Sam soon felt a trickle of blood flow from his nose.

A moment later the pummeling stopped. T.C., straddling Sam and panting hard, just stared at his brother, at the blood. Then he rolled off and sat in the dirt, elbows propped on his knees, head in his hands. They were silent for a long time. Sam took his handkerchief from his pocket and dabbed at his bloody nose. He looked around, surprised they had not awakened everyone in the barracks. Maybe they had, but folks probably had more sense than to get involved.

Finally Sam spoke. "Toshio, you called me *inu*. Did you mean it?"

Toshio merely gave a shrug of his shoulder, not lifting his head from his hands.

"Do you think I'm a traitor? Do you think I'm a stool pigeon?" Sam pressed, and only as his voice shook with passion did he realize how deeply that accusation had cut. "Please, Toshio, I need to know. I need for you, if no one else, to believe I am not those things."

"Then why did you not marry your own kind?" said Toshio from the depths of his hands.

"I married the woman I loved."

"It was wrong."

"I don't think so."

Silence again. Sam had hoped that by admitting his need for Toshio's support, he might draw his brother back to him. But he saw it was going to take more than that.

"I feel much the same as you do about what's happened to us," Sam admitted. "I'm angry, too, and you may not want to believe this, but Jackie is even more angry than I am. It is all very wrong, but I don't believe we can do anything about it by hurting and harassing people, especially our own people, who are just as confused as we are."

"I am not confused!" Toshio lifted his head, eyes flashing. "Many of our own people are to blame for what has happened. They sold us out in order to appease the government. They have blackened the name Nisei and brought shame upon us."

"What would you have had them do? Rebel? It would only confirm what white people already think we are—anti-American, pro-Japanese. It is not a black and white issue. Can't you see that?"

"You think I'm just a dumb kid, don't you, Sam? Your little brother eternally. I understand a lot more than you think. I know there are many sides to this, but unlike you I won't let that detract me from the basic truth that what has happened is wrong, and any one who appeases the wrongdoers is just as wrong."

"Toshio, I am proud of you for taking a stand." Sam reached out and laid a hand on his brother's shoulder. Incredibly, Toshio didn't shake it off. "I truly am. But—"

"Ah, here it comes!"

"I'm sorry there has to be a 'but.' It doesn't mean I'm less proud. I just think you need to realize that harassing people, harming them, like Fred Tayama was harmed, is no way to take a stand." When Toshio opened his mouth to protest, Sam quickly added, "I know you personally wouldn't hurt anyone, but if you are associated with those who do, with the Black Dragons, then you must share their guilt."

"But the Black Dragons are the only ones doing anything about the injustice."

"You've got to find another way. Mama and Papa would be crushed if you went to jail."

"Sometimes a person has to break the law if it is wrong, and they might have to go to jail." All at once Toshio looked like a man, not Sam's kid brother. "But I promise you that I will never hurt anyone who doesn't deserve to be hurt."

Sam rolled his eyes at the lame promise.

"Okay," Toshio said, "I will add this: I will never bring shame to Mama and Papa . . . or you."

Sam smiled. "I can accept that."

"Now I want a promise from you," Toshio said, and when Sam nodded for him to go on, he continued. "I want you to promise you will never stop being Japanese."

"That's easy," Sam replied. "I won't, and I mean it in the same way you mean. It will never stop being part of who and what I am. I wouldn't want it to. Neither would Jackie."

"How's your nose?"

"I'm gonna have an ugly bruise in the morning. It'll make me look more manly, I guess." He chuckled and was pleased his words brought a small smile to his brother's face. "Come on, let's go in. Now that we're not at each other's throats, I'm feeling how cold it is out here."

When Sam crawled into bed beside Jackie, he discovered she was awake.

"What happened?" she murmured softly.

"Toshio and I just had a little talk."

She reached up and gently touched his swollen nose, visible in the moonlight that came through the window. "Talk, eh?"

"I had to straighten him out a bit."

"Looks like he straightened you out, too."

"The strength of his anger shocked me, Jackie," Sam said more seriously. "But I realized I am almost as angry. It just escaped a little. I fear this whole camp is full of anger, and I think when it erupts, a scuffle between brothers will be small potatoes by comparison."

"Is there anything we can do?"

"Pray and keep the family as safe as possible. I'm glad you don't have to go out to work anymore. I wish I could keep the little sisses in."

"God will care for us."

He nodded, then wrapped his arms around her and held her close, basking in the security of her nearness.

19

THE NEXT DAY, they heard at breakfast that the administrators had brought Ueno, the Kitchen Union organizer, back to the camp jail. In exchange for this concession, the administrators declared there were to be no more public meetings. The protesters weren't satisfied and decided they wanted Ueno and the others involved released altogether. That afternoon about a thousand internees gathered in the compound near the administration buildings with the intent of rescuing Ueno, then ferreting out informers and punishing them.

But Jackie lost interest in politics when she began having mild labor contractions after they returned home from church. Sam was ready to rush her immediately to the camp infirmary, but Mrs. Okuda said it was too early, that sometimes such pains occurred days before the actual birth. Jackie was relieved.

"Are you sure you want to wait? The hospital is a long walk away," Sam asked anxiously.

"Please, Sam, tomorrow is December 7. I don't want to have our baby on that day, of all days! And I'm not due for another week. My mother is supposed to be here then." She knew it was unreasonable to think the birth of a child would follow one's plans, yet Jackie was suddenly afraid of what was about to happen to her, and she thought she could bear it better if her mother were at her side. She had come to love Mrs. Okuda, but it wasn't the same as having her own mother here. And she quickly saw that Sam, level-headed, well-meaning, dear Sam, was about to fall apart. Too bad it was

Sunday and he didn't have to go to work. It would have afforded a means to occupy his mind.

Sam was looking out the window, and Jackie knew his anxiety was compounded by what was happening in the streets of Manzanar. If she had to go to the hospital, they would have to pass the place where the rally was being held. Right now things were relatively calm with men delivering speeches to the crowd, but who knew what would happen later. Tempers were hot.

As it grew dark late that afternoon, Toshio burst into the apartment, slamming shut the door behind him.

"Lock this door," he ordered, "and don't leave the apartment."

"Jackie's going to have the baby soon!" Sam exclaimed. He was not overstating the situation. Contrary to Mrs. Okuda's prediction, Jackie's pains had continued, steadily growing more intense.

Toshio went on, "I couldn't stop what's happening out there, Sam. They are rampaging all over the camp looking for informers. I can't guarantee they will leave you alone because of my known loyalty."

"Jackie may have to go to the hospital."

"No! Not there. That's where they are hiding Tayama, and the Dragons want to find him and finish him off."

The little sisses started whimpering. Kimi tried to find out if her friend George was all right. He had been among the few who had enlisted in the Army, though he hadn't left the camp yet, and thus was sure to be a target of the protestors. Mrs. Okuda tried to comfort all her daughters at once, including Jackie, who had turned white with fear.

A quiet steady voice rose above the clamor. "They are all fools," Mr. Okuda said in English. "I hope you are not one of these fools, Toshio." Toshio did not meet his father's eyes. The older man continued, "No one will harm me. I will go to the camp police and make them protect Sam's wife." That was as close as he had come in months to even acknowledging that Jackie existed.

He rose from his chair and left. No one tried to stop him. They were simply too shocked to do so, not only because of his acknowledgment of Jackie, but also because it was the first time since the evacuation that he had acted as the true head of the family.

Mr. Okuda returned a couple of hours later. No police were

with him. He conferred with Sam in Japanese, then went to his chair, falling silent once more.

"Papa says the police are in the process of taking those who are in immediate danger to a military camp a few miles away," he explained to Jackie. "That would include JACL and Citizens Federation leaders as well as known informants and their families. We're not high on the list. They are also busy trying to keep the mob in hand. They'll send someone to guard us when they can, but Papa doesn't expect it. Come here, though." He walked to the window and gestured for Jackie to follow. The rest of the family came, too, except for Mr. Okuda, who remained in his chair.

Out the window Jackie saw four men standing in front of the apartment door. She recognized two of them as Sam's friends Charlie Tetsuya and YoYo Inoki. All four men were armed with baseball bats. She looked at Sam and smiled. He let a responding smile displace some of his tension. Then Jackie glanced at Mr. Okuda, now with a pipe in his mouth and his nose buried in a newspaper. She wondered what he had said to Sam's friends to induce them to come out so openly in his defense.

For supper that night they stayed in the apartment and ate from the small store of food Mrs. Okuda had put by for emergencies. When Sam took food out to their guards, they told him that passersby reported that nothing had changed, and if anything, the mob had grown and the speeches had become more rabid. Inside the apartment, however, things were changing rapidly. Jackie's contractions were becoming more regular and more intense. Even Mrs. Okuda was growing anxious.

Around ten o'clock that night Jackie's water broke. It frightened her because no one had informed her that this was a normal part of labor. She thought the baby was going to come on the heels of the rush of warm fluid. Mrs. Okuda assured her otherwise.

"But, Jackie, you must go to the hospital now," she added urgently. "Your pains will get worse, and the baby will come soon."

Jackie had never felt such panic in her life. She wasn't ready for this—not for braving a mob to get to the hospital, not for the terrible pain that was sure to come—and in her jumbled emotional state she wasn't even sure any longer if she was ready to be a mother. She shot a terrified look at Sam. He seemed to be fighting similar panic. He was looking at his mother!

"I will take Jackie to the hospital," Mrs. Okuda said.

"Are you crazy?" exclaimed Sam, losing the respectful tone he usually held for his parents.

"No one will harass two women, especially if one is with child," said the other woman calmly. "Jackie can use Kimi's hooded coat. No one will see in the dark that she isn't Japanese."

"No," Sam continued to protest, "I'll send one of the guys out front to look for Toshio. He can give us safe escort."

Toshio had left before supper. Jackie thought he probably felt he'd done his duty to his family and could return to his friends with clear conscience.

"I think we will have a better chance as just two women," insisted Mrs. Okuda.

Suddenly a hard contraction assailed Jackie, and unable to restrain herself, she cried out. Sam clamped his hand down on hers like a vise, then looked around wildly, as if searching for some means of rescue.

"Oh, God . . . oh, God . . ." he murmured. "What should I do?"

It wasn't God's voice that answered, or maybe in a way it was. Mrs. Okuda said, "We must go now. You give us about ten minutes, then you follow."

Jackie nodded, feeling an urgency in her body and trusting her mother-in-law's wisdom. She'd asked God to keep her child from being born on December 7, but she had thought at the time that would mean a December 8 child, or later. Was God going to answer her prayer by making this a December 6 baby? If so, it was going to happen soon, and she did not want to have it here in this cramped apartment with the whole family looking on.

"Sam," she said, forcing calm to her voice, "it's time to go. It will be all right."

As Kimi was looking for her hooded raincoat, another contraction hit Jackie. She wondered how she was going to walk all the way to the hospital like this. But before she could think more about that, the coat was slipped around her swollen girth, the hood was raised over her head, and Mrs. Okuda was leading her outside. The guards raised a mild protest, which Mrs. Okuda quickly hushed, telling Charlie to go in and have Sam explain what was happening.

The air was cold and the wind biting. Jackie couldn't button the raincoat all the way down, so it flew up around her, warming her little. Only the hood, which Mrs. Okuda had secured in place with a scarf, stayed put. The older woman, though several inches shorter than Jackie, kept her arm around Jackie's shoulder, surely putting a strain on the woman to keep it raised so. But when another contraction struck, Jackie was more grateful than ever for that arm firmly supporting her.

The mob was still throbbing around the jail. Soldiers and police carrying weapons appeared to have surrounded the crowd of protestors and were yelling at them to disperse. Mrs. Okuda could have taken a more circuitous route and perhaps avoided much of the mob, but Jackie's contractions were coming faster, making a shortcut a sheer necessity. She did cut a wide berth around the mob. A soldier with a machine gun suddenly stepped into their path.

"Where do you think you're going—?" He stopped as they came under the glow of a streetlamp and he realized they were women.

"We are not part of that," said Mrs. Okuda. "Let us pass."

The soldier studied them, taking special note of Jackie's condition. "You shouldn't be out at this hour."

"How else do we get to the hospital?" Mrs. Okuda demanded. "Now move aside, I tell you!"

Jackie had thought to speak up, as well, but decided her mother-in-law was doing just fine by herself, especially when the soldier obediently stepped aside.

But before they continued on, he said, "I hear some of this mob has headed for the hospital, so you better be careful. We can't spare any men, or I'd send someone with you."

"We need no one," Mrs. Okuda said as she shoved past and, with a firm grip still on Jackie, strode away.

When they had put a good distance between the mob and the soldier who had detained them, Mrs. Okuda muttered, "*Harrumph!* I would not want that one's help. Holding guns on those people for protesting isn't right."

"You agree with the mob, Mrs. Okuda?" Jackie asked, astonished.

"I am glad someone is protesting this injustice. I only hope no one gets hurt. Don't tell my husband, but I am a little proud of my Toshio for joining them."

"I would think—" But that was the end of any political discussion, for Jackie's unborn child waged its own protest. The pain doubled Jackie over, and Mrs. Okuda staggered to keep them both on their feet.

When they reached the hospital, protestors were milling about there. One accosted them, but Mrs. Okuda rounded angrily on him, notwithstanding her tacit support of his cause. "Don't you see my daughter is about to give birth, you fool? Do you want her to do it here in the yard?"

The man jumped back from them as if they had the plague. Mrs. Okuda bustled Jackie into the hospital, where a bed was quickly found for her. The pains came regularly now, nearly every five minutes, absorbing her completely until sharp sounds from outside penetrated the hospital's thin walls. When the *rat-a-tat-tat* sound burst out, she knew it was machine-gun fire.

What was happening out there? Where was Sam?

Sam, too, was tempted to take the long way around, but urgency forced him to take the direct route. As he neared the jail, the crowd started yelling.

"Free Ueno!"

"Banzai!"

While many voices took up the chants, others began to sing Japanese songs. Sam could identify the Japanese national anthem among the mix of voices.

He had nearly gotten around the mob when he saw them surge forward as though intending to physically breech the walls of the jail.

"Stop!" the police ordered again and again.

Several protestors began hurling stones and handfuls of sand at the soldiers and police, who responded by hurling tear-gas bombs and firing their weapons into the crowd.

Sam froze in place, stunned at what he was witnessing. In a moment his eyes started burning. He expected soon to be incapacitated by the tear gas but suffered nothing more than a burning sensation. It seemed to be having a similar effect on the protestors, as well. Only then did Sam note that the wind was carrying the gas away from the mob. But the gas bombs and the gunshots were still having some effect on the crowd, for they were scattering wildly.

Adding to the general mayhem, Sam saw two protestors send a driverless truck careening full speed toward the jail. The soldiers couldn't see that there was no driver and opened fire on it. Unde-terred, the truck crashed into the corner of the jail.

Sam was buffeted this way and that by the madly dispersing mob. He had to keep moving or be crushed. The soldiers pursuing the crowd could not tell that Sam wasn't part of the mob, and one grabbed him from behind. When Sam turned, he received the crack of a rifle butt to his head. He stumbled backward, and before the soldier could do any further damage to Sam, he was knocked down by the crowd.

Fighting dizziness from the blow, Sam forced himself to get up and keep moving. He had to get to Jackie. He had to be there when his child was born!

Jackie screamed. She couldn't help it. "Mama!" she cried.

"There, there," Mrs. Okuda comforted. "You are so brave, my daughter."

She didn't feel brave. Her father would cringe with embarrass-ment if he saw her now. How could she be so weak?

"This is transition," the attending nurse said. "It's the worst part."

Another contraction. Another scream.

"Can't you give her medicine?" Mrs. Okuda asked.

"It's too late. We don't want to slow the birth down now." The nurse then said to Jackie, "Are you ready to have this baby?"

"D-do I have a choice?"

The nurse laughed, but Jackie hadn't tried to be funny.

"Come on, into the delivery room," said the nurse.

She was being so chipper, Jackie wanted to scream. Instead, she said, "Please, no . . . my husband isn't here . . . ugh!" Another pain. "Sam!"

"Can't you wait just a few minutes?" pleaded Mrs. Okuda.

"Babies don't wait for anyone, dear," chirruped the nurse.

"No! I won't . . . I c-can't . . . Sam!" The pains came again and again. There seemed to be no pause between contractions. "Sam!" Jackie didn't care anymore if the baby was born today or tomorrow as long as Sam was there.

The curtain around her bed swooshed aside, and there he was! Jackie wondered for a moment if she was hallucinating. It was too perfect. Yet even in her physical distress she saw it wasn't totally perfect. There was blood on Sam's head, smudges on his face, and his shirt was torn—and he had no coat!

"Sam . . . my love . . ." She held out her hand to him—she had to touch him to know for certain he was real—but she jerked it away as she was wrenched again with a contraction. He bounded to her bed and grasped her hand, and she squeezed it tight.

"Sorry I'm late," he said.

"It's okay—" She groaned. Then her bed was moving.

"I'll be right outside," Sam called as she was swept through the double doors.

She didn't care about hospital rules. She wanted Sam to stay with her. It didn't seem right for him to have to stay outside.

But in a few moments she was staring up at bright lights and lying on a different bed. Her legs were propped up, and she could see the top of her doctor's head over her knees. Everything happened in a blur then. One instant she was experiencing the most excruciating pain she'd ever known, and the next she was hearing the most beautiful music she'd ever heard—her baby's cry!

There was no more pain. Only joy.

"Sam!" she called, hoping he'd hear her through the delivery room doors. "Our baby is here."

"I know," she heard his muffled reply. "I hear him."

"Nurse," she asked, "what time is it?"

"Eleven forty-five P.M. First time anyone asked that question before asking whether it's a boy or a girl."

"Well?" Jackie asked.

"A healthy little girl."

"Thank you, Lord," she breathed. "But you better let me break it to my husband."

Jackie had lived all her life with her father's disappointment over her gender, so she couldn't help being a little worried about Sam's reaction.

Back in her bed in the ward with her daughter in her arms, she was taken aback when Sam grinned and gazed proudly down at his daughter.

"She's fantastic, isn't she?" he beamed. "She's beautiful . . . incredible . . . marvelous."

"You truly don't mind that we have a girl?"

"You doubt!" He laughed. But he knew of her father's rejection and added more solemnly, "I would not have anything else. This girl, this daughter . . . she is perfect, exactly what God wanted to give us. How could I want something different?"

Jackie found herself weeping. The tears gushed, and she could not stop them.

Sam bent over and kissed her.

"Sam, I am the luckiest woman there ever was! She is beautiful, isn't she?" Jackie gently fingered her daughter's thick head of straight black hair. She'd never seen a newborn with so much hair! And yes, her eyes were tilted and black—or rather a murky gray at the moment—but they were lovely. Every tiny precious part of her was wonderful.

The nurse poked her head through the crack in the curtain. "There's a lady out here very anxious to see her grandchild."

"Yes, let her come in," Jackie said. "Sam, while your mother is in here, why don't you have one of the nurses tend your head?"

"You noticed?"

"Of course I did. You can tell me about it later. And later we can also pick a name for our daughter."

When Sam returned, a bandage over the gash on his head, they visited with his mother for a short time, then Mrs. Okuda left to find a male orderly who might be willing to take a message across the camp to tell her family the good news. Because the trouble in the camp had not abated, Sam insisted she spend the night in the hospital with them.

When they were alone, Jackie said to Sam, "We have put off choosing a name long enough."

"Talk about eleventh-hour decisions! But picking a name should be easier now that we have finally met our daughter."

Jackie nodded. "And I already know one thing. She must have a Japanese name." They had discussed at length, during the long months of pregnancy, whether to pick a Japanese name or an American name. They had looked at all sides, considering how either choice might affect their child. "Not because she looks Japanese," Jackie added, "but because I think it is important for this *Sansei* child to hold dear her cultural identity." *Sansei* was the term for third-generation Japanese.

"What do you think of Emi?" Sam asked.

"It is perfect!" Jackie knew that was the name of Sam's high-school friend who had committed suicide because of an ill-fated love affair with a white man. "This is what your friend Emi dreamed of, so perhaps it will always remind us of how blessed we are to have fulfilled that dream."

"She should have an American middle name," Sam said thoughtfully, "but I can't think of anything significant. We could name her for your mother."

"Mother never much liked her name, and I don't think she'd mind if it wasn't passed on. But . . ." Jackie paused, unsure of the idea that had just popped into her head. "There is another name, not exactly American. In fact, it is Irish . . . what do you think of Colleen?"

"Emi Colleen. It's like a song. Is Colleen your father's mother?"

A little embarrassed, Jackie nodded. "Do you think it is gross patronization? What a terrible way to try to win him over."

"Are you kidding? If she had been a boy, I was fully prepared to call him Keagan!"

They both laughed so hard the baby woke and started to cry— no, the tiny bundle bellowed!

"Don't worry, honey," cooed Jackie, "I would never name you after a man. You are Emi Colleen Okuda, and we love you as you are!"

20

A NEW CONTROVERSY plagued the internment camps after the new year, but Manzanar, still reeling from the December riots in which two Japanese men had been killed and several injured, was hit especially hard. It was at this time that the government decided to take stock of the loyalty of the internees.

"It is just another means for them to register men for the military," Sam told Jackie. He was pacing vigorously in front of her as she sat in a rocking chair nursing Emi. It was one of the rare times they were alone in the apartment. "I can't believe they would have the effrontery to attempt to test the loyalty of a people they have locked behind barbed wire!"

"I thought it was also to assess the internees for possible relocation out of the camps."

"I've heard that, too, so it only makes it that much more complicated," he groused. "I've no doubt it's an attempt to couch a travesty in a more positive dressing."

"If only everyone would simply refuse to fill out the questionnaire."

"There is too much division among the internees for any united front." He went to the table and plucked up a paper.

Jackie knew it was the loyalty questionnaire that all internees seventeen and older, male and female, must fill out.

"Have you looked at this?" he asked.

"I have, and I don't like it one bit."

"This is what's causing the trouble. . . ."

She let him go on, though she'd read it herself. He just needed to let off steam.

"Question twenty-seven: 'Are you willing to serve in the armed forces of the United States of America?' Question twenty-eight: 'Will you swear unqualified allegiance to the United States of America and faithfully defend the United States from any or all attack by foreign or domestic forces, and forswear any form of allegiance or obedience to the Japanese emperor, to any other foreign government, power, or organization?'" Sam's fist tightened around the paper.

"It really places everyone between a rock and a hard place," said Jackie.

"There is so much wrong with it, I don't even know where to begin to protest—"

The door burst open and Toshio strode in. "I'll tell you where to begin," he said.

"What? Were you eavesdropping?"

"These walls are paper thin, Sam. You don't need to eavesdrop to know everyone's business."

Jackie smiled. That was true enough. And one more grievance to heap upon the administrators. "Toshio, what do you think of all this?" Jackie asked as she tucked Emi's blanket a little more modestly around her.

He drew up a chair and straddled it, facing her. "I will burn my questionnaire. I refuse to answer it, and I further refuse to register for military service. I will not go into the Army when I turn eighteen. Those who believe as I do have been advising others against registering and have been told by the administration that we are in violation of the Selective Service Act."

"Many Nisei men feel that they are American citizens and therefore it is their duty to fight," said Sam, still pacing, still agitated. Relations with Toshio had actually improved since the riots, and he was a little more forthcoming with his family—one good thing, Jackie supposed, to have come out of it all. Now that the family knew where he stood in political matters, he was more open with them, less afraid of a backlash for his beliefs.

"They have taken away all our rights, and now the first right they are ready to restore is our right to get our heads blown off?" Toshio's eyes flashed, and he was barely able to stay in his seat. A moment later he was on his feet. Jackie thought it must be an Okuda trait, this need to walk off anger. "Only when they let me walk free will I consider military service!"

"It's voluntary now, but what about when there is a draft?"

"Let them try to draft me," growled Toshio, but he must have noted the look of dismay on his brother's face because he quickly deflected the subject. "It is question twenty-eight that is really confusing our people," he said, resuming his seat and trying to give the appearance of calm. "The Issei especially are torn in two by it."

"The part about forswearing allegiance to the emperor?" asked Jackie. She was glad not to talk about the Army. The brothers had argued about that often enough. Not that Sam was eager to join up, either, but he did not want to see his brother arrested, nor did he himself wish to be arrested for draft evasion.

"If they answer yes to that," Toshio explained, "they are as much as admitting they were loyal to the emperor in the first place. But if they answer no, they fear being shipped back to Japan or at the very least having to go to Tule Lake camp, where the trouble-makers are being sent. In any case the families will be ripped apart even more. And who knows if Japan would take them back? They could end up with no country at all." He paused with a quick glance at Sam. "I was tempted to answer no to both questions, but then I decided that by doing so I was acknowledging that the questionnaire was valid in the first place. They will probably take silence as a no anyway."

"Mama and Papa would be crushed if you were sent away," Sam said dismally. "Papa will answer yes to both just to keep the family together."

"And what about you, Sam?"

The question hung in the air for a moment. Jackie held her breath. As far as she knew Sam was still uncertain.

"I agree with much of what you say, Toshio," he answered finally, "but our parents have already been hurt so much by the evacuation, I don't want to hurt them further by being sent away. And I have Jackie and Emi to think about, as well. But Mama would be the most crushed if our family broke up."

"I guess it is different now that you are a family man. I don't hold it against you."

"I hold it against myself," Sam said dismally. "It galls me to have to concede. That's why I haven't filled the thing out yet. Answering yes to those questions will be among the hardest things I have ever done."

"Some believe the loyalty oath will also pave the way for some to be relocated outside the camps," Toshio suggested.

"Yes, sell our souls for relocation. But even at that, it most likely won't be to our former homes but probably someplace inland."

"The government realizes the evacuation was a mistake," Toshio stated with a scowl, "so they are using this as a way out. They can't admit they made a mistake and let us go, which in my mind is just another reason to disavow this oath. Why should we let them off so easily?"

"When I was young," Jackie offered, "my parents used to ground me when I misbehaved. Once my sister Blair and I were grounded at the same time, and we were raising havoc in the house. My mother threw up her hands and asked, 'Who is really getting punished here?' It is kind of the same here. Only the Japanese people are being punished by blocking relocation. It doesn't really hurt the government."

"But it makes a point, a statement to the government," insisted Toshio. "Sometimes that's all we can do."

"I don't know." Sam sighed, still pacing. "We are hurt no matter what we do. So perhaps the best thing is to affirm our loyalty, fight in the Army, and have done with it."

"Never!" exclaimed Toshio.

"Toshio, don't let your anger make you do something foolish," pleaded Sam.

"Toshio," Jackie interjected, "*are* you loyal to America . . . in your heart?"

He jumped up again, made a circuit of the small room before pausing before Jackie. "Has anyone ever asked you that question, Jackie?"

"No."

"When such a question is asked of you without cause, you find something strange happens inside of you." He glanced at his brother, who nodded slightly in affirmation. "I am an American. I have no other country, and it never occurred to me to be anything but loyal—until that question was asked. Now it is hard to say yes. If they didn't believe it before, when I did nothing to deserve being questioned, why should they now? And will they ever believe me? I feel as if my own mother has spit in my face. You don't recover quickly from that."

"But you will recover," said Sam. "You must! Our government has made a monumental mistake, something done in the passion of the moment. We can't hold it against them forever."

"Maybe if they beg our forgiveness, I can drop it."

Sam shook his head then glanced at Jackie miserably. She wanted to hold him and comfort him, but he started pacing again. Jackie thought of her sister Cameron and wished she were here so she could take all these things the two brothers had expressed and write them into an article for the newspaper. Jackie knew the *Globe* had attacked the evacuation order, but she hadn't seen any newspaper reporters come to the camp to interview the internees. In fact, few publications were opposing the evacuation. In any case Cameron would be great at this. The stories she was writing about Russia were so powerful, Jackie knew if she could do the same with the situation here, it might shake things up.

She didn't even consider the *Journal* in this. It had never printed a word about the evacuation, no editorials, at least, either for or against. Jackie's father was not touching the issue at all. Maybe she should be thankful for that. Perhaps he was ignoring it in order to protect her and their family. But it still made her sad when she thought about what an influential man he was and what he might do if he put the weight of his newspaper behind a protest of the WRA.

She was dreaming if she thought that would ever happen, as was Toshio if he believed there was a chance of the government asking the Japanese community for forgiveness. Yet part of her could not give up entirely. She had seen God do many good things here at Manzanar, and she could not believe He would stop now. He always managed to bring light into dismal situations.

Toshio left after the conversation—he'd only come home to pick up a baseball bat because a game was being organized in the yard. He may have disavowed his nickname, but he still loved the game, as did Sam, and it didn't take much to convince him to join his brother. She hoped the physical exertion would help them both to release some of their pent-up tension.

For herself, she just enjoyed the time alone with Emi. Jackie thought her daughter was incredibly beautiful, and though she didn't like to dwell on physical attributes, she couldn't help at times just gazing with wonder at the child. Her eyes were dark and shining now, and very large, with the thickest eyelashes Jackie had ever seen. She was round and healthy, and her hair was still a thick crop, with a tendency to stick up all over her head. Mrs. Okuda said that's how the little sisses' hair was when they were born, but their hair had tamed, and now they had long, straight, silky locks.

Even Jackie's mother had been impressed by little Emi when she had come to visit shortly after the child's birth. Jackie could sense a bit of awkwardness at first in Cecilia and a difficulty in warming up to a baby with Japanese features. But some of that awkwardness might well have been due merely to the fact that she and Jackie and the baby at first had to meet in the guardhouse. Jackie protested this and was joined by a few other internees who wanted visits from friends on the outside. Only when Cecilia casually mentioned who her husband was did they finally allow Cecilia to come to the Okuda apartment and to spend the night with one of the single white female teachers. The administrators didn't have to know her husband would never support such a protest in his newspaper. They were left to make their own assumptions.

It took about a half hour of tedious chitchat, with Emi exercising her lungs a bit, before Cecilia finally warmed up.

"Maybe I can quiet her," Cecilia offered when Jackie had no luck in getting Emi to settle down.

Jackie complied gladly and watched with a grin on her face as her mother cooed and rocked the baby in her arms, rising from her seat and strolling around the apartment.

"You used to like it when I walked with you," Cecilia said. She smiled at Emi. "Do you like it, too, sweetheart?"

Jackie stared in wonder, realizing that babies were babies and held a magic within them regardless of race. And grandchildren had the most potent magic of all. It had worked with Mr. Okuda, as well. If he wasn't eager to hold the baby, it was only because he, like many men, wasn't comfortable with infants. But on several occasions Jackie had found him watching Emi and talking to her in Japanese as she lay in her bassinet.

These thoughts begged Jackie's next question during her mother's visit. "Mom, what did Dad have to say about Emi?" She was disappointed he had not come, too, but hadn't really expected it.

"I wish he would have come," Cecilia replied. "One look, and I think his heart would melt."

One look, practically, had indeed melted Cecilia's heart, but Jackie thought it would take more than that to melt the stone of which her father's heart was made. She didn't say so, of course. She couldn't give up hope of his softening eventually.

"He was surprised when he heard her middle name," Cecilia went on. "I do believe he was touched."

"I was afraid it might make him angry."

Cecilia's brow quirked. Was there just a hint of scolding in her expression? "To have his grandchild named for his mother? How could that make him angry? You don't give your father enough credit, Jacqueline."

"Perhaps not." There was still the issue of his not coming to see his grandchild, but Jackie, ever the peacemaker, said no more on the subject.

The most amazing part of that visit had been when Mrs. Okuda had come home. She had been visiting friends in another part of the camp, and because she had expected Cecilia's visit to take place in the guardhouse, she hadn't known to stay away.

"I am sorry," she said as she walked in on them. "I will come back later."

"You mustn't leave," protested Cecilia. "This is your home, and I would feel terrible if I forced you away."

"That is kind of you, Mrs. Hayes. I would like to stay, if you don't mind, because it is too cold to take another walk." She smiled and added, "Not that it is much warmer in here. I have asked for a larger stove now that we have the baby. I hope it comes soon."

"Well, Emi seems healthy and content, so it must not be too bad." Indeed, the baby had stopped crying and was now cooing softly in Cecilia's arms. "Please, Mrs. Okuda, sit down and visit with us."

Jackie gave her mother and Emi the rocking chair while she and Mrs. Okuda took the two mismatched chairs.

"Mom, I have to thank you again for sending us the rocking chair," Jackie said. "I don't know how many times it has been a lifesaver."

"I'm glad you received it in one piece. I was worried."

"We almost didn't," said Mrs. Okuda. "The administrator must have thought it was contraband—that is the right word, isn't it, Jackie?" When Jackie nodded, Mrs. Okuda continued, "They wouldn't let us have it until Yoshito spoke to them and they examined it closely."

"Is Yoshito your husband, Mrs. Okuda?" asked Cecilia.

"No, Mom, didn't I ever tell you? That's Sam's first name. Samuel is his middle name."

"Just like Emi, a Japanese name and an American name," Cecilia said thoughtfully. "That is nice."

"Do you really think so?"

"I do." She paused before adding, "I have to say I had some anxiety about this visit. But here we are all sitting together, and it is quite pleasant. Mrs. Okuda, I am so happy for this chance to get to know you."

"It is the same with me. But I knew you would be nice because you have raised such a dear daughter."

"Thank you. And I do hope I will meet the rest of your children, as well as get to know Sam better. Do the others live in their own apartments?"

Jackie and Mrs. Okuda exchanged amused looks, then Jackie replied, "We all live here. Nice and cozy."

"Oh, my goodness!" Cecilia gazed at the apartment with a new appreciation. "Then I am more surprised than ever that I haven't met anyone else yet."

"The children are in school, except for Kimi, who works in the kitchen," explained Mrs. Okuda.

"And Sam is at his job in camp," added Jackie. "He tried to get off, but several people are out sick and he had to work."

"And Mr. Okuda? I will meet him, won't I?"

"We shall see" was all Mrs. Okuda said. "He is out now surveying a plot of ground the administration said he could use for a garden."

"Mom, let me show you the beautiful things Mrs. Okuda made for Emi." Jackie rose and went to the steamer trunk where she stored Emi's things.

The women oohed and aahed over the handmade things, then Mrs. Okuda made tea and they visited. Jackie's prayers were surely being answered, yet still she marveled at how wonderfully the three, or rather four, females got along. The two grandmothers shared Emi between them quite congenially, and when their attention wasn't on the baby, they regaled Jackie with stories of when their children were little, with special emphasis on Sam's and Jackie's childhoods.

Jackie feared it might all be spoiled when the rest of the family began to trickle in, but it all went quite smoothly. The Okuda children were like any children around an adult guest. They were polite and visited for a few minutes as was expected, then they politely asked to be excused and went outside to play with friends. Toshio, of course, did not show up at all. Neither did Mr. Okuda. But when Cecilia joined the family in the mess hall for dinner, he was there, though he said nothing beyond a cordial greeting.

Cecilia left for the bus station the next afternoon. Jackie could tell her mother had been encouraged by the visit—at least by the new relationships formed with most of the Okudas. But she still couldn't help her dismay over the living conditions of the camp, and she promised to be more faithful about sending packages of goodies.

As Jackie waved good-bye to her mother, a rather staggering thought struck her. Was it possible that Cecilia would influence Keagan to speak out against the internment camps? Maybe that was hoping too much, but just then hope was soaring high within Jackie. She had just witnessed a true miracle—she had seen two families take the first steps toward coming together.

As bad as the situation in the camp now seemed with the loyalty oath controversy, Jackie was not brought down, at least not to the depths she sensed Sam was heading toward. She needed to be positive and strong for him. It seemed that often when one of them was feeling weak, the other was strong. Sam had encouraged her many times, and now it was her turn to lift his spirits. She thanked God for strengthening her faith with the small miracles she witnessed.

Sam was naturally a positive, upbeat person, so it was difficult to watch him struggle over the political pressures placed upon him, not to mention the many other stresses he was experiencing. Jackie did not believe he would ever break. His core of faith was too steady for that, yet it was no less painful to watch him suffer. Emi's birth had lifted him for a time, but he was slipping down again, and Jackie felt that she and God and one little baby were all that kept him from drowning.

21

Moscow, Soviet Union
January 1943

THE CHURCH MEETING that evening had turned into a small celebration for one of the young members who had announced her recent engagement. Cameron appreciated the small touch of festivity the sweet pastries added to the usual after-meeting tea. However, it wasn't the rare sweets she was thankful for but rather a reason to be lifted a bit from the dreary winter rut that Moscow had become.

At least the war news was finally looking better. That had definitely not been the case a few months previously.

No time since the beginning of the war had been more depressing than the previous summer and autumn. For once, the press department had been candid in their communiqués. German advances in the Caucasus and the devastating loss of one of the richest agricultural regions in Russia were admitted with startling honesty. For a time it seemed the victories of the winters of '41 and '42 would be completely negated by what had come to be called the Black Summer of '42. The Germans appeared to have caught their breath and were raging forth as in the early days of the war.

Churchill's visit to Moscow in August should have been a highlight for the journalists, but apparently rumors that the British prime minister was "allergic" to the press were true. Cameron, after being alerted by a friend in the British embassy, managed to be at the airport for his arrival but caught only a mere glimpse of the man as his limousine raced away. At least she guessed it was he by the cigar clenched between the stocky man's teeth. Few Russians smoked cigars.

Feeling cheated after several days with no interviews, the correspondents gathered dejectedly at Spaso House, the American
ambassador's residence in Moscow, for their usual Saturday morning movie viewing. James Cagney's film *Each Dawn I Die* was suddenly interrupted with a call informing the correspondents that
Churchill would finally see them. Like eager puppies, they hurried
to where he was staying, only to be told after arriving that the prime
minister would not see them after all. The reason given was that
since he seldom received the press in London, it would not do for
him to break with tradition here.

The news that did filter down from Churchill's visit was not
encouraging, especially for Stalin. Hope for a second Front in 1942
was totally dashed.

One evening at dinner Carl Levinson quipped, "There's only
two ways a Second Front will be started: natural and supernatural.
The natural way would be for Gabriel and a band of angels to
descend and start it; the supernatural way would be for the British
to start it."

It was a strange irony that in the midst of the Churchill visit, the
full force of German might struck at Stalingrad with an incredible
raid by six hundred bombers, opening one of the bleakest phases of
the war for the Russians. When the German advance into Stalingrad
began in August, there was no doubt in anyone's mind that this
would be a pivotal military encounter. Besides its historical significance, this city was too closely tied to Stalin himself for his personal
honor not to be bound up with its fate.

Cameron felt a personal attachment to the city, as well, because
she'd heard Alex might be assigned there. Each dismal communiqué
tore her heart apart. Back in October when it had looked especially
bad for the Red Army, she had passed many a sleepless night with
worry. However, by the twenty-fifth anniversary of the October
Revolution, the situation began to turn around, and optimism again
could be seen in press communiqués.

The Allied landings in North Africa in November also gave reason for rejoicing. It wasn't a Second Front, but even Stalin appreciated its significance. For one thing, he was assured that his Western
Allies *could* mount a successful military campaign.

The Russian counteroffensive at Stalingrad began near the end
of November. By December the German Army was effectively

encircled and, for all practical purposes, trapped within a forty-mile salient. Cameron rejoiced with everyone at this news yet still despaired because there was no word from Alex. Sophia had said her father had written Alex a couple of letters but didn't know if the letters had gotten through. Certainly he had received no replies. Cameron knew Alex would have responded if he could. Perhaps he wasn't even at Stalingrad. He might have been there a short time then transferred to another Front. There was simply no telling.

Her greatest comfort in these months and weeks of separation and worry was the underground church meetings. She'd only been able to attend a handful, but each one restored her in a way she found amazing. She wasn't certain what it was about them exactly. Perhaps just the effect of hearing of other people's victories over trials and confirming the validity of her choice of faith.

At this particular meeting she found herself standing with Sophia and her grandmother Anna Yevnovona. "It's too bad Tina's fiancé isn't here to celebrate with us," she said, wondering even as she spoke why she was finding the downside to the event. She supposed she would never entirely shed her basic personality. But mostly she just felt huge empathy for the young woman.

"At least he had enough of a leave to come home and propose to Tina," said Sophia. She was grinning! "I hope we can attend the wedding. How I do love weddings!"

"Do you?" But Cameron wasn't really surprised. She would have been shocked if someone like Sophia *didn't* like weddings!

"I will never forget even the smallest detail of my own wedding. I was the first of my sisters to be married and the youngest. But neither Irina or Valentina resented that fact. It was such a happy time, wasn't it, Grandmama?"

"Oh yes. You were a beautiful bride. And Oleg! How dashing a figure he cut," Anna replied.

"It was the first time, and only time so far, he had worn a suit and tie." Sophia struck a dreamy pose, remembering the joy of that day and seeming to forget where her husband was now. But no, she couldn't forget that. "When my Oleg returns to me, I think we will have another ceremony to reconfirm our vows. I'll wear my wedding dress again."

"I hope it is soon," Cameron said.

"I pray every day it will be," Sophia responded with such

assurance that Cameron silently prayed it would happen one day soon.

"I do not believe God will keep you parted forever," said Anna with great conviction.

Cameron wondered by her tone if the old woman had had some direct communication from God himself regarding this.

"Nor do I." Sophia turned to Cameron. "What has happened to Oleg and me is very similar to Grandmama and Grandpapa's experience. My grandfather Sergei Viktorovich was in a gulag deep in Siberia, and Grandmama had no reason to hope she'd ever see him again. But she didn't give up on him, and they were finally joyously reunited."

Anna chuckled. "You make it sound like a fairy tale. I think I despaired many times, but there was no choice except to put my faith in God. So I did."

"Then he came to you. It was a miracle!"

"There was an even greater miracle than that," interjected Anna.

Sophia grinned and her eyes sparkled. She obviously knew this story well. "Oh yes, Grandmama. Tell Cameron about that."

"Please do, Anna," encouraged Cameron. "I enjoy a good love story as well as any."

"My Sergei had lost his faith while in prison. And I think that upset me as much as my losing him. I could do nothing to help him, and at times I wondered if my prayers were even touching him. There was no way for me to know if he was even still alive—"

"But God had been with Grandpapa the whole time," put in Sophia excitedly. "After he escaped from the gulag, he was rescued by a godly man who set him back on the path to God."

"You tell the story so much better than I." Anna laughed. "Why don't you finish it?"

Sophia took up the rest of the story eagerly. "One day Grandmama heard of an aristocrat passing through the village near where she was living. She thought it was someone else whom she also hoped to see for another reason—but that's a whole other story! Anyway, she ran to the village. A count or a prince in a peasant village was a rare thing even in the days of the tsar. And there Grandpapa was, seated on his horse. Though he was dressed simply, he could not hide his nobility. And despite the fact that they had been separated for a couple of long years, Anna knew her beloved Sergei immediately. As she ran into his arms, she also realized his heart had changed. He was hers, but he was also once again God's." Sophia ended the story with a sigh.

Cameron hoped that same story would one day be Sophia and Oleg's, for them to tell their children and grandchildren about their separation.

"That is a wonderful story," Cameron said. "No wonder you love weddings so much, Sophia. I'll bet your family is full of such romantic tales. And they are wonderful to listen to, but down deep I'm afraid I am not much of a romantic, though at times I do wish I were. I have never thought much about weddings."

"You will when you and Alex are finally together," said Sophia coyly.

"Oh . . . well . . . um . . ." Cameron found herself slightly embarrassed by the subject. Of course she longed to be with Alex, knowing that meant marriage. Yet it scared her more than a little. And the idea of a wedding was absolutely terrifying. Lace gowns and gardenias and cakes with iced roses were simply not for her. She regretted she had missed both her sisters' weddings, yet part of her was relieved. She might have had to be a bridesmaid, and that was surely worse even than being a bride.

Anna gave Cameron's arm a sympathetic pat. "Sophia just wants everyone to share the joy she found in marriage."

"Alex and I have talked of marriage." Cameron choked out the words. Why was this so hard? "It's just that . . . it seems rather impossible right now. For one thing, the Soviet government wouldn't permit a marriage unless I became a Russian citizen, and I doubt they would let Alex leave the country just to accommodate us."

"Yes, that does make it rather difficult."

"That's part of it, anyway," Cameron admitted. Then she realized that here was Anna Yevnovona, perhaps one of the wisest women she knew. Maybe if she could be honest with her, she could come to understand this bewildering fear at the subject of marriage.

But Anna was a step ahead of Cameron. "When the time is right, Cameron, I believe God will take away from you the fearsomeness of it."

"I hope so. But how can I want something so desperately yet be afraid of it at the same time? I think maybe I am just too independent to be a good wife. I have always gone my own way, done what I want. I know Alex wouldn't make undue demands of me, yet by the very nature of marriage, I will have to consider him. Am I really so selfish that this element of marriage scares me?"

"You modern women have it harder than I did," Anna replied. "Girls in my day expected to be married and to be cared for by a man. We usually thought we needed that protection. Today, women have so many more choices. I expect the war will only add to that. Women are doing men's work now, and they are the ones making decisions at home and taking care of their families. I wonder if they will find a need for men at all when the war is over." She added that final sentence with an amused twinkle in her eye.

"Oh, Grandmama!" Sophia giggled, then added with more solemnity, "Women will always need men. Not for things, maybe not even for protection, but for their hearts." She smiled at Cameron. "When you find the right man, you are not complete without him."

Cameron nodded. She still didn't know how it could be, but she knew without doubt she was not complete without Alex. "I guess that means I am going to have to marry Alex eventually," she said with a mock put-upon sigh, then grinned.

Sophia and Anna laughed with her. Anna said, "I think you will find many more benefits to the situation than drawbacks!"

22

After the new year, in late January, the journalists were treated to a tour of the Stalingrad Front. Cameron didn't care that most of the action of the battle was over. The German Sixth Army under Paulus was still trapped in what had come to be called the Cauldron, but the Russians had repelled an attempt a couple of weeks earlier to rescue Paulus's army, and now it was just a matter of waiting out the starving Germans. There would still be plenty for the newspeople to see and nearly fresh battlegrounds to inspect. But more than that, Cameron could not keep from hoping that Alex might be there and some miracle would bring them together.

On first sight Cameron thought the pre-Revolutionary train cars they were to travel in were rather quaint, even luxurious for Russian travel. These were likely the very cars reserved for aristocracy in the days of the tsar, but now the reporters shared them with high-ranking officers and Party officials. The trip would take longer by train, but the skies over Stalingrad were not yet secure for civilian air travel. She tried to quell her impatience by looking forward to seeing some of the countryside en route.

What she saw on the first leg of the journey was the scars of war: Kashira, its blackened remnants left from the German advance on Moscow last year; Tambov and Kirsanov, towns burgeoned with wartime influx; soldiers packed together on the station platform, either coming from or going to battle, and with them women weeping for joy at greetings or with sorrow at partings. At Saratov, where they met the Volga River, there was an air of prosperity rather than the bleak taint of war. But it was the war that had brought the prosperity, for to this city many of the country's leading universities and schools had been evacuated, bringing a huge influx of people, along with their money.

Now when they debarked the train to stretch their legs, they began hearing stories about the struggle for Stalingrad, which was felt even this far away. The greatest danger had been to the railwaymen, as the enemy attempted to cut off the Russian supply line.

"We are just like soldiers," said an engineer. "Many of our own were killed and are buried not far from here."

"The worst of it came in October," said another. "But considering all the traffic on these tracks, the Fritzes didn't hit many trains. We were lucky."

As the temperature dropped, the train crossed endless miles of steppes. The ground was only lightly brushed with snow, allowing brown grass to push through, and for hours on end Cameron saw few signs of human habitation. She opened her Underwood and set all her thoughts and experiences thus far onto paper. Some of it might pass the censors and make an article for the *Globe,* but most would simply take the form of a memoir. It all might matter someday after the war was over. She had no doubt Russia would continue to be a major player in the forum of world politics, and people would be interested in life over here. Maybe after the war she would continue in Moscow as a correspondent. It wouldn't be a bad life, and Alex would be near even if they couldn't marry. And there was always the hope that Soviet repression would loosen after the war.

Odd, but Cameron did not often let herself think in terms of after the war. At one time she might have actually thrived on the war and all its inherent adventures. She hated to think such a thing was true, but as a journalist she had to admit a wartime milieu did give her much grist for the mill, as it were. Now, however, she was fairly certain she could find success in her career with or without war.

Her avoidance of thoughts of postwar life had more to do with the fact that it would force her to make decisions. Now they were pretty much made for her, but later it would be different. She would, without doubt, have to choose between her career and Alex, her country and Alex. Her faith—

Strange, but her faith seemed to be the one constant in her life.

Everything else might crash, but that one element did not have to unless she chose to resent God for the loss of Alex. But God had made her no promises regarding Alex. There were many, many promises in the Bible, she knew, though she couldn't quote most of them. God promised to be with her, He promised to give her peace. But if she had learned nothing else in the last months since she made her commitment to God, it was that God's presence, His peace, were not the same as getting what you wanted. The people at the Turkins' church meeting had offered her the best example of this. God with you through good and bad times. This was faith.

Cameron sighed, her breath making a small puff of steam in the chilly air. She felt both contentment and resignation. Was it possible for those to go hand in hand? Well, she felt it anyway. And she felt cold, as well. She rubbed her hands together briskly. Taking off her gloves to type hadn't been a good idea. The thin walls of the railway car, for all its superficial luxury, offered little barrier to the cold outside, which at times reached twenty degrees below Celsius. The woodstove and hot tea from the constantly steaming samovar helped but not much.

Soon the train came to the end of the line to a town called Leninsk.

Igor Raspopov, who was filling in for Palgunov on this trip, stood as the train pulled to a stop. "This is Leninsk, which is the principal supply base for the Battle of Stalingrad. Also, this is where most of the wounded from the battle are evacuated. We are thirty miles from Stalingrad."

Cameron didn't know what to respond to first—the patter of her heart when she heard that the wounded came here, so there must indeed be doctors here, or the fact that they were only thirty miles from the scene of one of the greatest military confrontations in history.

Oh, definitely it was the doctors! Alex could be here! Dear God, let it be so!

"We will stop here for lunch," added Raspopov. "And it has been arranged for you to speak with some officers who fought at Stalingrad and also with some medical personnel."

Cameron's heart clanged again. She hardly noticed their surroundings as they debarked the train. Yet it was impossible not to note that Leninsk was a shabby town with some brick buildings on the main street but mostly composed of little wooden cottage-type structures. These might have been quaint, but the posters tacked to their walls were jarring—taking you from the old-fashioned backwater feel of the place to the harsh present. *Drive the German rats from Stalingrad! Glory to our brave soldiers!* That was all her knowledge of Russian could make out, but there were many more, she was sure, in this vein.

In the officers' mess they were served a substantial lunch of borscht, beef stew, freshly baked bread, and the usual flood of wine and vodka. Toasts were made to the allies and to a Second Front. But the words seemed a bit rote and tinged with irony. A major told them about the present situation in Stalingrad.

"Those Germans have pluck, I'll say," he boomed. Apparently his hearing had been slightly damaged during one of the air raids, and now he had little control over the volume of his voice. "They still have the gall to call out to us, 'Russian dogs, surrender!'" He laughed loudly. "If it were up to me, I'd bomb the entire caldron out of existence, with the German Sixth Army in it! But powers greater than I choose to wait them out." He shrugged. "There are loudspeakers in the city informing the enemy that every seven seconds a German dies. Over and over they are told this. I think they would surrender if they could, but that madman in Berlin forbids them."

Talk of irony! Cameron knew there were many times the Russians should have surrendered but were forbidden by Stalin. That's what happened when *two* madmen clashed in battle. She kept silent about this, of course. Nothing could convince this major that there were any similarities between his glorious Russians and the filthy Fritzes.

In the midst of this discussion two men entered the mess hall. Cameron knew they were the medical personnel sent to talk with the journalists not by the medical insignias she knew were on their uniforms, though they were too far away for her to make out such details. She knew because one was tall with pale hair fringing his cap, and though his face was rather more gaunt than she remembered, it was still as handsome, with its clear blue eyes, as always.

Every instinct within her wanted to jump up and fly into his arms. What kept her in her seat when her emotions were raging for release, she did not know, but one look told her Alex was experiencing the same emotions. She tried not to dwell on the unfairness of it, that even acknowledging the man she loved could land them both in serious trouble.

"Ah," said Raspopov, "our doctors have finally arrived." Apparently he could see the medical insignia the men wore, but at least he did not see the drama sparking in the eyes of Cameron and the taller of the two physicians.

"They must be busy men," Cameron said, so casually she was certain the phoniness of it was obvious to all. "We are pleased they found the time."

"We have very few patients at the moment," the other doctor replied in English as both men now came to stand before the table of journalists. "No new wounded for several days now."

Alex was silent, but he never did have the ability to mask his emotions as well as Cameron. She hoped he would stop staring at her, or their ruse would be blown completely. As for herself, she forced her eyes away from him, focusing entirely on the other doctor.

"Can you give us an estimate of the number of casualties during the battle?" asked Jed Donovan.

"Significantly more Germans than Russians, I can tell you that," said the second doctor. Only then did Alex take his eyes from Cameron so as to cock a brow as his colleague's glibness.

"Unfortunately, we are not at liberty to give out figures," Alex said finally, a resolve in his tone as he must have realized he would soon draw undue attention to himself if he didn't respond in some way to the gathering. "We can say," he went on, "that the percentage of seriously wounded is much higher in this war than in the previous one. In the Great War perhaps twenty percent of the cases one saw were serious. Now it is more like forty percent." Cameron noted that his English was more deeply accented than she recalled, and he seemed to have to grope for the appropriate English words.

"Why is that?" Cameron asked. The question wasn't important, neither was the answer. But now she could look fully at him. Oh, Alex, just to look at you! I never dreamed what a pleasure that could be.

But the other doctor answered, and Cameron was forced to shift her gaze to him.

"A greater proportion of mortars and bombs, and of better quality, have produced a greater number of head injuries. These, of course, are most often fatal under battle conditions."

"Still, we see more frostbite than anything," said Alex, his voice luring Cameron's eyes back to where they wanted to be. "It's worse among the Germans. They have no proper winter gear. They expected to take the city by September."

Cameron rifled in her mind for another question but found only a whirling mess and no coherent thoughts. She didn't want to interview this man—she wanted to kiss him!

Dear Carl Levinson saved her. "What are the chances of touring the hospital? If you've no patients, perhaps there is time?"

Cameron's mind *was* in a mess if she hadn't been able to think of that! But she quickly came on deck. "Oh yes! My readers have responded favorably to my articles about Russian medical care."

"I am sorry," said Raspopov. "We must get back on the road."

"Surely you can spare an hour," persisted Levinson.

"Yeah," put in Donovan, "my readers love that human interest touch."

"A hospital in Leninsk," offered Ed Reed, "that's what the people back in the States want to hear about."

Cameron wanted to hug each one of them. She knew none of them had any interest in hospitals. But they all knew about her and Alex. Those scruffy men couldn't have been sweeter if they had been Cupid himself.

"No, we must keep on schedule," insisted Raspopov.

"We have a new X-ray machine from the States," Alex said, "that I am sure these journalists should see. Their readers will want to see lend-lease in action."

"Oh yes, we must see it. I've got a camera, too, for some photos. Comrade Stalin couldn't ask for better PR," said Levinson.

"Oh, come on," said Donovan. "One lousy hour isn't going to kill your schedule." They all knew that schedules in Russia were never kept.

"An hour, then." Raspopov rolled his eyes, adding in a mutter, "I didn't know you reporters were so interested in hospitals. I thought you wanted to see battlefields."

"I can act as guide," Alex said. He added to his colleague, "I'm sure you have other important things to do."

The other doctor gave Alex a look as if he thought he'd finally gone crazy. "I do indeed!" And he hurried away as if afraid he might still get roped into this unsavory chore.

"Then I will leave them in your hands, Doctor," said Raspopov. "If any wish to remain here, I think there is more vodka, yes? And the major might have more to tell you. . . ."

Cameron, Levinson, Reed, and Donovan heard no more as they hurried after Alex, exiting the mess hall. And Alex was hurrying as if he feared this opportunity might be lost with dallying.

But Levinson paused a moment when they were outside. "Cameron, I'm sorry we have to tag along."

"Don't even think of apologizing!" Cameron said. "I love you, Lev, and I owe you a big one."

"We'll try to stay out of your way—"

But Alex turned impatiently. *"Pashli!"* he said in Russian, giving a hurrying motion with his hand that clearly translated his words. "We have only an hour!"

Cameron smiled but even now was careful to keep her distance since they were still very much in the public eye.

Cameron prayed her colleagues were not caught wandering the hospital corridors alone, but that was as much thought as she gave them in the next hour. The moment Alex closed the door of the small examination room where they at last found themselves alone, she did what she had been yearning to do since first seeing him. He met her halfway.

Gathered in his arms, she felt so alive, so whole, so complete. And, oddly, safe. Odd, because before she hadn't felt particularly *unsafe*. It was the same sense as being home, protected from the buffeting of the world outside.

"Cameron, I love you so!" His kisses kept her from responding with her own words of love. But there would be time for talk later. Or would there? The hour was ticking away. It was only fifty minutes now. She'd be content if time stopped altogether.

At least ten more minutes were burned away in their embrace, their kisses punctuated only by murmurs of love. Cameron didn't begrudge a moment of it, but she had to stave her natural tendency to think more of the time lost than of the time that lay ahead.

Finally they had to pause for breath. Alex brought together two chairs and they sat, still gripping each other's hands.

"How am I ever going to repay those reporter friends of yours?" Alex said.

"Give them each an exclusive of what really happened at Stalingrad."

"I owe them but not with my life." He tried to speak glibly but failed because the truth of his words fell heavily upon them. Even now they were risking his life or at least his freedom.

She tried to lighten the momentary shadow. "Didn't you see the looks on their faces? They are romantics at heart and loved playing matchmaker."

"How have you been, my Camrushka?"

She smiled. It had been a long time since he had used the Russian diminutive of her name. She liked it.

He took her expression differently. "I'm sorry. I haven't spoken English in ages. I'm becoming more Russian than ever."

"We could speak Russian if you'd like. I might be able to manage."

"You've become that good, yes?" But he shook his head. "No, I should keep up my English. It is becoming more and more difficult. It isn't my first language anyway, and now I have to think before nearly every word."

He took her face between his hands—strong, supple hands of a surgeon. Gentle, yet sure of themselves. Her body tingled at this touch, for it was different from his kisses. There was more of a reverence in it and in his eyes, as well, as they roved her face, seeming to memorize even the tiniest detail.

"I wonder now how I have survived these months without you," he said.

"I know. I feel the same." She laid her hands on his as they still cupped her face.

Then the same thought assailed them in the same instant, and their eyes flickered to their wristwatches.

"Someday," he said, "we'll have forever. I know it for a certainty, Cameron. God couldn't have brought us together just for a temporary lark. Patience is all we need."

"And you know that patience is my worst thing!" She smiled wanly. "But I do believe you are right. Something tells me, as well, that this thing we have is for a lifetime. But this is war. Lifetimes change with each moment."

"Shush . . . let's not think of that. It does no good. Let's just think of the—" he glanced again at his watch—"forty-three and a half minutes we do have."

"This is why I need you, Alex. And why I love you!"

And she forgot all about the lost minutes and thought only of what lay before them. She lost the inhibition the press of the clock had placed on her. She told him details of the last months instead of trying to squeeze in as much general information as she could. They spent a lot of time talking about the church meetings. She gave him her impressions of all the people, especially the Turkins, and he listened intently because he knew many of the people, though she had a feeling he would have listened just as carefully to anything she would have said just to hear her voice. She told him the story of Anna and Sergei Fedorcenko, including the many details she had learned later from Sophia. Alex knew the story, but he listened as if he'd never heard it before. He told her that the story was as important as was her "take" on it, her particular viewpoint. He hadn't realized she was such a romantic. She blushed a bit at this observation and admitted it surprised her, too, but she was certain her opinion of romance had changed drastically since meeting him.

They laughed, and they talked more. He told her about Stalingrad. Not the kind of stuff a reporter needed to know for an interview. Instead, he opened his heart to her about his fears, his feelings of inadequacy, his failures, and his triumphs. She didn't like hearing about the terrible danger he faced in Stalingrad before his transfer to Leninsk. There had been a hundred moments when he could have been killed, and the thought was like a knife in her gut. She clung harder than ever to the hope they both had of a long future together.

All too soon a soft knock came to the examination room door. It was Lev.

"The bus is downstairs waiting to pick us up," he announced when Alex opened the door.

"*Spasiba,* Carl," said Alex. "She'll be there in a minute."

"We'll wait here in the corridor. It's best if we all go down together."

"Yes, of course."

He closed the door and turned back. Cameron was standing now, wondering if she looked as forlorn as she felt.

"It's not fair," she muttered in spite of herself and all her previous success in accepting their lot.

"We have had a whole hour together! Let's not be robbed of that joy by—"

"Ungratefulness," she finished for him.

"I wouldn't have put it so bluntly. I am thankful for this time." He reached for her, and she melted once more into his embrace. "I . . . am . . . th—ankful. . . ." But his voice broke at the end, and she could feel the dampness of his tears on her hair.

She put the voices outside the door far from her mind. Lev and the others would just have to be patient. Alex was ignoring them, too, as he lowered his lips once more to hers. They were truly stealing that final kiss, but neither could let go. When the door burst open, they did not fall immediately apart like guilty lovers.

"Lev . . ." she murmured around the kiss.

But the response was in Russian. "What is—? Oh, I am sorry— Dr. Rostovscikov?"

They quickly let go and spun to face the nurse at the door. There could be no denying their embrace or the likelihood of stories about "just getting a medical examination" being accepted. The woman's red face indicated she knew what was transpiring between the doctor and the woman, the *foreign* woman, in his arms.

Lev was at the woman's shoulder. "Cameron, I tried to stop her!"

"Americans. . . ?" the nurse said. She was in her middle years, with a round and dumpy shape and a plain face made more so with her hair covered by a white cloth cap.

"I was giving the American journalists a tour of the hospital," Alex replied in Russian. His tone was lame and confused. He was so terrible at masking his emotions, even worse at lying.

"This is not right," the woman said sternly. "Bad for the hospital."

"No one need know," Alex said desperately.

Cameron wanted to speak but even in her shock realized it would do no good to reveal how much she understood. She could think of nothing to say that would help anyway.

Then a new voice entered the verbal fray, that also in Russian. "We are late. We have a schedule—is there a problem?" That was Raspopov.

"No . . . no problem," said Alex in Russian. Then in English he said to Cameron, "Go to the bus."

"But—"

"Now. Go."

Never more helpless, Cameron knew she had to obey. She knew there was nothing else for her to do. Levinson, Donovan, and Reed joined her, uttering effusive apologies all the way to the bus.

In another ten minutes Raspopov climbed aboard the bus, where everyone was waiting. He gave Cameron a look that was a chilling mix of disapproval and disgust, but he said nothing. Cameron wanted to return that look with one of defiance, but she couldn't stop her tears to do so. The man definitely had no sympathy for Cameron's reddened, damp eyes. Her colleagues did, though, and they were so gentle and kind with her, she cried all the more. She found a seat at the back of the bus, laid her head against its back, and pretended to sleep. She couldn't even let herself fret over what kind of trouble she might be in. Maybe the nurse had kept quiet about the incident. Yet that hard look in the nurse's eyes did not seem that of a romantic. But even if she had told Raspopov what she had witnessed, maybe he would simply let it pass in the interest of maintaining good Russo-American relations. In any case, she couldn't dwell on it. All she could do was feel a deep sense of emptiness, that she had left part of herself behind, the best part. She could not let herself fear that this might be the last time she'd ever see Alex.

By the time they made their next stop, she had pulled herself together—on the outside at least. And by the time the journalists returned to Moscow the next week with no mention of the incident, she felt hopeful that she had managed to dodge retribution for her actions.

23

YURI FEDORCENKO did not enjoy intrigues and did not know why he had so often in his life found himself in the midst of them. Perhaps it was because he simply could not say no. And it had been especially difficult to refuse his dear daughter Sophia when she had approached him about helping her friend Cameron Hayes. However, he would like to think the reason was more altruistic, that he had such deep distaste for watching wrongs committed that he was compelled to act to right them. And there could be no question it was wrong that a young woman could not even *look* for her brother whom she'd never even met.

Ah, so much was wrong with Russia that he wondered why he loved this country. So many thought only of escape, and indeed, he'd thought of it a few times, as well. But he stayed, and despite his innate pessimistic nature, he hoped. He knew God had not abandoned Russia. There was still a chance one day for it to be free.

In the meantime he must look constantly over his shoulder—literally, in this case. He was not being followed, that he knew. Yet it wasn't easy to shake that constant *sense* of being followed. After nearly twenty-five years of a Communist police state and hundreds of years of tsarist oppression before that, he feared paranoia was inbred in Russians.

His heart raced in spite of constant reminders to himself that he was safe. He did not know if the man he was about to meet could be trusted. Not only was he a stranger, he was a Soviet bureaucrat, a somewhat low-level one, but often those were the most dangerous, especially if they were the ambitious sort. His name was Vasily Zharenov, and by all appearances he *was* ambitious. He had worked in the mines of the Ural region as a youth and joined the Party shortly after the Revolution. He worked his way up to a position as a clerk of some sort on the Council of People's Commissars in the Ural region, where he somehow became involved in arranging the adoption of Cameron's half brother. That "somehow" was what interested Yuri, because the man's general résumé had little to do with the system of orphanages and other matters related to children's services. Why had he personally handled this matter? Alone, this was unusual, but even more so was the man's rather impressive advancement in the Party afterward. Shortly after the adoption he was made chief assistant to the head of the Ural Soviet, eventually working his way to a place on the Ural Central Committee. In the early thirties he moved to Moscow for a high-level position in the building of the metro, apparently because of his mining experience.

Yuri had learned a great deal about this Zharenov fellow since his daughter had given him the name along with the story of Cameron and her half brother. He hadn't even had to leave Moscow to do so. Though the man had begun his Party career in the Urals, Yuri had decided to search Party records in Moscow before risking a trip to Sverdlovsk. Yuri was still in a bit of shock over the fact that his daughter had done that very thing—gone to Sverdlovsk and Vdovin on some wild chase to contact relatives of the half brother. The child was often as timid and shy as a mouse, but she still had a wide streak of adventure in her, at least as wide as Cameron Hayes's own streak. In fact, the great irony of this whole business was that Sophia and Cameron would no doubt have greatly savored the intrigue Yuri was now set upon.

In any case, Yuri had found the name and tracked the man's career. He'd used several simple ruses in order to gain access to the records—all he felt quite aboveboard, never lying outright. Long years of life in a police state had made Yuri rather pragmatic about lying. His faith was built on truth, and he conducted his actions in a way he believed honored Christian godliness. Yet God did not expect him to be guileless about it. Or stupid.

So here he was, going to meet a stranger who could well have Yuri tossed into a gulag for his efforts. Yuri was using the guise of medical research, looking into lung-related illnesses among those in the mining industry. This was certainly an area that *could* use some research.

Zharenov's apartment was located in a typically drab, utilitarian building not far from Gorky Park. Yuri had agreed to meet here rather than at the man's office nearer to downtown Moscow because he felt it would be safer away from official surroundings. If he was followed, it would appear more like a doctor on a house call. Yuri shrugged. If Zharenov chose to report him, no ruse in the world would suffice.

Yuri took the elevator to the sixth floor, located the apartment, and knocked on the door. In a moment the door opened.

"Yes?" said the resident with what appeared to be natural suspicion on the fringes of the man's greeting.

"You are Vasily Zharenov?"

The man only nodded, giving Yuri a thorough looking over. As for himself, he was a rather nondescript sort. Shorter than Yuri by several inches, he had a medium build and was about the same age, but his thinning hair had more gray than Yuri's. His skin was ruddy but not in a healthy manner. Yuri guessed the red spots on his cheeks and nose were symptoms of heavy drinking. A cigarette dangled between the man's lips. He was dressed in an old ill-kept suit of brown wool. His necktie, even at that early hour of the morning when, presumably, he had just put it on, was crooked and loosened at the neck.

Finally Zharenov said, "And who might you be?"

"You are expecting me. I am Dr. Fedorcenko." When Zharenov made no move to invite Yuri in, he added, "I believe it would be best if we spoke in private."

Reluctantly the man stood aside, and Yuri stepped into the apartment. He followed his host down a short hallway and into a parlor that seemed to reflect Zharenov perfectly. It was shabby, messy, reeking of stale cigarette smoke and other unpleasant odors. Yuri was not offered a seat, so the two men conversed standing in the middle of the room.

"I am a very busy man," Zharenov said, "so I hope this will be brief. I checked after you called me and discovered you are rather a prominent man in the medical field. That is the only reason I kept the appointment. I must, however, be at my office in a half hour."

"It shouldn't take long." Actually, Yuri had no idea how long this would be, nor did he have any idea how to proceed. He'd given his approach much thought but hadn't reached any conclusions as to the best way to get his information. Mostly he'd thought of just making contact with the man.

"Do you mind if I finish my breakfast?" Zharenov asked, and when Yuri shook his head, the man picked up a glass of clear liquid from a table. A bottle of vodka was sitting next to the glass. "I'd offer you some, but—"

"I'm not interested, Comrade Zharenov. I, too, must be at my work shortly."

"So what is this about lung disease? I had a physical exam a year ago. Surely nothing has surfaced since then, and even if it had, why would one of the most important doctors in Moscow be bringing me the bad news?" Eyeing Yuri with narrow, suspicious eyes, he removed the cigarette from his mouth and tossed back half the contents of his glass, replacing the cigarette immediately afterward as if it were a vital part of his anatomy. "And I don't much buy this hogwash about a research project, either." He took a puff from the cigarette, then a drink, alternating these actions throughout the conversation and filling his glass once more from the vodka bottle.

"Why, then, did you agree to see me?"

"I was curious about why you were nosing into my records."

"You don't accept that I was doing background checks into miners and ex-miners with a potential for disease?"

"It looks very thin to me."

In that moment Yuri decided to take a risk. Not because he thought he could trust this bureaucratic cretin but rather because he knew that was the only way he could help Cameron. Also, he could see no harm in putting forth the truth, at least a safe version of it.

"I am looking into the adoption of the child of a patient of mine."

"Who?"

"The patient is deceased now."

"Did he give his child some disease?"

"There is always that chance. At any rate, the child was given up for adoption about twenty years ago, and my understanding is that you handled the adoption."

"You have the wrong man. I have worked solely for the Party in the last twenty years." He gulped more vodka, obviously aware of the fact that he was not a good liar. "And why didn't you give this story at the beginning instead of that lung disease business?"

"I realize adoptions are confidential, thus, if you were the wrong man, as you claim to be, I did not wish to break confidentiality. You have now given me no choice, but it seems for naught anyway."

"So that's all, then?" Zharenov finished his drink and set down his glass with a definite touch of finality.

"I suppose so." Yuri turned to exit the room, then paused. "Comrade Zharenov, there is one thing that still bothers me. You see, the adoption I am concerned about took place in the Ural region. In fact, it was near Sverdlovsk, where you yourself were based twenty years ago. Such a coincidence, don't you think, that your name is the same as the name on the adoption document."

"You did not mention you had a document."

"Didn't I?" Yuri gave a bemused shake of his head. "Does that change anything?"

"No . . . it doesn't matter. I did not handle adoptions."

"Not even one . . . for a man named Leo Luban?"

"Never." Zharenov also moved toward the door. "I must go. Before I am late."

At the front door, Yuri said before leaving, "Thank you for your time."

"Listen here, Doctor, it is a mistake to stir up an old hornet's nest, even if it is life or death."

"But, Comrade, if the young man's health were imperiled, don't you think the adoptive parents would want to know and deal with it? Don't you think the young man would want to know? In fact, if he is alive, he has a right to know."

"And you would like the names of the adoptive parents so this information could be passed on to them?"

"I would like the names of the adoptive parents."

Zharenov eyed Yuri dubiously, not appearing to fully accept the implication of the young man's physical danger. Yuri had danced around the issue, his tone lacking confidence, because it was not a lie he felt comfortable in promoting.

"Even if I knew the names, which I don't because I am not the man you are looking for, I still could not give them because I am sure they would want to remain anonymous."

"As I said—"

Zharenov just shook his head and closed the door in Yuri's face.

Walking to the elevator, Yuri gave much thought to stirring hornets' nests, old or new. He prayed no one would get stung by his actions.

———

Vasily Zharenov was late for work that day. He spent most of the morning trying to locate his old boss, Stanislav Tveritinov, not an easy task considering that the man moved around a great deal with his important job in the war department. The best he might be able to do was send a wire to his last known place of assignment and hope for a quick response. It would have been far easier if he could have gone to Tveritinov's wife, who resided in Moscow, but he had no desire to deal with a woman nor to be responsible for causing her worry, especially if that worry was undue. Best to approach the man and let him handle it.

Yet something within him urged him to approach cautiously. What good would it do, and more importantly, what harm would it do to alert Tveritinov about that peculiar visit by the doctor? Yes, he owed a great debt to Tveritinov. He had been quite generous with him after the arrangement of the adoption. Zharenov was not an educated man, but he was smart enough to know he could never have risen to his present position in the Party without the intercession of his mentor. He had been smart enough at the time to refuse monetary payment for the adoption, rather assuring Tveritinov he merely wished to give joy to his employer while subtly hinting that a promotion would be appreciated more than money. Tveritinov had seen to several promotions, which led to a much-desired move to Moscow.

It was odd how one simple adoption could have had such far-reaching effects on a man's life. For he hadn't been lying when he said he'd never arranged adoptions—save for that one. He'd been in the right place at the right time to put together the nephew of a starving farmer of Zharenov's acquaintance with Zharenov's affluent superior, who had just suffered the tragic loss of his six-year-old son. And he had made sure that he alone had arranged the matter so all the credit would be his.

Warning Tveritinov of this possible breech of his closely guarded secret might also warrant even more of a reward. And if the child's health were endangered, the parents would be that much more appreciative of the information. Yet an old proverb his mother used to tell him came into his mind. "Do not dig a hole for someone else, for you might fall into it yourself." An attempt to bleed Tveritinov further in this matter, even in the guise of trying to help the man, might well blow up in Zharenov's face. For one thing, Zharenov was not convinced the doctor was being forthright regarding the boy's health danger. There was something more to it, and it was that *something* that worried Zharenov.

He must weigh all the possibilities. Of course, he had a greedy streak that yearned for more power, but that vied with a more pragmatic side. Perhaps he should be content with what he had.

In the end he delayed sending a wire, deciding a face-to-face encounter would be best. Mostly he was simply buying time until he was certain which way the wind blew in this matter.

24

THE MORNING AFTER Cameron's return to Moscow, Sophia reported to the Metropole as usual to work. Cameron was in her room at her typewriter jotting down notes from her recent tour of Stalingrad—at least they got within twenty miles of the city. Sophia had barely removed her coat before she regaled her employer with the news of Yuri's adventure.

"He found Zharenov! I can't believe it!" For the first time in days Cameron forgot about Leninsk and all that had happened there. Her attention was fully on her secretary now. "Tell me everything, Sophia!"

"The man denied being the person who arranged the adoption, but the *way* he denied it made my father certain he was the right man." Sophia recounted in detail the conversation between her father and Zharenov.

"I suppose under the circumstances, the fellow wasn't about to admit anything," Cameron said, her mind racing with all the ramifications. "And if indeed his rise in the Party was due to the adoption, he'd have every reason for continued silence. But even his silence tells me something. The adoptive parents must be important people if they were able to intercede on the man's behalf. It is good for Semyon that perhaps he spent the rest of his childhood in some comfort."

"Yes, it is good . . . for him. It is a surety that the family was affluent. Few poor families could afford to adopt when they could barely sustain their own children. But, Cameron, consider this: The

family must be important in the *Party*." She arched her brow significantly. "I don't think that can be good for you."

"Surely the fact that they adopted a child can't be a huge secret.
You can't suddenly have a six- or seven-year-old child in your home
and expect secrecy. Even if, as Marfa Elichin said, they had just lost
a child of the same age, it is too farfetched that they would try to
pass Semyon off as that child. Their Party associates must know
they adopted a child. Heavens! The child himself must know, since
he was six or seven at the time of the adoption. What is the secret?"

"But Semyon is the child of a subversive and a Jew," said
Sophia. "They would want this kept quiet. They probably put forth
some other more acceptable story about the child's origins."

"What if the child himself blabbed?" At the confused look from
Sophia at her final word, Cameron clarified, "I mean, what if
Semyon told where he came from? He and his father were close, so
surely he would have deep memories. They can't make him forget."

"I have no answers, Cameron." Sophia sighed.

"I hate to admit it, but if Zharenov is denying having a part in
it and is maintaining secrecy, then I must accept that the adoptive
parents aren't going to be easy to locate." She slapped her hand
against the table, making the typewriter jump. "If only I could talk
to the man, I know I could get the information out of him."

"My father feared you might want to do this," said Sophia, "and
he told me to make sure you understood how impossible that is."

"I'm not a complete fool. I know the risk it would be." She
wanted to pound the table again in frustration. She drummed her
fingers instead. She thought about what had happened in Leninsk.
Perhaps she had dodged Soviet retribution for the heinous crime of
embracing a Russian citizen, but she could not expect to be so lucky
if she stepped out of line again. And even if she did decide to hang
caution and see Zharenov, and if by some miracle she did get the
information from him, what then? At some point in her investiga-
tion she was bound to get caught and deported. How could she
confront a high Party official, as Semyon's father likely was, and not
find herself in immediate hot water? So it would still do no good. If
Zharenov didn't turn her in, the adoptive parents surely would,
especially if they were also Party bureaucrats.

No matter which way she turned, she was likely to fall into a
trap.

And her caution had far more to do with good sense than with Alex. As it stood now, it seemed hopeless that she would ever see him again. However, thinking that thought with such finality made her insides ache. Yet how could she see him again with war and the police dogging them at every turn? So what would she lose by pursuing Zharenov?

Everything.

The word seemed to come from outside her own careening thoughts. Was that how God spoke? His way of urging caution? Telling her that even though all appeared hopeless, she must still act out of hope, the hope He had instilled in her when she had committed herself to Him?

"Cameron. . . ?" Sophia's tone and her large gray eyes conveyed concern.

"I'm not going to do anything stupid," Cameron assured. "I want to . . . oh, how I want to! But I know I can't."

"My father will continue to do what he can."

"No, Sophia. This Zharenov doesn't sound sympathetic, and if Dr. Fedorcenko pushes him, he could end up in a gulag. Somehow God will provide a way."

Sophia smiled. "I think so, too."

"I only hope it is soon. You know as well as I that I am not a patient person."

Cameron had heard things about God's timing. That a day is as a thousand years to Him. She had to accept the fact that she might be in for a long wait.

———

Cameron was returning to her hotel room after an evening at the theater with some embassy friends when two NKVD agents approached her in the lobby.

"You would to come with us, Miss Gayes?" The man's English was as choppy as could be, and she thought about feigning ignorance. But his tough bearing, not to mention his muscular body, indicated his words weren't really a request.

She went with them to a black vehicle parked in front of the hotel. She'd played this scene before a couple of times, except this time none of her friends were around to see her leave. The lobby was as empty of familiar faces as if an air raid had just sounded.

That gave her more of a sense of unease than anything. People had a way of disappearing in Russia, even foreigners, though more rarely. Yet her past experience bolstered her a bit. They probably just wanted to question her, probably about some silly thing she couldn't even remember doing. If it had anything to do with Alex, why had they waited this long? It had been a week since her return from Stalingrad.

At NKVD headquarters she was taken to a small room, not unlike the room she had been taken to when they had questioned her about Oleg. It was furnished with only a table and a couple of chairs. She took a seat as the agents departed. She noted no sound of the door being locked behind them. Maybe that was a good sign.

At least they didn't make her wait as long as they had before. That had been the day the foreigners were being evacuated from Moscow and she and Johnny had ended up missing the last train out of the city. This time the door opened in ten minutes. The man who entered was a rather typical agent—big, muscular, and dangerous looking. These men were not usually the ones to do interrogations. Was he going to take her someplace else? But a moment later another man entered. She recognized him as the man who had questioned her regarding Oleg. She could not recall his name. He was balding, rumpled, and though he looked like an elf next to the hulking agent beside him, there was a sinister aspect to the small eyes that peered at Cameron through wire-rimmed glasses.

"We meet again, Miss Hayes." He greeted her in a congenial tone that she didn't trust at all. His English was quite good.

She gave him a blank stare. Let him work for what he wanted. She did not rise from her seat.

"I am Major Smilga. If you recall, I spoke with you last fall." His eyebrow quirked as though he expected her to suddenly remember and greet him politely. She only shrugged. He glanced at his companion, who replied with a stony expression. "My associate here is Captain Bogorodsk."

"So you need *two* goons to question me this time?" Cameron said.

"Captain Bogorodsk wished to speak with you, but he needs an interpreter."

There was an unmistakable sneer to Smilga's tone when he said the word *needs*. Cameron wondered if Smilga didn't appreciate

Bogorodsk's muscling in on his area as NKVD interrogator. She also wondered about playing the two against each other, though she could see no purpose to such a tactic at this stage. She also saw no point in antagonizing them yet, or at least until she heard what this was all about. Though it galled her, she determined to cooperate.

"Captain Bogorodsk, what can I do for you?" she asked in English.

"Miss Hayes, I am sorry to have to inconvenience you," Bogorodsk said with Smilga interpreting.

The two men spoke their Russian quickly, and she had a hard time deciphering, catching only a word or two. She was as dependent on the interpreter as Bogorodsk. Her command of the language was simply not good enough to keep up with two natives.

"But I am trying to get to the bottom of an unfortunate incident that occurred several days ago in Leninsk," he said.

So it had finally caught up with her. But she kept her face straight and forced herself to be cool, though she felt like screaming.

"Do you know of what I speak?" prompted Bogorodsk.

"Leninsk . . . we had a bit of a tour there, as I recall." She couldn't help herself, but it went against her grain to admit anything to these men. "A hospital is located there."

Bogorodsk and Smilga now took seats. Bogorodsk leaned back in his chair and appeared quite relaxed. Smilga looked like a nervous rat by comparison.

"I can understand your reticence to speak plainly of that visit." The man actually did seem to understand. Was there something resembling a heart beating beneath all that brawn? Bogorodsk continued. "You found yourself in a precarious situation. But it is hardly worth denying, since I am aware you are not a stranger to Dr. Rostovscikov."

"He was my doctor here in Moscow when I was injured last year. Naturally I was happy to see him." She knew her denials were moot, but she could not do otherwise.

"Happy . . . hmm." The brute of an NKVD agent seemed on the verge of a smile. With a more businesslike demeanor he added, "There was no choice at the time but for you to be treated by a Russian."

"He did an excellent job."

"Yes, I am sure he did. He is a superior physician." He spoke with enough conviction that it made Cameron wonder if the man knew Alex personally.

Wait! She recalled Alex mentioning that he was on friendly terms with an NKVD agent. A situation that had been very helpful to them in the past because the agent had been willing not to look so closely at her and Alex. Could this be the man? Cameron didn't think a name had ever been mentioned, but she was now almost certain there was a grain of sympathy in the man. Might it help if she could get the man alone? Would it be worth the risk of revealing the extent of her knowledge of Russian? Furiously, she tried to work out in her mind all the pitfalls of a variety of actions.

But Bogorodsk spoke before she could make a decision. "You have made the mistake of becoming emotionally involved with a Russian citizen, Miss Hayes. We cannot let this situation go without being dealt with."

"Why?" she said desperately. "What is so terrible about mingling foreigners and Russians? I have never had this problem in other countries—"

"You must accept the way things are in the Soviet Union. You should have abided by our rules."

"Now what?" she asked peremptorily. She was sick of playing the game, sick of ridiculous Soviet rules.

Bogorodsk glanced at Smilga, then they spoke together in Russian. They were having some kind of dispute. She distinctly heard Bogorodsk say he could speak some English. Finally, in an undeniable huff, Smilga rose and exited the room.

When they were alone, the big agent said in broken English, "We can speak frankly now, yes?"

"I'm not sure what you mean."

He tried to reply but with great difficulty because of his limited English. The gist that Cameron understood was that he had convinced Smilga that she would talk more freely with him alone.

"I do not to want to cause for troubles on my good friend," Bogorodsk said.

"And your friend would be. . . ?"

"He is too your friends, also, I think."

Because he used the plural of *friend* Cameron wasn't certain what he meant. Was his friend Alex? Or was he speaking in more general terms? Should she continue to deny her relationship to

Alex? Yet her gut told her this man, against all reason, was on her side, or at least on Alex's side. With an inward sigh, she replied in Russian—slowly, picking out each word as she went, but probably her Russian was better than this man's English. At any rate, they managed finally to communicate clearly, helped along by switching back and forth with their native tongues when necessary.

"What are you telling me, Captain? Am I in trouble for what happened in Leninsk or not?"

"You are in trouble, I am sorry to say. I tried to intercede as best as I could—that is why it took so long for us to act upon the incident. I now hope for things to go as easily on you as possible."

"What about Alex? Is he in trouble?"

"Aleksei was isolated after the incident—" When Cameron gasped, Bogorodsk added quickly, "He is fine and will be back to his work soon, I assure you. But he was questioned and refused to cooperate. Because I have worked closely with Aleksei almost since he first came to this country, I was called in on the matter. I convinced Aleksei to support the story I would put forth to the authorities."

"What story is that?"

"Simply that you were overcome by Dr. Rostovscikov's handsome charms, and in the brash manner of all Americans, you threw yourself at him. He was in the process of fighting you off when the nurse came upon you."

Her first instinct was to be offended at being presented in such a horrible light—like some giddy, mindless woman. But immediately she could see how this was the best stance to protect Alex. Yet reason also told her Alex would never agree to such a tale. She said as much to Bogorodsk.

"You are right," said the agent. "He was most adamant against the lie. He was furious when I told him I would give that story the minute I left the room, and no one would listen to his denials after that."

"I thought you were his friend," she said coldly.

"I am, and my first concern is to protect him. But I sense there is more between you and the doctor than simple friendship. And it would devastate him should you be disgraced, as a deportation most certainly would do. In that case you would never be permitted back into this country. It might even do great harm to your career after you leave. You would no doubt be a risk for your newspaper to send on another foreign assignment."

Her hope soared. She wouldn't have to leave Russia! But why all this rigmarole?

"What is to become of me, then?" she asked with great misgiving despite the moment of hope she'd experienced.

"There have been hints of other indiscretions during your stay in Russia, nothing that can be proved, but still even hints are dangerous, Miss Hayes. My superiors were bent on deportation. I was involved in some of these investigations of your previous actions, and I managed to convince them that you were innocent, merely caught in the wrong place at the wrong time."

"Why . . . why would you do this?" Her thoughts were in complete disarray. There was hope, yet she knew something terrible was about to happen. And in the midst of that, here was an NKVD agent actually lying on her behalf! It befuddled her mind. It went against all reason.

"Maybe with this I will have finally paid a great debt. . . ." He paused thoughtfully, then gave his huge head a shake. "No . . . I will never completely pay that debt. But you may not think I am helping you when you hear the rest."

"I have no idea what to think. What is the rest?"

"When I leave this room, I will tell my superiors that you have confessed to being a silly female smitten, for moments only, in the hospital by the handsome doctor, perhaps a carryover from when he cared for you last year. I will mention the phenomena of patients falling in love with their doctors. You will not deny this."

"Then what?"

"I think you will have to leave Russia—"

"What! Then what is the good of these lies?"

"Miss Hayes, you will not be deported. You will leave Russia of your own will."

"It's the same thing to me!" she groaned.

"Have you not heard a word of what I've said? It is *not* the same. If you leave on your own accord, quietly and willingly, this incident may one day be forgotten. New men will be in power. Who knows, maybe I will even have such authority! You could perhaps return to Russia one day if you wish. At least there is a small chance, yes?"

She hated it all, but she had to agree the man was right. It galled her, but like Alex, she really had no choice but to agree. At least she knew Alex would be all right, though before she agreed to anything, she had to make certain of that.

"I have your word that Alex will be free?" she asked.

"He will be as free as he was before."

She caught more than a hint of irony in Bogorodsk's tone. Free of barred doors, free to practice medicine, but not free to leave or to be with her. Ah, freedom. Such a frail business it was!

Bogorodsk left the room, and another hour passed before Cameron saw him again.

"You will come with me," he said in English when he returned. Smilga and another agent were close at hand.

"Where?"

"To the airport."

"What! I'm leaving now . . . I . . . there are things . . ." she sputtered as a million loose ends sprang into her mind. It couldn't be this sudden. Yet she couldn't tell them that she had friends—some of them Russian!—to tell good-bye. She had dispatches to finish. She had . . . she didn't know what else, but she was not ready to leave Russia yet.

"Your things have been packed and are in the car," said Smilga with, Cameron was certain, just a hint of triumph in his eyes.

They had been going through her things! What had they found? Was there anything incriminating? Thank goodness Sophia had suggested not long ago to hide the material regarding Semyon under the lining of her suitcase. But still, she had other personal belongings. Her diary wasn't hidden. What if—?

But she suddenly realized the greater tragedy. She was leaving Russia. Maybe forever. . . . Please, God, not forever! Somehow, please get me back here! Alex, I won't let go! I won't!

She didn't know how, but she managed to make her leaden legs move. She was supposed to be leaving Russia willingly, and she could not reveal to these men just how this action was tearing her to pieces. They must never know the depths of her emotional ties to this place. But she knew. Her heart, and even a part of her soul, was going to remain behind in this cockeyed country. The only thing of value she had found in Russia that would go with her was her faith in God.

25

CAMERON TOOK a taxi from the airport in Los Angeles, but she didn't go directly to her parents' home. Everything had happened so suddenly she hadn't had a chance to notify them of her return. She thought she would stop by the *Globe* and see Max, then settle herself in a hotel before she called them. She knew her mother wouldn't like that, but Cameron simply wasn't ready to face her father.

Max Arnett was shocked when she walked into his office.

"I am so sorry, Max," she said after she relayed the story of what had happened. She was seated on the sofa in his office. "Whatever losses you incur because of this, I will try somehow to make up to you." She knew that was a lame offer, because it could involve thousands of dollars of accreditation money, but she needed to offer something. She owed so much to him, and she hated herself for having failed him.

"Let's just see what the Soviet government does," he said in his mild fatherly tone. He sat adjacent to her on the matching chair in his elegantly appointed office. "Don't think they have kept this quiet entirely to suit you. It is in their interest to prevent an international incident. Imagine what we could do with that story. Woman deported for love! What villains that would make of Stalin and his bunch."

"But it is my fault. Getting personally involved like that goes against any journalistic precept ever invented. But honestly, I couldn't help it, Max."

"You are not the first journalist to fall in love with a local while on assignment," he assured. "I have known many a *male* to do that very thing and to get into far more trouble over it. Now, Cameron, let's put the past behind us and consider your future."

She gazed at him in wonder. She could not help making the obvious comparison with her father. What would *he* have done under the same circumstances? She thought of Johnny Shanahan's impropriety during the Spanish Civil War. Her father hadn't fired Johnny, merely demoted him to the city desk for several years. But Johnny was a man, and Cameron knew her father would have a very distinct double standard in such an instance had it been a woman. His own daughter? She did not want to think of that!

But now, for the first time since she had been escorted onto that plane in Moscow, she did begin to consider her future. She had no idea what it held. Or what she wanted. She looked hopefully at Max, not afraid to admit for once in her life her confusion, her concern.

"What do you think I should do, Max? If, indeed, I do still have a job with you?"

"Don't even question that," he said firmly. "As far as I am concerned, you can name your next assignment."

Stunned, she shook her head. "I don't know what to say."

"Give it some thought. There are many options for you. One would be the city desk. With so many men in the Army, women are stepping into hard news areas in droves. Why, I even heard the *Journal* has hired a female Washington correspondent, not to mention others doing national and city news. We also once discussed the Pacific Theater. I could get you to Australia within the month."

"What about Europe?"

Cameron had considered the Pacific before but mainly because of Johnny. Not that it wouldn't be a fantastic assignment in any case. But she knew the allies were gearing up for the much-touted Second Front, and an invasion of Europe could not be far off. When such an invasion happened, it would be massive in scale, an event not to be equaled in the history of the world.

"Yes, that is certainly a possibility," said Max. "With the buildup of troops in North Africa, I wouldn't doubt if an invasion of Italy might happen soon."

Cameron's head nearly spun with the options before her. Had it really been less than two years ago when she had been unemployed and given the impression by many in the business that a woman simply had no future in hard news reporting? Her own father had refused to send her as a foreign correspondent merely because of her gender. Truly much had changed in two years. Cameron recalled Anna Yevnovona once commenting that the war would change the situation of women because they were now handling duties once solely male dominated. Of course this boon could well have a certain backlash, but for now Cameron knew to ride with the positive wave of it.

"I'll give it some thought," she said. "But for now, if you can use me on the city desk, I'd like to get right to work."

"Don't you want some time off? A little rest and relaxation?"

"That will just make me crazy. Since going to Russia I have longed for some real newspaper work. I want to pound the sidewalks, I want to hang out in police precincts, I want to chase a few ambulances."

"And here I thought I wouldn't be able to 'keep you down on the farm,' as it were." He smiled with understanding. "But I know the repression in Russia was frustrating."

"Thank you, Max. I'll report to work tomorrow if that's okay."

"I'll inform our city editor that we have a new gal on the job."

———

Cameron hoped her next hurdle would be as easy and as positive. She called her mother from the hotel she'd checked into and was immediately taken to task for being at a hotel at all. But there was more than scolding in Cecilia's tone. Cameron denoted a tremor in her mother's voice, as if she was trying, not very successfully, to conceal hurt.

"I can't stop you if you want to stay in a hotel," Cecilia said. "Even if there is this big rambling empty house available. It's . . . your choice."

"I just thought it might be a bit more . . . peaceful this way," Cameron said into the phone receiver.

"Perhaps if you gave your father another chance. You have both changed."

Cameron considered the changes within herself but wondered if she was ready to put them to such a test. She'd read that nothing was impossible with God. Did that include God's interceding with Keagan Hayes? And what did her mother mean in saying they *both* had changed? Surely if Keagan had had a religious experience, such a monumental event would have been felt even as far away as Russia.

Nevertheless, with an inward sigh she dared not express to her mother, she relented and said she'd stay at home. But she still kept the room in the hotel. Then she surprised herself by calling a taxi and asking the driver to take her to the *Journal* offices. She was still not ready to see her father, but it occurred to her after her mother said he was at work that it might be better for their first confrontation to be there, though they'd had their share of shouting matches at the office. Still, it seemed a safer, more controlled environment than home.

First she stopped by the pressroom, hoping to see some old acquaintances, but there were only a couple left. Most of her past colleagues had been men, and now, except for a few older ones, they were in the military. But no one she knew was in the office just then, so she sought out Harry Landis, catching him between meetings. Having taken over the job of managing editor last year and with such a scarcity of workers, he was a very busy man.

But when he saw Cameron, he said, "Never too busy for you, Cameron!" With a friendly smile he invited her into his office and offered her a seat. This place was a far cry from Max's orderly, stylish office. The sofa where she sat was old and worn, the desk piled with paper work, and the telephone rang several times as they visited. "I was just in to see your father, and he said nothing about you being home," he added as he swept some folders from the other end of the sofa and sat next to her.

"I had to leave Russia quite suddenly," Cameron explained. "He doesn't know I'm home yet."

"I'm not surprised the first place you'd come is here." He grinned. "Always in the blood, eh?"

"Well, the first place I went was the *Globe,* but I never really worked at their office, so this is where I feel at home. Though a lot has changed here."

"Yes, the war touches everything."

"Still, it feels good to be in the middle of a newspaper office with phones ringing, typewriters clacking, people rushing around to meet deadlines. I've missed it."

"Does that mean you are coming back?"

"I have many options to consider. But for now I suppose I'll work on the city desk of the *Globe*."

"I'd offer you a job here, Cameron. I pretty much have autonomy in hiring and firing. But . . ."

She smiled wryly. "I know, Harry. In my case other rules apply."

"You will go up and see your father, won't you?"

"That's why I came."

"Good. I know he'll want to see you. He's been very proud of your work, Cameron."

"That's nice to hear, even if I've never heard it from him."

"You know your father. He doesn't like to mollycoddle anyone."

"Especially his daughters."

"Well, I do hate to cut this visit short, but I'm already late for a meeting with the mayor. But I want to talk more with you. I want to hear all about Russia."

"Okay, Harry. It was wonderful to see at least one friendly face here."

As they rose, he said with a sigh, "So much has changed. . . ." He paused with a thoughtful expression on his face, then added, "Let's have supper together soon. We'll drink a toast to Johnny and talk old times as well as new."

"I'd like that. I'll talk to you again after I get settled."

They walked to the elevator together. He took a car going down while she stepped into the one going up and rode to the top floor. Her father's secretary, Molly, was still there in the publisher's offices and welcomed Cameron in her usual friendly but businesslike manner. When she spoke to Keagan on the intercom, he told her to send Cameron right in, which surprised Cameron. She thought her father would make her wait or do something just for spite. She thought a silent prayer as she opened his door. She didn't ask God for a pleasant visit with her father but merely that they wouldn't start yelling at each other.

"This is a surprise, Cameron," he said, rising from his desk. "Does your mother know you were coming home? She certainly said nothing to me." He did not walk around his desk for a more personal greeting. It was almost as if the desk formed a safe zone.

"No one knew," Cameron replied. "I left rather suddenly."

"Do you have time to sit for a few minutes?"

"Yes."

He, too, had a sofa in his office and a matching chair. His was leather, expensive, but soft and well used. Having been in the offices of three important newspapermen that morning, she couldn't resist the temptation to compare them. She'd felt most comfortable in Harry's cluttered office, knowing that every bit of clutter had to do with putting together a newspaper. Max's office had made her want to mind her p's and q's. Any warmth it held came entirely from Max, though his natural reserve kept that in careful control. The office of Keagan Hayes held a scent of old leather and stale cigar smoke, and while not stylish, it was comfortable and even inviting. The rich leather furnishings were offset by walnut paneling and a large red Persian carpet. In all, the room seemed to say, "Here works a very important man, but he isn't about to hit people over the head with that fact." Keagan Hayes didn't have to tout his own value. He just *was* important, and he expected people to *know* it.

For Cameron, the office held another level of ambiance. Yes, many fiery arguments had unfolded here, but she also had pleasant memories from her childhood of coming to work with her father. How many hours had she spent curled up on that sofa watching her father talk on the phone, wielding the power of a newspaper publisher? And here was born her dream of being a journalist just like Daddy.

Her stomach clenched as she thought of these things. Her father, indeed, had been her model—not Max Arnett, not Harry Landis. Those two men probably would have been better models, but she might not have turned out as she had if they had shaped her. She was a fighter because of her father; she was strong because of her father; perhaps she was even sympathetic because of him, because of the hurts he'd caused.

"What happened in Russia?" Keagan asked, resuming his seat behind the desk. Oh yes, and she was direct and no-nonsense because of Keagan Hayes.

How she hated to tell him all that had happened to lead up to her leaving, but she knew he'd find out easily enough from other sources, so she spilled out the whole story, at least about Alex.

"Stupid," he said after a long pause.

She bit back a defensive retort and instead nodded. "Yes, it was."

"And yet another argument against sending women overseas," he added smugly.

"Men fall in love, too, Dad."

"It is usually not love that fouls up men but more in the way of lust." Again he paused.

Cameron could not read his expression, though she tried. She was, however, almost certain he was not mad or even disappointed. But what was he? What did he really think about what she had told him? Perhaps he did understand because he'd been a foreign correspondent once, too.

"But you are right," he added, "male correspondents get into trouble, too."

She nearly gaped at him. *She was right?* Had she heard clearly?

"Don't stare at me like that, young lady," he said. "I can give credit where credit is due, you know."

"I appreciate that, Dad." Okay, he was honest with her; she would return the gesture. "But I know I fumbled the ball in Russia."

"Let's just hope you learn by your mistake."

"Well, I know one thing, I won't fall in love again on assignment because I still love Alex—"

"That's the most ridiculous thing I have ever heard, Cameron." Keagan shook his head censoriously. "Don't you realize how slim the chances are of your getting back into Russia, or of his getting out? I tell you this for your own good—forget about that man. You've not a prayer of seeing each other again."

"Dad, I've come to believe more in prayer than I used to." She swallowed nervously. This was perhaps an even more difficult admission than that of falling in love. Even now she wanted his approval, not his disdain, which she knew her new faith would no doubt garner from him.

"You are just full of surprises, Cameron" was all he said.

Several moments of silence followed, and when he didn't come back with a sharp uppercut, she gained confidence to continue the conversation.

"I think I will get back into Russia someday, Dad. The door was closed, but it wasn't locked. This NKVD agent I mentioned assured me the possibility was open."

"This doctor aside," Keagan asked, "do you *want* to go back— as a correspondent?"

"I believe my expertise in Russian affairs will be indispensable, not only as the war continues but afterward, as well." She sounded like Johnny Shanahan—confident, even arrogant in that confidence. But why not? It was true. She and the handful of journalists who had served in Russia in recent years definitely had to be the undisputed experts, so why disparage the fact?

Her father grinned in response. Was that pride glinting in his sharp green eyes?

"When the war is over," Keagan said, "Russia will be a major player in world affairs. They will not let their part in the war go unrewarded, nor will they let the Germans go unpunished. The Allies have already established that they will accept nothing but an unconditional surrender from Germany. Russia will not be edged out of the spoils, as they were in the Great War."

"That was their own fault because of the Revolution and Lenin's determination to make a separate peace."

"True, but Stalin will make up for that this time. We are going to want our best correspondents in Russia as much after the war as now." He leaned back and eyed his daughter as if sizing her up. "I only hope you haven't burned your bridges."

"I'll have to wait and see, I suppose."

"You were never a patient girl."

She smiled and nodded. "I have no choice now."

"What will you do in the meantime?"

"I still work for the *Globe*," she answered noncommittally.

"Come and work for me again, Cameron," he said, and the entreaty in his tone shocked her.

It suddenly occurred to her that no real mention of the past had yet been made. It almost seemed as if Keagan had forgotten the harsh words exchanged at their last meeting. But Cameron knew her father better than that. Keagan never forgot anything. Nor did he ever apologize. Perhaps this glossing over of past confrontations was the only way he could make it up to her short of saying he was sorry. She was ready to accept it as such, at least until he proved otherwise.

"I owe the *Globe* a measure of loyalty." She carefully left Max's name out of it because of the history of animosity and competition between the two men. She knew, even as she uttered the words, that they were risky. But if she was going to be honest, she had to do so regardless of the risk.

"Don't you owe any loyalty to your own father?" he asked caustically. She marveled at how quickly the tone of the conversation could change. "Never mind," he quickly added, shocking her yet again by his sudden reversal of tone. "I fired you—"

"I quit," she shot back before she could think.

He laughed, green eyes practically twinkling, shaggy red head shaking with mirth. Now she did gape. She couldn't help it. But his laughter made her remember why she had once adored her father. His amusement was by no means jolly, but it was genuine and infectious. She chuckled, as well, despite her emotional imbalance.

"Regardless," he said as his merriment faded, "we were both complete fatheads. Let's put it in the past, and you come back to where you belong."

"Max Arnett assured me I could write my own ticket at the *Globe*," she said, throwing aside all caution. If she came back to the *Journal*, it would be on her own terms. She was no longer a green upstart hoping for a few crumbs from the table of her betters. Her father may well know that from the start.

"I'll double whatever Arnett is paying you, and I'll make you chief crime reporter."

That was Johnny's old beat. And her old dream. But her dreams had changed.

"Dad, there's a war on, and that's where I want to be right now."

"You said you could write your own ticket at the *Globe*. What exactly does that mean?"

"I want to be in on the invasion of Europe. Until that can be arranged, I wouldn't mind doing the crime beat." She folded her arms smugly. She knew her father would never hire her on these terms, yet at least she could say he'd had the chance.

"How about you stay away from the war, work the city desk, and when the war is over, you will be the *Journal's* first female correspondent to the Soviet Union?"

"Oh, I'll have that, too," she said casually. She felt like a cocky gambler who couldn't lose. Yet part of her knew she could lose in this, because all at once she *wanted* to work for her father again.

She didn't know why. The man was impossible and would probably drive her mad. Yet, of all her dreams, that was the one that meant the most.

"Where'd you learn to be such a horse trader?" he asked.

"Must be in the blood."

"How would you like to be city editor?" he tempted.

Thinking he must be joking, she laughed.

"I'm not kidding," he deadpanned.

When she thought of a twenty-six-year-old woman as city editor of the *Journal,* she wondered if she should take the position just for the sake of irony. But it wasn't what she wanted.

"Dad, I am honestly not trying to hold out for better. I've told you what I want. I can get that at the *Globe.* To tell the truth, I'd rather work for you but not if I have to compromise my desires."

"I guess you don't have to compromise," he said flatly.

Her heart sank as she took his words for rejection, and at the same time she realized just how much she did want to work for her father—more than she'd ever have guessed a mere hour ago.

Then he said, "Okay, report to work tomorrow morning. I suppose your mother is anxious to see you today. I'll get the ball rolling on a European assignment for you. But you realize there won't be an invasion this year."

"An invasion of Italy is in the works," she said evenly, barely managing to cover her utter shock at his acceptance of her terms.

"Don't push me, Cameron!"

"Okay, okay!" she chuckled.

And when they rose, he finally moved away from the protection of his desk. He came up to her, stopped short, then patted her shoulder affectionately. She had a huge urge to throw her arms around him and give him the hug there ought to be between a father and daughter, especially when they hadn't seen each other for a year. She sensed he really might want to hug her but just didn't know how to put something like that into motion. Before she could mount such a personal "invasion" herself, he had opened the door and stepped into the outer office, where Molly was typing and his afternoon appointments were seated in chairs. She could not make herself take such a risk in public.

As she left, she comforted herself with the memory of one of the best encounters she'd had with her father in years. They had both

240

changed. She was certain of that. But she couldn't quite define the changes in her father. He was still himself in many ways, yet she knew something must have happened to him in the last year to soften his sharp edges. Like a victim of an explosion, she mentally assessed her emotions and could feel no new wounds within herself for having come close to him. Amazing! She silently thanked God and wished Alex was here so she could share this triumph with him.

26

CAMERON DID NOT start work in the morning, because Cecilia had other plans. Perhaps she knew that once Cameron became involved in her job, she would have little time for her mother. Thus, Cecilia suggested they take a few days and travel to Manzanar to visit Jackie. Cameron actually thought it a great idea. She had been disappointed to find her sister wasn't home and was anxious to see her new niece.

On the train to Lone Pine, Cameron and her mother had their first chance to talk seriously since she'd come home.

"Mom, I wish I had more news about Semyon." Cameron glanced at her mother to gauge the level of the other woman's disappointment. Of course Cameron had not been able to inform her mother of anything regarding her son while in Russia.

"I want you to tell me honestly," Cecilia said, "that it wasn't because of him that you had to leave. I know you said it was because of your doctor, but . . . well, I know your tendency to take risks."

"It had nothing to do with Semyon." Cameron was a little ashamed to admit just how few risks she had taken in the matter of her half brother.

"So you didn't find him." Cecilia gently edged the conversation back to the beginning.

"No, however I did learn a few new things. But before I proceed, I should tell you about Yakov—"

"You found him?" Something sparked in Cecilia's eyes. She had always firmly assured Cameron that she had never loved Yakov. Their relationship had been based more on mutual need. But that look . . . no, it could only be surprise. Nothing more.

"Mom, Yakov Luban has died."

"I knew it must be so. How?"

"I believe he had cancer. He died less than a year ago. But he was in prison—"

"No! Not Yakov. He would never do anything—"

"Mom, remember, it is Russia. People often go to prison for doing nothing."

Cecilia seemed relieved. "Yes . . . I did forget. Do you know why he was in prison? He was never very political."

"I think it was because of his Christian faith," Cameron answered. "His letters seemed to indicate he first ran afoul of the Soviet government because of his bookstore. I later learned the trouble over the bookstore very likely made him more outspoken about his faith, and he was known to distribute religious tracts. But I am getting ahead of myself. I had a friend who ended up in a gulag about a year ago. While there he met Yakov, and they became friends. Oleg—my friend—was with Yakov when he died. Before he passed away, Yakov gave Oleg some of his personal effects, which Oleg in turn smuggled out of prison, and eventually they were passed on to me. I have them and will let you see them, but among them was a letter from Yakov's brother. His name was Leo. He's also dead. Yakov left Semyon in his brother's care when he knew he was soon to end up in prison. Semyon was about five years old at the time." Cameron paused at a strangled groan from her mother. Surely Cecilia must be thinking of the terrible hardship of father and son parting. Cameron went on. "Leo had Semyon for a couple of years. There was a terrible famine in Russia at that time. Leo's youngest child died, and he could not afford to keep Semyon any longer, feeling he was depriving his own children, so he found a way to get the child adopted."

"Oh, that poor child," sighed Cecilia. "How traumatic for him to lose his father, then so quickly lose the only other family he had known."

"Mom, I spoke with Leo's daughter, Semyon's cousin. She is a lovely girl, a year younger than Semyon, and she adored him. Would you like to know what she said of him?"

Cecilia hesitated, a look of almost panic in her eyes. "Knowing would make me become more attached, Cameron. Should I let myself get attached? I know you didn't find him, and now you have been forced to leave the country. How much hope is there of ever finding him now?"

"I have come to place a lot of stock in hope, Mom. I've heard you talk about God opening doors. Well, it seems some doors were opened in Russia regarding Semyon. I truly don't know what God intends, but I really do believe He has been a part of this. I think it is safe to hope He will make something more of it."

"My, my!" exclaimed Cecilia. "I wonder if I will ever get used to you talking like this, dear. It warms my heart, and it does make me believe God can indeed do anything. Tell me, then . . . tell me about my . . . about Semyon."

Cameron grasped her mother's hand and shared what Marfa Elichin had said about her cousin, how he had always been a champion of righteous causes, even young as he'd been at the time; how he had fought for her and others when they had been wronged, even when it meant standing up to bullies much bigger than he.

"Mom," Cameron finished, "I was afraid of becoming attached, too, but it's too late, I think. I want to know him, and I am almost certain he is still alive. Marfa had the name of the man who arranged the adoption. My friend Yuri Fedorcenko, Sophia's father, found this man and spoke to him! He was very defensive and secretive. Why would he be that way unless he was protecting someone? If only I could have spoken to the man, but I had to leave the country shortly after I learned of Yuri's encounter. I doubt, though, that I could have gotten near him without causing an international incident."

"I'm glad you didn't. You've had enough troubles in Russia." Cecilia paused, glanced for a moment out the train window. "What will you do now, Cameron—I mean about your doctor?"

"Somehow, I will get back into Russia," she said with a confidence that she truly felt. Alex had always assured her they would have a future together. She had to believe him. "Mom, I haven't told you something about him because there has never been the chance. But even if Alex could get out of Russia and make it back to America, it is doubtful he'd be able to practice medicine here because of some problems he had in the past."

"Then you would stay in Russia?" Her tone was tinged with disbelief. Cecilia's experience in Russia had never been positive, so how could she imagine anyone wanting to stay there if they didn't have to? Cameron herself had often pondered that possibility. She loved Russia, but live there forever? She knew it would be a huge sacrifice.

"I don't know," she replied honestly. "I love Alex so, and he is such a huge part of me. People are supposed to make sacrifices for love, aren't they?"

"Cameron, don't ever make any so-called sacrifices that you will later resent your man for."

Cecilia, of course, was speaking from experience. She had sacrificed her own child for the sake of her marriage.

"I would like to meet this man who has won the heart of my independent, self-reliant daughter. He must be remarkable."

"He is. So strong, but so tender." She suddenly felt her cheeks heat up, and she laid her chilly hands on them. "Goodness! See what he does to me? I swore I'd never become giddy over a man."

"Oh yes, I remember that well."

"But you always said I'd change my tune when the right fellow came along."

"I did indeed." Cecilia chuckled. "I am a wise old gal, aren't I?"

"Mom, I was so worried about coming home, but everything has been wonderful. I missed you more than I knew."

"I'm happy you are here. I hope you stick around for a while." When Cameron opened her mouth to gently clue her mother in to reality, Cecilia added wryly, "I know it won't be forever, maybe not even a month. I'll appreciate what I am given, but I know your father will do what he can to keep you here."

"He has promised me the moon." Cameron still couldn't believe that encounter with her father.

"He'll never show it, but I know he is ecstatic about your coming back to work for him. Did Max take the news well?"

"He wasn't happy, but I think down deep he knew if Dad ever offered me another job, I would take it. I'm still not entirely certain I've done the right thing, that it will work, especially if Dad tries to control me too much. But I had to try. I had to give him another chance."

The conversation lulled a bit, and Cameron's gaze focused out the window. She wondered if her eagerness to take this trip was just a way to postpone the true test of the arrangement with her father. She wanted to cling to their last meeting, and she feared their fragile bonding would crumble too easily. Her father had not changed *that* much. It was in his nature to control all he could. Well, Max had told her she could always come back to the *Globe*.

As the scenery slid past the window, she thought about Jackie. The closer they came to Manzanar, the more dismal the landscape became. Her mother had told her it was Jackie's choice to join Sam and his family in Manzanar, but could she truly be happy here locked behind barbed wire? Cameron drew the all-too-obvious comparison between Jackie's situation and hers with Alex. Jackie had truly made that ultimate sacrifice. Was that the power of love, then? Would Cameron act in the same vein when her moment of choice came? Or had it already come and she had chosen selfishly? Might she have been permitted to stay in Russia had she committed to relinquishing her citizenship? Perhaps she would never know.

Cecilia had said Jackie was free to leave the camp at any time— but her baby would have to stay. What kind of world had this country become? Cameron had come to idealize America in the face of Russian repression, but now she was about to be thrust into the reality of Americans locked up merely because of race. Of course racism had always been a sickness in America, but was she ready to look into this blatant face of it? And not do something about it? Perhaps that's one reason why she had been forced home. She had the power of the press at her disposal.

The eight-mile bus ride from Lone Pine was not pleasant. Cameron had been toughened by far worse excursions in Russia, but Cecilia did not take the winding roads well and was quite green by the time they arrived at the tall gate of the concentration camp. Cameron's own stomach lurched when she viewed the guard towers manned by armed soldiers. That was disheartening enough, but to think her sister lived here! When Cameron had heard about the internment of the Japanese in America, she had never dreamed it would touch her personally.

Cecilia had called ahead, so Jackie was expecting them and greeted them in the administration office. After hugs and kisses, she took them across the camp to her apartment, where the baby and her family were waiting.

Cameron was stunned at how many people were expected to stay in the small apartment. She was more astounded at how naturally Jackie fit in. Cameron did not believe herself to be a racist, but she was acutely aware of the roomful of Japanese faces and her own contrasting Caucasian face. Even little Emi Colleen had distinctly Japanese features, but Jackie flowed with it all as if she did not even notice.

The Okuda clan was warm and friendly, those present at least. Sam was expected at any minute and had planned to be there for Cameron and Cecilia's arrival but had probably been held up at work. Sam's brother wasn't there, and no explanation had been given for that. Nevertheless, the oldest member, and patriarch, Hiroshi Okuda, rose and formally shook Cameron's hand and, after acknowledging Cecilia in the same manner, resumed his chair and said nothing more the entire time. Not so the rest of the family. The three daughters asked about news from the "outside."

"We don't get much news in here," Jackie explained.

"Well, you have come to the right person," Cameron chuckled. "The war—"

"Oh, we don't want to know about the war," the girl named Miya said. "What are the new styles? I heard skirts are shorter in order to conserve fabric."

Cameron laughed. "About style, I am the *wrong* person. I haven't been here long enough to know anything current. I've been in Russia, where most people still dress in styles of the thirties."

While Cameron chatted with the girls, Cecilia and Mrs. Okuda put their heads together over Emi's bassinet while Mrs. Okuda shared with the baby's other grandma a detailed report of all her newest feats and wonders. Finally Cameron pulled herself away from the younger girls and went to the bassinet to view her new little niece.

"Jackie, she is beautiful!" Cameron said dutifully, though it was true enough. In this child the races had come together in a perfect blend.

"Come and hold her," offered Jackie.

"Oh . . . uh . . . maybe later," Cameron hedged. When was the last time she had held a baby? Perhaps never? But when she glanced at her sister, there was a look of deep disappointment on Jackie's face. "Jackie, I—" What could she say? Admit that she was afraid to hold her niece, that she was certain once the child got trapped in her awkward arms, she would surely start to wail?

"I'll fix us some tea," Jackie said, her tone suddenly formal, though it also held a slight tremor.

No one else seemed aware of the emotion in the exchange between the sisters. The grandmas continued to coo over the baby, the other girls went about their own business, and the oldest of them asked to be excused and left the apartment.

Cameron watched her sister go to a corner of the room where there was a small table with a hot plate on it and a teakettle on that. She tried to puzzle out the meaning of her sister's reaction. Wouldn't Jackie normally have just kidded Cameron about her lack of maternal instincts? But they had been apart so long, how could she know what was normal for Jackie anymore? Jackie had been a teenager when Cameron had truly known her last. Her baby sister must certainly have gone through tremendous changes in the last two years. For one thing, she was married and a mother, not to mention the challenges her special circumstances must surely have placed upon her.

Cameron went to the table where Jackie worked. "Can I help?"

"There's really no room for help." Jackie filled the kettle with water from a bottle on the table. Cameron saw no sink or other plumbing in the apartment.

"Somehow I put my foot in my mouth, Jackie. I didn't mean to hurt your feelings."

"I'll recover." Jackie took cups, Japanese style without handles, from a shelf and set them on a tray.

"Then I *did* hurt your feelings?"

"Well, what do you expect when you don't want to hold my child?" She took down a tin of tea and, perhaps more forcefully than necessary, scooped out tea leaves from it, dumping them into a china pot that matched the cups.

"You know me, Jackie. How I am around children."

"Are you sure it is children in general or just those with slanted eyes?"

Cameron gasped. She'd never suspected this to be at the core of her sister's reaction. "Jackie, I am shocked you would even think such a thing of me!" She gently placed her hand on her sister's chin and nudged her face so she would look directly at Cameron. "Listen to me and know without a doubt that my refusal to hold Emi has *nothing* to do with that. I was—" she gulped and made herself admit it—"afraid. Afraid that she would scream once I touched her or spit up or whatever else babies do when they are unhappy. The last thing on earth I'd want is for my own niece to hate me, her totally inept aunt, which might not happen if I just avoided her. Please believe me, sis."

A small smile played on Jackie's lips. "I'm sorry I thought such a thing of you. I guess I am a bit touchy." Lowering her voice, she added, "Even Mom had a hard time warming up. And Dad has never even come to see his granddaughter. That hurts me so much."

Cameron put her arms around her sister. "I am so sorry, Jackie!" Tears moistened her eyes.

Jackie sniffed back her own tears, then said in a lighter tone, "I'll tell you one thing, sis, I know for sure my daughter *won't* like you if you avoid her, but if you reach out to her, at least you have a fifty-fifty chance of being accepted. You always did like to take chances."

"Those are pretty good odds, I guess."

"You might even grow to like the feeling. There's really nothing like holding a child in your arms, especially if it is your own."

"I've been thinking about that lately," Cameron admitted.

"Oh, you have? Could it be because of a certain doctor?"

The kettle began to boil, and Jackie lifted it from the burner and poured water into the pot.

"Yes, sis, it is exactly because of my doctor." Again Cameron felt a blush rise in her cheeks as she thought of her feelings for Alex. "I am very much in love with him, and I could easily forget my fears and have his babies."

"I am so happy for you, Cameron!"

"Unfortunately half a world separates us, and an entire government is bent on keeping us apart."

Jackie placed a comforting arm around Cameron. "God will work it out."

"I believe that, too."

"Mom told me about your new commitment to God. I—"

"You wouldn't believe it until you saw it, eh?"

Jackie laughed, as Cameron had obviously guessed right. "I truly believe anything can happen now," she added, her earnestness still touched with amusement.

"That's really something coming from you, Jackie, forced to be in a place like this. I'm sure it hasn't been easy for you."

"I hope we have time later to talk all about it."

But there was something in Jackie's tone that seemed to say the opposite, that she didn't want to talk about it at all, not so much because she didn't want to confide in Cameron but more that she just wanted to talk about anything else but this place.

"Now, let's serve this tea before it gets cold. And maybe we can pry Emi from Mom's arms so you can practice a bit on her."

27

CAMERON GAZED down at the child in her arms. She wasn't screaming. Wonder of wonders! The two-month-old child was awake and cooing, a little drool dribbling down the corner of her lips and bubbling each time she made a sound.

"I think she likes you," Jackie said.

"I know I like her." Cameron grinned.

"I think if everyone was given a baby to hold, there would be peace in this world," said Mrs. Okuda as she looked on. She and Cecilia had been offering motherly suggestions whenever Cameron's technique became awkward. Everyone was seated in chairs that Sam had borrowed from neighbors in preparation for their visit.

As the women were agreeing with Mrs. Okuda's wisdom, Sam finally made his appearance.

"I'm sorry I'm late," he said, removing his jacket and hanging it on a nail in the wall. "The freeze last night broke some pipes, and that backed up everything." First he greeted his mother-in-law. "Mrs. Hayes, I am so glad to see you again."

"Thank you for having us, Sam."

Though they spoke formally to each other, both their tones held warmth. There was no animosity between them, that was clear.

Sam turned to Cameron. "At last I meet my world-traveling sister-in-law. Jackie speaks so highly of you."

"She does the same with you, Sam." Cameron held out her hand, and Sam grasped it warmly. "I owe you a hug when my lap isn't occupied and I can stand up."

Sam gazed down at Emi with a look of wonder in his eyes. "I understand completely. She is the most incredible creature, isn't she? I still can hardly believe she's mine."

Jackie rose and came to him, linked her arm around his, then clearing her throat daintily, said, "I had a little something to do with her, too, Sam, my love."

"You are everything that is beautiful about her," he said gently, and somehow the words came off genuinely without being sticky sweet.

Cameron took a moment to study her sister and brother-in-law covertly while their attention was on the baby. They seemed very comfortable close to each other. There was still some of the newly-wed intensity about them, for they had not yet been married a full year, yet Cameron sensed a depth to their affection that wasn't dependent upon physical gestures. When Jackie resumed her seat, a definite connection remained between husband and wife, and when their gazes happened to meet, there were many levels of meaning in the momentary exchanges, as if already they could communicate reams to each other with a mere look. Cameron wondered if she and Alex were the same way. Though they had known each other as long as Jackie and Sam, their time together had been so limited, perhaps too much to have reached that level. But Cameron longed for it to be so.

Everyone visited for a time. Jackie made more tea and asked if Cameron and Cecilia could wait a couple of hours and eat dinner with them in the mess hall. They assured her they could, but in the meantime she found a box of crackers and served that with the fresh tea. Before long Emi fell asleep in Cameron's arms, and fond aunt though she was, Cameron began to grow restless. Well, she couldn't expect to change overnight! It was enough that at least on this first try with tending a baby, she hadn't dropped the poor thing on her head.

"I was wondering," Cameron said, "is anyone up for giving me a bit of a tour of the camp before dinner?"

"That's a great idea," said Sam. Cameron sensed that perhaps he'd grown a bit bored with the visiting, as well.

"Why don't you children go," offered Mrs. Okuda, "and unless Mrs. Hayes wants to go also, she and I can watch Emi."

"I am more than willing to help with the baby-sitting," Cecilia said with a smile.

Everyone else bundled up in their coats and left the apartment. The two younger girls, whom Cameron had heard the Okuda clan refer to more than once as the little sisses, joined them but only for a short way before they went off to find their friends.

A chilly wind gusted around the remaining three, blowing dust all around them. Cameron pulled her neck scarf up around her mouth and nose and noticed Jackie did the same. Sam had no scarf but managed by using his hand to cover his mouth when the dust became too intrusive. They kept to the more sheltered areas nearer the barracks.

"There really isn't much to see," Sam offered apologetically. This was now his home, and admittedly there was little to be proud of.

"I mostly wanted some fresh air." Cameron gave a cough, and they all chuckled. "What's it like here in the summer?"

"About the same," said Jackie. "Only hot and dusty instead of cold and dusty."

"They chose prime real estate for us," Sam said, and though he tried to infuse his words with humor, he simply could not hide his bitterness.

"Tell me about your life here," Cameron urged. "I really want to hear about it."

"Do you plan to write about it for your newspaper?" Sam asked.

"That would depend on many things. Would you mind?"

"Not in the least, but the administration might have something to say about a journalist roaming around here unsupervised."

"Of course I would have to go to the administration office and inform them of my intention." She gave her brother-in-law a side-long glance. "Is it far?"

"A good ways across the compound."

"I guess we better head over there then." As Sam nodded, Cameron laid her hand on his arm. "But, Sam, I am so tired from my trip, can we walk slowly? Very slowly, in fact."

Sam laughed. "And there is a way to avoid some of this wind. It's a bit circuitous but far better than breathing dust."

"Lead on, Sam."

Sam and Jackie accommodated Cameron by talking freely of their life at Manzanar. In one sense Cameron was given a picture of Main Street, U.S.A. There were high schools with football teams and pep squads, a drama club that actually did a production of *Our Town*. There were sock hops and bands emulating Tommy Dorsey and Glenn Miller. This youthful tendency, Sam pointed out, was because more than seventy percent of the Japanese interned were Nisei, and most of these were under the age of thirty.

"That means more than seventy percent are American citizens?" Cameron confirmed.

"That's right. Though most are not old enough to vote. I believe if the Japanese had that kind of political power, we might have escaped this as did the Germans and Italians."

"Still, many are old enough to be in the Army," Jackie added.

"I can still hardly believe something like this is happening in America," Cameron breathed. "Tell me more about this loyalty questionnaire you mentioned. That was for the purpose of military registration?"

"Yes, also for relocation."

"That would be good, wouldn't it?"

"Many, especially the elders, are afraid to leave the camps. They have nothing to go to. They lost everything in the evacuation. For example, what would happen if I answered yes in the oath and I was drafted? And then my parents answered yes and they were relocated? Who would take care of them? My father can barely speak English. Should my mother at age sixty start to work as a domestic? And in the present political mood, would anyone hire either of them?"

"That's a terrible prospect," said Cameron, "but what is even worse about that loyalty oath is that it presumes guilt."

"Exactly!" said Sam. "That is one among many reasons my brother has already answered no. He was going to ignore the thing but at the last minute decided that was the coward's way. We expect him to be hauled off to a special camp for disloyals at any time."

"If I understand correctly," said Cameron, "isn't he only seventeen?"

"Yes, but that was the age cutoff for the questionnaire because men of that age will likely be eligible for the military before the war ends."

"May I ask how you plan to answer the questionnaire?"

"I will probably have to answer yes so that my family isn't deserted altogether, but that may happen anyway if I must go into the Army."

Jackie put her arm around Sam's and held him close. "There is not a family in this camp that isn't experiencing intense torment right now. The family and honoring one's parents are such important parts of Japanese culture, Cameron, and the family is being torn to shreds."

"How do you feel about the Army, Sam?" Cameron asked. "Besides the obvious reluctance to leave your family?"

"I tried to enlist on December 8, 1941, and was turned away along with hundreds of other Nisei." Jackie seemed surprised and Sam added, "I never mentioned it to you because it came to nothing. But at that time none of us thought twice about serving our country. I met a Japanese fellow who was in the Army during the attack on Pearl Harbor. He said there were about five thousand Japanese in the Army at that time, and most were summarily discharged except for those needed as translators. So why this sudden interest in gauging our moral fitness for military duty? The recruiters who have come here say it is our golden opportunity to prove our loyalty. Why now?"

"I know you don't expect an answer," said Jackie, "but I heard the reason is that the U.S. Army has been quite impressed with the Japanese fighting men and would like a few on their side."

"I can believe that," added Cameron. "No one expected the sweeping victories the Japanese have made in the war."

"In any case, Cameron, I have yet to answer your initial question." Sam paused as they passed a small group of men coming toward them. One nodded toward Sam, almost covertly, Cameron thought. Sam gave a brief nod in response. No one else in the group was friendly at all. Sam continued, "I will go if I am drafted, but I won't go voluntarily. That is expecting too much of a man locked behind barbed wire. But if I have to fight in this war, I will do so with my whole heart. I still love this country. I am not like some who would rather go to Japan than serve America."

"Is that how your brother feels?"

"I hope that you can talk to him before you leave." Sam smiled with affection. "He will talk your ear off about politics. But I

believe I am right, I hope at least, in saying that Toshio has no desire
for Japan. In his heart and experiences he is as American as you. He
has become very active in lodging protests with camp administrators and the WRA, but he doesn't want to leave America. He wants
to change it for good."

"Cameron, do you think Dad will let you print any of this?"
Jackie asked. "So far, he has supported the decisions of the WRA.
He hasn't been as vicious as some, but with his ties now to the Jap-
anese community, you'd think he'd be more supportive of us."

"I am not surprised he isn't," Cameron replied. "He has probably convinced himself that he's helping you by supporting the WRA.
Who can say what his reasoning is."

"You would think because he's an immigrant himself he would
have more sympathy."

"Dad remembers every wrong done him with a vengeance."
Cameron shook her head, thinking ruefully of the dichotomy that
was her father. "But he only wants to remember his immigrant
status when it benefits him. Most immigrants want to forget as soon
as they lose their accents."

"If we Japanese could lose the marks that set us apart, we
would," said Sam. After pondering a moment, he added, "In a way
this evacuation has changed that attitude a little. Many of us are
drawing closer to our Japanese culture. And that's good. It wasn't
healthy when we wished so hard that we could be white."

Cameron placed an arm around Sam's shoulder. "I am so glad
I've had this chance to get to know you, Sam. My sister made the
perfect choice for a husband."

Sam grinned and pulled Jackie close on his other side. "A true
miracle of God."

"Somehow," Cameron added emphatically, "I am going to do
something to help this situation."

"That, too, will take a miracle. Few newspapers, or any
publications for that matter, have dared to speak out against the
evacuation. Since this has the approval of the president himself, any
protest is thought to be un-American."

"I don't mind going up against FDR," Cameron said. "It's Keagan Hayes I worry about."

Jackie laughed. "That never bothered you before."

"Now I have a bit more of a conscience," Cameron said with a chuckle. Then more seriously she added, "Maybe no one realized it, but it did bother me a great deal. I hate always fighting him."

"Then don't," said Sam. "The fact that you're working for him again must mean things are better between the two of you. Don't risk that over this story."

"But this is important."

"Yes it is, but there will be other champions of this cause. You may not have another chance with your father. I have told Jackie this, and I tell you—I do not ever want to come between you and your father. I know he is not the most accepting of our marriage, but it's not because I haven't done everything that could be done to make it so."

"That's just it," Cameron replied. "Sometimes it's impossible to please him."

"Still, don't risk your relationship because of this."

"You're a very fine man, Sam. I'll take your words under advisement."

A few minutes later the administration building came into view, and the three stopped. But Cameron had learned an important lesson in Russia—to take every opportunity presented and worry later about the censors. In this sense her father was the biggest censor of all, but even she knew he had experienced some changes, no matter how small, in the last two years. Maybe he was looking for a reason to alter the *Journal*'s stand on the WRA. If not . . . well, she had learned another lesson in Russia—how to back off when necessary. Perhaps she and her father had both come to the place where they could actually compromise.

Cameron's articles on the concentration camps and the WRA did not get published. They were good, too.

"There is not one iota of editorializing in these," she told her father as he looked over her submissions.

"Not per se, of course. You're too good for that," he replied. "But you and I both know the news can be subtly slanted by canny omissions." He arched a brow. "Which is quite obvious in what I read."

"Why? Because I don't sing the praises of the WRA?" She leaned across his desk and shuffled through the pages. "But there"—she

stabbed a finger at one of the paragraphs—"I clearly state the difficulties the War Relocation Authority has had in administering such
a diverse group of American citizens."

Keagan rolled his eyes. "Don't make me laugh."

"All right, Dad, there are omissions, I admit. But you have also
slanted the news by omitting from the *Journal* anything about the
camps at all."

"Touché!"

"Dad, you must know that what has happened to the Japanese
is wrong. You and I have clashed about many things, but I have
never doubted your honesty as a newspaperman."

He lifted his eyes to meet hers. The green was sharp and hard
like the edge of an emerald, but the look emanating from them was
not malicious. "It isn't widely known, yet it is no huge secret, either,
whom my youngest daughter married and what has become of her."
His even tone betrayed the merest hint of a tremor. "Do you not
think that if I came out in opposition of the WRA, I would also be
accused of using the paper to champion my personal cause?"

"You wouldn't be the first newsman to do so."

"It would still be just as wrong."

"Is that why you've shied away from it altogether?"

He hesitated, but that honesty she respected about her father
came through. "No, not the only reason, but putting everything
together, I've decided this is one matter I shall not meet head on.
Whatever I did, my credibility would be in question, so I will do
nothing."

"But you can't simply ignore the news."

"Don't tell me what I can and can't do! I'm the publisher of this
paper, and that is my prerogative." Calming his tone, he added,
"For once in your life, Cameron, give *me* a break and try to see
matters from my perspective."

She did not like backing down, and she liked even less realizing
that her father had a good point. At least the battle for the Japanese
in the United States was not dependent on her or the *Journal* as its
champion. There were others, as Cameron learned while she
researched her articles, fighting for the cause of the displaced Americans. She made it a priority to use the one tool she still had—she
would pray for those warriors.

PART IV

"Go for broke!"

Motto of the 442nd
Regimental Combat Team

28

Luzon, Philippines
March 1943

TENDING SICK MEN was becoming a routine chore for Blair. There were always two or three down with some tropical ailment, mostly malaria. Then after each mission the company of partisans carried out, one or two usually returned with wounds of varying intensities. This time was no different. Ralph had a gash on his head, Marcos had a bullet in the arm, and Tony Hillerman had been bitten by a snake. The snakebite was the worst. The men had removed most of the venom at the scene but at the cost of a terrible infection growing in Tony's right calf. There were no drugs left to fight the infection. Blair could only keep it clean and pray.

At least there had been no deaths this time. Of course she never saw the dead—the men simply didn't have the strength to haul them back to camp. But in her worst nightmares someone was always carrying Gary's dead body on his shoulders and dumping him on the ground at her feet. They had both accepted the very real possibility that their lives were going to be short. She felt prepared to die but didn't think she could take it if Gary went first, yet that was the most likely scenario because he put his life on the line nearly every day. Lately a rumor had reached them that the Japanese had put a price on his head, making matters worse, because if he was captured, he was likely to be summarily executed once they figured out who he was.

Blair tried not to dwell on the grim reality of life as a fugitive in the Philippine jungle, though there was little to distract her thoughts. Yet a new circumstance made her think on these things more than ever, made her more afraid of dying, more desperate for a future for her and Gary.

"You okay, Blair?" asked Ralph, sitting up on his bed mat. The bandage wrapped around his head was already soaked with blood.

"Ralph, you are supposed to be lying flat, at least until the bleeding stops," she scolded. There simply weren't enough bandages for frequent changes.

"You were hovering there over Tony's leg. I thought you were going to be sick or something," he replied as he lay back on his mat.

"I just got distracted with my thoughts." She began again to vigorously clean Tony's leg.

Just then Gary strode into the camp, two full water skins slung over his shoulder. He handed the skins to Tom Morris, who usually did the cooking, then came over to the makeshift infirmary, which was outdoors because the little hut was hot and stuffy this time of day. The rainy season was over and the temperature had cooled but that still meant ninety-degree days.

"How are these layabouts coming along, Blair?" he asked, amusement taking the edge off the sarcasm.

"Hey, you're just jealous you didn't get wounded so you could get tended by the prettiest nurse on Luzon," said Marcos.

"I've been suspicious you fellows have been standing in front of bullets on purpose," Gary countered. "Now I know the truth of it."

Everyone laughed. Blair forced her amusement and hoped no one noticed. She was too muddled right now, realizing she was going to have to talk to Gary soon, and she didn't know how he would take what she had to say. She wasn't sure how she herself felt about it.

"I'll never take a bullet, or a snake, on purpose, Captain," said Tony, "but it makes it easier knowing we're gonna get cared for so well."

Blair smiled in spite of herself at the sincerity of his words. These men seemed to truly admire and respect her. Maybe that was only because they respected Gary. But still, it felt good. She'd never been good at much of anything except singing, and it never ceased to surprise her that nursing, even her trial-and-error brand of it, should be something she'd excel at.

She finished cleaning Tony's leg, put on a clean bandage, then rose. Gary had crouched down by Ralph, and they were conferring in low tones, probably planning a new mission. The group had grown to about twenty since last fall, though usually there were never more than ten in the camp at any one time. Most of the newcomers were Filipino guerrillas, who often went to their villages to gather information. There was also a wide network of locals, perhaps a hundred, who spied out information, scrounged supplies, or helped occasionally with various attacks against the enemy. This expansion of operations was one reason why the enemy knew of Gary and was on the lookout for him. Not that they had a reliable description of him, but they had learned enough from captured operatives to know he was out there and that much of the havoc raised against the Japanese could be attributed to the Jungle Fox, Gary's code name in honor of another guerrilla fighter, Francis Marion, who had harried the British during the Revolutionary War.

Blair checked with Tom to see if he needed help with dinner preparations, but he had everything under control. Growing impatient to talk with Gary privately, especially if he was planning something that would take him away again, she walked casually over to where he was still talking to Ralph.

"Gary," she broke in, "when you and Ralph are done, can you and I talk for a bit?"

Gary and Ralph exchanged looks. Ralph shrugged.

"We're done," Gary said, rising. "You want to walk a little?"

"That would be good."

They strolled into the jungle—not far, of course, not even close to the first perimeter of sentries. Blair breathed in the lovely jungle fragrances, hoping to steady herself. Gary took her hand in his, and a little electric tingle coursed up her arm. Every time he touched her, it was like the first time, and she never failed to marvel at the sense of security his nearness gave her. And it wasn't entirely a physical security, for a sniper could pick them both off with each step. No, it was the security of being loved—a love without bounds or conditions. She wondered why she was so afraid of telling him what she must.

"What's on your mind, Blair?" he asked gently. "You've seemed tense for a couple of days."

"How long do you think the war can last?" she asked, hedging.

"You know I can't answer that." He paused, and she knew he was determined to give her some answer if only just to please her.

"Any news we get is so jumbled that we have a hard time knowing if it is Jap propaganda or even American propaganda. But I think it's safe to say we've had some big victories against the Japs in the last six months. We're finally getting back on our feet after Pearl Harbor, and you know as well as I that when we do, there'll be no stopping us."

"Then it's only a matter of time?"

"That's safe to say."

"Can we hold out long enough, Gary?"

"It doesn't help to talk about that." He paused in their slow amble, turned toward her, focusing his intense dark eyes down on her. "What's the matter, Blair?"

"Let's sit down." She glanced around, then shrugged. "I guess this is a good enough spot." It was jungle like everything else, but there was a fallen log, half rotten, on which they could sit. There was just enough room for them to sit close side by side. "I know we are trying hard to accept the present and not look too far ahead. But lately all I can think of is the future, and I want so desperately for us to survive to enjoy it. We . . . must have a future, Gary."

"I am so sorry you must endure this—" He stopped suddenly. "What are you trying to tell me? Are you . . ." He closed his eyes and inhaled a breath. "Blair, are you . . ."

"Yes, Gary, we are going to have a baby." She caught her lower lip between her teeth. She wasn't certain how to read his reaction. Joy? Surprise? Disappointment?

"Wow!" A slow grin spread across his face, darkened only by the two days' growth of beard he perpetually wore.

"You're not upset?"

"We did our best to take precautions under the circumstances," he said. "So I look at it as out of our control."

"Like it's God's will?"

"Something like that."

"I never thought it would happen," she said, "what with my poor nutrition and the malaria and who knows what else. I'm not even sure how far along I am because I haven't been regular for months. Maybe I'm wrong altogether. . . ." She paused and shook her head in answer to her own doubt. "But I feel different. A little sick in the mornings, more tired than usual, and . . . I don't know, just different."

"What should we do?" She had never heard him sound so help-less before. "Maybe we could find a doctor in one of the villages."

"There isn't much a doctor can do at this stage," she replied, as if she knew anything about the matter. Whatever nursing she happened to know was entirely limited to wounds and tropical diseases. There had been no call to learn anything about maternity in an Army field hospital. And Blair had never been blessed with an abundance of common sense until lately. But the little that she did have gave her some aid now. "A doctor might be able to confirm it," she went on. "But what else will he tell me? Eat well, drink plenty of milk, that sort of thing?" She gave a shrug. "I can only do what I can do."

"Are you happy about it, Blair?" The intensity of his gaze deepened.

"I feel a little selfish admitting it, but yes, I am. I'm happy to be having our child. I can't help being happy even though everything is against it."

He took her in his arms and held her close. "I'm happy, too. We must trust him or her to God."

"I'll do my best to take care of myself."

"I know you will."

But they both knew how difficult that would be. A baby needed vitamins, calcium, protein. An expectant mother needed those things, as well. Part of Blair hoped it would turn out to be a false alarm. Even if she was capable in her present physical state to bring a baby to term, what then? How could an infant survive this life?

So while accepting the joy of new life—which she knew in her heart was not a false alarm—she also tried to prepare herself for losing it. For the next couple of weeks she fully expected a miscarriage. Though she was trying to spare her mental health by hedging against the worst, it was not a healthy way to live. When she was struck with a bout of malaria, she expected that to be the end. She didn't know what to think after the worst of the attack had passed and nothing happened.

Gary, on the other hand, knew exactly what to think. "Blair, you can't risk another attack. You've got to see a doctor. What if the quinine is hurting the baby?"

She knew he was right. "Have you found a village doctor?"

"I've sent a couple of men to look, but there's no one we can trust." He paused, looking uncertain. When he spoke, his words were slow and conflicted. "You need to go to Manila."

"No," she said flatly.

"Listen to reason, Blair—"

"I don't care if I lose the baby. It's more important that we stay together."

"You don't really mean that."

"I do!" she insisted. "We can have other babies, but who knows what will become of us if we're separated again. I don't think I could bear it."

He gently lifted back a damp strand of her hair. Her fever had just broken, and sweat still ran down the sides of her face. There was only love in his eyes as he responded. "I don't care only for the baby. I worry what it would do to you to have a miscarriage under these conditions. And I've seen men healthier than you die of malaria. I won't risk that. You can use the false papers that Reverend Sanchez got for you and you'll have no problem being treated in a hospital. I'm sure the reverend will even let you stay with him. Now that Mateo is well, he can be our contact with his father."

"You've got it all figured out, then?" she said petulantly. She knew he was only caring for her as he felt a husband should, but the thought of being separated from him again frightened her to her very core.

"Come on, Blair!" he pleaded.

Tearfully she said, "I've been so happy these last months, I can't bear for it to end. And I have a horrible feeling that something awful will happen if we part again."

"I have an awful feeling of what could happen if you stay. I don't want to watch you die. I couldn't bear that." He lifted her hand to his lips and kissed it. "Blair, we've lived each day of the last year on the edge of disaster. This isn't any different. It's just another downslope to the roller coaster we're on."

"Can you promise there will be another uphill, then?"

He shook his head. "But I do know this: Every time I've gone down, I've seen God at the bottom, and when I'm flying to the top, He's been there, too. That's what I can promise. God will be with us together and apart. He'll be the link holding us together."

"Gary, I just remembered something Reverend Sanchez told me." Blair brightened a bit. "Can you get that Bible he gave me?"

Gary searched in her pack and returned with the Bible, handing it to her. She opened quickly to the chapter in Psalms, glad that her memory was still as sharp as ever despite illness.

"'If I take the wings of the morning, and dwell in the uttermost parts of the sea; even there shall thy hand lead me, and thy right hand shall hold me,'" she read, then added, "I guess I'll learn now for certain the truth of that."

"I believe it's true, Blair, or I wouldn't send you away from me."

"I do, too. It's the only way I can find the strength to go."

29

BLAIR WALKED down Dewey Avenue carrying a basket filled with papayas. She hoped the basket made her appear to have a sense of purpose—that is, one besides her true purpose. She was wearing the blue skirt and blouse from Fernando's girlfriend but felt rather conspicuous. She tried to think of why a German woman would be dressed in old country-looking clothes. She recalled seeing some German women who had come to the nightclub before the war, and they had tended to be rather more fashionable than this.

But no one stopped her, no one questioned her. Was it so common, then, for a white woman to be strolling down the street? Or was it just assumed that because of her boldness she must be legal?

As to the first question, Blair saw few white faces. There hadn't been that many Germans or Italians in Manila in the first place. Most white faces had been American or other Allied nationalities, and of course they were now all either in hiding or POWs. So despite her deep tan, she still stood out among the Oriental and Filipino faces. She also still could not help a sense of panic each time she passed a Japanese soldier, which was frequently. They were now the rulers here, and they made their presence clearly felt. But the day-to-day activities of the city had for the most part resumed. Department stores, restaurants, and other businesses were busy. Taxis still raced up and down the avenue, though most other traffic was light because of the limitation on gasoline use imposed by the Japanese.

"Blair!"

A woman's voice called her name. An electric shock of panic raced through her. She nearly stopped and turned, but by some force of will within, she made herself keep moving and not respond. She was not Blair Hayes. Her papers said she was Frau Elsa Dengler. Her story was that she was the widow of Albert Dengler, mining engineer, who had died of a heart attack two months ago. They had come to the Philippines shortly before the war in order to research the purchase of a gold mine.

Blair continued walking as casually as her racing heart would allow, but she now had the feeling of being followed. Who had called out her name? Blair knew very few people in Manila. Her first instinct was that it might be Claudette, but she knew her friend's voice too well for it to be her. Blair had been thinking a lot of Claudette since coming here. This was where they had met. If her friend was in Santo Thomas prison, where mostly civilians were kept, she wouldn't be too far away. Blair silently prayed again, as she had so often, that Claudette was safe wherever she was.

If not Claudette, then who? Only one other name came readily to mind. But if Silvia Wang had somehow come out of hiding and was living in Manila, wasn't she smart enough to know not to call attention to Blair in public like that? More than that, though, did Blair want to run from her?

If it was Silvia, she was a friend, wasn't she?

Although many questions bombarded Blair's mind, she knew she had to find out who it was. Moreover, if whoever had called her name was following her, she could not lead that person to Reverend Sanchez, no matter if it was friend or foe.

Quickly she turned down the next side street, went to the next corner, and turned again, trying to appear elusive, yet at the same time not wanting the person tailing her to lose her. She'd seen this scenario in a movie once. She turned down yet another side street. The narrow street was empty, no pursuer in sight, so she ducked into a recessed alcove of a building. Then she waited.

A couple of moments later a figure appeared at the end of the street, pausing and looking both ways as if uncertain of how to proceed. Blair studied the figure carefully, then stepped into view. The woman looked Blair's way, then hurried toward her.

"How careless of me!" she exclaimed when she reached Blair. "I was certain it was you and knew I'd made a mistake by calling when you kept walking. I was so surprised to see you, I just wasn't thinking."

"Let's keep walking," Blair said as she casually swung back into motion.

"Can you forgive me?" the woman asked as she walked at Blair's side.

"Of course, Silvia," Blair said, smiling at her old friend. "I only hope you can forgive me for ignoring you and for playing this little game."

"What's going on, Blair?"

"Please call me Elsa. I'm a German national now."

"Have you escaped the prison camp?"

"I never was in one. I've been hiding from the Japs since the islands fell."

"My, my!" Silvia was obviously impressed. "We shouldn't talk here. Can you come to my place?"

"It could be dangerous for you."

"No, I'm sure it will be all right. I'm back at the nightclub. It's quite safe there."

Blair did not know where her sudden sense of misgiving was coming from. Silvia had been a good friend. But how could she be so certain her place was safe? Was there any truly safe place in this city unless you were a Jap or a collaborator? But Silvia was neither. She was half Chinese and, because of that, hated by the Japanese. Yet here she was back in Manila and apparently back in her old nightclub. Blair remembered how kind Silvia had been to her and to Claudette. She had given Blair quite a bit of money, calling it severance pay, when they were evacuating. She was a friend.

As they came to the end of the street, where it bisected a busier street, a group of Japanese soldiers, laughing and talking, ambled past. Silvia glanced at Blair and laughed merrily as if at some wry joke. Blair, with hardly a second thought, responded in kind. They were just two women out for a walk. Two beautiful women, unfortunately, because the soldiers noticed them. Ogling them briefly, they made some comments in Japanese, probably the kind soldiers were apt to make at pretty females, then they strutted on.

That helped Blair make her mind up. Silvia's quick wit, despite her initial faux pas, made Blair realize this woman would be a good ally to have. She might be able to give Blair far more help than

273

Reverend Sanchez. Besides, Blair had been having misgivings all along about endangering Sanchez by staying with him. The guerrillas still depended upon him for many of their supplies, and if he were in any way compromised, the band of men, including Gary, would suffer. It would be far harder for a man like him to explain the sudden appearance of a German houseguest than it would for a woman of the world like Silvia. Blair would still make contact with the pastor, but for now she thought it a good idea to feel out these new possibilities.

Silvia's Casa Mañana was exactly as Blair had left it over a year ago. The inside walls and the bar were lined with bamboo, and the ceiling was partially bordered in thatch to give the appearance of a tropical hut. A couple dozen small round glass-topped tables and a few larger ones, all with wicker chairs, dotted the floor. There was a large stage at the front, and between the tables and the stage, a dance floor. Two ceiling fans turned lazily overhead to disperse some of the sultry afternoon air. There were no customers at that time of day because the club didn't open until four o'clock. It was now two in the afternoon.

"I can't believe you're back here," Blair said as she sat with Silvia at one of the round tables. Silvia had gotten them both some cold papaya juice.

Blair noted that Silvia hadn't changed much. Still beautiful and regal in a silk Manchu-style dress, red with embroidered lotus flowers set in a stunning pattern. There was also still a white hibiscus flower tucked behind her ear, enhancing her jet-black hair that was twisted into an intricate bun at the back of her head. Her dark eyes, though as lovely as the rest of her, were still shrewd as a street vendor's. She was half Chinese and half Spanish. Her mother was the daughter of a rich Spanish family, and her father was a Chinese diplomat. Both sides of her family had disowned her and her mother.

"It wasn't by choice," Silvia answered, sipping her drink. "The Japs took over my villa in the mountains. Be glad you never made it there!"

"Did they arrest you? What happened?"

"We made some mutual accommodations," said the older woman cryptically. When Blair cocked a puzzled brow, Silvia added, "I won't go into the grim details, but I did what I had to do to survive. There was a Jap general who wasn't too disgusting. . . ." She gave a shrug to finish her thought.

"Silvia, are you collaborating with the Japanese?" Blair asked bluntly, unable to hide the repulsion in her tone.

"Surviving, Blair."

"There's a difference?"

Blair truly didn't want to judge her friend. She could still remember when she was trying to survive back in the States and how the criticism of others had infuriated her. She also thought of her attempts to survive since the war began. Maybe she hadn't done anything truly dishonorable, but she certainly had been forced at times to live like an animal. How could she judge anyone?

"I'm sorry, Silvia," she added more thoughtfully. "It must have been hard for you."

"Maybe I cared too much about staying alive. Maybe I was too much of a coward to want to face prison. Blair, you should see how they are forced to live in the camps. Maybe—and I guess this is how I sleep at night—I thought I could do more good on the outside." Pausing, she gave a quick glance around, though they were obviously alone, "You know, in the Resistance."

"I knew you couldn't be a collaborator, not really!"

"I've had to do a lot I'm not proud of."

"Gary has said the same thing about what he's had to do since the war began. I've felt that way, too. Maybe God will have a special dispensation for those of us caught in this nightmare. He knows what is in our hearts."

"I've missed you, Bl—I mean, Elsa." Silvia smiled and grasped Blair's hand across the table. "Let's speak of more pleasant things. You mentioned Gary. Did you find him, then?"

"Oh yes, I did! I only just left him yesterday. He's—" But Blair felt a sudden inner check. Maybe she trusted Silvia, yet for everyone's good, it was probably best to keep details vague, for now at least. "He's out there still. He escaped from the Japs early on and has been hiding ever since. I found him a few months ago."

"You've also been a fugitive all this time?"

"Yes. Can you believe my having survived in the jungle like Jane and Tarzan? I still can hardly believe it when I think of it."

"What made you come back to Manila?"

Blair saw no reason not to tell the truth, especially if her friend might be able to help. "I'm pregnant, Silvia." She smiled and felt a blush rise on her cheeks. That, too, was something she still found hard to believe. "I've had malaria, and Gary worried about my health, so we decided I should come to Manila and try to get medical care. I've got forged papers."

Silvia gave a low whistle. "You have been busy, haven't you, dear? And I'll wager that's only half your story. But I don't want to hear everything. I have a feeling that if I know less it'll be better for everyone. I give my word I won't tell the enemy, but . . . in this world, ignorance isn't always a bad thing."

They both fell silent, each absorbing what they'd heard and assessing what to do next. Blair still was uncertain of what to do about Sanchez. She did know she should not tell Silvia about him.

"Do you have a place to go?" Silvia asked.

"Nothing definite."

Silvia smiled knowingly. "You can stay with me . . . Elsa. And you can work here in the club if you are up to it."

"The danger—?"

"No one will think anything of my having a dear old German friend come for a visit and fill her time with singing."

"I'm a recently widowed wife of a mining engineer," offered Blair.

"All the better. You are probably quite desperate for some means of supporting yourself and your expected baby. By the way, when do you expect your little arrival?"

Blair shrugged and gave a frustrated sigh. "I can't tell for sure. I think I'm two or three months along."

"Then you might have a couple of months before you start to show." Silvia scrutinized Blair carefully. "We might be able to concoct some costumes that could extend that a bit."

"Truthfully, Silvia, this is probably the best option I have."

Silvia continued to eye Blair before adding solemnly, "You can trust me . . . Elsa, I swear it."

"It's not that," Blair replied. "This was not my initial plan. I never expected to see you." As Blair heard her own words, she realized that was a good point. This meeting with Silvia could not possibly have been planned as any entrapment by anyone. This could very well be God's answer to the misgivings she'd had all along about endangering Reverend Sanchez. Or was it just impulsive, flighty Blair?

I need to decide now, she thought. God, what should I do? She looked again at Silvia, who was sipping her juice. Suddenly whatever reservations she had before dissolved. Something made Blair certain that God, for whatever the reason, had put Silvia in her path today.

"Silvia, I would happily accept your offer."

———

Of all that had happened in the last few days, nothing was stranger to Blair than this evening, standing on the stage of the Casa Mañana and singing "If I Didn't Care" to a roomful of primarily Japanese faces. Silvia's band wasn't as good as the one she'd had before the war—half of those musicians were now in POW camps. But it was adequate, especially since most in the audience weren't experts on Western music. That was still what they wanted to hear, though, even if it wasn't the best.

Besides the music, a murmur of voices and the tinkling of glassware filled the room, but as always, Blair absorbed herself in the music and heard little else.

When she finished her set for the evening—she did only one show because she was still not physically fit for more—Silvia took her by the hand.

"I'd like to introduce you to some of my regulars," she said quietly.

Blair gave her a slightly panicked look. She wasn't sure she was ready for this.

"Better get it over with," Silvia answered her look. "It's always best to be right up front, give your own answers before their questions catch you off guard."

Blair could see the logic of that, but she could also see how a mere introduction could raise many questions. But before she could protest, they were standing before one of the larger round tables. There were five Japanese officers seated with two pretty Filipina women who Blair thought were probably also *surviving* the best way they could—at least that was better than thinking they were collaborators.

Blair did not remember any of the complex Japanese names as

Silvia introduced the men. One man was a general, three were no less than colonels, and one was a lowly captain. Chairs were brought up to the table when she and Silvia were invited to join the group. The general was quite handsome, Blair thought. He was about forty, with a slight brushing of gray in his dark hair. The corners of his eyes crinkled when he smiled, and he had a rather decent smile, which disconcerted Blair because she did not wish to think of any Jap as decent. He spoke no German but fair English, so they communicated in that language. The other officers, Blair assumed, spoke only Japanese, for they did not join in the conversation except occasionally when the general translated a comment or two. The Filipina girls also did not take part but spent the time mostly clinging to one or the other of the officers in rather seductive ways. The general seemed more interested in Silvia than the Filipinas, and Blair was certain this must be the general of whom Silvia had spoken earlier.

Questions, of course, were asked, but only conversationally, never with the tone of an interrogation. Blair managed to keep her story straight and was quick to answer *Cologne* when asked where in Germany she was from. She'd spent two weeks there when she'd gone to Europe on tour after graduating from high school, so if any of these men happened to know anything about Germany, she could be fairly intelligent on the subject. She also spoke her English with a good German accent.

After ten minutes of conversation in this vein, she was beginning to think of a way to excuse herself when the captain asked her to dance.

Not revealing the dismay she felt inside, she gave the man a wide smile and said, "I'd be delighted." What else could she do?

They rose, and he took her hand, leading her out to the dance floor. The band was now playing "Penny Serenade." The captain placed his arm around Blair's shoulders and his hand at her waist. Inside, Blair cringed at his touch. Unlike the general, this man looked so much more like the Japs she'd encountered all too often in the jungle. Perhaps because he was young, of small stature, and dark of hair and eye. She thought of the wounds he, as a representative of all the enemy, had inflicted upon her friends. She thought of the suffering she herself had experienced because of those like him. She thought of the danger Gary was still in of taking a Jap bullet to the heart. Her stomach churned so wildly that she wanted to vomit.

But she danced and smiled. What an actress she was!

He could speak better English than he had let on at the table. "I greatly admire your Hitler," he said in thickly accented tones, mixing the pronunciation of r's and l's.

"Do you?" she said. "I didn't know you could speak English."

"Best not to know more than general, eh?" He smiled, his lips parting into what seemed to Blair a devilish grin. Her insides quaked.

"You are Nazi, yes?"

"Of course," she said. "My husband was a Party official back in Cologne," she added, just for the sake of talking, hoping that would calm her raging emotions. She amazed herself at how readily the lies flowed from her, but she was glad now she was so adept at thinking on her feet.

"Together we be victory!" enthused the officer.

"Victorious," she corrected.

"I go to the field tomorrow." This he had to repeat twice because he so mangled the final word.

"Really? You won't be in danger, will you?" She feigned concern.

"Always danger out there. But we have many new equipment recently arrive. We take care of them enemy who now sneak around in most dishonorable way. But maybe you and me say good-bye later . . . at my place, yes?"

"I have a previous engagement. I am so sorry. Perhaps another time?" Unless Gary finds you and kills you before then, she thought ruefully.

The dance lasted another minute, and then they returned to the table, where Blair remained only a few more minutes before an opportunity to leave arose. She quickly took it and went backstage to her dressing room. Once there she shut the door and sank down on the upholstered chair by her makeup table, gasping in several deep breaths before the trembling stopped. She had been steady as a rock while out there with the soldiers, but the trembling had begun the moment she was out of sight of them. She supposed that was something to be thankful for.

She thought of that dance, of the horrible touch of the enemy, and she desperately wanted to get away, back to the guerrilla camp. That dirty primitive place with its disease and starvation seemed a haven compared to this. Some part of her knew that a good Christian should not hate others, yet she feared she did hate the Japanese. How could she continue here surrounded by these loathsome people who tortured and killed?

But she had to for her baby's sake. She'd had a brief visit with Reverend Sanchez since her meeting with Silvia. He had supported her decision to stay with Silvia. He was deeply involved in the underground and feared he was being watched, so he felt certain her appearance would only endanger them both. He also thought Silvia would be better able to get Blair medical aid, which turned out to be true, for Silvia had already gotten her an appointment to see a doctor. So Blair had to go on. She told herself that perhaps once she saw a doctor and got some medicine, she could return to Gary.

Almost anything would be better than having to keep up her act, smiling, dancing, conversing with the enemy. She thought of her fake concern when that captain had told her of his next assignment. Ugh!

Then another thought edged around her revulsion. His next assignment? What Gary would have given to hear about that! And the fact that a large shipment of matériel had recently arrived in Manila. If only Gary knew, he could have planned an operation to blow the stuff up.

She hadn't even tried to get information from that stupid officer. What might he have told her if she had applied a few more feminine wiles?

Blair started trembling again.

What was she thinking? Well, she expected a nightclub full of Japanese soldiers was probably a treasure trove of loose tongues. How hard could it be to extract a bit of information and then pass it through the underground to Gary? And how much trouble could she get into for doing it? It was a sure bet the hapless soldiers who talked were never going to admit they'd spilled secrets to a pretty nightclub singer.

Whoa, girl! A minute ago you were shaking just at the thought of touching one of them. Now you want to make a living of it?

She wouldn't go beyond a dance and a wink and a smile, that

was certain. But if a dance could help Gary, wasn't it worth the sense of revulsion it produced in her? Look what he risked every day. And the risk to her would be minimal, far less than what she risked just sitting in the guerrilla camp. She would be sensible about it. The safety of the baby would always come first. But this was war, the world was in flames, and there could be no true safety for her or her baby until the war was over. She would do what she could to bring that end about sooner.

30

Manila, Philippines
July 1943

As Blair approached Reverend Sanchez's church on this morning in late July with rain splashing freely off her umbrella, she felt more buoyed in spirits than she had been in a long time. She went in through the front door and slipped into one of the back pews. No one had cause to question her attendance, as she was a German Protestant attending one of the Protestant churches in the city. She came today because it was Sunday, and she'd established early in her stay the habit of attending church. She and the pastor did not usually meet personally when she came to church, or any other time for that matter. But occasionally she would linger after the service, as any parishioner might, and they would speak for a few moments. Usually if she had information to pass on, she did so by way of a go-between, seldom giving it directly to Sanchez.

She enjoyed the service, the hymns especially. But unlike previously when she had attended church before making a commitment to God and had ignored the sermons with daydreaming, she now listened carefully to Sanchez. She discovered he was a wise man. His sermons were not fiery admonishments to walk the narrow way. They were, in fact, not very fiery at all. When he spoke, it was more like teaching. He'd choose a passage from the Bible and explain it. Blair was so ignorant of biblical matters that she truly appreciated this style. There was so much for her to learn that she needed a teacher far more than a preacher right now.

An hour later the congregation exited the sanctuary, and she waited patiently, still seated in her pew, as the minister greeted his departing flock.

She thought about the last months and marveled at how right it had been for her to come to Manila. She was glad Gary had been strong for them both and had insisted she do this. Blair found herself in a fairly comfortable niche in Manila. She'd been seeing a doctor at a clinic and had learned her baby would be due sometime in September. Her malaria was under control, and with vitamins provided by the clinic and a decent diet provided mostly by Silvia, her general health was improving. She was up to her prewar weight, though now she was over six months pregnant.

"Ah, Elsa, I am glad you stopped for a moment to chat," said Sanchez. He glanced toward the narthex, where a few folks were still standing around visiting. They must keep up appearances until they were certain they were alone. "Is there anything specific I can do for you?" he added as he slipped into the pew beside her.

"No, Reverend, I just wanted to let you know how much your sermon meant to me today," Blair replied, her words honest enough. She maintained her German accent, though they conversed in English. "The Twenty-third Psalm is one passage I have heard often and thought I knew it, but you made it come truly alive by relating some of the history of King David."

"David is one of my favorite biblical personages. He was so human, made many mistakes, yet always his heart was pure toward God."

"It gives us all hope."

"Yes, it does, my dear."

Just then the outer church doors banged shut. Sanchez rose, went into the narthex, had a look around, then returned. "We are alone." He smiled. "In the human sense at least!"

"Have you heard anything lately from Gary and Mateo and the others?" Over the months Sanchez had delivered verbal messages from Blair to Gary because they had not felt it safe to see each other. Gary was apprised of her returning health, and she knew from the last contact that he was safe.

"Mateo came himself this last time." Sanchez shook his head with a slight smile on his lips. "A father cannot stop his children from growing up, though I did try with him, my youngest. He has become quite a young man, and I don't mean just because of the three inches he has sprouted in the last six months."

"He was always an admirable person. You have every right to

be proud," said Blair, thinking of the responsible, even-tempered young man she had spent so much time with before the fall of Bataan.

"It almost makes up for the loss of my firstborn." Sanchez sighed.

"Are you sure he is dead?" asked Blair.

"I have not heard from him since before the fall of Bataan."

"But there is no conclusive proof. He could be in a POW camp."

"I will keep hoping and looking." He didn't sound very hopeful. Then he added in an obvious attempt to divert the subject, "Gary sends his love to you, of course." He glanced down at his hands folded placidly in his lap. "I do not like deceiving him about where some of my information is coming from, Blair."

"Neither do I, Reverend. I swore when I found him that I would never lie to him again. But what good would it do for him to know what I am doing here? He would only worry unduly. You know I am not taking any huge risks."

"Just being in that nightclub is a risk." His tone, though quiet, betrayed misgivings. "I know I supported that path at first, but that was before I learned how deeply your friend is involved in espionage. She makes my operation seem puny."

Blair had learned shortly after coming to work at the club that Silvia was engaged in spying on some of the people at the highest levels of the Japanese hierarchy in Manila. But for everyone's protection Silvia didn't share details of her work with Blair, nor did Blair share with Silvia anything about Reverend Sanchez's dealings. Only recently had Blair learned her friend was operating, indirectly at least, on behalf of Douglas MacArthur himself. She was part of a network, set up by his order, to gather information that would aid in retaking the islands.

"I don't think there are degrees in this business—" Blair said, then stopped short. She'd only meant to emphasize the importance of what Sanchez did until she realized how her statement reflected on what she was doing.

Sanchez nodded smugly as he noted her slip.

She shrugged wryly. "Well, take heart, soon I'll be too big and awkward to do anything useful."

"I do have some other good news for you, Blair. I have some information about Claudette—"

"You've found her!"

"I think so, and it is as you thought. She is a prisoner at Santo Thomas."

"Can you smuggle a message to her from me?" She knew the bulk of Sanchez's work involved smuggling food, money, and sometimes messages into the various POW camps.

"I believe it could be slipped in with the food and money we deliver." He smiled again. "Mateo was also interested in getting a message to her. Is there something between them that I don't know about?"

"I do think they were growing quite fond of each other, Reverend." As Blair spoke she took a slip of paper and a pen from her pocketbook. "It sounds like all these months haven't dulled Mateo's feelings."

"He seemed reluctant to confide in me," said Sanchez, his dismay clear. "We were once very close. I feel I have missed so much of his maturing into manhood because of this war."

"I probably wouldn't know of their fondness for each other, either, except I was there and saw it happen. They were very shy about their feelings, not quite sure what to make of them. Perhaps Mateo still feels shy having been separated from her for so long."

Blair wrote as she talked, just a few lines, using no names while trying to make clear who she was. *I was thrilled to hear you are alive and well. It was like a happy scene in our favorite movie. By the way, I found what I was looking for. And it gives me hope all will be well. Like Claudette Colbert kissing Clark Gable and living happily ever after. I know that's how it will be for us. Just be strong and trust God.*

She handed the paper to Sanchez, then told him the little bits of information she'd learned over the last week. Nothing momentous. A new road being built, a convoy departing Manila for the north. Probably nothing that could help Gary, nothing that would bring them together any sooner.

When she finished, she hugged the pastor and then left the church, stepping out into the unrelenting rain.

————

Two days later it was a usual weeknight evening at the Casa Mañana. Blair finished her performance for the night and was making her way to her dressing room when Ricardo, the bartender, waylaid her.

"Where is Silvia?" he asked.

"I don't know. Isn't she mingling with the crowd as usual?" Blair glanced out toward the tables but didn't see her friend. "Maybe she's in the basement getting supplies."

"I will look. Let me know if you find her," he replied with a creased brow as he strode away.

"Wait a minute, Ricardo!" she called, turning and catching up to him. "Is something wrong?" She was getting to know the business of the club well enough so that sometimes she filled in for Silvia if she had to be away.

"No, but she was here, then just disappeared."

The bartender's concern seemed out of proportion with the problem. Silvia was answerable to no one, except perhaps the Japanese, and if she was just going to be gone for a few moments, she never found it necessary to inform everyone. Perhaps it was Ricardo who bore watching. He'd only been employed at the club for a few weeks, and though he was congenial enough, he had not warmed up to the other employees. It might be simply that he was new and the others had all been there since the occupation. The previous bartender had been well liked by everyone, and his sudden disappearance three weeks ago had left everyone in shock, fearing he'd fallen afoul of the Japanese. Blair did not know the details of Silvia's operation, but she suspected the old bartender and one or two of the waitresses worked with Silvia in the underground.

Five minutes later Silvia was back. She'd gone to the cellar to find one of her good bottles of champagne for a special customer. Seeing that all was normal, Blair went to her dressing room to change into street clothes. She was tired this evening and, since it was slow, decided not to mingle with the customers for her information-gathering routine but rather to turn in for the night. She went upstairs to Silvia's apartment over the club, which she now shared with her friend.

She was just falling asleep, stretched out on Silvia's sofa, when the creaking of the floorboards was followed by a soft "Elsa?"

"Hmm . . ." Blair murmured, a bit foggy from sleepiness.

Silvia came to the sofa and knelt down beside it. "Are you awake?"

Blair's eyes popped open. "Y-yes, sure . . ."

"I hate to wake you," said Silvia, "but something's come up, and I need you."

Propping her head in her hand, Blair was now fully awake. "What's happened?"

Silvia lowered her voice to a bare whisper. "I heard something important tonight. Sometime in the next two days there is going to be a huge raid on guerrillas. The Japs arrested some key operatives, and I guess they have learned how to locate some of the partisan groups."

Blair's heart nearly stopped. "Which groups?"

"I don't know, but as many as possible have to be warned. I have contacts who can get word to several groups, Gary's included."

Blair swung her legs off the sofa and rose. "I'll get dressed. Reverend Sanchez can help if I get word to him—" She stopped, realizing too late that she'd never before mentioned Sanchez's name to Silvia. But there could be no harm in it now that she was sure of Silvia's loyalty to the resistance. And the pastor surely could help in this situation.

Silvia, rising also, put a restraining hand on Blair's arm. "No you won't! This is dangerous. It means being out tonight after curfew. I'll take care of it. I can come up with a good story for being out. But I need you to keep an eye on the club while I'm gone. There's only one waitress on tonight, and she and Ricardo can't handle everything. Besides, I think maybe Ricardo is stealing from the till, and he needs to be watched. Are you up to this?"

"Of course. Let me get dressed." Blair was already heading to the closet where she kept her clothes. Thanks to Silvia, her wardrobe had improved since coming to Manila. She had the means now to look a far more sophisticated German woman. She chose a black brocaded Manchu dress that fit loosely and had a dress-length matching jacket that hid her pregnancy nicely. She would have preferred a more practical skirt and blouse in case she did have to find Reverend Sanchez, but for now this was more suitable evening wear and would not draw attention to her.

A few minutes later she and Silvia descended the stairs and returned to the nightclub. Silvia explained to her waitress that she'd just received a phone call from General Shougo, and he wanted her to join him at the Manila Hotel for a late soiree. Blair decided this waitress must not be one of Silvia's operatives, because Silvia did not even hint at the truth to the woman. Silvia departed.

The band played, several customers danced, and all was quite normal. Blair began to circulate among the tables, greeting regular customers whom she knew and inquiring of others if they had any needs, as she'd seen Silvia do each evening. Immediately a table of two couples clamored to have their drinks refreshed. Blair noted the waitress was busy so she took their order and went to the bar to have Ricardo fill it. She didn't see him right away and quickly her eyes jerked toward the cash register, but he was nowhere near it. Well, at least Silvia's receipts for the day were safe, unless the man had already absconded with them. Then she saw him back in the dark recesses adjacent to the bar. He was talking to a Japanese soldier.

Pretending to be occupied polishing glasses behind the bar, she waited. He returned in a moment.

She handed him the slip with the drink order. "Can you fill this?" she asked. "When you are done with that soldier's order, of course."

But as she glanced to where Ricardo and the soldier had been talking, no one was there. However, the entrance door of the club was still swinging from someone just having exited.

"He only wanted directions," said Ricardo quickly.

Blair sensed then from his explanation, which was too quick and too casual, that Ricardo was doing far worse than stealing. Perhaps that's why the man had appeared suspicious all along, not because he was a thief but because he was spying for the Japs. It all made sense to Blair as she began to put it together with other suspicious activities. And now he somehow knew what Silvia was up to, and he must have sent that soldier after her to stop her. Blair wanted to turn and run out that instant to find Silvia, to warn her. But she had no idea where her friend had gone. Her only hope was that the soldier who had just left would not be able to track her, either. Blair hated being so helpless, knowing her friend might be in trouble and unable to do a thing about it. Her frantic look must have been clear to the bartender.

"It's no use," said Ricardo dryly.

"What do you mean?"

"Don't get mixed up in things that are none of your business." Those words cemented her suspicions.

And it was her business! More than he could know. Not only was her friend in danger, but if Silvia was not successful tonight, then Blair's husband and many of her friends could be dead in two days.

"I don't know what you are talking about, Ricardo." She rolled her eyes. "I only know the receipts better tally tonight, or you may well lose your job. We know you have been dipping into the register."

This appeared to have caught him off guard, as Blair had hoped. He'd been certain she was working with Silvia. Now he no doubt didn't know what to think.

"Just because Silvia's gone to that party doesn't mean you can get away with anything," Blair added.

"Is that what you think?"

"I'm not as dumb as I may look. Now please take care of that order."

Ambling away, she began circulating again. Her behavior in no way hinted at her churning insides. Even as she laughed and talked to customers, most of them Japanese, her mind raced trying to think of what to do. She could go to Reverend Sanchez, and perhaps he, at least, could find a way to warn Gary. But there was no way to leave without rousing Ricardo's suspicions. If he could send someone after Silvia, what was to stop him from doing the same with her? No, she would just have to leave it to Silvia and pray she was successful.

The next hour before closing passed with agonizing slowness. Finally at midnight she locked up the club and balanced the receipts. Then after helping the other staff clean up, she watched them leave and at last felt free. By then it was one o'clock in the morning. Ricardo was gone, and she could easily slip out now. But it was a terrible risk to be out at that hour. She did not have an official pass. Perhaps she could use her pregnancy as an excuse—a problem had forced her to seek medical aid. But that reminded her just why she couldn't take the risk. The child also kicked in her womb as if to help jog her sensibilities.

"I'm sorry, sweetheart," she murmured, gently patting her

slightly rounded abdomen. "But it is a hard choice—you or your daddy."

What finally made up her mind was the very real possibility that if Ricardo suspected her in the least, he would almost certainly be watching the club or having someone watch it. If she left now and was followed, she could risk bringing the enemy down on Reverend Sanchez.

Feeling miserable and helpless, she returned to the apartment, pacing as she waited for Silvia's return. When her legs tired of that, she sat on the sofa and tried to read, but within minutes of opening a book, she had slumped over and was fast asleep.

When Blair awoke at dawn, the first thing she did was check Silvia's bed. It had not been slept in all night. Her friend had not come home. Blair's stomach lurched. She knew something awful had happened. Even if Silvia had gone to a party with the general after making her underground contact, she would certainly be home by this hour. Trying to quell her rising panic, she forced her mind to think straight. But all she wanted to do was run and warn Gary.

Now that it was daylight and the curfew lifted, Blair decided she could finally try to do something without too much danger. In a rush, relieved to finally have something to do, she started for the door but then noted the severe wrinkles in the dress she'd fallen asleep in. The last thing she needed was to draw attention to herself by rushing out dressed like that. So hurriedly she changed out of the brocade dress. Her hands fumbled so over the buttons in the back of the dress that she finally just ripped them out. Tossing aside the dress, she slipped quickly into a more sensible skirt and matching jacket. Hearing a noise outside, she nearly panicked, but looking out the window, she saw a man in the street below pushing a cart full of things for market. A pottery jug had fallen out and crashed into the street.

That didn't ease her panic; it only emphasized that at any moment the police could explode into the apartment. She flung open the door and on the porch noted the basket Silvia used for market. She grabbed it, thinking it could provide her with a good reason to be out.

There didn't seem to be anyone watching the building, but she gasped in a deep breath and forced herself to take care anyway. She had to pull herself together. It was imperative that she wasn't followed as she went to Reverend Sanchez's church, even if at this hour of the day she could come up with a plausible reason for going to the church. Still, no sense inviting questions.

She stopped at the market in order to keep up her ruse. She put a few items into her basket, but when she went to pay for them, she realized she had forgotten her pocketbook. She put the things back, then with a shrug at the disgusted look from the shopkeeper, left. Still there seemed to be no one suspicious around. But she paused at a few more shops and meandered a bit. The church was a good two miles from Silvia's. She considered taking a taxi, but even if she could get the pastor to pay the driver when she arrived at her destination, she didn't want to risk another person knowing what she was doing. Taking the time to walk was agonizing but necessary.

The church was deserted when she finally arrived, so she went to the parsonage nearby. The reverend was having breakfast. She told him what had happened.

"I am glad you waited till morning to tell me," he assured her.

"I have never been more torn in my life, Reverend," she admitted. "But when I woke this morning and Silvia wasn't there—oh, do you think she's been captured?"

"It doesn't look good."

"Do you think it's too late to get a warning to Gary?"

He rubbed his chin thoughtfully, and when he spoke, his tone was far more encouraging. "I will get on that right away."

"What can I do to help?"

"I think you should stay here for now. It might not be safe for you to return to Silvia's place. If she has been captured, who knows what she will tell them."

"She would never betray me!"

"Who knows what anyone will do under interrogation?"

Blair groaned as she considered her friend suffering. How much could Silvia take? She'd said before that she liked the comforts of life. Maybe she would be too pragmatic to suffer for another. No, Silvia was a survivor, but she was still a decent person, not one to give up her friends for a few comforts.

Resolved to do what Sanchez told her, she remembered something. "Reverend, I forgot my pocketbook at the apartment. My papers were in it."

"You went off without your papers?"

"I was in a hurry—"

"Never mind. They won't do you much good if you are betrayed. I'll send someone over there later to see if the coast is clear, and maybe then you can go back." He rose. "I must go now. Help yourself to some breakfast."

"Reverend Sanchez, are you sure I am not placing you in jeopardy?"

"There is no way Silvia can lead the Japanese to me, is there?"

"No, I never told her—" Blair stopped short as she recalled her conversation with Silvia last night. Blair now remembered she had suggested that she go to Sanchez with the warning. She had spoken his name. Had she used his title? Dismally, Blair realized she never spoke of Reverend Sanchez without his title. There were many in Manila with the surname of Sanchez but few who were also pastors. Would Silvia reveal this if captured? It might not have even registered with her.

Sanchez must have noted the blood drain from Blair's face as she recalled these things. He said, "It's all right, Blair. God will protect us." He strode to the door. "Stay put. I'll be back as soon as I can, though it might take a couple of hours."

31

AFTER REVEREND SANCHEZ left, Blair forced herself to eat something. She wasn't hungry, but she knew she must eat for the baby she was carrying. Then she cleaned up the pastor's kitchen and put away the leftover food.

By noon she was pacing up and down Sanchez's cozy living room. He should be back by now, but she tried to calm her rising panic by reminding herself that he wasn't on a set schedule. It would be a small wonder if he finished as quickly as she hoped he would. She tried to distract herself by playing the piano that sat in the corner of the room. Her hands were shaking, and she flubbed several notes of "The King Shall Come."

She almost giggled at her choice of hymn, but when she saw the section in the hymnal titled *The Coming of Christ,* she couldn't resist, what with her present waiting for Reverend Sanchez to come, as well. But thinking of Christ's returning in glory, perhaps to rain judgment on the marauding Japanese, was a nice diversion. Better, at least, than thinking about Reverend Sanchez not returning at all.

By three o'clock in the afternoon even the music failed to soothe Blair. Acid gnawed in the pit of her stomach as she feared the worst. Was it possible that both Sanchez and Silvia had been captured? Even if Silvia had been arrested and spilled out everything, the Japs couldn't have acted this quickly. But if they had, wasn't it more likely they'd come here to the parsonage first to find the pastor? The Japanese could not have known to look for him elsewhere.

Her mind spun with possibilities. Anything could have

happened. She sighed with frustration.

After another hour passed, Blair knew she had to do something. If Sanchez had been captured, the occupation police would most certainly make it a priority to search his house. If they found her here . . . well, she could think of few believable explanations for that, especially if they connected Silvia to her. The only thing she could think to do was to leave the city and find Gary herself, but that was not so easily done, either. It would be next to impossible to leave without her papers, which she'd left at Silvia's. Even if she did find a way out of Manila, could she find Gary? He'd probably moved his camp several times since she'd last seen him.

Perhaps she could seek refuge with one of Silvia's waitresses, Rosa, who Blair was almost certain worked in the underground. If Silvia had been captured, no doubt all of her associates would be questioned, but Blair could make a better case for herself being at Rosa's. Yet without those all-important identity papers, she was all but lost.

As it grew dark outside, she feared she had waited too long, and she imagined police crashing into the house at any moment. Yet she didn't want her panic to make her do something else stupid like she had in leaving her pocketbook behind.

Her heart leaped when she heard a noise at the back door. Her mind raced with fabrications to tell the police.

"It's me, Blair," came Reverend Sanchez's voice from the kitchen.

She jumped up from the sofa where she had been waiting and raced to the kitchen. "You scared me!"

"I'm sorry. I thought it would be best to come in this way," he said, "in case the place is being watched, though who is to say the back isn't being watched, as well."

"Did you see your contact?"

"No. He wasn't there. I'm going to try again in a couple of hours. His wife said he would be back."

"It'll be too late," groaned Blair.

"We must hope not," soothed the reverend. "Gary and the other guerrilla groups live under fear of discovery all the time. We've got to trust they know how to take care of themselves."

She'd lived among the guerrillas long enough to know the truth of this, yet it did not entirely dispel the awful gnawing of fear inside her.

"Do you think I should return to Silvia's?" Blair asked, mostly so as not to dwell on her fear for Gary.

"I've sent someone over there. Let's wait until she reports back."

Wait. How she hated that word!

But it wasn't long before the girl Sanchez sent knocked on his door. She said there was a guard posted at the door of the club, which was closed for business. If Blair had any hope that Silvia had not been captured, that dashed it completely. If she'd been able, Silvia would have opened the club. Beyond this guard, however, the girl hadn't seen anything else suspicious.

An hour after the girl departed, Sanchez also left. Blair ate some toast and jelly and had a hot cup of tea. And she waited. Sanchez returned a few minutes before curfew and reported his sucess in finding his contact and relaying the information about the raids. She agreed with him that the best thing for her was to stay the night. Perhaps by morning the police would have given up their surveillance of Silvia's place and it would be safe to return there at least long enough to retrieve her purse. It was now twenty-four hours since Silvia had left the Casa Mañana to warn her contact about the raid.

After tossing and turning all night, her mind plagued with indecision about her next move, Blair welcomed the dawn, even if it brought another day of worry as thick as the falling rain. In a way she found the steady beating of the rain on the roof soothing. She thought she could lie there forever listening to the sound. Could she be blamed for not wanting to leave that bed in the minister's spare room? Once she rose from bed, decisions would have to be made and actions taken.

After she washed up and dressed, she went to the kitchen and found Reverend Sanchez already fixing breakfast. He told her to sit at the table, then he placed a dish of scrambled eggs, toast, and sliced bananas in front of her. Her appetite had not improved since yesterday, but again she forced herself to eat.

As Reverend Sanchez poured tea, he said, "I've been thinking about what to do next." He sat in the chair opposite her. "I will go to Silvia Wang's apartment to fetch your papers—"

"No! You can't do that," Blair said firmly. "If anyone goes, it will be me. I can at least come up with a plausible reason for being there."

"If Silvia has talked, you will surely be implicated."

"We all could be implicated." Blair's mind raced over the many scenarios she'd considered, but only one appealed to her. "Reverend Sanchez, I feel it is time for me to return to Gary. I think you should consider that, as well. Manila is no longer safe. The police could come here at any moment."

"I have thought of that." For a moment a look of longing eased his tense brow. "To be with Mateo again, ah, that would be wonderful. I think of it often. But there are many here besides Mateo and Gary who depend on my organization. We have been able to reach nearly all the POW camps and to ease the suffering of many of the prisoners." He gave a self-deprecating shrug. "I suppose it is arrogant to think this organization will crumble without me."

"Then you will come with me?"

"This network may continue without me, but this is where I feel I belong. I could not go off and be safe with my son and do nothing in the cause of liberating my home."

Blair chuckled lightly. "You have never lived among guerrillas, have you, Reverend Sanchez? It is hardly a safe place. Still, I understand what you are saying. I've had similar thoughts. But you won't push it to the edge, will you? I mean, you'll know when to head for the jungle, won't you?"

He nodded. "And I feel you are probably right in your decision to return to Gary when we are certain the raids have been unsuccessful. I will give you what quinine I have and a few other medicines."

"That's another reason for me to return to Silvia's. Besides my papers, I have quinine and vitamins there."

"It would take too much time to have new papers made for you."

"I'll have to try for Silvia's."

"You must be careful, and if there is even a hint of a trap, you must not do it. We'll find some other way to get you out of the city."

She thought of how Sanchez had smuggled her out of Manila several months ago by hiding her in a false compartment of a wagon. She'd been folded up like a pretzel for hours. She supposed she could do it again if she had to, but she had a bit more bulk now than she'd had then. And almost as important as her papers were the medicines, the vitamins especially. She could not expect a decent diet back with Gary, and if she was going to have her baby in the jungle, she was at least going to do everything she could to ensure the child was healthy.

They decided she should wait until evening to go to Silvia's so that she'd have the cover of darkness. Also, it might play to her advantage if she was caught. It could simply appear as if she was showing up to work unaware of the club being closed.

"But you cannot get caught," emphasized Reverend Sanchez. "Even with a cover story they might still take you in for questioning. It is possible they would question you just because of your association with Silvia. Try to slip in and out unseen. If you can't do that, then do not make the attempt."

As Blair traversed the streets of Manila once again, she wondered if her stay here was about to end. How she longed to return to Gary! And now she knew it could not be more dangerous there for her than it was here, where she couldn't seem to avoid hotbeds of espionage. But she still needed a doctor. Her health had improved, but could she really consider having her baby out in the jungle with no medical supervision? These thoughts weakened her earlier resolve.

"Don't think of that," she murmured to herself. Anything could happen between now and her due date. However, at the moment all she could think of was possible disasters. It seemed as if any security she might have found in Manila was crumbling by sure degrees. In the world she now lived in, a world where time was measured by the present, where the future was too elusive to hold, three months was a long time, a lifetime. If she lived three more months, if Gary lived three months, that was more than could be expected.

The two miles between Reverend Sanchez's and Silvia's used to be a nice constitutional on a Sunday morning that Blair hadn't minded. She had deemed it a good way to build her stamina. But making that trek now, at night, looking over her shoulder the entire way, fearing the sound of footsteps coming near, her heart thudding with fear at what she was about to encounter at the end of the journey, was another matter. She should have had more to eat at Reverend Sanchez's in order to keep up her stamina, but her stomach had been far too knotted to take in much nourishment. At least at this hour of the evening the heat wasn't so oppressive; nevertheless, by the time she came to Silvia's street, she was drenched with perspiration.

Pausing at the end of the street, she surveyed the area around the club. Nothing seemed out of order. A couple of children were playing a game. A bicyclist wheeled past. A woman was sweeping her front porch. And there was the guard posted at the front door of the Casa Mañana. Blair figured there must be a guard in back, also, so she kept to the shadows as she made her way into the back alley. Surprisingly, there was no guard at the back door of the club, and the back stairs leading up to the apartment were unwatched, as well. Perhaps the guard in front was just for show. Perhaps they felt no real need to guard the premises. Perhaps no one suspected Elsa Dengler of having any part in Silvia's side business of espionage. Maybe they had forgotten about Frau Dengler completely.

She began to sense she was truly safe. So much had gone wrong in the last two days, it was only right that something should finally work out. Still, she was careful as she trod up the back stairs that led to the apartment. She pushed open the door, not surprised that it was unlocked, because she had failed to lock it when she rushed out two days ago. She stepped inside and closed the door behind her. For obvious reasons she couldn't turn on a light, but she knew the apartment well enough to get around in the dark.

Carefully she felt her way along the furniture to where she thought she had last left her pocketbook. A floorboard creaked behind her, and she stopped, her heart doing at least one flip in her chest. Then the lights burst on. For a brief moment she was nearly blinded, and when her eyes adjusted, she almost wished she was blind.

Two Japanese soldiers were facing her. She immediately recognized one of them as an officer who was a regular at the Casa Mañana. The captain she had danced with on her first night.

"Goodness! You startled me," she said peremptorily. Then realized belatedly she hadn't used her accent.

"Forgive me, Frau Dengler . . . it is Dengler, is it not?" said the captain. Again he conversed in English, still not improved in all these months, though he replaced fewer r's with l's.

"Yes, of course," she replied, her accent back in place. "What are you doing in my apartment?"

"Your apartment? I thought it belonged to Silvia Wang."

"Of course. I'm her houseguest is what I meant."

"Do you know where Miss Wang is?" he asked.

She looked around as if surprised that her friend wasn't there. "I have no idea. I have been out of town for a couple of days visiting a friend in the north. I thought perhaps she was ill and in bed, since I saw the club isn't open."

The captain strode toward the bedroom door, the only other room in the small apartment. He flung it open. "She is not there."

"I really have no idea where she might be, then. And I still don't understand why you were here sitting in the dark."

"We thought it more efficient place for guard, yes?" He smiled ominously. "For instance, would you come if you seen a guard posted?"

"Why shouldn't I? I live here." Though she infused her tone with indignation, inwardly she couldn't believe she'd fallen into such a simple trap.

"You say you be out of the city. How you leave without these?" The captain reached toward a table. Blair saw her purse lying there and beside it some folded papers, which the captain took in hand.

She stared at the papers he held, her identity papers no doubt. She had absolutely no ready answer to his question. But something told her that it wouldn't have mattered if she did. It was possible the captain and his cohort might even have specifically been waiting for her. Had Silvia talked, then?

"Ah . . . no good answer to my question?" Tapping his fingers thoughtfully against his lips, he added, "Frau, I do, in fact, know where Miss Wang is."

"You do? Then why ask me?" Her confusion was only partly feigned. What was his game? How much did he know? Was he merely baiting her, hoping she would slip up? In her present state of mind, she might just end up accommodating him. She had to make herself think clearly.

"Would you please to come with me, Frau Dengler?"

"Why? Where?"

"We are questioning all of Miss Wang's associates."

"Can't you do it here? Someone needs to be here to open the club."

"The club is the least of your worries," he said dryly. "Will you please come?"

Though he was the picture of proper decorum, she had a feeling the word *please* was a mere form. But she had to try to stall. Maybe she could think of something to do if she had a few minutes. What would that be? Escape? Would she try to outrun two Japanese soldiers who were no doubt in prime physical condition?

"Could I get a drink first? I am dying of thirst . . . from my walk, you know. It's warm even for this hour."

"There will be time for that later."

Blair knew it was no use to fight it further. Perhaps if she remained cool, she could wheedle her way out of this. There was still the chance this was just a routine questioning and she would be quickly released once they were convinced she was just an acquaintance of Silvia, an innocent bystander. The trick would be to convince them.

She was bustled into a car on the street and taken to the Japanese administration building downtown. Should she take heart that it wasn't one of the POW camps? There were only four cells here for temporary use. She was shoved unceremoniously into one.

"Why are you locking me up?" she asked with misgiving.

"Only for your safety and comfort," said the captain. "See, here is chair for you to sit. Someone will be with you soon."

She sank down on the chair as the door was shut and locked, then noted her surroundings. They were spare and, despite what the captain said, completely lacking in anything even vaguely resembling comfort except for the wooden straight-backed chair. There was no bed to sleep on and only a hole in the floor for a toilet. Her hopes of a quick questioning and release plummeted.

She remained there alone for several hours, until the light from the rising moon started to shimmer through the barred window high overhead. She had feigned thirst back at the apartment in order to stall, but now her mouth was so dry she began wondering what she would have to do to get a drink of water. What *would* she do? Would she betray her friends for one? Not yet. But what would it take? Would she die first, and her child, also?

She kept telling herself it might not go that far. Perhaps the captain was telling the truth. But why were they taking so long to question her? Not that she was anxious for an interrogation to begin. She had been through so much suffering in the last year and had survived by God's grace. She knew He would continue to be with her, yet there remained within her a deep fear that she was weak at heart and always would be. Her earthly father had had far more time to beat that perception into her than her heavenly Father had had to work it out of her. What if, in the end, her weakness proved more pervasive than all else?

"Oh, God, give me strength! I don't want to betray my husband or my friends!"

As the darkness in the barred window turned to the gray light of dawn, she struggled to grasp hold of her faith, her God, knowing she would fail without them.

32

FINALLY TWO JAPANESE soldiers came into Blair's cell. One was much taller than most of the Japanese she had seen. He was about fifty years old and had the look of a chunk of granite. She didn't think he could be fooled easily. The other was more squat, solid in build, but wire-rimmed spectacles seemed to soften his features.

"Frau Elsa Dengler," said the tall man in excellent, nearly unaccented English. "I have a few questions for you. Answer them honestly, and there is no reason why you cannot soon be free."

"I will try to accommodate." She licked her lips. "But I am very thirsty, and it's hard for me to talk. May I have a drink of water?"

"Of course, but first—"

Blair's heart sank, and she feared it would be a long time before her lips felt some moisture.

The tall Jap continued, "But first will you clear up some confusion regarding your identity? We have called the German consulate, and they have no record of an Elsa Dengler. So perhaps you can tell us who you really are?"

"I'm Elsa Dengler. I don't know why—"

Slam! Out of nowhere a hand struck the side of her head. The bespectacled man who had appeared so much more benevolent than the tall man now had an evil glint reflecting off his eyeglasses as he withdrew his lethal hand.

The blow made Blair's eyes water and her ears ring.

"Your name?" said the tall man.

She didn't know what to answer, what lie to give.

The bespectacled man loomed.

"Wait," said the tall man to his partner. Then to Blair, "Perhaps you would rather give us other names? I already know some. We need only verification from you. You will not have to betray anyone, you see."

"My name is Blair Hayes. I'm an American citizen," she answered smugly. They wanted a name, so now they had one. See how much it helped them.

"Using forged papers?"

"Yes."

"Where did you get the papers?"

"I don't know. They came to me by way of a third party."

"Who was that?"

"My name is Blair Hayes. I'm an Am—"

Wham! Another blow to the other side of her head. It rocked her chair so that it wobbled precariously on two legs for a moment before it righted itself. Blair still felt as if she were wobbling.

"You are wasting our time," said the tall man. "We know everything. All we want from you is confirmation."

"I can't confirm what I don't know!"

"We have all your accomplices in custody—Silvia Wang, Manuel Sanchez, Ramon Olivera, a pretty little waitress named Rosa Figueras. They have all talked. They have told us how you have been passing information from the nightclub to the underground."

Had they really captured Reverend Sanchez? And Ramon Olivera was the go-between she used to deliver her information to the pastor. That meant his organization had also been compromised, not just Silvia's. Blair thought dismally of her small slip of giving Silvia the pastor's name. Small slip? One that would no doubt be the death of them all.

"I don't know any of those people," she said. "Except of course Silvia. I had no idea she was involved in espionage. I just worked for her."

"It is useless to act ignorant, Miss Hayes ... or is it *Missus*?" He glanced at the protuberance of her stomach. "We know you have a husband who is a partisan. Give us his name, and we will let you go."

Blair's stomach lurched as her heart skipped a beat. They knew about Gary! Then it had to have been either Silvia or Reverend Sanchez who had talked, for only they of her current associates knew about him. Did it matter which one had talked? One of her dearest friends had betrayed her, but could she hate that person even if she knew who it was? What had they suffered that had forced that person to talk? She could not think of hatred, only that her friend had suffered. And it occurred to her that whoever had talked had not given Gary's name. That was something. Or had they? Her interrogators seemed to know everything else.

"I don't know what you are talking about. My husband is a mining engineer. He died—"

Another blow struck the corner of her eye, and she felt a trickle of blood. Then came another blow and another. Her vision blurred and her head spun. Only one other time in her life could she remember being hit by another human. It had been a sleazy blackguard of a man she had worked for in California. He'd hit her once or twice, but back then she thought she deserved it. Gary had saved her from that man, that life.

And now she could save him by taking blows that this time she knew she didn't deserve.

"A name," said the tall man, "and it will stop."

She clamped her mouth shut. The bespectacled man grabbed the collar of her blouse and, yanking her from the chair, slammed her up against the stone wall.

"I-I d-don't know any names," she stammered, still reeling inside and out.

There were more blows; she lost count of how many. When the beating stopped, she slumped to the floor. Then the men went to the door and opened it. But the tall man paused.

"We have been gentle with you because of your condition," he said, his tone even, no sneer, no malice. Very civil. "We will give you time to think about our questions. Perhaps your memory will clear. When we return, all you have to do is give us what we ask for. Then it will all stop. Otherwise we will no longer show restraint." He left the cell, pausing only to grab the chair and take it with him.

After the door slammed shut, all Blair could think about for the first few moments was that those loathsome creatures were gone and no one would hit her again. She felt a deep sense of relief, but

307

it lasted only a minute before she became aware of every part of her body searing in pain. Curling up on the filthy cement floor, she wept.

She did not see another soul for two days. Nor was there food or water. During that time, as the physical pain eased, she wondered about her friends. Had their interrogations been worse than this? Those poor people! They could not be blamed for talking. If those two beasts who had questioned her returned, if that four-eyed monster hit her again, she would tell them everything she knew. She might do it just for a glass of water.

What would it hurt for them to have Gary's name? They probably knew it anyway and were just trying to confirm it, as they had said. Gary wouldn't want her to suffer, to risk their child. He'd want her to talk.

She had no idea, then, why she didn't talk when those two sadists returned to her cell two days later. She defiantly didn't speak one word. But deep down she knew it had nothing to do with bravery or nobility. She knew, instead, that if she uttered one word, everything would belch out in a torrent. And she indeed knew enough names to keep these animals in business for ages. Gary Hobart, Ralph Senger, Mateo Sanchez, Tony Hillerman, Woody Woodburn, Fernando Segundo, Tom Morris. Some she only knew by one name, Albert, Marcos, Costas, Roxas. She could bring them all down if she opened her mouth. And she couldn't deceive herself that they would be only captured, forced to sit out the war in a POW camp. Many of those men, like Gary, would be summarily executed if caught. Nor could she truly believe that giving a few names wouldn't hurt. Look what Silvia's or Reverend Sanchez's talking had done. Two important underground organizations had no doubt been destroyed. She no longer believed that the guerrillas could take care of themselves. They were as vulnerable as anyone else. And if the Japs broke down the guerrilla organizations, the entire war effort could be jeopardized. One name was like the bottom card in a house of cards. Remove it, and the entire precarious structure would crash.

When the interrogators departed this time, they left a bucket full of dirty water. She drank of it as if it were an artesian spring.

Day after day her captors returned to her cell and continued to beat her for her silence. They were not gentle, though they did not beat her so as to incapacitate her completely, not while they thought she might yet spill out information. Between the interrogations and the beatings, she was fed only a small bowl of rice each day, along with what water remained in the dirty bucket. Perhaps they thought if the beatings did not work, starvation might.

Every day as the sun sent a thin ray of light through the high window and she broke through the haze of sleep that bordered on stupor, she had to convince herself to wake at all. She faced each day with dread of the inevitable interrogation. She cringed inside at the prospect of facing those slant-eyed beasts. But worse than that, she had to begin each day forcing herself to remember why she couldn't talk.

For Gary . . .

Who . . . is Gary . . . ?

You know him . . . he is . . . husband . . . yes . . . my husband . . .

Who . . . ?

The lowest moment was when she feared her sanity was slipping. If she lost her mind, then she'd have no control at all over what she said. She might reveal all.

She forced herself to play games in an attempt to keep her mind sharp. She recited all the lines she'd ever memorized for movie parts and auditions. Perhaps she should have been truly frightened by how much of that she could recall to memory. If only she'd memorized more verses from the Bible. Someday she would have to make up for this present lack.

Each day became a struggle, against the Japanese and against her own weaknesses. And when she made it successfully to the end of the day without talking to the enemy and was still sane, she counted it a great victory.

She lost track of the exact number of days the interrogations continued but thought it must have been eight or nine when the most vicious beating of all was delivered to her.

"You have tried our patience to the limit, Miss Hayes," scowled the same tall granite monster who would forever haunt her nightmares. "You will save lives if you give us the information we want. Tell us what you know of the partisans."

"No . . ." Blair rasped. She had no strength for any wittier response.

"I am sick of you, then!" yelled the tall man, for the first time losing his reserve. To his henchman he added, "Show her the full extent of our displeasure."

She hoped it greatly disappointed the squat four-eyed ogre when she fainted soon after he began beating her. She had no idea how long it was before she came to, but the fact that she was alone when consciousness returned gave her little comfort. The Jap had said he'd reached his limit. Well, she was fairly certain she had, too. Her body could not live much longer. She certainly would not survive another interrogation.

Silently she begged her child to forgive her. She had made the choice to sacrifice her life and that of her child for the lives of countless others.

All she had left as she lay on the dirt floor waiting to die was the comfort of the kicks of her child.

The subsequent pains came on so gradually, she wasn't sure what they were at first. Cramps no doubt from drinking contaminated water. Then they became too regular for ordinary stomach cramps.

"God, no!" she groaned. "Please, God, it can't be." Though on one level she had expected to die and her baby with her, she realized she hadn't truly accepted that fate.

Frantic, she started screaming for the guards, and when there was no response, she pitched the water from the bucket and began slamming the empty bucket against the cell door in desperation to get someone's attention. Over and over, like the blows she had received.

Crash! Clank!

"Help me, Lord!"

Finally the guards came. She screamed, "My baby! I'm having my baby!"

Outside the still closed door, she heard the guards talking, and though they spoke Japanese, she knew they must be deliberating about what to do. Most likely they hadn't understood a word she'd said, but perhaps they might think she was ready to talk. A few minutes passed, then the door opened and the tall interrogator was there with a guard. Thank God his partner was not with him!

"Take her to the infirmary," he ordered after assessing the situation.

Three hours later Blair delivered her child. They told her it was a boy, but considering the conditions of his birth and Blair's physical condition, both in the months before the birth and during her imprisonment, he was too premature to survive. They said he stopped breathing only a few minutes after his birth. The doctor in attendance was a benevolent Jap—he instructed a guard to take her to the morgue to see the dead fetus, saying he felt that would be best for her mental recovery.

The word *recovery* echoed in her mind as she gazed at the bundle of blankets on the bed. She wasn't supposed to recover. She had chosen to sacrifice them *both*. This wasn't how it was supposed to have happened.

Without thinking, she rose from the wheelchair on which they had transported her to the morgue.

"No, no. You must not stand," said a voice behind her.

But she did not listen. How could she know for certain this was a real child? Perhaps her cruel captors had lied about the baby's death and hidden her living and healthy baby from her.

A hand from behind grasped her arm, but she defiantly shook it away, then reached for a corner of the blanket and drew it back. She had not expected to see such a perfect whole being. It made the sight far worse than if it had been deformed and unrecognizable as a human. Something inside her crumbled and cracked as the reality of her loss bombarded her senses. With a gasp of misery she turned away from the painful sight and immediately felt light-headed. Her knees began to buckle. Someone caught her before she hit the floor. As unconsciousness engulfed her, she thought, "Maybe there is still a chance that I will die, too."

———

It both amazed and befuddled Blair that the same people who had beaten her nearly to death, who had caused the death of her child, were now nursing her carefully back to health. But even more astounding was that she let them. She was that weak in character, she supposed, that after the death of her child, she still had a basic desire to live. She hated herself for it, but there it was. She did not want to die.

She consoled herself with the thought that perhaps her desire to live was a twisted form of self-punishment. By living she would prolong the suffering of her grief.

She didn't know. She hardly cared. She only knew she wasn't ready to give up on her life. Maybe, too, she believed that giving up on life meant giving up on God. She wasn't ready to do that, either.

Words came to her mind: "Lo, I am with you always." "With God all things are possible." "I will never leave thee, nor forsake thee."

Words from sermons returned to her and words from Meg Doyle's talks, which Blair thought she hadn't been listening to at the time. Words she'd had to memorize in Sunday school to make her mother happy. Words spoken by her mother that Blair had rolled her eyes and sighed at hearing. Funny, they hadn't popped into her mind when she had been in her cell trying to hang on to sanity. Maybe she'd been too befuddled to remember them, or maybe it had been easier to recall movie lines.

Now they came to her in bits and pieces, washed over her, and somehow made her fight to live. Hope and despair truly were two sides of the same coin, and now that coin stood on edge as she wavered between the two.

She remained in the hospital for two weeks and did indeed begin to regain her health. The Japanese doctor told her she'd almost bled to death after the birth of the baby, and when she looked into a mirror, the pasty white countenance that stared back at her proved the truth of his words. She was thin, too, because try as she might, she simply could not conjure much of an appetite. So being healthier merely meant that she was stronger than the half-dead woman she'd been two weeks ago. She had a long way to go to reach even the health of the woman who had first come to Manila after leaving the guerrilla camp.

The door to her ward opened, and a Filipina nurse bustled in pushing a cart with breakfast trays for the four patients in the ward. She set trays on the bed tables of the other women and helped adjust their beds so they could eat. Two of the women were Filipinas from the Santo Tomas prisoner-of-war camp. They were middle-aged, and Blair didn't know what their ailments were. The other patient was an American. She was partially comatose. The nurse told Blair she had tetanus. She was probably about ten years older than Blair and quite attractive despite the ravages of her illness. Blair wondered what had brought her to this place and thought it would be nice to talk to another American if only the woman would wake up.

The nurse smiled as she brought Blair her tray and set it on the bed table. She cranked up the back of the bed, then came and began lifting lids on the various bowls.

"You must eat," she said in Tagalog because she knew Blair understood that language fairly well.

"I try, but . . ." Blair shrugged, not caring to explain yet again why she had no appetite.

"It is very important now, Miss Blair." The nurse leaned close, apparently attempting to adjust Blair's pillows. "I have heard you will be transferred to Santo Tomas soon," she whispered. "You won't get such good food there. You must eat while you can."

"Where did you hear this? How soon?"

"A day or two, I think. Please eat."

"Do you know," she asked the nurse, almost afraid to hear the answer, "are they finished interrogating me, then?" In addition to all her other emotional upheavals, the fear of another interrogation was always with her.

"I have heard they feel you must truly not know anything if fear of losing your baby didn't make you talk."

So she had succeeded. She had managed not to betray her friends and the cause of the war. She felt no pride at all in such a grim accomplishment.

Nevertheless, Blair forced down the gruel and milk and banana. And she wondered what it meant to be moved to the POW camp. Were they really finished questioning her? Had her son died not only to save his father and his father's comrades but her, as well? Her child was the true hero, then, like his father, and he didn't even have a name. Should she name him? Would Gary mind if she did so without his approval? But she had not the vaguest idea what to name him, for she'd never given thought to names while she had been pregnant. She had always believed she would see Gary again before the birth, and they would find a name together.

She thought of naming him after his father, but she could not bring herself to name a dead child for someone who she desperately needed to believe was still alive. She could not have death and grief associated with that dearest of all names. So searching in her mind, she decided upon Edward. That was Gary's father's name. Gary would like that. And now she knew there was one thing she must do before leaving the hospital.

Later, when the doctor came to examine her, she asked, "Does my baby have a grave?"

"Of course. We are not barbarians, madam!"

"I did not mean to offend. I merely wanted to make sure he has been properly . . . cared for. There has to be a name on his grave. He should have a birth certificate, as well."

"That can be arranged if you wish," said the doctor. "What name have you given him?"

"Edward H—" Stopping suddenly, Blair realized she'd almost said Hobart. After all she had done and suffered to hide that name, she'd almost revealed it now! How stupid of her. Yet she hadn't. She added smoothly, "Edward Hayes."

"Is there a middle name? I understand you westerners often have these."

"No, there isn't."

"I will take care of the matter." He turned to go.

Blair laid a hand on his sleeve. "Doctor, will I be released from the hospital soon?"

"I suppose it can't hurt for me to tell you. Yes, you will be going to Santo Tomas."

Blair knew something of Santo Tomas. She'd learned of the place before the war, when it had been a Dominican university. She and Claudette had once gone there on a sightseeing trip. Of course, that was before the school was abandoned a week after the first bombings of December 8, 1941. The school had been founded in 1611 and still had an Old World flavor. The main building was stately and charming, three stories high, and larger than a city block. Its highest tower was topped by a huge white cross that could be seen for miles around. The grounds, which sprawled over roughly sixty acres, were surrounded by a twelve-foot-tall stone fence. It was now home to just under four thousand internees, most of whom were enemy nationals working in Manila at the time of the Japanese occupation. Nearly a thousand of these were children, while more than half were women. The rest were men, most over the age of sixty because, of course, most of the younger men had been in the Army and now were either in military POW camps or were fugitives.

These last figures Blair had learned while helping Reverend Sanchez in his efforts to aid the prisoners. Now she would be one of the prisoners —with no Reverend Sanchez to aid her. She now knew what had become of him and Silvia. She had learned from one of the nurses who had attended the pastor's church that he had indeed been arrested. He had been beaten quite badly during his interrogation, and in the middle of one of those sessions he'd suffered a heart attack and died. Blair had wept for hours after hearing this news, nearly inconsolably. Would the war take from her all she held dear?

But perhaps even worse than this news was what she learned on the truck on the way to Santo Tomas. There she met the waitress, Rosa, who looked as battered and bruised as Blair. She also had been captured as a result of Silvia's arrest.

"Silvia told the Japs everything she knew," Rosa said.

"I can't believe that. How can you be so certain?"

"Perhaps we will never know for sure." Rosa's expression was hard with her own certainty. "But I do know with little doubt what became of her. A nurse in the hospital told me that Silvia committed suicide. That, to me, is proof enough of her guilt."

Maybe so, Blair thought sadly. Perhaps Silvia had talked, then despaired so deeply afterward that she took her life. Nothing would surprise Blair any longer. But she seethed inside as she imagined what those Jap animals must have put Silvia through to drive her to that extreme.

As the truckload of new arrivals pulled through the iron gates, she put these thoughts from her mind. She had to concentrate now on beginning a new phase of her Philippine experience. What lay ahead, she did not know. More torment? More torture? More drudgery? Maybe it didn't matter. She sensed within, for good or ill, she would likely survive whatever crossed her path. That was her curse, she supposed, and maybe her hope.

Blair noted a new addition to Santo Tomas from when she had visited this place before the war. There was an ominous layer of barbed wire topping the stone and concrete wall. But Blair felt no sense of dread or fear as she approached what would be her prison, probably for the duration of the war.

She remembered as the truck rumbled along that this place held more than misery. Thinking of this, her anticipation grew. Claudette was here. Finally she would see her friend and know she was all right. Perhaps other friends were here, as well. This bolstered her spirits as nothing had in weeks.

She was taken to a women's dormitory in the main building. This had once been a classroom and now was home for twenty women. Half of the women had iron beds to sleep on, but the rest, including Blair, had to content themselves with bamboo cots. Blair didn't mind. She'd slept on far worse. There was barely space in this area to move about and no privacy at all. She was greeted, though, in a friendly manner by the women present. Some were Americans, and she never thought hearing an American accent could sound so good. But they were all strangers to her.

She was shown to an unoccupied cot, and then her Japanese escort left. She looked around, a bit bewildered, unsure of what to do next. She was soon surrounded by a handful of chattering women. She realized what a new arrival must mean to these who had been locked up perhaps since the beginning of the war—news and information of the outside world. She was bombarded with a flood of questions all at once. Now she probably looked more bewildered than ever.

"Hey, give the girl a break," broke in one of the women. She was quite tall, and that seemed to give her a rather commanding bearing, for the others quieted long enough for Blair to get in a word.

"I think the war is going well," Blair said. "I don't know a lot, but America is gaining much of the ground lost in '41."

She tried to answer a few more questions but had little of the kind of information the others wanted to hear. Eventually, one by one they wandered back to their own beds and activities. Blair once again looked about, wondering what to do next.

The tall woman who had spoken before was still standing nearby.

"I'm Dorothy," she said. "You'll get used to the routine real quick."

"Hi, I'm Blair."

"That's an odd name—pretty, though, just different, you know."

"I'm named for my uncle. My father wanted a boy."

"That's a man for you, isn't it? They all want little replicas of themselves running around." Dorothy was at least six feet, and looking down on Blair, she grinned. "I have a feeling we wouldn't be in this fix if it wasn't for all those males strutting and shaking their sabers."

"Well, I can't complain too much. One of them is my husband," said Blair wryly.

Dorothy laughed. "Mine, too. A Navy lieutenant. He's in Bilibid Prison . . . I think. I hope."

"Mine's . . ." Blair paused, looked around, and thought better of talking too freely. "I'm not sure where he is. Safe, I hope."

"I see." Dorothy nodded knowingly. "It's almost time for supper. Let me show you the ropes."

Blair walked with Dorothy out to the grounds as she explained that Blair needed to get a meal ticket before queuing up at the dining hall. "Standing in line is what we do most around here."

"Miss Blair!" called a voice that Blair recognized.

She turned and saw the one face besides Gary's that she most desired to see.

"Claudette!"

She ran toward her young friend, the first person she had met when she came to the Philippines, who was also running toward her, and they flung their arms around each other.

Dorothy laughed. "This is the best part of this place, when long-lost friends find each other."

Blair kept her arm around Claudette as they both walked back to where Dorothy was standing. She made introductions, but Dorothy understood that they would want some time alone, so she went on her way, assured that Claudette would show Blair the ropes.

"I was so worried about you for so long," said Blair as tears leaked from her eyes. "Then just a couple months ago, Reverend Sanchez discovered you were here."

"He has been so good to send me packages since then," said Claudette, her own eyes moist. "And I got your messages. Until then I worried so about you."

Blair hadn't the heart just then to tell her friend about the reverend. She was hungry for just a few moments that weren't tainted by grief. They found an old tree stump and sat together, talking continually about everything else, catching up on over a year of separation. Claudette had made it to Corregidor, and when "the Rock" fell to the enemy, she was captured with the nurses and finally ended up here. She was especially pleased to hear Blair's reports about Mateo, though Reverend Sanchez had informed her of his safety and she had received Mateo's messages.

But before they covered just a fraction of the time of their separation, Claudette had other news.

"Mrs. Doyle is here, too!" She beamed.

"I hoped she would be. But what of the girls?"

"She knows nothing of where they might be. Anything could have happened to them. And also, Reverend Doyle died in Bilibid Prison from complications after his leg was amputated."

"Oh, poor Mrs. Doyle. It must be so hard on her."

"Shall we go see her?"

"Of course, you ninny! Let's go."

Meg Doyle was already in line at the dining hall, so it wasn't difficult to locate her. Blair felt as if she were meeting her sister. There were hugs and kisses and tears. And the three of them chattered through a meal that Blair hardly noticed, not that it was much of note anyway. Later Claudette mentioned that she had not seen Mrs. Doyle so happy in a long while. But Blair had noted how Meg would fade every now and then, grow distracted and lose her smile. Blair understood, for she felt at times she did the same when she would suddenly feel guilty for being so happy, when she would remember burying her baby and losing Gary.

Yet despite the undercurrent of grief she knew they all shared, she could not help the joy in at last being with her dearest friends. At one point during the meal as they sat on benches at the long tables, Blair just gazed with quiet wonder at her friends. Two weeks ago she had reached the lowest point in her life. She'd been in an abyss, dark and frightening. Now she felt showered in light. Clear, beautiful light! It seemed so impossible. Then she remembered, "With God all things are possible."

And she broke down and wept. Not just tears of joy, but uncontrollable, hiccuping sobs. Meg Doyle was at her side in a moment, her arm encircling Blair's thin shoulders.

"I . . . I'm j-just so h-happy," Blair stammered tearfully.

"I know . . . I know," Meg murmured softly.

Claudette, seated on the other side of Blair, put an arm around her, too.

"It's kind of why we came to God, isn't it, Blair," said Claudette, "so we could find happiness in the middle of a Jap prison."

Blair nodded, unable to speak further. Claudette always had been the wise one.

33

Manzanar, California
September 1943

JACKIE WIPED another bead of sweat from her brow. The heat was as oppressive as if it were the middle of summer. If only the wind would bring relief, but instead it only stirred up the dust of the dry desert earth. She balanced nine-month-old Emi on her hip and adjusted her daughter's sun hat so the glare wasn't in her eyes. Jackie wished she'd brought her own hat but hadn't given it a thought because she hadn't known their wait would be so long.

The bus was late, or maybe the white drivers simply relished making their Japanese passengers wither in the heat. She glanced at Sam. His jaw was set, and he was gazing straight ahead. This was not a happy day for him, but no doubt it was worse for Toshio. It was he who was to be a passenger on the bus when it came.

"Toshio," she said, mostly to break the oppressive silence, "your mother wanted me to make sure you had your winter coat."

He gave a shrug. "Yeah, I got it. It'll probably be just as cold and miserable there in the winter as here."

"Yes, I think so, too," Jackie said. "Sam, what do you know about the weather there? I'm not even sure where Tule Lake is."

Sam looked at her as if not appreciative at all of being dragged into the inane conversation. Yet he had chosen to go to the bus stop and see his brother off. No one had coerced him. It might have been better if he had remained back at the apartment with his parents. What good would another good-bye do?

"He's still furious at me, Jackie," Toshio said.

"I don't think he would have come here to see you off if he was mad at you," offered Jackie.

"Would you quit talking about me as if I'm not here?" Sam snapped.

Jackie restrained a smile. She'd had a feeling that ploy would goad him into talking. "Well, Sam, you're acting like you aren't here. I thought you wanted peace with Toshio."

"I want peace," Sam replied. "But I am still furious. He could have answered yes on the questionnaire."

"I couldn't," countered Toshio. "And now I have to pay the price."

The price for Toshio for answering no to the key questions on the loyalty questionnaire was to be hauled off to the internment camp at Tule Lake, where rebels and malcontents were kept. Everyone was sick over this, his parents especially. In their eyes he was still just a child with a passion for baseball and an interest only in goofing off with his friends. Though Sam knew better, down deep he probably wanted to keep thinking of his little brother like that, as well. It was so hard at times to accept how drastically their world had changed.

"What's done . . ." Sam gave a frustrated shrug.

"Will you write me letters?" asked Toshio.

"Do you really want me to?"

"I don't want to get cut off from my family. I told you before I don't want to go to Japan. This country is still my home."

"Then I'll write."

Just then Jackie saw the cloud of dust that preceded the bus. Her stomach knotted. She wished she could have gotten to know her brother-in-law better. She knew his family was still upset over the stand he had made, or at least at the repercussions it had caused, but she respected him for it.

"I'm sorry I couldn't go along with the powers that be, Sam," Toshio said, as if the approach of the bus placed an urgency upon things that must be said. "But I don't think it should ever be said that all Japanese Americans went like lambs to the slaughter. Some of us tried to buck the system."

"Everyone has their reasons for what they have done," Sam said a little defensively. He would never be quite comfortable with his own decision not to protest. He had his reasons, too.

"I know that," conceded Toshio with true understanding. "But, though my family is ashamed of me, I will never feel shame for doing what I felt I had to do."

"We aren't ashamed of you!" exclaimed Sam. He seemed surprised his brother should think this, but even Jackie had wondered at times if that had not been the case.

"I wish I could feel that was true, but if you say so, I'll try to believe it."

In a swirl of dust and fumes the bus pulled to a stop. Jackie coughed and drew Emi close so the child wouldn't have to breathe the foul air.

"Can I give my niece a hug before I go?" asked Toshio.

"Of course."

When the dust settled, Jackie let Toshio take Emi, and he gave the child a hug and a kiss. Then, before handing Emi back, he leaned over and gave Jackie a kiss on the cheek.

"I'm glad Sam has you, Jackie," he said, sounding more like a wise old sage than a nearly eighteen-year-old. "You're good for him."

"You take care, Toshio, and you write to us, too," she said, tears rising in her eyes.

"Okay, move along," said one of the guards who had herded most of those waiting into the bus.

Toshio placed Emi back into Jackie's arms, then turned to his brother. "You gonna hug me or something?" The flippancy of his words only partly hid the tremor in his voice. His eyes glistened with unshed tears.

For a moment Sam looked as if he was trying to think of a snappy comeback, but no words came. Finally he just threw his arms around Toshio. His eyes were damp, too, and as he stood back, he still seemed to be having trouble speaking.

Toshio nodded, understanding, then strode toward the bus and climbed in. Jackie and Sam watched as the bus pulled away. They didn't move until it was out of sight. Sam continued to be silent on the walk back to their barracks, but when they were a couple of minutes from their destination, he stopped.

"I'm not quite ready to go in," he admitted.

"Let's walk some more," Jackie suggested.

"Okay, but you must be tired holding Emi. Let me have her."

Jackie gladly relinquished Emi to her father. Her arms were

getting tired holding the bundle. Precious though she was, Emi weighed twenty-two pounds. Jackie worried that she was too chubby, but Mrs. Okuda was quite pleased with her "butterball" grandchild and said all of her own children had looked the same at that age.

The little family walked for a short distance, but Sam quickly realized it was too hot for a leisurely stroll. "Let's go to the mess hall. It should be open now."

The mess hall was not much cooler, but at least they were out of the direct blast of the sun. Jackie made no complaints, and Emi seemed content. Jackie knew her husband needed to talk, but it usually took him time to ease into unburdening his heart. So while Sam and Emi got settled on a bench by a table, Jackie went to the kitchen to see if she could pilfer a little snack for Emi to keep her occupied. The kitchen workers generally didn't like to give out food outside the given schedules, but they conceded when they saw Sam holding Emi in the dining room. It seemed all right for them to give a bit of food to a baby. One of the men found some saltine crackers, wrapped them in a napkin, then looking furtively around as if breaking a serious law, handed them to Jackie.

When she returned to the table, she found Sam playing peeka-boo with Emi. He seemed to have relaxed a little. Jackie slid onto the bench opposite Sam's. She gave a cracker to Emi.

"Eat slowly, Emi, sweetheart," she said. "I think those crackers are made of gold."

Emi didn't seem to care. She shoved the whole cracker into her mouth, then proceeded to spit bits and crumbs right back out as she giggled and tried to talk.

Sam laughed. "Who taught this child to eat?"

"I'm surprised she gains any weight at all, since it seems so much of her food ends up everywhere but in her stomach."

"Thank God for the joy she brings us," said Sam, "when we need it most."

"Cheap entertainment."

"I think I could watch her all day."

"I wish we could. I wish that was all there was to life."

"But it's not."

Jackie shook her head in agreement.

Sam added with a grunt, "You know what I really wish? That I wasn't so angry all the time. I was always Mama's good-natured kid. Now I'm changing. And no matter how much I pray about it, the anger is still there."

"There is such a thing as righteous anger, Sam," Jackie said. "Like when Christ turned over the money changers' tables."

He barked such a dry, harsh laugh that Emi stopped her cooing and her attempt to mangle another cracker in order to stare at this odd, discordant sound coming from her gentle father.

"I didn't mean to scare you, Emi, sweetie," he murmured softly. He kissed her forehead. "Daddy's just a little nuts lately." To Jackie he added, "Maybe a small part of what I feel is righteous indignation over a terrible injustice, but I can't let myself off that easily. This anger eats away at me, makes me want to smash things sometimes. That's not right. Yet I can't let it go. I have tried so hard all my life to do the right thing, to be a good citizen. Every year I was in grade school, I won the good citizenship award. Maybe if I hadn't tried so hard . . ."

"How many citizenship awards did your brother win?"

"He was too busy having fun with his friends. He was a good kid but not as over the top about it as I guess I was. I *had* to win those awards. I went out of my way to do it. But you never think when you are proudly standing in front of everyone holding that engraved certificate that you will one day end up in prison."

"Sam, it doesn't help to dwell on it."

"I know . . . I know." He took out his handkerchief and wiped away some crumbs from around Emi's mouth. "But I stew over it, and it becomes more entrenched. I try not to, then something crops up to emphasize it again."

"Like Toshio leaving?"

He nodded. "I worry that that's the *straw*. Not only the straw that will break his back but mine, as well."

"No, Sam!" Jackie could not keep the fear from her voice.

"He's never been away from his family. He'll be only eighteen in a couple of months. I know lots of eighteen-year-old boys are having to leave their families now for the war, but . . ." He gave a shrug, obviously not knowing how to voice what worried him most.

"He'll be all right," said Jackie. "He has grown up so much since coming here. I wouldn't be surprised if he did great things."

"He told me last night that when he is drafted he will resist. He will go to jail if he does—real jail, not just some internment camp. And when he told me that, I knew what I must do if—no, *when*—I am drafted."

"What, Sam?" she asked, though she feared she already knew the answer.

"I'll go. You know, one brother must balance out the actions of the other—"

"No, Sam!" she cut in sharply. "No wonder your anger is eating you up. You must do what you believe is right, not what you think you have to do in order to save face from your brother's actions."

"It's not that simple, Jackie, and you know it. I guess it is stupid of me to try to make my actions sound more noble by using my brother as an excuse. Still, taking Toshio out of the equation, I don't see how I have any other choice. For one thing my sense of pride far outweighs my sense of outrage over the injustices done to the Japanese people. To put it simply, I am just too proud to go to a federal penitentiary. And I guess I am too weak, as well."

"Listen to what you are saying," Jackie said. "I would almost laugh at how ludicrous it is if it didn't make me sick at heart. You say you're going to fight in a war because you're too weak to go to jail? It doesn't make sense. Yet I know what you mean. I know how many different directions you are being pulled. No matter what you do, it's going to be the wrong thing—or the right thing. It's hard even to distinguish which. I don't think you're angry because you hate America or its government, at least not entirely. I think it's because you feel helpless."

He looked at her with wonder in his eyes. "Jackie, my dear wise wife." His lips twitched in a slight smile. "Do you think that might be so? That wouldn't be so bad because—" his voice broke as emotion suddenly struck him—"I don't want to hate my country. I have no country if not this one, and there is so much about it I love." He cleared his throat and blinked away the threat of tears. "I've been afraid to admit even to myself the real reason for wanting to be in the Army. It is for patriotism. It is my duty to fight in this war like any other American. That's all I want, all I have ever wanted my whole life, just to be like any other American."

Jackie rose and went to him, sitting on the bench close to him and putting her arm around him. Emi tried to grab Jackie's nose.

Jackie gave her child a kiss, then did the same to her husband. When Sam's lips touched hers, there was far more fervency in them, and he reached an arm around her to pull her close. Emi was wedged between them, but the child didn't seem to mind at all.

"Sam, the last thing I want," Jackie breathed, her face still touching his, "is for you to go to war, to leave Emi and me. Part of me would almost rather you went to Leavenworth. No one would shoot at you there. But no matter what happens, you have my love and support."

"It would be so easy for me to use all that has happened here as an excuse to stay out of the war. And for me it would be an excuse, not a matter of principle as it is for Toshio." Pausing, he moved his head back a bit so he could see both Jackie and Emi. "You two are the dearest things in my life, and the thought of leaving you is almost unbearable. Yet I know it's the best thing I can do for you, to protect this country, to protect you, and to see that this war ends soon so that our lives can return to normal."

She tried to fight back her own tears as she nodded. She took some comfort in knowing that thousands of men and women all over the country were having to face what she must soon face. But there was a knot of fear inside her that went beyond what most couples were feeling. Jackie had heard men in the camp talk about fighting in the war, and some had already left to join the all-Japanese unit formed earlier in the year. These young men, in preparing to go to war, were saying that this was their chance, once and for all, to prove their American patriotism. Though Sam hadn't said exactly that, Jackie knew the idea was in his mind. And men who had so much to prove often took dangerous chances.

34

Jackie wasn't surprised when Sam told her he had decided to enlist rather than wait for his draft notice. She knew his going willingly rather than by force, so to speak, was just another part of his strong desire to prove himself loyal.

Sam's parents not only were surprised by his decision but were reluctant to give their support.

"You must not do this so that we can be relocated," Sam's father insisted. "I will not have you risk your life for that."

"We do not wish to be relocated, anyway," Mrs. Okuda put in. "We have no place to go, no way to support ourselves. Who will hire an old man and an old lady?"

Jackie's heart ached when she heard this because her mother-in-law's words were true. Once released from the camp, especially with both their sons away from them and unable to offer any financial support, the elder Okudas would have to start over with absolutely nothing to their name, just as it had been when they had come from Japan more than a quarter of a century ago. But then they had been young and ripe for such a challenge.

"Mama, Papa, that's not why I am going," Sam said.

Jackie could tell he didn't believe his words to be much of an assurance. There was really no way to turn any of this into a comfort for his worried parents.

"Is it because of Toshio?" asked Mr. Okuda.

"It's because of *me*, Papa. I must serve my country." He paused, then added because there was more to it, "It is also because I want to prove my loyalty."

With a tremor in her voice Mrs. Okuda said, "I have heard rumors that these all-Japanese units will be used by the Army as suicide squads."

"That's not true, Mama, I am sure."

It surprised Jackie when Mr. Okuda turned to her since he seldom spoke to her. "You will leave the camp when Yoshito go to Army and take my grandchild with you?"

"I will stay if you need me," Jackie said.

Sam added, "I talked with Kimi, and she assured me she will settle down and look out for you. She is twenty now and mature enough to help."

"She will want to marry sometime soon," Mr. Okuda said.

"She is waiting for Susumu."

Kimi's fiancé had been evacuated to the Heart Mountain Camp in Wyoming, and despite the fact that she was casually seeing other boys at Manzanar, she still planned on marrying Susumu one day.

Sam glanced helplessly at Jackie. She knew the deep responsibility to care for his parents that he bore as the eldest child. She understood the weight upon him and the emotional toll it carried.

Perhaps his father understood, for he barked a dry laugh. "You make it sound like I am wretched old man! I can still care for my own family!"

His eyes flashed, and Jackie thought this must be a picture of the man of old, the man before the camp had sapped him of his manhood. His English had even improved over the last year, as if he'd been expecting this day to come. Nevertheless, he did indeed sound more like the head of his household than he had since coming to the camp.

"Now go. Do your duty," Mr. Okuda added, "but do not go in order to make me proud. You have already done so!"

Sam left in early November. Jackie didn't depart the camp until the end of the month because it took three weeks for her to receive clearance for Emi to leave. She had already written to her mother and was told in no uncertain terms that she was more than welcome to come home to stay. Jackie knew her mother wanted her and wanted Emi, as well. It was her father's reception that worried her. He had never yet made an attempt to visit his granddaughter, and Cecilia had made no reference to Keagan when she extended her welcome.

The taxi driver carried Jackie's luggage up to the front porch of her parent's home. She paid him, fumbling a bit with her purse because she held a squirmy Emi on her hip. As the driver pulled away, Jackie took in a breath and rang the bell. She had been relieved that the time of her arrival occurred when her father would most likely be at work. But since he was not tied to a regular schedule, it was possible that he would be home. She hoped not. She needed a little more time before she was ready to face him.

When her mother answered the door and it became apparent her father was not home, Jackie felt as if one hurdle had been crossed. They greeted each other with warm hugs despite the fact that Emi was quite shy with her grandmother.

"I suppose she doesn't remember me," Cecilia said, for when she held out her arms to the child, Emi clung all that much more tightly to her mother.

"She'll warm up quickly," assured Jackie. "She is more shy than usual because of all the changes she's gone through lately."

"I understand. I'm just so glad you're here." Cecilia seemed to suddenly check her joy. "Of course, I wish it were under better circumstances. You and Emi must be missing Sam terribly."

Jackie nodded and felt the emotion that was always bubbling close to the surface. She shook it away as best as she could. "He has written me a couple of times already, and his letters are so vivid that I almost feel like I am there. Well . . . almost." She paused, not doing a good job of curbing her emotions. Then changing the subject, she asked, "What shall I do with the luggage?"

"Let's just bring everything into the entry for now. We can take it upstairs later. I'm afraid I have no regular servants these days. The gardener comes only twice a week and the housekeeper three times. There's such a manpower shortage that we all have to make do. Cameron helps with some of the heavier jobs."

"She is still staying with you?"

"She gave up on the idea of finding a place near the paper or, for that matter, of finding a place of her own at all. There is a housing shortage here. People have poured into southern California from all over the country to work in the defense industry."

"I'll be happy to see more of her, then."

"Don't expect much, Jacqueline. She is as much a work addict as your father. They seldom come up for breath."

"But they are getting along?"

"You can judge for yourself. I have ordered them both to be here for dinner tonight for your homecoming—not that they wouldn't *want* to, you understand." She gave an awkward smile. "Cameron is really looking forward to seeing you."

Jackie wanted to ask, "And Dad?" but couldn't bring herself to do it. She'd find out soon enough. It was three in the afternoon. Dinner would be in a few hours.

They went into the front parlor, and Cecilia continued to talk as they settled themselves into seats. "I have brought down your old highchair from the attic for Emi, and I also brought the cradle, but I see it may be too small."

Jackie chuckled. "My little butterball!" She had Emi on her lap facing her and was entertaining her with games of peekaboo and pat-a-cake as she and her mother talked. "She can sleep with me in my bed, Mom. She often did at the camp, especially when she was first born and it was so cold."

"Oh, but Jacqueline, it isn't good for a child to sleep with her parents. Teaches bad habits. Perhaps that's what makes her cling to you so."

Jackie blinked in surprise at her mother's rare criticism and opened her mouth to try to defend herself when Cecilia gave an embarrassed chuckle.

"Oh, how I hated when elders tried to tell me how to raise my children!" Cecilia said in an apologetic tone. "My mother wasn't alive when you were born, but there were many other nosy women who tried to fill the void. I'm sorry, Jacqueline. I will try to hold my tongue."

"Well . . . I may not like it, Mom, but I don't want you to have to walk on eggshells, either. I'm sure you have much wisdom to offer. I know I'll ask your advice often."

"And I'll try to give it only when asked."

"You are probably right about Emi sleeping with me, but there was often no other choice."

"I wish I would have saved more of your baby furniture, but when we moved into this house it seemed pointless to lug it all along. If you like, we can go shopping for a crib tomorrow. It will have to be used, no doubt, because a new one will be hard to come by with war shortages and all."

"That would be nice, Mom. Emi has never had a real crib."

Jackie and her mother visited for a short time longer until Emi began to nod off to sleep in Jackie's arms. Truth be told, Jackie was tired, too. She'd had to catch the bus from Manzanar to Lone Pine quite early that morning, and then the train ride hadn't been pleasant because Emi had had motion sickness and been quite restless. Cecilia seemed to understand when both of them retired upstairs for a nap. Secretly Jackie also thought she was going to need the rest for what lay ahead.

When Jackie came downstairs at six, she found her mother in the kitchen putting the finishing touches on dinner. She explained that their cook had gone to work at Douglas Aircraft for much more money, and thus far it had been impossible to find a replacement. Jackie put Emi into the highchair that Cecilia had brought into the kitchen, then offered to help. All that was left to do was set the table in the dining room. The minute Jackie left the kitchen with a stack of plates, Emi started crying. Depositing the dishes on the dining room table, Jackie returned quickly to comfort Emi, who stopped fussing the minute Jackie came into view. In order to finish the job, Jackie had to carry glasses and flatware in one hand, making several trips, with Emi propped on her hip. Cecilia made no comment the entire time, but one glance at her told Jackie she was biting her tongue. Maybe Emi *was* spoiled. Jackie gave an inward shrug. Mrs. Okuda had never chided her for spoiling Emi, though Sam believed it was because culturally the Japanese were notorious for spoiling young children. He admitted his mother had spoiled hers.

At seven o'clock sharp, the time Cecilia had said dinner would be served, Cameron came home. She and Jackie, with Emi still clinging to her mother, greeted each other with hugs. Keagan did not come home until seven-fifteen. Cecilia thought that was doing quite well for him. But before coming into the dining room, where everyone was now congregated, to greet his daughter, he stopped at the wet bar in the parlor to pour himself a drink.

"Hello, Dad," Jackie said when he finally made an appearance. She had put Emi back in the highchair, which Cameron had moved into the dining room. The child was content for the moment, chewing on zwieback toast.

"Good evening, Jackie," he said. He set his drink down by his place at the table but made no move closer to Jackie.

"It's been a long time," she said. Then boldly she added, "Can I have a hug?"

"You know I don't go in for such sentimentality." But he gave a shrug and a bit stiffly strode to her and put an arm around her shoulder. "Good to have you home."

Jackie smiled. The greeting held more warmth than she should have expected. But he never once mentioned Emi nor looked in the baby's direction. She was reminded of Sam's father. What irony that those two men were so much alike!

Cecilia came in carrying a platter with a fragrant standing rib roast. Jackie wondered how many ration coupons that had taken. She and Cameron helped bring in the rest of the food, and they all sat at the table. Jackie marveled at how they all naturally gravitated to their old places. Sadly the chair next to Jackie and adjacent to Keagan was empty. That's where Blair had always sat—near her father, Jackie recalled, because Blair was the one who most often needed disciplining at the table. Emi's chair was placed between Jackie and Cecilia.

Keagan carved the roast, then bowls of side dishes were passed and plates filled. The conversation was genial though rather superficial, as everyone was on their best behavior. They talked of rationing and new items on the list. Jackie asked questions because it was still new to her. They hadn't had to deal with that at Manzanar. They also talked about mutual friends they knew, men who had gone into the military, marriages, births.

When the conversation turned to the weather, which was warm and balmy for the end of November, Cecilia remembered something. "Emi will have her first birthday next week—December 6, isn't it, Jacqueline? We should have a small party."

"I'll be busy," said Keagan in almost a preemptory fashion. "We are putting out a special Pearl Harbor Day issue."

"But your granddaughter's birthday is the day before."

"Yes . . . well, because of the issue, I've had to move several important meetings to the sixth—"

"Hogwash, Dad!" Cameron said. "The so-called special issue is little more than an extra banner headline. What extra work is there for you?"

"It's okay, Cameron," put in Jackie, trying to keep her tone even, though her lips trembled a little with emotion. "If Dad doesn't want to be around Emi, there's nothing we can do about it."

"That's ridiculous!" Keagan said, but his voice lacked its usual effrontery.

"Well, you haven't even looked at her since you've been home," said Jackie.

"What do you mean I haven't looked at her? I'm in the same room, for heaven's sake." But even as he spoke his eyes were still averted from his granddaughter.

"Never mind!" Tears sprang into Jackie's eyes, and she had an urge to jump up and run out of the room, but she was determined to handle this in a mature manner.

"Well, maybe you're expecting too much." Haughtiness mixed oddly with defensiveness in Keagan's voice. "I haven't turned you out, have I, or your Jap baby?"

"Thank you very much," Jackie retorted with sarcasm, having a hard time remembering to be mature. "If you want us to leave—"

"You'll do no such thing!" said Cecilia, glaring at her husband. "Keagan, you promised me you would be on your best behavior."

"I didn't promise to be lovey-dovey over the child!"

"I don't expect that, Dad," said Jackie, making herself calm. She could not alienate her father so soon. He just needed time to warm up to reality. "I know it must be hard for you, but she is your grand-child, and you might come to enjoy her if you just gave her a chance. You could start by simply looking at her. She is so pretty and sweet."

Keagan drummed his fingers on the table a moment. Everyone was silent. Then as if to mock the silly adults around her and fill the uncomfortable silence, Emi began to chatter, mostly in her usual gibberish, but she had mastered two words, *mama* and *cracker,* which came out more like "ker-kak," and these she now uttered several times in singsong fashion. Jackie saw that Emi's bowl of mashed potatoes, smashed cooked carrots, and a bit of the pot roast, chopped finely, was empty. Jackie had the package of zwie-back and gave Emi a piece.

"Dad, she looks so much like Jackie," Cameron said, her voice soft and gentle, as if with entreaty.

Jackie was reminded that her sister had indeed softened quite a bit over the last few years.

"Well . . . um . . . if you say so," muttered Keagan. Then he added, still without looking at Emi, "Maybe I can clear up some time on the sixth."

After dinner Jackie and Cameron insisted on cleaning up, but Emi was still not willing to be separated from her mother. When they tried to sit her in her highchair back in the kitchen, she kept standing up, teetering precariously. Jackie was forced to give up her good intentions of helping with the cleanup.

"I'll wash up," Cameron said. "You and Emi can keep me company."

"If you have it under control, I'll go see if your father needs me," said Cecilia.

Jackie could not see what her father could possibly need, but she had a feeling Cecilia was just giving the two sisters some time alone.

With the kitchen door closed, Jackie was able to put Emi on the floor to crawl around a bit. "It'll be nice when she learns to walk." Jackie took a dish towel in hand.

"She should be doing that soon?"

"I think Mom is concerned that Emi hasn't started walking already, but to tell the truth I hardly encouraged her to crawl much at Manzanar. The floors of our apartment were so rough and dusty, no matter how much we swept them. Mom's floors are so sparkling clean, she can crawl to her heart's content."

Cameron chuckled. "Mom complains all the time at how messy her house is now that the housekeeper can come only three days a week."

"It's paradise compared to the camp. I guess I've learned to appreciate many things I never did before." Jackie took up a dish her sister had set in the drainer and began to dry it.

"So how about Dad?" Cameron gave her head a frustrated shake.

"He's come a long way!"

Now Cameron laughed outright. "I guess you could say that."

"Again, it's appreciating the little things," said Jackie. "He didn't turn me away when he well could have, and he is going to come to

Emi's party. For him, that's incredible! How has it been for you to work with him?"

"Kind of like taming a wild elephant. We have our good days, and we have days when I feel like I have been stampeded by a herd. I don't see him every day, and that helps. I'm just a reporter, and if he wasn't my father, I'd have no reason to see him at all." She dipped a soapy dish into the rinse water. "Can you tell me something, Jackie? Has your faith helped you much in dealing with Dad? Sometimes I feel like I'm back to being my old self with him—you know, snotty, stubborn, sarcastic. It's a bit discouraging."

"Maybe just *surviving* life with Dad proves God is with us," Jackie answered glibly, then added more earnestly, "but I know how you feel. All my life I have tried to be a good Christian, to show him a good example that might draw him to God. I haven't always been successful. I get angry, answer sharply, storm out of rooms. I've finally come to the conclusion that God mainly cares that I am trying. You know, 'the spirit indeed is willing' even if 'the flesh is weak.'"

"That makes me feel better."

"Dad would try the patience of Job."

The sisters laughed. Then a loud clanking and banging intruded into the quiet kitchen. Emi had opened a cupboard and was enthusiastically emptying it of its pots and pans. She seemed so happily occupied that Jackie shrugged.

"Do you think she can hurt anything?" she asked.

"What do I know?" Cameron replied. "But I say as long as she's happy and there are no sharp implements involved, there's no harm. By the way, what does your little cherub want for her birthday?"

"I haven't given it any thought. I really didn't think there would be any fuss over it."

"My first niece turns one only once in her life. At the moment I'm rolling in dough, so I want to indulge her a little."

"Thank you," smiled Jackie. "Well, to be honest, Emi needs so much. She's nearly grown out of all her clothes."

"Let's go shopping tomorrow!" Cameron said brightly. "You, Mom, and me . . . and Emi, too."

"You *want* to go shopping?" Jackie grinned wryly. "You have changed, sis."

"We all have." Cameron held a soapy goblet midair. "At least I know you and I have, and it seems a safe bet that no matter what Blair is doing, she's changed, too."

"What do you think she is doing? Mom says she's probably in a POW camp."

"Yes, I'm sure she is," Cameron said vaguely.

"Come on, you know more about these things than anyone I know. Tell me what you really think."

Reluctantly Cameron complied. "Well, we've seen some lists of prisoners, and she hasn't been on them. But the lists are by no means complete. Neither has she been on any casualty list. It's very likely she's in hiding. I truly believe she is still alive. She's probably having the adventure of her life."

Jackie nodded, not completely convinced, but Cameron's view was better than the alternative. "How I resent this war for altering our lives so," she said. "I know God is with us and He will make it all right. Yet we will never be able to go back to the way it was, the way it would have been without a war. Sam and I would have a little house, he'd be teaching high-school English, Blair would be a famous actress, you would be chasing the news."

"Well, I'm still doing that, at least."

"Yes, but there's an empty place in you now, Cameron. Not in your spirit—God has filled that quite well—but in your heart. A huge chunk of you is thousands of miles away in Russia, and until you and your doctor are reunited, you will just be going through the motions of life."

"In a way that is true. But I would never have met Alex if there hadn't been a war, so I guess that's one reason why I can't resent the war entirely." She took a handful of dirty flatware and dropped it in the wash water. "Sometimes I fear I thrive a little too much on the war. Then I remember all the destruction it has brought, the horrible things I have seen, and I realize I need not fear. I'd go back to reporting society news if it could all be over. Just to know Alex is safe, even if I never—" She broke off suddenly as her voice caught on emotion.

Jackie laid a comforting hand on her arm. "I forgot that your Alex is also in the Army. And it's worse for you since you can't even get a letter from him." Her stomach twisted and she glanced down at Emi as if seeing her child happily emptying her grandmother's cupboard would ease her anxiety, but it didn't help. "The Bible says

God will deliver us from our fears, and I try to abide by that, yet I can't seem to shake the gnawing worry inside me since Sam left. Does it ever go away, Cameron?"

"I'm newer at this than you, at least this matter of faith," Cameron replied. "But I have had to deal with Alex being in the Army a bit longer, and honestly, there is a knot inside me that is always there. Work takes my mind off it for a time, but the worry never disappears. Can any woman whose man is facing terrible danger be expected to shake all anxiety?"

Jackie shook her head. "Another thing God understands, I hope."

"If I know nothing else, I do know He is an understanding God," Cameron said with a conviction that warmed Jackie's heart and made her feel safe in sharing more of her feelings with her sister.

"I dreamed of Sam the other night," murmured Jackie. "He was on a battlefield like those I've seen in newsreels. He was standing all alone, covered in blood. Oh, Cameron, I know I can't dwell on pictures like that, but it is hard. The Japanese men who have gone into the Army are so determined to prove their loyalty, I fear what lengths they will go to."

"Sam seemed like a level-headed fellow to me."

"Normally he is, but the evacuation has changed him. He has so much anger in him now and, I fear, so much to prove. I guess I just have to trust him to God and know that his personal faith is strong, too."

"It always comes down to that, putting ourselves in God's hands. I wonder now how I managed before I knew to do that."

"Cameron, I am so glad we can share both our pain and our faith. I know you plan to go to Europe the moment Dad lets you, but I'm glad you're here now."

"Me too, sis. And I am going to take some time away from the paper so we can spend more time together."

They finished up the dishes, then Jackie took Emi up to bed. She had fears and worries in abundance, but Jackie also realized she had much to be thankful for. Her homecoming had gone quite well, her father would celebrate Emi's birthday, and her sister shared her faith. She'd put off writing Sam for a couple of days because she'd been feeling down and didn't want to bring him down, too. Now she took out some stationery and a pen. She could send him words of hope now to go with her expressions of love.

35

Jackie closed the blinds to dim some of the afternoon light, then looked over at the new crib nestled against the wall in her bedroom. Emi had already fallen asleep. Her little birthday party had exhausted her. In addition to family, Cecilia had invited two of her friends from church, who brought their grandchildren—Cecilia thought a child's party wasn't complete unless there were other children present. The five juvenile guests ranged in age from one to five. There had been moments of pure mayhem. Some of the other children were not completely willing to give up the gifts they'd brought for Emi, nor did Emi think much of the concept of sharing. There had been tears and struggles, alleviated a little by cake, which had not always ended up in mouths but also was smeared in curls and on carpets.

But all in all it had been a good day. The most interesting aspect had been Jackie's father's presence. He'd mostly been a quiet observer, though she had caught him once or twice rolling his eyes in his usual disdain during some of the more chaotic moments. And he had not interacted very much with Emi, though he did sing "Happy Birthday" to her with everyone else and may have glanced in her direction more than once.

Sighing, Jackie took an envelope from her pocket and sat on the bed. She'd received her own gift that morning. A letter from Sam had arrived just before the party. With company arriving, there hadn't been time to read it until now. She slipped off her shoes and put her feet up on the bedspread, then tore open the envelope but was a little disappointed to find only one short page. Sam said he was all right and loved her and Emi and that he would write more later, but they were so busy now with field maneuvers, he could barely eke out a few lines. Needing more, she took his other two letters from her nightstand drawer and reread them.

November 15, 1943
Dearest Jackie,

This is the first chance I have had to write since I got here. I think of you every day, and if I could I would write you as often as that. But so far they have kept me hopping here. We later recruits have a lot of catching up to do with those who came in the summer. We go from dawn to dusk, and by the time I drop into bed after dinner, I am too exhausted to even lift a pen. A sedentary year at Manzanar has made me a softie, but I don't think even working on Papa's farm would have prepared me for this.

Let me first tell you a bit about Camp Shelby here in Mississippi. It is much improved from when it was first occupied in the spring. There are a few fellows still here who were here then, and their descriptions make anything at Manzanar seem like the Ritz. Sagging floors, leaky roofs, doors hanging off hinges. Much of that is fixed now, but it still is rough. I suppose that is okay since it helps in the Army's job of trying to toughen us up. As I said, my basic training is more concentrated in order to catch me up to the others. Oh, by the way, my friend Charlie Tetsuya is here, too. He came a few days after me, so we are able to moan and groan together. There are also a few others I knew from Manzanar.

Jackie, we are hearing great things about the guys who have already shipped out. The 100th Infantry Battalion, mostly made up of Hawaiians, has been fighting its way through Italy and doing themselves proud. I think our white officers here at Shelby have gained a real respect for the Nisei soldier.

Well, sweetheart, my eyes are falling shut. There's so much I want to say to you. Every time I turn around, there is something I want to share with you, but I have to get a quick letter off to my folks, too, so forgive me for cutting this short. Anyway, I'll write more when I can. Give Emi a great big hug and kiss for me. I have practically worn out the photo of you both with my looking at it. And I don't want to forget to mention

the little New Testament you tucked in my duffel bag. I'm read-
ing that as much as I can, but there isn't as much time as I'd
like. I decided to just choose one verse each day and memorize
it because I can do that even when the lights are put out.
                                    All my love,
                                    Sam

His next letter had come ten days later.

November 26, 1943
Dearest Jackie,

Here I am again, sitting on my cot, my body screaming with
exhaustion. But I guess it's not screaming as loudly as it did
when I first came here. As I mentioned before, we are getting a
concentrated dose of training. We eat, drink, sleep war . . .
war . . . war. It is all very serious. We all know—and our offi-
cers know even better—that we can't fool around. You should
see how I have perfected close-order drills, military discipline,
military jargon, and military courtesy. I can take apart my rifle
in no time flat and put it back together, too. I can also hit the
bull's-eye pretty regularly. Hunting with my dad and T.C.
helped me, but my sarge reminds us often that shooting rabbits
and geese is not the same as shooting Germans. Sometimes I
wonder . . .

Ah, never mind that. I want to tell you about something
that happened the other day when we got a pass to go into
town. This is the smaller town near the camp. They tell us we
may get a leave to New Orleans, which isn't too far, but I'm
learning to take Army rumors with a grain of salt. Well, any-
way, about our trip to town. Most of the civilians around here
have pretty well accepted having us Nisei in their backyards.
They realize we are trying to serve our country just like any
American. Our officers and NCOs feel the same. They support
us and believe in us. They will not abide the use of the term Jap,
especially in reference to us. I never much liked the term, either,
but since I've been called a lot worse, I just tolerated it. But here
it seems more important for there to be a strong separation
between Japs the enemy and us Nisei, though sometimes even I
think of the enemy as Japs. Anyway, I have felt a lot more
acceptance here from whites than I thought I would. But there
are always a few rotten apples—I'm talking about among the
civilian population, not at the base, because as I said, racial
slurs are firmly not allowed here.

We went into town, saw a movie, then went to a tavern for a bite to eat. I sensed hostility the minute we stepped into the place, but there weren't many choices for food and we were hungry, so we sat down at a couple of tables. There were six of us. Immediately some of the other customers started in on us. "How's come we have to eat with Japs?" "These cursed Japs are shooting at our friends." And so forth.

Well, our sarge—he's white!—threw the first punch. The rest of us had to back him up, not that we weren't ready and willing! I guess I am corrupted now, Jackie. My first barroom brawl! But don't worry, I was soundly punished for it. Our COs don't like it when we're called Japs, and if they had been there, they might have slugged a few of those bigots, too. But, just as much, they don't like their men involved in fights with civilians. I scrubbed latrines for a week.

All in all the 442nd Regimental Combat Team is doing pretty well. We passed our last inspection with flying colors, and all of us Johnny-come-lately recruits are shaping up well, if I do say so myself. You may have heard this, but just recently the War Department reclassified all Nisei as eligible for military service. On top of that, Japanese aliens are also eligible for military duty if they pass a couple loyalty tests. This has come about in large part due to the excellent showing of the 100th and the 442nd units, mostly, of course, those already overseas, but I guess the dedication of us still at Camp Shelby has helped, too. Our basic rights as Americans have begun to be restored. I'm not sure if that's enough for Toshio. Mama wrote and said he is still firm about resisting the draft and will probably go to jail, as we feared. And now that he has turned eighteen, he's eligible for both.

Yesterday, Thanksgiving Day, found us in the field practicing maneuvers. We still had turkey and all the trimmings, even though it was in our mess kits and it rained most of the day. I wasn't the only one down in the dumps missing my family. I have this wild fantasy that the war will end tomorrow and all this will be for nothing and they will send us home. Wish it were true. Wish it would happen. We are forced to think about the war all the time here, though I would so much rather think about you and Emi. I have no idea what will happen when we finish training, but even if I knew, I couldn't tell you. Guess I will just have to trust tomorrow to God. He's done okay by me so far. Well, sweetheart, 5 A.M. is going to roll around awfully

early, so I better get some sack time (that's what we call it in the Army!). My love for you never dims or alters—unless it is to grow, which it does every day. God be with you and Emi.
All my love,
Sam

Jackie was in tears by the time she finished Sam's letters. She tried to keep from reading between the lines, but it was hard not to sometimes, especially when he spoke of the future. He tried to put a casual face on it, but it must gnaw at him as much as it did her. They were preparing him to go to war, to fight, to . . . die perhaps. There was no other way to look at it. Fear clung to every word he wrote, even those that were determined to trust God. But courage was stronger even than the fear, and that was what scared Jackie most. Sam was the kind of man who did nothing halfway. If he was determined to prove himself, he would not hold back.

Well, she just had to follow Sam's own advice and trust their tomorrows to God.

———

Cecilia was happy that Jacqueline had decided to join some of her young friends from church on an outing to dinner and a movie. It was nice some of them were still calling Jacqueline after all that had happened, though Cecilia knew many were snubbing her. And Jacqueline seemed to need a bit of a distraction, as she was having a hard time hiding her worry over Sam.

However, Cecilia had to admit she had an ulterior motive for encouraging her daughter to go out for the evening. It meant Cecilia would have baby-sitting duties. Emi had begun to warm up to her grandmother, even letting her hold her when Jacqueline was in the room. Tonight Jacqueline had only been able to get away by distracting Emi, then slipping out when she wasn't looking. It took Cecilia ten minutes to soothe the child afterward, but now all was well.

"Pat-a-cake, pat-a-cake baker's man," sang Cecilia to Emi as they sat on the sofa.

Emi responded with "pa, pa, ba ca ma!" as she tried to mimic Cecilia and pat her grandmother's open hands, missing more often than not.

Cecilia giggled at the child's antics, and Emi giggled right back.

She was such an adorable child that Cecilia no longer noticed her racial differences. She was sweet and funny and beautiful—that was all Grandma saw.

"Emi, sweetie, can you say *grandma?*"

Emi replied, "Pa, pa, ba ca ma!"

"Oh yes. You say that very well. And I know you can say *mama* and *cracker*. I'm sure you could say *grandma*. Gr-and-ma! See, very simple."

Cecilia tried a few more times. She knew Emi had not learned this word yet because Jacqueline had told her how Mrs. Okuda had been trying to teach her without success. That had made Cecilia even more determined. But Emi was more interested in pat-a-cake. So with a smile, happy that she simply had the opportunity to play with her granddaughter, Cecilia held up her hands again.

"Pat-a-cake . . ."

"Ga-pa!" Emi said in reply.

Cecilia laughed. "Well, we weren't exactly going for *grandpa,* but it's a start. Gr-and-ma!"

When Cecilia heard the front door open, a twinge of disappointment shot through her as she feared Jacqueline might have cut her evening short. But it was Keagan, not Jacqueline, who walked into the front parlor.

"Goodness, you are home early," she said to her husband.

"Early? It's six o'clock," said Keagan as he hung his coat on the hall tree and strode into the room. He went directly for the wet bar.

Cecilia said nothing about the fact that his usual time for getting home was more like seven, eight, or even nine. Instead she realized something else.

"I better start dinner," she said.

"No dinner yet? I'm starved."

"I've been busy with Emi."

Pouring himself a drink, Keagan said, "So Jackie's finally letting you alone with her?"

Cecilia hadn't known Keagan had noticed. "Yes. And you will be pleased to know I have gotten her to say *grandpa.*"

Keagan laughed dryly. "I'll believe that when I hear it. Why *grandpa* and not *grandma?*"

"Well, seems she has a mind of her own. I tried *grandma*, but 'ga-pa' is what came out."

"Oh, Cecilia, even you should know that's just her usual gibberish and not a true word."

Cecilia cocked a wry brow. "What would you know of her *usual* gibberish? You haven't actually been listening, have you?"

"Hard not to with her yammering all the time." There was just a touch of defensiveness in his tone as he plopped down in his favorite chair, drink in hand.

"Keagan Hayes, why don't you stop trying to be so hard-nosed," Cecilia upbraided him gently. "Perhaps you should just admit you like having a little granddaughter, especially our Jacqueline's baby. I know you always favored her."

"Not favoritism," he said quickly. "She was just the only one who didn't constantly try my patience."

"And perhaps for that alone you owe it to her to give her child a little attention."

"You know I was never one for pandering after babies. Maybe when she gets older I can teach her how to ride a bike or something."

Cecilia did not mention the fact that he had never taught his own daughters that particular activity, or many others. Perhaps he *would* be different with his grandchildren.

Then he said, "Why in heaven's name couldn't she have had a boy?"

Cecilia let out a sharp sigh. So much for being different. She rose from the sofa.

"I'd best start dinner," she said. "Can you keep an eye on Emi?"

"What?" he retorted. "You never made me do that with our own kids."

"I was younger then. I could do a dozen things at once. If you want dinner, you'll have to help out."

"This is ridiculous!" he grumbled. "Make it fast. That's all I have to say. And I will not touch her diaper!"

Cecilia wore a small smile as she left the room. Maybe there was hope for the man. Indeed, he had never helped with his own children in this way. But she paused just outside the room, out of sight of Emi, just to see if she would accept being left with this man she hardly knew. Emi did not let out a peep except to look at Keagan, lift her hands, and merrily utter, "Pa, pa, ba ca ma!"

Cecilia interpreted it for her husband. "She wants to play

pat-a-cake." Then she went to the kitchen.

From his chair Keagan glanced at the baby. It did not occur to him that this was the first time he had ever really looked at her. In any case, he did not allow himself to be caught up in any emotional sentiment over it.

She *was* pretty. Like a china doll, but in an odd way, very much like Jackie, too.

"So, little girl, you want to play pat-a-cake, do you?"

She looked at him with wide eyes. "Ga-pa."

"You and I both know you aren't saying *grandpa*. And if you were any kind of a grandchild, you would say *grandma*, not *grandpa*. She's the one who wants to hear it, you know." He sipped his drink, still gazing at her over the rim of his glass. "And I must be loony to be talking to you as if you could understand a word I am saying."

The child, who had been sitting on the sofa, rolled over on her tummy, then, feet first, scooted off the sofa until she was on all fours on the carpet. Then she crawled around the coffee table, chattering all the while. Grasping the edge of the table, she pulled herself up, and apparently quite pleased with herself, her chattering rose to delighted squeals.

"Pretty clever of you." Keagan had seen her stand like this before, at least he had glimpsed it out of the corner of his eye when he had been pretending not to be interested in the child.

He wondered why he had done that. It was obvious, of course. It was because the child was a Jap . . . no, not exactly because of that. He refused to believe he was *that* bigoted. It was because this Jap child was his daughter's . . . his grandchild. It was hard to get over his resentment. Why had Jackie done that to him?

Disgruntled, he tossed back the rest of his drink as the child stood at the table bouncing up and down, lifting one of her hands and waving it triumphantly. She was totally oblivious to all the bitter thoughts he was thinking.

And that amazed him as he considered it. She did not know, nor did she seem to care, how he felt. Suddenly it dawned on him that this baby, who cried her eyes out the minute her mother was out of sight, was standing here chattering and giggling with only him in the room.

"You don't know what's good for you, girl," he said roughly. "Little Colleen . . ." He'd never spoken her name, either, but for the life of him, if he must accept this child, he was going to use the name he preferred, not some foreign appellation.

"Ga-pa. Ga-pa!"

There! He thought smugly. She liked her good old American name better, too.

All at once she let go *both* of her hands as she tried to do pat-a-cake. An instant later she realized what she had done. A look of utter surprise momentarily replaced her merriment.

"Now, that is something, isn't it?" Keagan said. "But why don't you show me what you are really made of. Walk to Grandpa, then maybe I'll have a better opinion of you." Setting aside his drink, he held out his arms in an entreating manner.

She tottered a moment longer, and then she did it. She took a step. And another.

"Oh, my goodness!" breathed Keagan, truly unable to believe what he was witnessing.

It was about four steps to where Keagan was sitting, but he had a feeling she wasn't going to make it that far. So before she tumbled down, without thinking, he scooted to the floor on his knees, and as she took the third step, he was there to catch her as she tottered forward. Into his arms she tumbled. And she was giggling, not crying, as he awkwardly took a secure hold of her.

He thought she would scream at his touch. But the silly child was giggling!

"Ga-pa. Ga-pa!"

"Well, I'll be," he said, shaking his head in utter disbelief. "Cecilia," he called out, "come quickly!"

But he knew he was too far away for his wife to hear, so he picked up Colleen and carried her to the kitchen. When Cecilia turned upon hearing him enter, a look of astonished wonder crossed her face.

"Is something wrong?" she asked, drying her hands on a tea towel and gaping at the sight of the baby in Keagan's arms.

"You'll never guess what this little munchkin just did," said Keagan. "She walked to me!"

"No! Really? And I missed it." It looked like Cecilia didn't know whether to laugh, cry, or call the police.

"Come on, Colleen, let's show your grandma what you did. She won't believe me otherwise."

Keagan put Colleen down and told Cecilia to kneel a couple of feet away. The child stood for a moment, then bent over on all fours and crawled to Cecilia. They tried again and again without success. Cecilia even tried to use a cookie as a bribe, but it didn't work. Then they changed places and tried to get Colleen to walk to Keagan again, but still no luck.

"Well, she really did walk to me," Keagan said, a bit miffed that the little imp had made a liar of him.

"I believe you, dear."

"Do you?"

"Yes. She has excellent taste." Cecilia smiled. "I mean, she did say *grandpa* first, so I'm not surprised she chose you to take her first steps with. She sees something in you that the rest of us sometimes miss. Your bark is far worse than your bite."

"I still have a bite, woman, and don't you forget it," he growled, but there was just a hint of humor in his green eyes. "I expect little Colleen is just smart enough to know which side of her bread the butter is on."

"She's a very smart girl, your little *Colleen*." Cecilia picked her up and kissed her chubby cheek.

Keagan looked at Colleen for a very long time, and for a brief moment he did not see those slanted eyes. She was only his beautiful granddaughter.

PART V

*"The eyes of the world are upon you. The
hopes and prayers of liberty-loving people
everywhere march with you."*

GENERAL DWIGHT EISENHOWER
TO HIS TROOPS, JUNE 6, 1944

36

A<small>N AIR OF ALMOST</small> electric tension resided among the press community in London. They could feel something big was coming, though no officials had ever given any hint of exactly when Operation Overlord would begin. They had no date, no time, but these journalists were trained observers. The long-awaited event was coming soon. The Allied invasion of mainland Europe, which Stalin had been clamoring for for years, was about to begin—the Second Front. Huge in scale, it would dwarf even the invasion of Italy, which had occurred the previous fall. The outcome of the entire war now seemed to hinge on Overlord.

But Cameron was not about to sit on her haunches and just wait. For the last two months she'd been sniffing all over the south of England for stories. She'd see to it, if it was the last thing she did, that her father received his money's worth for taking—what he saw, at least—a big chance in sending a woman overseas. By January, however, even Keagan could smell which way the wind was blowing. Many newspapers were sending women to Europe because they had been proving themselves as capable as men since the war began.

The hardest part for Cameron had been waiting in the States after learning that her father's Christmas gift was giving his okay for her to go to England to cover the cross-channel invasion they knew was coming soon. It had taken three months for all the paper work and the security clearance to come through, which luckily her father had begun even before he'd made the announcement to

Cameron. She finally left for England in early March.

Now it was May, and the waiting continued even if she was in Europe instead of the States. Today, for a change, Operation Overlord was far from Cameron's mind. As she climbed up the steps from the Tube station to ground level, she looked again at the directions on the paper in her hand. She was in Whitechapel, but the street wasn't going to be easy to find with all directional signs removed. This was an area hit especially hard by the bombings during the blitz, and signs of devastation were everywhere. Many residents were already clearing away rubble and trying to put their homes back in order. Cameron had done an article on these brave folks a few weeks ago.

She had to pause frequently to inquire of these same people but eventually came to the street on her directions. The apartment house was located easily once she located the street. Inside, she found number twenty-five on the second floor and knocked on the door.

The woman who answered was middle-aged and matronly, dressed in a drab housedress. Her graying hair was fixed in a bun, and she wore thick glasses.

"Hello. I'm Cameron Hayes, correspondent for the *Los Angeles Journal*," she said with a warm smile. "I was told there were some folks here who would be interested in granting me an interview."

"Yes, of course, you are very welcome. Come in." The woman spoke in a thick eastern European accent, which Cameron assumed to be Polish because of whom she intended to interview.

Stepping into the room, she felt a twinge of homesickness, not for California but rather for Russia because this room had such a distinct flavor of the homes, such as the Fedorcenkos', that she had visited in Russia. There was nothing she could definitely point to besides an Old World look, the samovar, steaming on a side table, a key element.

"Josep," the woman called down a hallway, "the woman reporter is here." Turning to Cameron, she added, "I am Lidia Wilkins. Please sit."

"I'm happy to meet you," said Cameron, taking the upholstered chair Lidia gestured toward. "You don't have a Polish surname."

"No. I came to London in '35 and married a Brit." She took a seat on the sofa. "I was an adventurous girl. My family stayed behind . . . unfortunately."

Just then a man entered. He was tall, lean, perhaps a few years younger than Lidia. Cameron could see a slight resemblance between them, mostly in the eyes, both pairs of which were dark brown. His hair was probably a shade or two darker than hers but cut so close to the scalp, it was hard to judge the exact color.

"This is my brother, Josep Dlugosz," said Lidia.

Cameron rose and held out her hand. "I am—"

"I heard from the back, Miss Hayes." He spoke English, but his accent was even thicker than his sister's.

There was an intensity about this man that gave Cameron a shiver. He reminded her of Oleg Gorbenko, Sophia's husband, who had once told Cameron a shocking tale. Was this man about to do the same? That's why Cameron had come. One of her press colleagues had spoken of some Polish refugees who had amazing stories to tell of their lives in Nazi-occupied Poland. Cameron knew it was too late to help Oleg, but she had never really let go of that painful incident and her feeling of having let Oleg down. Perhaps now that such stories were not so isolated, she could tell them back in the States.

"What do you want to know, Miss Hayes?" asked Josep unceremoniously.

Cameron opened her mouth to reply, but before she could get a word out, Lidia said in a scolding tone, "Josep, please sit and relax a little. Miss Hayes is our friend. You have nothing to fear in England."

The man obeyed his sister, then said, "It isn't easy to shake the fear."

"I understand," Cameron said. "I recently spent a year in the Soviet Union and have a small conception of what it is like living in a police state."

"Bah! Russia—that is no friend of Poland." He shook his head. "However, they now look good compared to our present oppressors."

"Where did you learn such good English, Josep?"

"We often sheltered American and British escaped POWs. They taught me. I believed that one day I would escape to freedom, and then I would tell my story. I was in the Warsaw underground for years. I left three weeks ago only because the Nazis found out who I am and put a death sentence on my head."

"Are you Jewish?'"

"No, but I knew many good Jews who fought next to me in the underground. You know, then, what they are suffering in Poland?"

"I have a vague idea. A few years ago I heard a rumor of German atrocities against Jews in Russia, but I could never find proof." This was essentially true, for if she'd had such proof, she would have forced her American editor to print the story. That's why she had tried to get Oleg and Sophia out of the country but had failed miserably.

"Do you know of the Warsaw Ghetto?" When she shook her head, Josep went on. "The Nazis have built a wall around it so the Jews there cannot get out even to work. They are starving on meager rations. Part of our work in the underground was smuggling goods into the ghetto. But, Miss Hayes, that is only part of what I have seen. My work often took me away from Warsaw into the countryside. I once saw a train of cattle cars. But instead of cattle, there were Jews packed in the cars, over a hundred to a car. They were starved and wretched looking. I am sure many did not survive that trip."

"They were going to concentration camps?" Cameron asked, though she already had guessed the answer. "Did you ever see one of these camps?"

"They call them death camps."

Cameron had not heard this term before. Though it really didn't surprise her. She had always believed Oleg's story of the massacre by Germans of hundreds of Jews. She talked with Josep for another hour and left feeling drained. He gave her the name of another refugee in London. She would make arrangements to see this man as soon as possible. The prospect of yet another hour of hearing similar horrors made her sick inside, yet she thought of those actually *living* those horrors, not just hearing about them, and she knew she must do something about it.

———

Absorbed as Cameron was in interviewing Polish refugees, the big story was still Operation Overlord. The tension in London grew to nearly a fevered pitch. Rumor had it that the operation had already been scrubbed a couple of times and that the next attempt would be based almost entirely on the weather, which had thus far not been cooperative. So Sunday, June 4, with winds battering the coast and the skies thick with clouds, seemed to be an unlikely time for it to take place. Even when there was some clearing on Monday, many remained skeptical. Cameron went to bed Monday night quite late, certain she'd be able to sleep in on Tuesday, June 6.

The phone in her hotel room rang at four o'clock in the morning. She grabbed for it, knocking over a glass of water in her sleep-muddled attempt.

"Yeah," she said thickly.

"Wake up, sleepyhead!" came the voice of her friend and colleague Edna Townsend, who had also been the one to share the leads on the Poles, "unless you want to miss the party."

Cameron didn't waste time with questions. She knew what it meant. It took her ten minutes to get dressed in the military uniform she was now expected to wear on official business, but in her haste, she realized after leaving her room that her skirt was twisted, her stocking seams were crooked, and she'd forgotten her hat and umbrella. She wasn't about to waste time fixing such trivialities. She met Edna in the hotel lobby, and they shared a taxi to the Ministry of Information. There they showed their accreditation papers and were admitted. All the journalists waited in a room together. Most of them were in as much physical disarray as she, some worse. Obviously no one had been given much notice.

The men in the group would soon be following the troops across the Channel. The female correspondents had already been given the news that they would not be permitted into France on D-day or on any day soon thereafter. They had fought and argued with the ministry over this but to no avail. Now Cameron was determined to find a way to make the best of what she had been given. As she waited, she worked out in her mind the lead to her invasion story.

Finally, just before 6 A.M., a British officer came into the room. "In a few seconds," he announced, "the first communiqué will be dispatched informing the world of the beginning of Operation Overlord. Then you will be free to send your own dispatches."

Cameron could almost feel the seconds tick off. Every journalist sat on the edge of his folding chair like a runner awaiting the gun to start a race.

"Go!" said the officer finally.

And the race was on. Cameron and Edna had made their taxi wait, so now they tore out of the ministry building, jumped into the cab, and ordered the driver to race to where they had already scouted out a telephone in a newsstand about two blocks away. They had stopped briefly on the way to the ministry building and paid the proprietor to keep the phone free. Cameron made the first call and asked to be connected directly to her father. This was a story she wanted him to hear directly from her.

"It's started, Dad." She had to speak loudly because of static on the overseas line.

"What's it like there?" he boomed back.

"A light drizzle, overcast skies. You should see the planes overhead! The skies are practically black, there are so many. The sound is like having a swarm of bees in your ears. Their destination, we now know, is the coast of Normandy."

She thought she heard the scratching of a pen—or was it just static?—as her father jotted down her comments.

"Is that all?" Keagan asked.

"The invasion only started a few minutes ago," she replied.

"All right. Keep on it."

As if she wouldn't! She realized her father's sharp tone was probably not so much directed at her as it was at the fact that he couldn't be here himself. Reporters often spoke of the big story. Now every journalist who knew anything at all knew this was it, the story of a lifetime, very likely the story of a century.

"I'll call back in a couple of hours," she said after giving him every other detail she could summon of the little she knew.

When she hung up the phone, she was determined, even if her father's frustration was not directed at her, to astound him with her next dispatch.

Besides talking to refugees in the months since coming to England, she had been working on currying sources in the military. She went to parties, got to know officers, listened to them talk of their families, and remembered every detail of what they said, even the names of their dogs. If she happened to see them again later she'd always mention the small details of their lives they had shared.

"Hi, Captain, how are you doing? Did your wife's roses win that blue ribbon at the fair?" "Has little Jimmy learned to ride his bike yet?"

She remembered how Johnny Shanahan had always prided himself on his memory for such details and knew this was another lesson she owed to him. But just as she had never truly believed Shanahan was just trying to do a good job in listening to details, she found she enjoyed getting on this level with others. She wanted to know people and as a result be true to who they were in her writing. She saw it as merely a side benefit if it aided her in getting news.

Cameron went to an air base where a flight commander she'd met was assigned. She learned he was out on a mission and waited a couple of hours for his return. When he didn't return, she prayed he was all right. She spoke with other flyboys who had returned from bombing runs over Normandy, though she knew this was probably against regulations. Then she went in search of another lead. She sent another more lengthy dispatch that afternoon but still wasn't satisfied because the content was far too general for her standards. That evening, when D-day was only twelve hours old, Cameron made her way to the south coast of England, where she knew a nurse who was assigned to a field hospital. The nurse took her down to the docks as minesweepers brought in the first casualties from the invasion.

But all Cameron could do was watch. One of the soldiers on guard, noting her press insignia, told her quietly, "My orders are to shoot anyone who attempts to talk to anyone debarking the transport."

She groaned with displeasure but was still determined to find a way to personalize this event, to bring it to life for her readers.

She continued to call in regular dispatches to the *Journal*, talking to either her father or to the managing editor, Harry Landis. But still she had nothing spectacular to report. After spending the night in the same field hospital, she faced D-day plus one with renewed determination. Back at the docks she noted a hospital ship preparing to debark. A half dozen nurses were walking up the gangway, chatting and laughing. They paid no attention to Cameron as she slipped in among them. Before she knew it, almost before she had given it much thought, she was on board.

She meandered around the ship, talking mostly to the nurses, getting their feelings about what was happening. Many were on their first run to pick up wounded soldiers. They were afraid of what lay ahead, wondering how they would react to seeing their "boys" wounded from battle. But they were a lot like Cameron in one sense—they were anxious to get into the fray, to finally have the chance to *do something* in the war.

"We'll be leaving soon," one of the nurses said to her, seeming to at last take note that she wasn't one of them. "You should disembark."

"Oh yes . . . sure . . ." Cameron smiled, now realizing why no one had paid her mind. That would change once they were underway.

She ambled away from the nurses, found a latrine, went inside, and stayed put until she felt the ship's movement. Her heart was pounding, knowing at any moment someone was going to want to use the facilities and betray her hiding place. She tried not to think of all the regulations she was breaking. She also tried to ignore her heaving insides as the ship got farther from the relative calm of the docks. She'd forgotten she had no affinity for water.

Waiting a half hour, until the ship was far enough out to sea so there was no chance of them taking her back to port, she left the latrine and went above deck. Everyone was too busy to take note of her presence. Landing craft and water ambulances were coming alongside the ship and offloading their wounded. It was a harrowing process in the rough seas and took no small amount of time because the smaller crafts were full of injured men.

Cameron went below with a group of wounded. First she asked one of the nurses for something to calm her stomach, then she helped with the men. Perhaps it was due to her willingness to help that no one made any attempt to upbraid her for her presence. She talked to the men, listened to some of the anguished tales of the first landings, and believed the story of their incredible heroism had to be told. She also doubted the male correspondents on Normandy were facing such stiff censorship.

She helped to feed the wounded, many of whom had not eaten since before the invasion had begun. Those who had managed to choke down breakfast yesterday morning had for the most part lost it during the Channel crossing. She did other menial tasks that helped free the nurses to do more skilled treatments. She felt oddly at ease in the surroundings of the hospital, perhaps because it made her feel closer to Alex. She thought of some of the things he'd told her of treating the wounded during battle. She wondered where he was now and what he was doing.

Had he been in the Battle of Kursk in the summer of '43? There, what was already being lauded as the greatest tank confrontation in history had been fought. All Russia had rejoiced at their final victory, knowing Hitler's last hopes of defeating Russia had died there. But if she knew Alex, he would have agonized only at the dead, the wounded, the senseless blood spilled. No matter where he was, she stopped a moment to utter a silent prayer for his safety.

Since Kursk, the Russians had been steadily moving west. January of '44 saw the Leningrad Blockade finally broken. By May the Crimea had been cleared of Germans. Was Alex with the Red Army as it moved? They had previously been reluctant to let him leave the country. Would extremity of need force them to give latitude to one of their finest doctors? If so, it could be her and Alex's one chance to be together. When the Russians pushed into Germany—and she had no doubt they eventually would—Alex might be within her reach. All she had to do was get into the mainland of Europe. She knew this would happen eventually. The female journalists would be allowed into France and beyond—when it was safe, of course.

If she needed more motivation than merely covering the war, the possibility of meeting up with Alex was it. She would somehow push east just as tenaciously as the Red Army was pushing west.

When she went back above deck to observe more patient transfers, she jumped at an opportunity to board one of the empty water ambulances returning to Normandy. Even the fear of drowning while the smaller boat heaved up and down against the side of the ship as she climbed from one to the other did not deter her. How she hated boats and water!

She tore the sleeve of her uniform jacket as one of the men grabbed her while she hung precariously in midair. Her backside hit the deck of the ambulance hard, shaking her teeth in the process, but she otherwise made it without injury.

A few minutes later the skipper called out, "This is as far as we go!"

Cameron had been wondering how they were going to land on

the beach with waves crashing wildly against the sand. Now she knew. She and the corpsmen aboard had to debark into chest-high water and wade ashore. She said nothing about the fact that she couldn't swim. One of the men told her to ride the waves in. She watched what they did when a wave came at them and tried to imitate them, swallowing half the sea in the process. But five minutes later her feet were firmly planted on what she would soon learn was Omaha Beach.

Rain began to pelt her and her companions as they trekked up toward the rocky cliffs above the beach. Cameron stumbled over a rock and started to careen off the path. A corpsman caught her before she did so.

"Whoa, miss!" he said. "Don't set foot off the path. This is the only place I can guarantee doesn't have mines."

Gulping, she looked to her right and to her left. All thought of setting off on her own vanished. But she appeased herself with the fact that just being here, in France, on the beach where just hours ago history had been made, was good enough for now.

For the next couple of hours she gathered what were truly the stories of a lifetime. She learned that Omaha Beach had seen the worst resistance from the Germans and, though no one was clear with the figures, probably the highest casualty rate among all the landing sites. The sounds of explosions and gunfire were not so far away even now. The battle still raged. The outcome was still uncertain.

It was more clear than ever that the Germans still had a lot of fight in them when an air raid siren blared and German bombers attacked an area quite close to the Red Cross tents. Cameron dove for cover in a ditch along with several other personnel.

Her new corpsmen friends marveled at her relative composure during the deafening bombardment.

She shrugged. "It's not my first, fellows."

She helped them load wounded back on the ambulance.

"I didn't think they were letting nurses out here yet," commented one of the wounded.

"I'm a reporter, not a nurse," Cameron said.

"Well, I'll be!"

"You gonna write about us?" asked another.

"If the generals will let me."

Those who could yelled out their names and spelled them for her if they thought it would help. She took out her soggy notebook and pencil and wrote them all down. She would write about each one if the powers that be would let her.

She had never been more tempted to do anything than she was to stay in Normandy. But a corpsman told her the hospital ship was nearly loaded and would return soon to England. Still, she wavered until she observed two officers, one a colonel, having a talk some twenty feet away from her. They kept glancing in her direction as they conferred. Had they finally realized this female definitely didn't belong here? Taking that as a sign that her welcome was soon to be over, she headed back to the beach with the corpsman.

She was a bit disgruntled when, upon her return to England, she was immediately confronted by a pair of MPs who escorted her off the hospital ship. Maybe she should have risked staying on the mainland. She was told she wasn't being arrested, but for her own safety, she would be confined to the nurses' quarters until further notice.

"Next time you see France, miss," said the officer who gave her a formal reprimand, "will be when the other female journalists are *permitted* to go!"

She apologized profusely and even somewhat sincerely. She figured her adventure had been well worth a few days cooling her heels in England, especially since she wasn't going to lose her accreditation for it. She *would* return to France. That's what was important.

37

June 20, 1944
Dearest Jackie,

You'll probably get all the letters I wrote you on shipboard in one big pile. I'm not really sure how the mail works for GI's out at sea. You'll now know what I couldn't tell you until after the fact because of security—we shipped out on May 2. Twenty-eight days at sea on a Liberty ship gave me lots of time to write letters, but there sure wasn't much to write about. You'll see that because I really rambled on so. At least I wasn't seasick like so many of the guys. Maybe I should have gone into the Navy.

We landed in Italy on June 1. I can't say exactly where, but yes, I'm in Italy! I wish I would have paid more attention to the Italian aspect of the war, but last July when the invasion of Italy began, I had a few other things on my mind with all that was happening at Manzanar. When Mussolini was deposed a few weeks after the invasion, I was worrying over the loyalty oath. When Italy signed an armistice with us in October, I was looking forward to—or should I say dreading?—my induction into the United States Army. As our troops were fighting through the south of Italy, I was busy learning one end of a rifle from the other. All that seems a distant memory now, kind of vague, almost like it happened to someone else. And, Jackie, I haven't even been "blooded" yet—that's what they call it after a soldier fights in his first battle. Don't take it literally!

I wish I could have seen Italy as it was before the war—I

hear it was a beautiful country. What I have seen so far is a land devastated by war. The waterfront areas, especially, have been ravaged. Rome wasn't as bad, but there was a fellow in another company who saw the ancient ruins of the Coliseum and said, "I didn't think we hit Rome that hard!"

I have one other funny story about Rome. I think I can tell it because the Germans already know we were there, so no need for security. Anyway, they say, "All roads lead to Rome," but several of our units have decided that the reverse of that isn't true. That is, all roads don't lead out of Rome, or it sure appeared so! We call our encounter with Rome "The Second Battle of Rome" because we had such a hard time finding a road that led north out of the city. Our unit was lost for hours around the Vatican.

I'm not complaining that we haven't seen action yet, but I do at times wonder what we're doing here. Most of Italy appears to have been conquered already. Maybe they're saving us Japanese for the crossing of the Alps, though I can't see the logic of that, since most of us are hardly mountain people and even fewer are used to snow. I just pray we get across before winter. But for now we are bivouacked and spending time in training. Our commanders think—they are probably right—that we got terribly out of shape during the ship crossing. And my fears about the Alps might well be true because we have been doing a lot of mountain hiking—mountains like none we had in Mississippi.

We've heard some scuttlebutt that we're moving out tomorrow. I don't know because rumors are one thing the Army has in plenty. They also say there will finally be some fighting. I don't want to think of that. I'm just lying here trying to picture you, my love. The shape of your face, the glow of your eyes, the shine of your hair, the feel of you when I hold you close. I miss you so! I miss the sense of belonging when I am with you. Do you know what I mean? With you, I know who I am and where I am going. It's like on a human level what I feel with my Lord. But it is hard to hold on to you sometimes, and to God, as well. I feel in limbo, like my breath is held and I can't let it out until this is over.

One of my buddies says he's afraid if he thinks of his wife, he will get killed, so he is trying real hard not to. Everyone has their way of coping with the fear, I suppose. Some say things like "I won't get it because I'm too young . . . too thin . . . too *handsome . . ." One guy says if he shaves, he'll get it, so he hasn't shaved in three days. We're all waiting to see how long before the CO makes him shave. Luckily, he's only nineteen and hasn't much of a beard in the first place.*

Well, it's "lights-out," so I will finish this later or send it as is if someone takes the mail. Oh, before I forget, you know the New Testament you gave me? Well, since landing in Italy, I have been carrying that in my inside jacket pocket, right over my heart. Maybe I have heard too many stories of Bibles stopping bullets, but that's not the real reason I carry it there. When I feel it press against me, I think of how good God has been to me, and no matter what happens here, He has given me, with you and Emi, more happiness than any man has a right to.

I love you!
Sam

———

June 25, 1944
Sam, my love,
I received several letters from you all at once! It was like Christmas all over. I am praying for you harder than ever knowing you are now on your way to war. It must be difficult being so bored. I know how you like to be productive. But the hardest part must be all the idle time to just think about what is ahead. I've heard they are making small-sized books specially to give to soldiers overseas. I hope you can get ahold of some because you love to read, and it will be a wonderful diversion. Maybe they will have A Tale of Two Cities! That always reminds me of when we met, and for that reason alone I will always love that book.

Oh, before I forget, I must tell you about the money the Army sent me—your paycheck. You asked me to send part to your parents, and I did, but your father sent it back to me and said, "I will not take money from a son who has a wife and child to support." I tried to explain that my parents refuse to take money from me for living expenses, so I don't need it, but he was adamant. He did say if they are evicted from Manzanar, he may change his mind. So here is what I have done with the money—I hope you approve. Half I have put in the bank for expenses other than those which my parents are taking care of and also for emergencies—perhaps should your parents have need later. With the other half I have bought war bonds. It is one way I feel I can help you. When the war is over, we will probably have a nice little nest egg to get started again. How I look forward to that! We'll have a little home, you'll teach high-school English as you write your book, and we'll produce brothers and sisters for Emi.

Speaking of Emi, she is waking up from her nap, so my peaceful moment is over. Now we will be going at breakneck speed till bedtime. Since she started to walk, I seldom see her actually walk—she is usually running! I have never seen a child more full of energy. I will give her a kiss from you. I show her your picture every day, so she knows who her daddy is.

> All my love,
> Jackie

June 30, 1944
Dearest Jackie,

Sorry I haven't written for so long, but we have had little free time for the last ten days. We have seen our first combat action. We gave no one any reason for regretting the recruitment of Japanese Americans. Several men have been put in to receive the Distinguished Service Cross. I want so desperately to talk to you about all that has happened, yet part of me just wants to gloss over it. Jackie, I have killed men! It is horrible, utterly horrible. I am sick now even thinking about it. But you can't think—that's the only way to survive. So I'll say no more about it.

July 21, 1944
Dearest Jackie,

We're getting a few days of rest after a month of combat. I'll try to make up for lost time in my letter writing. I am also going to make up for many missed baths! Never thought a small thing like a bath could feel so good. When you're grunting through dirt and grit for days on end, you almost forget what it's like to be human.

I have learned one thing: there is no glory in war. It is all dirt, dirt, and more dirt! And meaning no disrespect to your *father, when you read all those glorious headlines in the paper about battles, take them with a grain of sand—very dirty sand! "Driving the enemy back." "Charging forward." I have never seen any of that. It is all slow, tedious labor. If we take a hundred yards in a major battle, that is good. And each inch of ground, each foot, each yard has a terrible price tag. Our friends have fallen, our innocence gone forever.*

We have had some hair-raising times. The worst was when we went into this town to meet with some partisans. We thought the town was cleared of the enemy, but as we were in the house of one of the partisans, having coffee—here, because of shortages, they have no real coffee. It is some bitter stuff made of hickory—we heard trucks coming down the street. It was a German patrol! There were five of us, and we were quickly hustled into an attic to hide. There we waited while the Germans came into the house to search. That was as close as I ever want to come to Germans! It's a lot different from seeing them across a battlefield. But they didn't find us.

Another funny incident happened in a village we liberated. Charlie was searching a basement to make sure it was clear of the enemy when he stumbled upon fifteen thousand gallons of Italian wine. I've never acquired a taste for wine myself, but most of the men were sorely disgruntled when the CO made us move out before even a drop of the stuff could be tasted.

I got your letter about the money, and I think what you are doing is fine. I'm glad to know the Army checks are coming through. I always knew my dad was stubborn!

I really appreciate that you are trying to keep Emi from forgetting me. That worries me a lot. I am missing so much of her growing up! But I have to say that what you told me about her taking her first steps for your father almost makes up for me missing them. How good God is to us for providing moments like that.

I love you,
Sam

July 28, 1944
Dearest Jackie,

Yesterday we had a ceremony for the combat team that I thought you'd like to hear about. Lieutenant General Mark

Clark, commander of the Fifth Army, came to our unit to award decorations. The 100th Battalion, mostly made up of Hawaiians, received the Distinguished Unit Citation. They have truly been heroes in the fighting. I guess I should tell you that I received a Purple Heart. I didn't tell you before because I didn't want you to worry. The wound was minor, and I didn't even want the medal, but Charlie said I deserved it and it would reflect on the entire unit. I just got some shrapnel in my back. I was laid out for a couple days, then returned to my unit. I am perfectly fine. It, the medal that is, will be sent to you. Maybe if I get two, you can have some earrings made. I'm sorry, I don't mean to sound glib. I just don't want you to worry.

The other reason I am writing is because of what happened today. I met the king of England! Okay, not personally, but I did see him close up. Several from our unit formed part of the honor guard for His Majesty George VI as he inspected the area.

Well, it's my turn in the bathhouse, so I better move before someone else gets my hot water. We should have a few more days of rest, so I will write more later.

Love,
Sam

———

August 20, 1944
My dear love, Sam,

I just received your letter about your Purple Heart. I can't help worrying. Please, I don't need earrings! I need you and nothing else. They say the Germans are faltering all over Europe and that the war can't last much longer. I count each day and will dance in the streets when it is over—no, I will dance only when you are back in my arms.

Until then I am doing all that I can to make the end come quicker, though I have never felt so helpless. I wish I could work in one of the defense plants, but it wouldn't be right to leave Emi for the long hours that requires, though many women have left their children in the care of others to do such vital work. Each of us must do what we feel is right. Mom would be thrilled if I worked and let her care for Emi. But I feel Emi needs her mother. So I have become involved in the Red Cross. I volunteer two hours a day at the blood bank. Even Emi is *doing her part! They are making the nipples on her baby bottles smaller in order to conserve rubber. However, Mom thinks she is too old to still use a bottle, so I am trying to wean her.*

I made another sacrifice for the war. I needed a new swimsuit because my church was going to have a Fourth of July party at the beach, and I have gained a few pounds since Emi's birth. Well, you can now buy a two-piece swimsuit. My mother was appalled at how skimpy they are! But this has reduced the amount of material used by a good ten percent so that more can go to defense use. Should I make a "pinup" photo of me in it for you? Goodness, I am blushing!

> *All my love,*
> *Jackie*

———

September 10, 1944
Dearest Jackie,

I can't wait to see you in that new swimsuit, but don't send a photo because I don't want to watch all the guys drool over my beautiful wife!

Things have been pretty confusing around here lately. Our combat team has been reorganized, though that doesn't affect us lowly foot soldiers much. However, what does affect us is that we have had to move three times in the last week. I guess the officers can't decide what to do with us. We are sick of packing and unpacking. There are rumors now that we might be heading to France. That's where most of the guys want to go because we hear the Seventh Army is ripping through the Germans there and the war could end any day, so they don't want to miss all that action. I have told you before that we have changed our ideas about the glories of war, but that doesn't lessen the appeal of some action. It is better, I guess, than the waiting and all that goes with it. We want to fight, knock out the Germans, and get this war over. . . .

———

September 20, 1944
Dearest Jackie,

Well, looks like we will be off again soon, though I can't say to where, even if I knew. We have a lot of spare time now. I have toured Naples and Pompeii. I want to be able to say I saw more of Italy than battlefields. Maybe I will run into Cameron. Didn't you say she was over here? That would be a treat to see someone from home. Has it really been almost a year since I have seen you? It seems longer, so much longer! The war has to end soon. We hear Paris was liberated a couple of weeks ago and the push into Germany is on. Why can't Hitler see it is a lost cause and give up before more lives are lost? Of course once we finish Hitler, there still is Japan to take care of. But it can't go on forever.

Jackie, home is all I think of now. If the way home is through Germany, that's okay. I will fight the devil himself to get back to you!

Give Emi a kiss from me.

Love,
Sam

September 21, 1944
Dearest Sam,

I want you home so badly. But wouldn't it be marvelous if you ran into Cameron? I told you she is there now, didn't I? I don't know exactly where, though. She was mad as a hatter because she and the other female journalists had to wait until it was safe to enter France. But she has been there a couple of months now and having all kinds of adventures, I am sure. . . .

September 30, 1944
Dearest Jackie,

I can't say where we are, but we have reached our destination. I have never seen so much rain, and the wind blew down our tents. Everything we own is soaking wet. And again we are just waiting around. That's what war is for the most part— waiting! And more waiting. We are just itching to get this over with. That's what makes the waiting so hard. It's not that we want to get shot at. . . .

October 15, 1944
Dearest Jackie,
    We started moving shortly after my last letter, and there just hasn't been time to write. Sorry. This is the most miserable place I have ever seen. Rain, wind, fog, and the worst rocky terrain to cross. It wouldn't be so bad fighting over a strip of land if it wasn't so worthless. . . .

———————

October 18, 1944
Jackie,
    Charlie was killed today. I can't believe it. I feel so sick and alone. I've lost many friends here, but Charlie was different. We grew up together, and he and YoYo were my best friends. I don't know if I can deal with this. I've prayed, but where is God? Why can't He stop this insanity? I have never felt such despair.
                                        Sam

———————

October 19, 1944
Dearest Jackie,
    I wish I could take back yesterday's letter. I should never have sent it, but the fellow came by collecting mail, and I didn't have my wits together. Disregard it all, please! I am fine. I haven't lost my faith in God. It's hard, I'll admit, but you go on. I have to go. They're shelling us.
                                I love you,
                                Sam

38

FOR DAYS IT SEEMED they were climbing up one hill after another. Sam hardly remembered hiking *down* those hills, just up. The earth was rocky and muddy, and when it wasn't raining, there was often low-lying fog that made them feel as if they were in a nightmare.

Only because he was exhausted did he welcome hearing their unit would be relieved for a few days' rest. He almost hated the rests as much as the action. It gave too much time to think, to stew, to worry. But after only one night, they were wakened and ordered to move out once again.

"Okuda, come with me," said Lieutenant Yumi.

"What's up, Lieutenant?"

"I just got word before we bedded down. You got a promotion to sergeant. You're gonna be a squad leader."

"Oh." Sam didn't know what to think about that. More pay was all that came to mind. The rest, the idea of leadership, was just a thing to take in stride. He only cared about the war ending soon.

As the men were packing up their gear, Sam joined in on a squad leaders' meeting.

"The First Battalion of the 141st Infantry is trapped behind enemy lines," Yumi said. "They've been trying for two days to get out but are pretty well pinned down. So we gotta go in and get 'em out."

"Aren't they a bunch of Texans?" asked one of the men.

"Does it matter?"

"No, just thought it's kind of keen that we get to rescue the cowboys is all."

"Be ready to march at 0400."

When Sam returned to his squad, he was pleased to see they were nearly ready to leave. There was time for a quick cup of coffee.

"Sarge," said Private Ichiro, coming up next to Sam and speaking softly, "I can't go out there again . . . I just can't."

"You sick or something, Gordon?" Sam asked.

"It isn't that. Look." He held out his hands. "I'm shaking. I'm scared. That means I'm gonna get it this time. I know it."

"Weren't you ever scared before?"

"Not like this."

"You don't have a choice, Gordy." Sam hated his cold tone, but there wasn't time for sympathy. There wasn't time for fear. They were moving out in five minutes. Then relenting because he couldn't stand the forlorn look on Gordon's face, Sam added, "We're gonna get a rest after this operation, a few days I hear. We're due. Okay? You can hold out for that, I know."

Gordon swallowed and nodded, a kind of grim acceptance of his fate. He stuck his shaky hands into his pockets.

It was so dark when they departed that they had to hang on to the backpack of the man ahead so as not to get lost. But advancing daylight didn't make the path appear any better. Before them lay a steep forested ridge. At least it wasn't raining. During the march Sam had time to think about his recent letters to Jackie. He could really kick himself for sending that letter about Charlie. What a selfish fool he'd been! But she was the person he talked to about everything. She always made his hurts feel better. Yet she was hurting, too, with worry and fear. He had to remember that.

God, just let her get that second letter soon!

He felt hypocritical praying for that because the second letter had been such a lie. He *wasn't* okay, as he'd tried to convince her. Inside he felt empty and used up. There were days when he couldn't even see Jackie's face in his mind's eye anymore. He told himself over and over that faith was especially for times like these. He clung to God like a man gripping the ledge of a building, the ground and death looming a thousand feet below.

He was clinging. Maybe that was enough.

By late in the afternoon they met with heavy enemy resistance led by a tank and half-track. His unit was stopped dead.

"We can't get around 'em, Sarge, so let's go through them!" said

Private Ichiro, patting his bazooka with a grin plastered on his young face. He seemed to have gotten over his earlier fear, but Sam wasn't convinced. Sometimes battle fatigue disguised itself in the oddest ways.

"You okay, Gordy?"

He shrugged. "Guess if you can't beat 'em, join 'em, huh?"

Sam knew everyone had his own way of accepting what lay ahead. Maybe Gordy was so sure of his own portending death that he had decided to face it with bravado.

"All right, then, give it a try," said Sam. "But stay under cover."

Ichiro didn't obey that last order. He crawled to within twenty-five yards of the tank, stood to get the best vantage, and fired. The mortar practically went right down the tank's hatch. It burst into fire. Gordy managed to blast out of commission a couple of machine gunners, as well, before he raced back to the cover of the trees.

The young private wore a look of utter shock as he faced Sam a few moments later. Shock that he was still alive, no doubt, but surely also shock at his boldness.

"Sarge," he breathed as the unit pushed through the hole he'd made in the German defense, "I know it's true now, all you say about God."

Sam couldn't disagree. He knew then that God hadn't deserted them.

Keeping up a barrage of fire, they moved forward, continuing to widen the gap in German defenses. But after gaining only a few feet, they were met with more enemy resistance. Men were falling all around. Most, Sam feared, were his comrades instead of the enemy. The German defense was incredible. Sam could little believe all he'd heard about defeating the enemy in a year. They were well armed and in no way resembled a defeated foe.

The Nisei units pushed against the Germans for three more days, their losses heavy. The "lost battalion," as the 141st was being called, grew more and more desperate, running out of food, ammunition, and medical supplies. The condition of their wounded was getting critical because there was no way to evacuate them.

Command ordered the Nisei units to push forward at all costs.

The terrain became treacherous, with steep ridges and sharp precipices along many trails, and the Germans made the Americans pay for each inch of ground they took. By the fourth day Sam was sure they must be getting close to the stranded men. It seemed only one line of Germans was left between the Texans and the Nisei rescuers.

Maybe Sam was just as crazy as Gordy, for after having been dulled so long, his mind's image of Jackie cleared for a moment, like the fog clearing on the treacherous mountainside. Suddenly she seemed to finally be within his reach. Perhaps this would be the last battle, and if he could get through it, he'd see Jackie for real.

In an instant he lost patience and opened up fire with the tommy gun given to him with his promotion. He sprayed the next ridge with fire, and Gordy, taking heart, laid in with his bazooka. This action seemed to invigorate the rest of the unit, for they were right there offering corresponding fire. With renewed energy they nearly surged right over the Germans.

The enemy fell back, but the men of Sam's company did not let up. They kept coming on until they ran into an enemy machine-gun nest. These Krauts apparently didn't need the rest of their men—with the nest alone, they had total and lethal control of the ridge. Because of its sweeping vantage of the men below, it was as good as a tank for defense. With curses all around, Sam's company was forced to halt.

The advance thus far had been costly and now it seemed it had been for nothing. Since he had been the impetus in starting the initial advance, Sam was loath to see it all wasted. Perhaps over this ridge they would find respite. Maybe even an end to this carnage. And he still could see Jackie's face so clearly, like a promise beckoning him. He could hope because there was hope. He knew that.

"Cover me!" he yelled to his squad, then dropped to his knees and scurried forward on his belly.

He'd seen many a Kraut machine-gun nest go down, so he knew this one wasn't invincible. Veering to the left, he saw what looked like good footholds in the side of the ridge leading to the nest. His men were doing well keeping the machine gunners busy with a blanket of gunfire, enabling him to keep moving closer until he could land a good pitch. So far he had not been spotted by the enemy. The trees and brush hid him but also made a clear toss impossible. He crawled to the right, but no matter what position he took, he couldn't get a clean shot. Nevertheless, he had come too far to give up.

Pulling the pin from his grenade, he rose and stepped to the right into a clearing in full view of the nest. He didn't hesitate, knowing he had only fractions of a second to act. He pitched the grenade at the same moment they opened up fire on him. As enemy fire riddled the dirt a mere two feet in front of him, he saw the grenade hit its target, blowing the nest out of existence. By then he was already on the ground, snaking his way back to his men, keeping low in case he'd missed anyone.

"Looks like you've got nine lives, too, Sarge," Gordy said.

Sam shrugged in response, then called to his men, "Move out while it's clear!"

They didn't have to be told twice. As he started to jog after them, the lieutenant came up beside him.

"That'll earn you a medal, Sam."

Sam shook his head, feeling incredibly foolish. He'd done it because it had to be done and because he wasn't about to let his men take all the risks. He'd only done it, if he were honest, to hurry them closer to home.

"All I want, lieutenant, is to get home to my wife and baby."

"It won't be long—"

The sharp report of rifle fire cut off the rest of what the lieutenant had been about to say. Sam heard the sound and a moment later felt a terrible pain in his head. He crumpled to his knees.

"Sniper!" a voice shouted.

Sam heard men hit the dirt. His vision was blurred, but only as he tried to rub his eyes did he realize he couldn't see because blood was pouring down his face.

I'm hit. He didn't know if he thought the words or said them out loud. But a moment later he heard from one of the men, "I got him!"

"Medic! Medic!"

"Someone's gonna be here, Sam. Hang on!" That was the lieutenant's voice, though Sam still could see nothing but blurred images. "We got the sniper."

"My head hurts," Sam mumbled.

"Medic!"

"I'm . . . not . . . going . . . home. . . ."

"Yeah you will. Hang on!"

But the lieutenant's voice seemed far away. Everything surrounding Sam began to spin and blur. What was real began to slip away. But what was even more real came clear. Jackie's face . . . like before, only now he was sure he could touch it. He just had to reach out. . . .

Jackie and her mother were in the kitchen fixing lunch, and Emi was chattering in her highchair when the doorbell rang.

"I'll get it," said Jackie. She grabbed a dish towel, quickly dried her hands, and bustled from the kitchen.

She saw the uniform and the badge on his shirt. Western Union. It took only that for her whole world to crash. She stumbled back against the open door as the fellow held out the telegram.

"Ma'am, I gotta have you sign for this." There was sympathy in his eyes.

She just stared with disbelief.

"I'm sorry, ma'am. . . ."

He looked about somewhat wildly, no doubt wondering what to do if she fainted on him. Despite the blur that suddenly engulfed her, Jackie noted the boy looked so young. How many of these terrible telegrams had he delivered?

Then he took a step forward and stuck his head into the doorway and called, "Hello! Hello . . ."

A few moments later Cecilia came into the entryway carrying Emi. "Jacqueline, what is it?"

Her mother's voice seemed to galvanize her a little. "Mama . . ." Jackie breathed.

Cecilia rushed forward, perceiving the meaning of the scene. Emi was still chattering merrily. Cecilia signed the delivery man's clipboard, took the telegram.

Before turning away, the fellow said, "I'll be eighteen next month, and I'm gonna go whop me some Japs, and some Germans, too."

"Thank you," Cecilia said vaguely, whether for the delivery or the sentiment, Jackie didn't know.

Cecilia placed her free arm around Jackie, closed the door, and led her into the house. She started to open the paper.

Jackie grabbed her mother's hand. "No. Don't open it."

"Jacqueline, it might not be the worst—"

"I can't stand it . . . I can't . . ."

"Yes, you can. Come, let's sit down."

In the front parlor they sat down close together on the sofa with Emi nestled between them. Cecilia opened the telegram. When she finished scanning the lines, she turned and threw her arms around her daughter.

"It's true, then, Mama?" murmured Jackie plaintively.

"Oh, my dear! I am so sorry—" Cecilia's voice broke on a sob.

They clung to each other for a long time with little Emi squirming about between them, having no idea what was happening.

Somehow her mother got her upstairs and into her bed. Jackie let herself be led because she had no strength of will to do anything for herself. Still crying, she crawled beneath the covers that her mother held up. She made no protest when her mother carried Emi out of the room. In the dim corners of her mind she knew that soon she would need Emi desperately, but now she simply could not bear the baby's happy oblivious chatter.

Jackie thought she'd never sleep but only cry forever and ever.

Then, amazingly, she was waking up. The bright noon sun that even the drawn shades hadn't dimmed but nevertheless had ushered her into that impossible sleep was now dim. The sun was surely setting on the gray autumn day. She must have slept for hours. She had the thick sluggish feel of it, not helped by her red puffy eyes.

Glancing at the crib beside her bed, she saw that Emi was asleep. Mom must have crept in while she slept and put the child to bed.

Jackie's gaze fell on the framed photograph of Sam, so regal in his uniform.

Oh, God, he's dead!

Tears assailed her once more, but she fought back the worst of it because she didn't want to wake Emi. But she had little control, and when hiccuping sobs started again, she buried her face in her pillow. *I'll never see him again. I'll never hear his laughter or his dear sense of humor. Emi will never know her father. I am broken without him. How will I—*

More sobs erupted. Emi stirred. Only then did Jackie realize she wanted—*needed!*—Emi to be awake. She rose and laid a hand on the child's back, rubbing it gently, though even as she did so, she realized she was being selfish. Still she did not stop. Emi whimpered a little, and quickly Jackie scooped her from the crib.

"Mama?" she said, rubbing the sleep from her eyes.

"I need you, Emi," Jackie said in a shaky voice, tears spilling once again from her eyes.

Emi reached up a little hand and seemed to attempt to pluck a tear as it fell on Jackie's cheek.

"Mama sad?" Emi's brow wrinkled.

"Mama very sad."

Gazing at her child through the veil of her own tears, Jackie remembered something Sam had written in a letter while on the battlefield. "I think of how good God has been to me, and no matter what happens here, He has given me, with you and Emi, more happiness than any man has a right to. I love you!"

She tried desperately to hold on to that knowledge. She knew it was true. Yet it was too hard to accept that there would be no more, that the mere two and a half years they'd had together was all she'd have. Perhaps one day she would be able to thank God for it, for the depth of their love, for the completeness of their lives. God *had* been good to them. So good.

So cruel.

I'm sorry, God. I know you are not cruel. But . . . why? Why couldn't your goodness include fifty years for Sam and me? Your Word says, "All things work together for good to them that love God . . ." Where is the good in this? Show me, she silently demanded.

She felt Emi's soft cheek press against hers and knew this was part of it, but it wasn't enough. If God was to take a fine man like Sam, if God was going to break a love made in heaven, there had to be more to it.

Help me to see it, God! Help me to see you in this. That is all I ask.

39

GARY GLANCED again at the paper in his hand. His first thought was that it had been foolish to trust information like this to paper. His second thought . . . he could hardly discern his second thought among the jumble that assailed his brain. But the runner, a boy, was panting hard.

"Get him some water," Gary told one of his men.

"What is it?" asked Ralph.

Gary looked at his friend, then turned to face the rest of the men, all of whom, except for the sentries, had gathered around the runner.

"American troops have begun landing on Luzon," Gary said, suddenly realizing his voice was shaky. The tears that sprang to his eyes surprised him, as well.

He wasn't the only one to react in this manner. Even Ralph's eyes were moist. They had been waiting for three years for this moment. All their suffering, all their struggling, had been for this. Even when they'd heard in October that MacArthur had landed on Leyte, an island south of Luzon, it hadn't seemed real. Gary knew a lot of fighting lay between that island and this one. A lot could happen. The Japanese position was weakening—he'd helped to make that so—but they still had much fight left in them.

Now it was truly happening. Soon the islands would be free.

"Where are they landing, Captain?" asked Roxas.

"They had enough sense not to put that in writing," answered Gary, "but we have informed them that Lingayen Gulf would be the best spot. We have to hope it's there."

"So what do we do?" inquired several voices at once.

"Roxas, you and Tony head out now and try to link up with the American troops. They'll want all the information about enemy disposition you can give them."

Tony gave Gary a look of gratitude. "Thanks, Captain."

Gary knew every American guerrilla had yearned for the day when he could connect with his own people once again. But something told him such a reunion wasn't going to be all warm and sentimental. Most of them had forgotten what it was to be a real soldier. What was he saying? They had nearly forgotten what it was like to be American, or even human!

He looked down at himself. Nary a soul would know that a West Point graduate lurked beneath his shabby mismatched clothing. He'd managed to cut out some of the insignia from his old uniform and sew them to his shirt, although it was too hot to wear it all the time. The shirt was khaki but had been pilfered from a Jap supply dump. His trousers were civilian, baggy, held up at the waist with a rope. On his head was a dirty blue bandanna topped with a hat of woven palm fronds, while his hair under that was greasy and hadn't been cut in months. His feet were bare now because his last pair of boots had disintegrated months ago and he hadn't found replacements, nor had he seen the need since his feet were as tough as a native's. His look was completed with skin as brown as a Filipino's.

His appearance wasn't all that bothered him, and he was acutely reminded of these other areas when Tony and Roxas packed up their gear and reported to him before leaving. They both gave him a rather sloppy left-handed salute. No one gave a regulation right-handed salute around here because that hand was almost always gripping a weapon. Most of them even slept with their weapons tucked under their arms.

As the two men hiked into the jungle, Gary knew he was being frivolous in his fears. So what if he made a fool of himself in front of the arriving army. After all that had been sacrificed for this day, that was hardly important. Gary thought then of the many who would not see this momentous time. His original unit from two years ago was diminished by half. Tom Morris, killed; Woody Woodburn, captured, probably executed; Fernando Segundo, captured and definitely executed. Gary had later found his body mutilated and strung up as a lesson to other partisans. Dozens of other names were etched into his mind, never to be forgotten. He had replacements, of course, but each man lost had cut him deeply.

Beyond that and in his heart was the most personal sacrifice of all—Blair. He put aside his niggling fears because of all she had given for him and for the cause of liberating the islands. He knew she was now at Santo Tomas, but because it had been too risky, he hadn't been able to get personal messages to her. Yet through a third or fourth party, he'd heard of what she had suffered at the hands of Jap interrogators. He knew that to protect him, she had never talked. He knew she had lost their child. He had suffered his share of grief over that, but his agony could be nothing compared to hers after having carried and nurtured the baby for over six months.

No, it didn't matter at all if he appeared a buffoon to the regular Army men. It only mattered to free the islands, to free Blair.

He turned to the men milling around the campsite. "We still have plans to destroy that supply dump near La Paz." Without thinking he spoke Tagalog because many of his men spoke poor English or none at all. Tagalog had nearly become his first tongue, he'd spoken it so much. He now had to think to speak English.

"Won't they be extra alert, Captain, with the Americans landing?" asked Mateo, who had become an important part of the guerrilla band.

Ralph answered him. "You want the new boys to get all the glory, Mateo?"

Mateo shook his head, but they all knew it had less to do with glory—they had been at this too long to believe in such a thing anymore—than with just finishing what they had started.

"Okay," Gary said. "We'll move out at sundown as planned. But take all your gear 'cause we won't be coming back here."

"We gonna meet up with the Americans?" asked Albert Pirro.

"We're gonna try."

———

On a warm January morning, seated in the grass under a clear blue sky, Blair listened with equal parts interest and fascination to Meg Doyle's sermon. Well, she was interested most of the time. Meg did have a habit of wandering off the subject and getting a bit long-winded. What was fascinating, though, was the woman's marvelous memory for Scripture. She hardly needed to refer to the New Testament she had scrounged from one of the other internees. Blair, who prided herself on having an excellent memory, hoped she could do as well one day.

When her turn came to lead the small congregation in a closing song, Blair also had to thank Meg's memory for that. With the help of a few other knowledgeable folks, Meg had written out the words to several hymns because there were no hymnbooks in the camp.

All in all, they had put together a fairly nice Sunday service. Blair had been rather surprised upon her arrival at the camp to find that Meg hadn't already whipped the other inmates' religious lives into shape.

"I'm afraid I haven't had the heart," Meg had admitted on Blair's first Sunday when she had inquired of the possibility of finding a service.

"Meg, you haven't lost your faith, have you?" Blair tried to hide her utter shock at the very idea.

"No . . . it's there . . ." But she had sighed as if she didn't have the energy to try to find it.

Blair remembered how strong Meg had always been for her, even to the point of bullying her. So she plunged ahead with the idea that suddenly formed in her mind.

"Meg, would you mind if I tried to put something together for Sundays? I know there are other church groups here, but I think the activity will be good for me."

"Why should I mind?"

"Well, I certainly would need your expert guidance in such an endeavor."

A little smile bent Meg's thin lips. "The tables have turned, eh?"

"I'm honestly not trying to trick you. And my reasons for wanting to do this in the first place are completely selfish, I am sure."

"Selfish?"

"I feel like a wraith half the time, Meg." Meg, of course, by now knew about all of Blair's recent heartaches. "Each day I am not sure I can stand on my own. But if I can surround myself with people of faith, maybe I'll be able to survive. Not to mention that the simple effort of planning services will keep me occupied."

"I never thought of it that way!" said Meg. "Since coming here,

I haven't been able to see my way to being a spiritual leader. But I didn't think of *them* holding *me* up. And something tells me it is not selfish at all. It is how Christianity should work, the strong ones holding up the weaker ones, and in lieu of strong ones, everyone taking turns holding up one another. Perhaps, then, we could give it a try."

One thing Blair quickly learned from the other internees was that keeping busy was a prime aid to survival. So besides the obvious spiritual benefits of having a church service, there was the element of it keeping Blair and Meg busy planning and organizing. Theirs certainly wasn't the only religious service in the camp, but they quickly learned that with a population of almost four thousand, there were many differing needs and desires. For their first service, two weeks later, they had about thirty in attendance, and it grew to fifty most days.

At first Meg demurred about speaking publicly. She didn't feel strong enough for that. Blair had no intention of stepping in, and Claudette laughed at the idea of giving any kind of sermon herself. They were both too new in their faith to have the confidence to teach others. Finally, when the Saturday before the first service came, Meg stepped up, as Blair thought she would. Meg would always be a leader at heart, and once she started a task, she was determined that it be successful. She was not going to see the effort of planning fall apart because no one wanted to preach. Eventually she admitted that giving sermons was such a balm to her that she feared she herself might not survive without them.

Those first six months at Santo Tomas were not too bad for Blair. It was prison, no question of that! The presence of the Japanese was constant and keen. The guards with their bullying and sneers made Blair cringe, though she hated herself for it. If they approached her, she would wince, never shaking the deep fear of another beating despite the fact that since her interrogations before coming to Santo Tomas, they had never struck her again. Such a deeply ingrained terror did not dissipate quickly or easily.

Nevertheless, existence here could have been worse, and she'd heard rumors of loathsome atrocities at the military prison camps. At first there had usually been enough food—never as much as before the war, but far more than Blair had been used to while hiding in the jungle. The administration allotted thirty-five cents a day per inmate for food and other necessities. For many this was augmented by packages from outside, usually from friends and relatives in Manila. These outside sources also managed to get money to inmates so they could purchase various items at the prison canteens, such as eggs, milk, and some toiletries. Reverend Sanchez had been instrumental in getting money and packages to many in the camp. Others took over after his capture and death, but their system was never as effective. Blair was often without means to procure amenities beyond the allotment because, of course, she had no friends left in Manila.

The camp ran like a small town, with elected officials, inmates who acted as liaisons to the Japanese administration. There was a camp newspaper and a library. There was even an adult school where Spanish and music appreciation were among the courses. Even golf lessons were given by two Americans who had been pros at a Manila country club.

When Blair thought how Gary must be worrying about her, she felt a little guilty that she wasn't suffering as much as would be expected at a prison camp. She'd tried to smuggle messages to him via the regular camp smuggling operation to let him know she was all right, but it was too risky to send anything directly to him without someone like Reverend Sanchez on the outside who knew him. So she never knew if her messages were received.

Then early in 1944 Claudette brought news that would change everything for the camp.

"I just heard that the Japs have changed command of the camp from civilian control to control by the Japanese Imperial Army."

Blair and Meg both responded with looks of dismay. The cruelty of the Imperial Army was well known to them. Blair had heard that it was a great dishonor for a Japanese soldier to get captured, and for that reason they treated their military prisoners not only with disdain but with terrible cruelty. This attitude had generally not extended to civilian captives, but would that change now?

"Why do you suppose they have done that?" mused Blair.

"It's obvious," said Meg. "They want us under a heavier hand."

"Maybe it's a good thing," offered Claudette. When both of the other women looked at her aghast, she added quickly, "Well, maybe it's because the war is going bad for them."

"Hmm, could be," said Blair. "They probably don't have enough food for their own army, so they're going to have to wring it out of us. But they need the army to keep us from rioting."

She didn't like it when she soon realized she might not have hit far from the mark. First the monetary allowance was cut off, and all food was strictly controlled by the administration and served in the mess hall. They also cut off outside packages and any contact with the outside world. The canteens were closed down or greatly limited in their wares. And over the following months, the daily ration of food was gradually cut back until it was less than a thousand calories per day and included little or no protein. In fact, most of the food was hardly recognizable as food at all. Usually it consisted of a gruel-type dish that resembled and tasted like wallpaper paste.

Blair's health began to weaken once again as malnutrition set in. She had her first bout with malaria since leaving the jungle. It was a mild case, and she didn't go to the clinic despite the urging of her friends. Many others in the camp were hit much harder, the older POWs and children especially. The nurses Blair knew said the death rate among internees was rising dramatically.

On a morning back in September of '44, when Blair was standing in line at the mess hall waiting for breakfast, she had beheld a sight that was better than even a steak dinner at the Brown Derby.

"Look!" someone yelled.

Blair had heard the sound of airplane engines but assumed it was the Japs practicing maneuvers. She looked up anyway for diversion and saw the stars on the side of the aircraft.

"They're ours!" she breathed.

For months, at the back of each inmate's mind was the thought, "They will come soon. Hang on!" Even after the disappointment of Bataan, when their "boys" had never come to rescue them, they still clung to hope. Finally it was being realized. For the first time in three years American aircraft was aloft over Luzon!

But now more than three months had passed. It was January of yet another year, 1945, and still no rescue. Blair looked out on the small congregation, now dwindled to about fifteen because so many were too weak with hunger to come. The death toll from malnutrition and disease in the camp had risen alarmingly. These voices, as they intoned the words to "What a Friend We Have in Jesus" a cappella, were almost lifeless. Blair's own voice was a mere shadow of what it had been a year ago. Yet they were all here, and they were singing. That was surely something.

Two weeks later Blair was awakened in the cold dark hours of the morning by the rumble of artillery fire, which by now had become all too familiar. But unlike in past times when that same sound had frozen her with fear, she now listened with growing excitement and anticipation. These explosions sounded closer than ever before.

Claudette crawled into bed with her. "Blair, they're ours, aren't they?"

"Yes!" She had no idea why she was so confident of that fact, but she was. Some assurance in her weak bones told her something good was finally coming.

All through the day they waited, the sounds of artillery drawing closer. The guards finally ordered everyone confined to their dormitories, and a blackout was enforced.

Well after dark Blair heard a loud crash down in the compound outside. A roar of what could only be tank engines accompanied it. Rumors had flown about all day that the Japs planned to blow up the camp and kill all the prisoners. Thus Blair couldn't help momentarily losing her earlier confidence.

All the women in the room crowded around the windows to see outside, but it was too dark to make out anything definite.

Then from below a voice shouted, "Hello! Anyone home?" It was a distinctly American voice!

The entire camp surged from the buildings to welcome the visitors.

Gary had made sure he and his men were with the troops entering Manila on February 3. The new GI's—that was a new term that he'd learned meant Government Issue and usually referred to the common soldier—had needed the seasoned guerrillas to help guide them through the jungle. And their troops had fought the enemy the entire way. The Japs were obviously defeated, but they refused to give up. The taking of Manila encompassed the most vicious Japanese resistance of the war. Just as the Americans reached the Grace Park suburb immediately north of Santo Tomas, Gary caught his first real wound of the war.

A sniper's bullet seared his right calf, knocking him off his feet and into a nearby irrigation ditch. Ralph, who had been marching beside him, got off a couple of rounds in the direction of the sniper.

"I think I got him," Ralph said as he rolled into the ditch next to Gary. He continued to hold his rifle at the ready, peering into the surrounding buildings.

Gary had yanked the bandanna from his head and was stuffing it into his pant leg to try to stop the bleeding. "Three years, Ralph, I never took a bullet! Why now?"

"How bad is it?"

"The bullet is still in there, and it hurts like everything."

The men who had been with him had taken cover, some in the ditch, others behind buildings. Every time someone tried to get back on the road, the sniper opened fire. One more man was wounded.

The larger portion of the company was making unopposed progress in other sectors. They were going to get to Santo Tomas and liberate the prisoners while he was stuck in a ditch, pinned down by a sniper. He knew at this point the idea was crazy, but he had wanted his to be the first heroic face Blair saw. He had even dreamed about their passionate reunion. Now the place would be liberated, and she would be there with no idea how close he was. The prisoners might even be moved away before he had a chance to get there.

One of the Americans—that is, one of the new American soldiers in the ditch—looked at Gary's leg and shuddered. "Is there a medic here?" he called to the others.

Ralph thumped his head. "Sorry, Captain, I didn't even think to call for a medic."

"Why should you?" Gary said. "We haven't had that luxury in three years." He ran a hand through his hair. "Anyway, I don't need a medic," he groused bitterly. "I need to get to the prison camp."

"Why's that?" asked the lieutenant who had called for the medic.

Ralph answered because Gary had tried to move and the pain had rendered him momentarily speechless. "His wife is in there." Ralph peered carefully up over the edge of the ditch. "There he is. I'm sure I saw light glinting off the sniper's scope."

The sun was setting and in the right position. Perhaps it was so. But what good would it do? Gary felt as if his spirit were draining out with his blood. He'd been so certain he would see Blair today.

Then Ralph started moving. Gary grabbed his sleeve. "What're you doing?"

"Hey, them Japs caught me twice. I'm gonna catch me just one before this war is over!"

"He's got too good a view of us," the lieutenant said.

"You keep him busy from here, Lieutenant," said Ralph, "but wait till I get to the end of the ditch before you open fire. There's just about fifty yards after that when I'll be in the open. I can run that far easy if he's distracted. Then no sweat flanking him."

"Be careful" was all Gary could say.

It was a big risk his friend was taking, and Gary knew Ralph was motivated in large part by his desire to get Gary to Santo Tomas. Nevertheless, the risk had to be taken eventually. The men couldn't sit here forever.

When Ralph reached the end of the ditch, several of the men opened fire in the supposed direction of the sniper. Some even tried a trick learned in cowboy-and-Indian movies of putting their helmets on the end of a bayonet and lifting them a tempting distance above the edge of the ditch in order to entice fire from the sniper. Gary fired a few times, as well, but the position he had to be in to do so sent shooting pains up his leg. He wondered, even if Ralph got the sniper, how he was going to rescue anyone when he could barely walk.

Before he had a chance to stew over this thought, he heard a loud whoop he recognized as Ralph's. In about five minutes his friend appeared, his rifle trained on a Japanese soldier.

"You should have killed him," said the lieutenant.

"It's not a true capture if I do that." Ralph grinned.

They trussed up the man with rope, then left him in the ditch as all the Americans climbed out, still cautious in case the fellow had friends. No one worried about leaving the sniper stranded in the ditch. Sooner or later he'd be discovered.

For a few minutes Gary thought he'd have to remain with the prisoner because he had a time of it trying to crawl out. But finally, with several hands pulling and several more pushing, he made it, but he needed a rest at the top before he could move again.

"I'm not gonna make it," Gary groaned.

"Is it that bad?" gasped the lieutenant.

"I'm not gonna make it to the camp," Gary elaborated with forced patience.

"Oh, yes you are!" Ralph insisted, then to back up his words, he grabbed Gary and flung him over his shoulder.

Gary groaned again but made no protest. He was glad now that he'd lost forty pounds in the last three years. He still was amazed that Ralph never seemed to show any physical effects from all their hardships. He'd starved, lost weight, and fought disease, but it seldom stopped him for long.

And that was how they marched into the camp sometime after dark. American tanks had already crashed down the front gates, and the swell of cheering internees had by now become knots of milling onlookers. Apparently a number of Japanese officers and guards had retreated into the education building with hostages and were demanding safe conduct before they gave up.

"Put me down," Gary said, and when Ralph complied, he began scanning the prisoners in the main courtyard. "I don't see her," he said dismally. It was hard to see anything in the darkness, even with the scattered lights the troops had set up.

"I don't, either," said Ralph.

Gary swayed against his friend.

"There must be a hospital here. Let's get you there, then I'll look for her."

They quickly learned from the other men that the holed-up Japs had cut the rest of the camp off from the hospital. So Ralph helped Gary, who refused to be carried farther, to a first-aid station that had been set up in the courtyard. Gary was a trained soldier, who in the last three years had learned to be far more pragmatic and practical than West Point had ever taught him. He was definitely not a starry-eyed romantic. Yet he'd so firmly planted in his mind that picture of his reunion with Blair that his present predicament brought him as close to despair as he'd been even in his worst days in the jungle.

"Captain Hobart!" yelled a voice out of the night.

It was Mateo. He had also been with the force that had come through Grace Park, but he had somehow forged ahead of his comrades, the guerrilla band. He was just as anxious as Gary to reach the prison camp. He had arrived with the first assault team.

"You've been wounded!" Mateo said as he came up beside the

cot where Gary now lay and where a nurse was tending his leg.

"Yeah, perfect timing."

"I found them," Mateo said with a big grin on his face.

Gary started to struggle to his feet, but the nurse restrained him with the help of Ralph and Mateo.

Finally Mateo said, "Be still, and I will get her for you."

It wasn't the reunion he had dreamed of, but once Gary laid eyes on Blair, none of that mattered anymore. The smile that nearly split her thin face in two even made him forget the pain in his leg. She knelt by his cot and showered him with kisses, further making him forget all but her and that they were finally together.

The others gave them privacy, as much as could be had in a busy compound with hundreds of people milling about on one side and a hostage crisis on the other.

———

As it always seemed these days, joy and grief vied for her emotions. Joy dominated for a time when she first saw Gary. They were together. The war was over—for them at least—and they were both alive. Then the sadness hit.

"Gary, the baby—"

"Hush," he said gently. "I know. I wish I could have been here for you."

"We'll have more babies," she promised. She had not wanted to think along these lines since their baby's death, yet now that she and Gary were together, there could be a future.

"Many, many more," he said.

"We'll go home soon?" That, too, was a subject that she had not wanted to think about.

"Yes," he said.

"It seems impossible, but I know now nothing is impossible with God. It is almost too good. I don't deserve—"

"You deserve every good thing there is, my love, and when we get home, I'm going to make sure you never forget that."

"I already have every good thing there is!" She bent and kissed him again, knowing the truth of it. She had him and her faith and a future. What else did she need?

PART VI

"I am become death,
the shatterer of worlds."

BHAGAVAD GITA
Ancient Hindu Philosophical Treatise

40

Germany
April 1945

By April Cameron felt as if she had fought a war right alongside the one between the Allies and the Germans. It was the war all female journalists were waging with SHAEF—Supreme Headquarters, Allied Expeditionary Force. While the invasion was still fresh, within a few days of D-day, female journalists were finding many creative ways to buck regulations and get into France for short jaunts.

Only by mid-July 1944 had female correspondents officially been allowed to enter France and only under very stringent rules. In short, they were not allowed to go any closer to the Front than the women's services, that is, for the most part the nursing staff. They also had to bunk with the nurses rather than in the press camps with the male reporters, which of course were the hottest bed of news and action. Though the men were allowed the use of jeeps, the women were not, so they were forced to be at the mercy of others.

Many of the women broke the rules whenever an opportunity arose. Cameron had been with frontline soldiers, and she had trekked through villages liberated only moments before she arrived. Finally, in April of '45 when the Nazis were on the run, the U.S. Army began to lighten its rules. They had no doubt begun to realize the futility of keeping the women out of danger and out of Germany, as well. By opening the press camps to them, the SHAEF bureaucrats thought to offer at least some protection from the danger of snipers or hidden ambushes by other desperate Germans. It also had the effect of placing the women more in the center of news gathering.

For Cameron, much of the last nine months had been a wild romp of exhilarating rides in bombers, dangerous negotiating over bombed-out bridges, and heartrending journeys through battlefields where the Allied dead lay on the ground, still fresh and warm. She'd seen refugees of German concentration camps as they made their way home, wraiths of skin and bone. Her emotions went in moments from high thrills to deep sorrow. Learning of her brother-in-law's death had shaken her terribly. And almost as bad had been when the news came on April 12 that President Roosevelt had died. At least he had known that victory was assured, yet Cameron thought it sad that he had not been able to see this war to its end.

She was marching with a troop of GI's when the news came. They were all stunned and saddened. FDR had been a symbol to them. He'd brought them through a terrible depression years before, and they knew in their hearts he would bring them through this war, as well. For a brief moment hope wavered despite the fact they all knew the Germans were near their end.

When the initial shock wore off, one soldier asked, "Who's going to be president now?"

"The vice-president," offered another dryly, some of his GI wit returning.

"And who's that?"

"Harry Truman," answered Cameron.

"Never heard of him," said another.

By April 25 Cameron had made it as far as the Elbe River in Germany and was attached to the First Army. She was having lunch with some other reporters, sitting in the open air under a crisp, clear sky, when a jeep raced into the camp. As it screeched to a stop in a cloud of dust, several soldiers and a few officers gathered around it. The reporters forgot their half-eaten canned sardines and hurried over. This smelled like news. But the men in the jeep were immediately herded into the general's tent and did not emerge again for several hours.

The reporters converged on the men the moment they exited the tent.

"What's going on?" Cameron asked.

"We met up with the Russians," the lieutenant from the jeep said.

The reporters surged forward in anticipation. They had all been waiting and looking for this moment. But none more so than Cameron. She pushed ahead of them all. She had more than a scoop urging her on.

"Where?" she demanded. "How many? Were there medical units?"

"It was by Torgau. You should've seen them. They was just like regular guys," said the driver.

Now everyone bombarded the GI's with questions, and as soon as they were milked dry of information, the journalists made a mad dash for idle jeeps. Cameron hadn't waited through most of the questioning. She had hurried off the moment she'd heard *Torgau* to grab the vehicle vacated by the GI's now being questioned, which was still near the general's tent. She started it up as her colleagues were searching for other transportation. Before racing off, she called to her friend Edna, who brought along two male correspondents. Cameron made no protest. It was pure foolishness to drive through this country alone, and male companions were certainly handy in such situations.

It was too dark when they arrived at Torgau to make any attempt at contacting the Russians without risking being taken for lost German soldiers. Cameron knew for a fact the Russians would shoot first, and if a rare one did ask questions, even she might not comprehend enough to give the right answer. So they spent the night in the village in an inn that wasn't too badly damaged by the bombings. In the morning Cameron hitched a boat ride across the Elbe with a couple of Ukrainian captains.

Thus her search for Alex began. She had no idea in which specific unit to look, for even while she had still been in Russia, Alex had moved around a great deal. There was no telling where he would be now, if indeed he had left Russia. The Russians Cameron encountered on the opposite bank of the Elbe were in a high mood. She had never seen so many laughing Russians before, even at the drinking orgies she had observed in Russia. She was welcomed among them with open arms.

"Bravo! Americanski!" they yelled.

"America, our friend!"

They gave her directions to medical units, her Russian holding her in good stead. But no Alex.

She was waylaid for a time in order to observe the ceremony in which the commander of the Sity-ninth Infantry Division, General Reinhardt, and the commander of the Red Army Fifty-eighth Guards met formally as Reinhardt crossed the river. She did have her job to do and an obligation to the *Journal*. She smarted a bit that she hadn't been the first to report the scoop about the Russians reaching the Elbe. That honor had gone to Ann Stringer of the *United Press*. At least it had been a woman.

This was a great moment for both armies because their meeting effectively cut the German Army in two. There was dancing and celebration in every corner of the various camps. Cameron was with Edna when they were grabbed by a couple of burly Siberians and led in a high-stepping folk dance. They found it hard to refuse the celebrating Russians.

Laughing as they took a moment of rest, Edna said, "Goodness! They are like big children, aren't they?"

"Don't underestimate them, Edna," said Cameron. "That's what Hitler did."

But evening was coming on again, and she had much more to accomplish that day besides celebrating. She'd heard from one of the Russians of a medical unit she hadn't searched yet that was located east of the village. When she asked for a lift in that direction, the fellow was happy to accommodate her. He was thrilled to have found a beautiful American female who could speak some Russian. She was the first American he had ever seen, so he was rather mesmerized.

"*Spasiba! Spasiba!*" she thanked him enthusiastically for at least the tenth time after arriving.

Observing the medical unit for a moment, noting the staff rushing around and the stretchers of wounded being wheeled here and there, she marveled once again at the price of the celebrating down by the river.

She glanced toward the command tent but did not head in that direction. She couldn't just ask a commander to see if Alex's name was on the roster. Regardless of all the gestures of friendship now bursting between the Americans and the Russians, it would be dangerous for one of those Americans to seek out Alex specifically. So she just wandered around the camp, and if someone made inquiries of her, she told them she was a reporter seeking a story about medical units. She cemented their sympathy by briefly interviewing them. She would get a story out of this, if nothing else.

She'd made the rounds to most of the tents, and since it was getting dark and her friends would start to worry about her if she was too late back to the inn, she decided to check just a couple more tents before leaving. She poked her head into one and knew enough now about medical units to guess this was a postoperative ward. Alex would be here if he was anywhere. She scanned the stretchers and the busy workers, sighed, and was about to turn away when a flash of pale hair caught her eye. How many times recently had a blond doctor, or even a medic, made her heart stop?

Regardless, her heart stopped again. But this time the man turned, laid a hand on a passing orderly, and was about to speak to him. Cameron gasped and came within a heartbeat of crying out his name. She stopped herself in time but cast desperately around for a way to get his attention more subtly. But as was so typical of him, he was absorbed in his work. Subtlety might not be the best approach.

So she casually shoved over a nearby instrument tray. It made the expected loud clatter as forceps and scalpels and similar items crashed to the canvas floor. Everyone turned toward the noise. Alex did, as well. For a brief moment their eyes met. She saw he was about to make the same mistake she had barely avoided. She could almost feel his intense effort not to run then and there into her arms.

"I'm so sorry!" she said in English, appearing flustered as she bent to gather up the instruments.

A nurse and an orderly rushed to lend a hand.

Alex strode over. "This is what comes of civilians invading my ward," he growled in Russian. "You are American, yes?" he added in English. "Come with me." He grabbed her arm, firmly but not harshly, and propelled her from the tent. He made the perfect picture of an offended doctor about to take an unwelcome intruder to task. He did not stop prodding her along once outside but kept propelling her forward until they were behind the next tent and well out of sight.

Then he just stood there and stared at her as if he'd used up all his quick reflexes and was now numb.

"We do meet in the oddest places." She finally broke the silence, a lopsided and quite silly grin on her face.

He nodded, and she watched as many different expressions flickered across his face. He'd never been good at masking his feelings, but she marveled now at the depth of his emotion.

"How did you—? What—? It's like—" He shook his head, totally at a loss for coherent words.

Cameron wanted no words right now anyway. Unable to resist touching him, she lifted a hand to his cheek and said, "Alex, would you please kiss me?"

That he seemed able to do. He enveloped her in his arms and drew her close as he pressed his lips against hers. She reached up around his neck and grasped him just as firmly. She had almost forgotten the smell of him, the strong soap for a surgeon's hands and more than a hint of antiseptic, mingled oddly and sweetly with a spicy scent. And the feel of him, the hard muscles of his arms, the sure but gentle touch of his hands. And she minded not a whit at the slight abrasion of his cheek against hers. She knew he worked too hard to shave regularly.

Neither cared for a long while if the entire Red Army converged upon them. And Cameron no longer cared about the approaching night. The shadows were now her friends. But soon the two lovers needed to rest from their passion, and Alex eventually found his speech.

"When I saw you standing there," he said, still holding her as if he feared she were but a dream that would slip away upon his waking, "I feared I had finally snapped. I thought I was hallucinating."

Their conversation, she realized, was a jumbled mix of Russian and English. As on their last meeting, he seemed to have to think in order to respond in English, though now his accent was more pronounced, and the Russian came out more naturally. She managed to understand most of it, but her own Russian had grown a bit rusty in her months away from the country. He stumbled over the word *hallucinating,* saying it in Russian, which she didn't understand, and when she shook her head in confusion, he smiled apologetically and repeated it in English.

"It's a wonder I didn't ruin your whole plan," he added.

"You were quick to recover." She touched his cheek again—she couldn't stop herself, he was so real. "It makes it all that much more marvelous at how fast you reacted and just as I hoped you would."

"Well, if it was a dream, a fantasy, I was completely willing to follow it. And when I grasped your arm and knew for certain you were real, do you know how hard it was to restrain myself?" His eyes roved over her with still a hint of disbelief. The intense blue of them startled her, for they had dulled in her memory.

"I know quite well." She smiled. She had been actively looking for him, yet even she feared this was all just a dream.

"What do you want to do? How long do we have?"

"I know exactly what I want to do, Alex." And though she had never given it specific thought until this moment, now that he was here before her at last, she knew what she wanted, what had subconsciously impelled her in her search. "I want to marry you tonight."

He laughed. "Dear Camrushka, I love you! You are the most audacious, marvelous woman I have ever known."

"And?" she prompted.

He drew her close again and touched his lips to hers, but this time the touch was soft, tender, as if with that initial rush of passion over, he now wished to savor a splendid morsel.

"Yes, I want to marry you!" he said when he finished kissing her thoroughly. "It is so crazy, it must be right."

"I thought you'd argue the practical reasons against it."

"There are too many practical reasons against it to waste breath and time mentioning them." His gaze, filled with tenderness, had not a practical iota about it. "But how will we manage it?"

"I'm staying at an inn in Torgau. It's the only inn still mostly intact, but I can't remember the name of it. Come tonight. I'll find a minister."

He shook his head. "It can't be tonight. I'm on duty, and I couldn't get away without questions being asked. I could do it tomorrow night. . . ."

She could not help the dismal look she gave in response. They both knew how quickly lives could be changed in a mere twenty-four hours.

"I know . . . I know . . ." he said miserably, "but the longer we can keep them from looking for me—"

"Alex, what do you mean?"

"I'm going to defect, aren't I?"

She stared at him in utter disbelief. She had not thought it through this far. But that had been for good reason.

"Cameron, did you think I would marry you, then turn around and return to my unit?"

"I . . . I didn't know. I just knew that no matter what happened, I didn't want to go another moment without being your wife." She squeezed shut her eyes, steeling herself against the inevitable dose of reality and practicality she knew was coming.

"I feel the same way," he assured her. "But we can be together now. This is the perfect opportunity, perhaps the only one we will have. I can seek asylum with one of the U.S. commanders—"

She took a shuddering breath as the joy she'd felt only moments before seemed to shatter inside her. "Alex, have you heard any of what transpired at Yalta earlier this year?"

He shook his head. He was a Soviet citizen, after all.

"The Big Three, I mean—"

"I know who the Big Three are," he said glumly.

"It's supposed to be a secret agreement. I heard it from someone . . . well, it doesn't matter who. The three leaders have agreed to repatriate one another's civilians—this is mostly regarding those prisoners and the like that they liberate here in Germany. But in the case of Russia, any Russian deserters and dissidents who have slipped into Germany would also be returned to the Soviet Union if they are found by the Allies. If you turn yourself in to an American commander, or any official, he is obligated to turn you back over to the Russians." She lifted her eyes to study him as she spoke. It sickened her to see the vitality she'd seen in him just moments before suddenly drain away.

"You'd think they were against us personally," he said, biting out each word with a bitterness so unusual for him.

Desperate for some way to lift him again, she quickly added, "We might find one who is sympathetic. I have some friends in high places—"

"Do you think any American official is going to be eager to risk his reputation for a man with my record in his country? Under normal conditions it might have been possible, but not now after what you have told me. Oh, Cameron, I thought my past was finally behind me. But here it is now returning to devour me . . . us. I am so sorry."

"No, Alex, it is not your fault." More sheepishly she amended her previous words. "Anyway, I don't really have that many friends in very high places."

A tender smile bent his pale lips. "I see you in my mind every morning when I wake and every night before I sleep. You, and my faith in God, keep me going, give me the hope and the courage I need to survive. I guess I will have to keep on in that way for a while longer. But seeing you in reality makes it so much harder to go back to an image in my mind."

"Alex, what I said before . . . I still want to marry you. I don't care what happens later."

He looked away as he dropped his hold on her. "You shouldn't be tied to me. You could meet someone else, start over—"

"Alex, you incredible, dear idiot! That is not going to happen. I am tied to you in my heart and my soul. As long as you live, I am yours. You are mine. Marriage is almost a mere formality—*but one I want.*" She grasped his arm and pulled him around to face her. "I deserve that, Alex. You deserve it, as well." Oddly, as she spoke it never once occurred to her that he might not feel the same, that he might wish to put their hopeless relationship behind him and try starting over with another. She didn't need to look up and see his blue eyes glinting in affirmation. But it was nice to see anyway.

She went on. "Beyond that, Alex, there is a power in the marriage bond. I know it! A deep spiritual power but also another kind of power, one that I know in my heart will bring us back together in the future."

Tears flowed from his eyes as he nodded understanding. He pulled her into his arms once again, and his embrace trembled with emotion. She wanted to stay like that forever, but they were standing behind a medical tent near a war zone, and it was already just short of a miracle they hadn't been discovered. Besides, they must talk. Arrangements had to be made, plans for their wedding.

41

"THERE'S NOT A DECENT white dress to be found in this town!" Edna exclaimed as Cameron let her friend into her room.

"I never wanted a white wedding dress or any such thing," Cameron assured. "I am quite relieved I don't have to fuss with such nonsense."

"Why don't you at least let me tell some of our colleagues? I'm sure they'll want to attend your wedding, and we can make an event of it."

Cameron knew Edna meant well. She wanted everything for Cameron's wedding day that she herself would have wanted. But Cameron had tried to explain why it must be kept quiet, not for her sake but for Alex's. In fact, Cameron had decided not to tell anyone and had only revealed it to Edna because, as hard as it was for her to admit, she needed to share this with someone. And she wanted at least one friend to be with her for the wedding.

"An event is the last thing I want," Cameron said firmly.

"I suppose I understand. I wonder how many *regulations*"—her slurred tone made clear just what she thought of such regulations, especially those that singled out the women—"you'll be breaking."

"I don't think there is a single one forbidding the marriage of a female journalist to a Red Army doctor." She smiled wryly, not mentioning the fact that even the most hard-nosed SHAEF officer would never have thought of such an occurrence in order to regulate against it.

After sharing a cup of tea and some conversation—Cameron

was glad for both because her tension was slowly building as the appointed time drew close—Edna returned to her room to finish an article or two before the ceremony.

Cameron consumed more tea, but it helped less and less. She wasn't nervous about the wedding or the marriage—she was rock-solid certain about that. What jangled her nerves was the thought of all that could go wrong. The plan was for Alex to slip away from his tent well after dark. During the day he would complain of fatigue and mild stomach discomfort so that no one would have cause to question his turning in early for the night. He had one friend, the doctor he shared a tent with, whom he felt he could trust implicitly. Alex hoped this man would cover for him should any need arise during the night, whether medical emergency or surprise inspection. But even to this friend he didn't reveal the entire truth of what he intended.

Alex thought he could get to the village around nine o'clock that evening. As the hands of the clock inched toward the hour, then passed it, Cameron's tensions mounted.

Edna, who had rejoined Cameron in her room, had a worried look. Though she didn't speak the words, Cameron knew she was thinking them: "I hope he hasn't stood you up."

Cameron answered the unspoken sentiment. "He's a doctor. He's always late."

She paced back and forth. At nine-thirty she asked Edna to go to the church and make sure the minister waited. Cameron had had a hard time finding a minister who would perform the rather unorthodox ceremony. And she had purposely failed to mention to the man that her intended was a Russian officer. These people in the village were Germans, and even the best of them had little love for Russians. For that reason Alex would pass himself off as a Polish refugee. Cameron had scrounged some civilian clothes for him in village shops—all well used, out of date, and in varying sizes.

As for herself, she had only her army fatigues to wear. She'd left everything else back at the press camp when she had hurried off to meet the Russian Army. And when she had been scouring the village for things for Alex, she had not even thought about what she would wear, not that the bombed village had much to offer. For years they had suffered terrible privations in order to feed Hitler's war machine. Even if she had found a dress, she wouldn't have had the heart to take it. She was satisfied wearing her fatigues.

There were so many other things to worry about than proper attire. What if Alex couldn't get away? What if they captured him stealing away from the camp? He'd be shot as a deserter. What if he did get away, and as they were standing at the altar, a squad of NKVD came and shot them both?

"Steady, girl . . ." she murmured.

She strode to the window and, pulling back the blackout shade, gazed at the deserted street below. There was a curfew . . . another worry.

Then she heard a tap on her door. She rushed to it and flung it open. "Alex!" She bustled him into the room.

"I am so sorry," he explained. "It was the stupidest thing. I lay on my cot waiting for things to quiet down, and I fell asleep! Stupid! So stupid!"

"When was the last time you slept before that, Alex?"

He only shrugged in response. She was well aware of the long, arduous hours he put in.

"We best hurry," she said, turning to gather up the bundle of clothes for him. "I hope they are okay. I won't look," she added as she turned her back. Soon she heard the sounds of his shuffling about as he shed his uniform and slipped into the civilian duds. She mused that soon they would be married and she wouldn't have to turn her back when he dressed, but that thought brought an ache to her heart. It would be a long time, she feared, before they were together long enough for the awkwardness of such a scene to wear off. Not tonight certainly. But she didn't want to think of the future. They would have to wait for the future. But she prayed it wouldn't be too long a wait.

"Okay, you can turn around," he said.

She did, and an immediate giggle escaped her lips. "I'm sorry, Alex! I didn't mean—"

"I thought Germans were larger people."

The trousers were several inches too short and baggy, as well. The sleeves of the white shirt were well above his wrists, but the wool argyle-style sweater, V-necked and long-sleeved, fit fairly well and covered the fault of the shirt. The necktie was rather nice, maroon silk with a fine gold-striped pattern.

"My groom!" she breathed.

He strode to her, scooping her into his arms as he fingered the coarse khaki of her fatigues. "My bride!"

"Let's pray the minister has waited," she said.

———

He had. Edna, true to her profession, had distracted the man by interviewing him extensively regarding his observations about the war. He wasn't a Nazi—most Germans one encountered in these conquered territories claimed they were not Nazis and never had been. But this man seemed sincere in this profession. Cameron wanted to believe it, for she did not like the idea of being married by a Nazi, even if he was a Lutheran. In any case Cameron hoped Edna received a Pulitzer for her efforts.

The minister's wife would act as the second witness and would provide music for the occasion. This was Edna's idea, for Cameron had not even considered music. Edna had also scrounged up a bouquet of scraggly daisies from someone's yard.

At this point Cameron had not the heart to protest any frivolity her friend chose to dream up. With Alex close at her side and their wedding only moments away, even Cameron began to experience a sudden surge of sentimentality.

The service was barely ten minutes long. The excerpt from the "Wedding March" that the minister's wife played on the organ was the longest part of the service. Their time together would be far too short, as it was, to spend it on a long drawn-out ceremony. It was slowgoing enough because the minister's English was hardly fluent. There were stops and starts as the proper words were chosen. Cameron smiled and tried not to grit her teeth.

The minister said to Alex, "Aleksei Rostovscikov, wilt thou take this woman to be thy wedded wife, to have and to hold from this day forward? Wilt thou love her and comfort her, honor her and keep her in sickness and health, and forsaking all others, keep thee only unto her as long as ye both shall live?"

Alex turned his gaze fully on Cameron. Indeed, she might have been the only person in the room, or in the entire world at that moment. His eyes washed her in blue light, gleaming with love.

"I will," he said, as if it were a prayer.

Then the minister turned to Cameron. "Cameron Hayes, wilt thou—?"

"I will!" she exclaimed, then turned red as she realized that in her eagerness she'd cut the man off. But precious seconds of their married lives were ticking ominously away.

He cleared his throat delicately. "Yes . . . ahem . . . of course you will."

Alex smiled, put an arm around her with reassuring pressure.

"Do you have rings?" the minister asked.

Now Alex grew flustered. "I'm sorry. There wasn't time."

Cameron seldom wore jewelry except for the chain with the key Alex had given her. She had a feeling if she tried to foist that unusual item on the minister as a substitute for a ring on top of everything else unconventional about this ceremony, he would throw up his hands and walk out on them. She had no need of a ring, yet she understood the importance of a token.

At that moment Edna stepped forward with her hand held out. In her palm was a plain gold band with three diamond chips set in its surface. "My wedding ring," she explained, "from my ex-husband. We're divorced, you know. I've been meaning to get rid of it."

Cameron knew otherwise. Edna was a romantic and kept hoping the man would come back despite the fact that he'd run off with his secretary two years ago.

When Cameron hesitated, Edna smiled. "Go on. It's time I moved forward with my life, too."

Cameron took the ring and handed it to Alex, and he repeated after the minister, "With this ring I do thee wed, and herewith I give thee my love and devotion so long as we both shall live."

She held out her hand, and Alex slipped on the band. It was a little big, but Cameron did not notice as her sight blurred with tears. She lifted her eyes to meet Alex's, and bending his head, he lowered his lips to hers.

"I truly love you as I love my own life," he murmured.

The minister cleared his throat again. "Ah . . . it's not time to kiss the bride. I must pronounce you first."

Oh, that German efficiency!

"Go on," said Alex with incredible patience, "because I am about to kiss her again very soon."

"Well, then . . ." The minister looked at his book, apparently intent on maintaining as much of the form as possible, but when

Alex gave him another somewhat less patient glance, the man closed the book and hurried on. "In the name of the Father, the Son, and the Holy Spirit, I pronounce you man and wife. You may now kiss . . ."

But he didn't have to finish, for Alex had Cameron in his arms and didn't let go for a very long time. Edna snapped photos of them kissing, then she took photos of them holding hands before the altar. Cameron knew she would appreciate these one day—they would be the only photos she had of Alex—but now she just wanted to finish and leave. It was almost eleven o'clock. She knew Alex couldn't have much more time. Finally the minister had everyone sign the marriage certificate. Cameron took it and put it carefully into her handbag. Alex, of course, could carry no evidence of what had happened this night.

Finally she and Alex were back in her room at the inn. They stood in the middle of the room, awkward for one of the few times in their relationship.

"How long do you have?" Cameron asked roughly. She didn't want to know the answer. It seemed always when they were together there was a clock ticking.

"Till morning. Boris, my friend, will be able to cover for me that long, I think."

There was no more time for awkwardness. She ran to him, gripped him in her arms desperately.

———

Hours later, still in each other's arms, they watched through the crack in the drawn shade as the first pale light of dawn tinged the sky. They had not slept all night, the press of the clock always upon them. But Cameron mused that it was probably the most extended length of time they had ever spent together, so that was something.

"What's the date?" Alex murmured.

"I'm not sure." She thought back over the last few days. The meeting of the Russian Army had been the twenty-fifth. She'd found Alex the next day. They were married the following day. "April twenty-eighth," she finally answered.

"So our wedding day was April the twenty-seventh?" She nodded, but he hardly noticed, his thoughts apparently focused on something else. "I cannot promise I will be with you on our first anniversary—"

Her arm was around him, and her fingers pressed hard into his shoulder. "Oh, Alex . . ." But she knew the truth of his words. "My father is already working on getting me reinstated to Russia," she said. "When the war is over, things will change."

He nodded grimly.

"This is not the time to turn Russian on me, Alex!" she implored. "Changes might be good . . . they might!"

As he brushed a strand of hair from her eyes, his gaze softened. "But just in case, my love, we must plan something to do together on that day, at least something for us to do at the same time, wherever we might be." He ran a hand though his hair. "Is that silly? I don't know, but wouldn't it be good to have some way to affirm our connection? Knowing that at the very same moment we are performing the same act? There's a certain beauty in that, yes?" He chuckled dryly. "We Russians can be very ritualistic when we want to be."

"I know." She kissed his cheek. "But what shall we do? Dance a jig? Sing a song?"

"I won't dance a jig until I see you again." He rubbed his chin. "If we were together on our anniversary, I would give you a dozen roses. I would take you out to a fine candlelight dinner."

"Then we'll do just that. A candlelight dinner across ten thousand miles."

"Will you feel foolish?"

"Perhaps we can do it in our own homes rather than in a restaurant," she amended. "That's better anyway, because I would not want a bunch of strangers around if we truly were together."

"No . . . no strangers . . ." He leaned toward her again, encircling her with his arm. "I'll never get enough of you, Camrushka," he said, kissing her.

She glanced toward the window. It was going to be a gray day. It might rain, but that did not keep the relentless dawn from lightening the sky.

"I would run away with you," he said. "We might find a place where no one would find us. Say the word, Camrushka!"

"Would that be admitting we had no other hope?"

He shut his eyes tight and nodded. "And hope is all we have . . . hope and five more minutes."

"We don't want to run and risk getting shot. Alex, we can trust God for a real future together." As she finished, she wasn't certain if she was making a statement or asking a question. She was glad that when he spoke, his tone held the confidence she seemed to lack.

"Yes, we can trust God. He has not failed us. We cannot fail Him by giving up. But, my dear wife, there may come a time when I *will* run, when I will flee Russia, and it will not be giving up. It will be a sure knowledge in my heart that the time has come. It is far too risky now. I accept that, but we will not wait forever. God would not have that, I am certain."

"There is still the possibility of my renouncing my U.S. citizenship and staying in Russia."

"Cameron, you are far too liberated to be happy in Russia."

"As long as I am with you—"

"It might seem that way now, but in time you would come to resent me for it." He let out a ragged sigh, and a veil of grief began to slip over him.

She understood. She, too, was fighting through a gamut of emotions. Joy, grief, hope, despair—they all fought back and forth inside her. One moment she felt like laughing, the next, tears were clogging her eyes. She had no doubt he felt the same.

"But might you not resent me one day for having to give up medicine?"

"I am willing to make every sacrifice for us to be together," he replied unequivocally.

"And I am not?" she responded sharply. She groaned inwardly. Was anger now to cloud the mix of emotions? Quickly she added, "Oh, Alex, let's not talk of these things. The time—"

"God will work everything out, Cameron, in good time, in His time. I know it."

"I do, too!"

"Then we will leave it to Him. And use the time He has given us now more wisely than to fret over the future."

And she quite liked his idea of wisdom when he took her again into his arms and for another few minutes the clock was forgotten.

Then with a sigh that mirrored an odd mixture of contentment and misery, he rose and put on his uniform. She, for one, liked the ill-fitting civilian clothes much better.

He held out his arms. "Come and say good-bye to me."

She was in those arms in a moment. They kissed, they cried, and then he was gone. She hurried to the window and watched as he stepped out into the street. Taking care not to be seen by others, he disappeared quickly from her view.

"Dear God, keep my husband safe. See him through this war unharmed. Bring us together soon."

It was an odd sort of irony when several days later the news broke that Adolf Hitler had committed suicide on April 30, two days after Cameron and Alex parted. It was no irony at all, just joy, even if bittersweet for Cameron, when Germany surrendered on May 7. Cameron moved through all the victory celebrations in a detached way. The end of the war would finally bring many sweethearts back together, but not for her. It would only take her sweetheart farther away.

The days immediately preceding the surrender should have given Cameron a small taste of things to come, for there were suddenly hordes of refugees clogging the streets and roads—Germans desperate to get into the western part of the country, away from the east, which by now all knew would be occupied by the Russians. No German wanted to fall under the merciless authority of their bitter enemy.

Cameron wondered over and over if perhaps in the mass of confusion the surrender brought, she and Alex could have slipped away. She told herself they had made the right choice. They did not want to live as fugitives. God would honor their faith in Him.

Alex's departure and the end of the war left Cameron feeling let down. She hated to believe that she thrived on the war, yet it had dominated every aspect of her life for years, so for a few days after the surrender, she felt intensely at loose ends. But she caught her stride again quickly. Because there was no more fighting didn't mean the battles were over. Germany was rife with political contention as the country was carved up among the victors. Oddly enough, Cameron did some of her best reporting during this time, perhaps because the Soviets were at the center of much of the infighting between the uneasy allies.

When her father wired her about coming home, Cameron found many valid reasons to stay. She needed the distractions found in Europe. And she was just a little nervous about seeing her family. What would they think about her unorthodox marriage? Her father would not approve of her marrying a Russian, especially these days as he was growing more and more anti-Red.

So she lingered in Europe, praying she would know when the time was right to go home.

42

YURI FEDORCENKO was in his office at the hospital when a knock came at his door. He had no secretary, though one was often promised him. Therefore he had nothing to insulate him from interruptions, which came frequently, so much so that he could never get through the mounds of paper work on his desk. Even with the war ended, the work of the hospital continued at its usual frenetic pace. Wounded were still coming in from German lines even though the shooting had ceased a week ago.

He considered ignoring the caller. If there had been an emergency, he would have been called over the loudspeaker.

But when the sound came again, he shrugged. He hated paper work, anyway.

"Come in."

The man who entered was a stranger to Yuri. He was tall and looked rather imposing. This impression was heightened by his black hair, peppered with gray, which was combed severely away from his face. Dark horn-rimmed spectacles added a faint scholarly ambiance while in no way detracting from the man's strong granite-like features.

"You are Dr. Fedorcenko?" the man asked. In contrast to his powerful appearance, his tone was soft, as if he never needed to raise his voice in order to be obeyed.

"Yes, I am." Yuri rose from his chair and extended his hand across the piles of papers on his desk. "May I help you, Comrade. . . ?" He quirked a brow and waited for the stranger to provide his name.

"I hope so."

Yuri was keenly aware that the man had deliberately not supplied his name. Instead, he turned, closed the door, then seated himself in the chair opposite the desk.

"Please be seated," Yuri said.

The man did not smile but rather set his fedora on a small cleared space on the desk and laid fine doeskin gloves beside it. Yuri noted the man was dressed well, at least if the expensive cut of his overcoat, which he did not remove, was any example.

"I am a man who does the asking and the telling, Dr. Fedorcenko," he said. "Don't expect me to ask to be seated or to inquire if you have time to speak with me. You will speak with me."

"I am quite willing to speak with you, sir, though I don't know your name or your business."

"My name you do not need to know. My business . . ." Pausing, the man leveled his sharp black eyes at Yuri in a manner that was surely expected to make most men tremble. Yuri had been through too much in his life to be cowed by a pair of intimidating black eyes. When he returned the gaze steadily, the man continued, "I see your dossier does not lie, Comrade."

"I hope not, though I have never seen it myself."

"It makes for interesting reading, to say the least."

"Should I be honored that a man such as yourself took the time to read about me?"

The stranger leaned back in his chair, though he did not for a moment relax. "I wanted to know why a man of your stature is involving himself in petty intrigues."

"Intrigues?" Yuri's stomach knotted.

There was only one intrigue in which he'd been involved recently. The matter with Cameron Hayes's half brother. It had been just over two years since he had first contacted the man Zharenov. Since then he'd tried to speak to the fellow two more times with no further success. He'd often wondered if the fellow had attempted to contact the boy's adoptive parents and had been a little surprised nothing more had come of the matter. Until now. How was this man seated before him involved, as Yuri's instincts indicated he surely must be?

"Come now, don't play ignorant," the stranger said sharply, though still his voice did not rise significantly. "You are a smart man and a survivor. You have successfully ridden the waves of many political upheavals."

"What do you expect from me, sir?" Yuri asked. "You refuse to give your name, you throw your weight around, you give me no choice but to go on the defensive. Perhaps if we ceased discussing *my* dossier and spent a few moments on yours, I might be able to help you." Yuri's tone remained steady, never once revealing the quaking inside.

"I didn't ask for help," the stranger said with irrefutable clarity.

Yuri let out a sharp sigh. "You are obviously an important man. Well, so am I, and I have work to do, as you can see. So stop talking in circles or . . ." Since he knew of no threat he'd be willing to carry out, he just shrugged to finished his sentence.

"A direct man. An honest man. I like that. Thus your inquiries confuse me even more." The stranger crossed his legs and fastidiously smoothed over the folds of his coat. Each of his next words was deliberate and measured. "It is obvious you have no true interest in diseases of the lung—"

"Ah, but you are quite wrong there," Yuri cut in smoothly. "Although my specialty is the cardiac and circulatory systems, the respiratory system is very closely related." Yuri suddenly realized that *he* was now the one trying to go in circles, so he added with a wry smile, "I see that directness goes against the Russian grain, does it not? Forgive me." Yuri was quite certain now that this conversation had to do with his earlier interviews of Zharenov. He also sensed who this stranger must be. And now he knew that although he must be cautious, he must also be forthright. This man deserved it. He was a worried father. But Yuri also saw no reason not to be honest, to a point at least. "You are right about lung diseases. I used that as a ploy because of the delicacy of the matter I wanted to discuss with Comrade Zharenov. That is the reason for your visit, isn't it? You are connected to Zharenov. You are in fact the father of the boy I was inquiring about."

The stranger's face remained like a stone wall, completely devoid of expression. When he finally spoke, his expression remained stoic, his voice still soft. Only his eyes changed. They became conflicted with emotion—tenderness, even fear, vying with an almost animal-like protective instinct. Yuri himself would probably have worn the same look if he'd thought the safety of his children was being challenged.

"I am," said the stranger. "My name is Stanislav Georgivich Tveritinov. I tell you this because now that you have seen me it would not be hard for you to identify me with a little effort. I am assistant to Comrade Nikita Sergeiovich Khrushchev, supreme political commissar of the Red Army and first secretary of the Ukrainian Party."

Tveritinov's words were like a punch in the stomach to Yuri. He'd thought the man was important, but *this*! Khrushchev had the ear of Stalin himself. He was, in effect, Stalin's top watchdog. As his assistant, Tveritinov was not far behind. With one word he could make men disappear. And the fact that he was a *political* officer made matters even worse. It was his job to know incriminating things about people in order to bend them to his will.

But Yuri regained his equilibrium as he realized something else: this man had his own secrets. If Yuri were a gambling man, he'd be willing to bet Tveritinov's boss, Khrushchev, did not know his assistant's adoptive child was the son of a Jew and a man who had just recently died in a gulag. Yuri had no intention of using this information for blackmail, yet it was certain Tveritinov had every reason to be as cautious as he did. Perhaps that was why he had waited so long to pursue the matter, though Yuri thought it also possible Zharenov might have taken his time in contacting Tveritinov. This was an extremely sensitive matter for all involved. Of course, an all-consuming war had also interceded, causing roadblocks of its own.

"Dr. Fedorcenko, tell me why my son is of interest to you," Tveritinov demanded.

"I approached Zharenov on behalf of a third party," said Yuri, "a person who happens to be related to your son."

"Is this for the purposes of extortion?"

"No. Your son's birth mother simply wishes to find him, to know he is well, and perhaps, though I doubt this would be possible, to meet the boy."

"You have been deceived, Doctor. My son's birth mother is dead. That I know for a fact. I also know the father died recently in prison."

"The boy's father's *wife* is dead," Yuri replied significantly.

"Are you telling me the boy was illegitimate?"

Yuri nodded. "It is even more complex than that." With each moment the conversation progressed, Yuri became convinced there could be no harm in the truth as long as names and certain other specific information was withheld. So he told a simplified version of Cameron's story, including all key elements but leaving out incriminating details. He was also careful not to mention Marfa Elichin, who could be most harmed by her involvement and who really didn't need to be mentioned.

When Yuri finished, Tveritinov let out a ragged sigh, the first time during the encounter that he let down all guard. "You are telling me my son's mother is a foreigner no longer in Russia?" Without waiting for a response he continued. "What is your involvement? How did any of this surface at this time?"

"Before I continue, I need certain guarantees that neither I nor my family will suffer repercussions, nor, for that matter, the woman I represent."

"Your guarantee is this, Doctor: I do not wish for any of this information to be made public. So as you are silent, so am I silent."

"That is good enough for me," Yuri conceded, then went on, "The daughter of the boy's birth mother was in Russia within the last few years—"

"A citizen?"

"No."

"An employee of one of the embassies?"

"Let's not play a guessing game, Comrade Tveritinov. Who this person is, for now, is not pertinent."

Tveritinov steepled his fingers and tapped them thoughtfully against his chin. "I will judge that eventually," he finally said, "but for the present, continue."

"I made her acquaintance . . . in one way or another," Yuri said, feeling as if he were dancing in a minefield. "We became friends and in time she confided her family story to me in hopes that I might help her find her long-lost half brother."

"How did you come up with Zharenov's name?"

"I am not going to reveal every detail of this story," Yuri said resolutely. "There is no point in dragging in the names of others who are only peripherally involved."

"Then tell me the name of this half sister."

"I think that information would be premature at this time."

"Then what do you expect to come of this meeting?"

Yuri smiled. "I did not instigate this meeting, sir. But I am sure the young woman would want to meet you if she were still in the country. Yet if I told you her name before such a meeting could be arranged, what is to stop you from making sure she never shows up at such a meeting?"

An amused smile very briefly quirked Tveritinov's lips. Yuri knew that had been the man's intent all along even before he spoke. "If I knew who she was, I would indeed see that she was promptly deported or blocked from entering the Soviet Union again. I do not want my son's life disturbed by the past. He is a fine young man and is headed for important things. I don't want that ruined, as it well could be by all this foolishness. He was seven years old when he came to us, but I have grown fond of him as if he were my real son. He knows nothing of the past, and that is how I want it to remain."

"But how can this be?" asked Yuri. "As you said, he was seven at the time of his adoption. Surely he has some memories of the past."

"The doctor who examined him as a child said he was quite traumatized by past events and consequently blocked memories of them from his mind. The boy's father was a subversive, probably a criminal, as well, and a fugitive for some time. What child wouldn't be deeply wounded by these things? Semyon had terrifying nightmares for years. I believe he still has them but will not admit it. So do you wonder that I want to protect him?"

"No, I would do the same thing," Yuri replied.

"We then are at an impasse."

"There is a mother in—" Yuri stopped abruptly. He'd been about to say in America. It would have been but a short leap to Cameron with this information, especially for a man of Tveritinov's resources. There were still a few female workers at the American embassy. There were also American female journalists who came and went. No matter how coy he tried to be, there were still a myriad of ways Tveritinov could link him to Cameron. In any case, he had to exercise some caution. He must also count on the fact that Tveritinov would also show caution in digging too deeply. He had a great deal of power in the government, but there were still others with far more power lurking over him.

"Think of the mother, Comrade Tveritinov," Yuri implored, smoothing quickly over the brief hesitation. "She has lived for years not knowing if her son is alive or dead. The war surely must have placed him in great danger. She only cares for his well-being. As I said before, even she must realize it would be impossible for her to ever meet him."

"But the sister would like a meeting, yes?"

"Of course, when she returns to Russia, as I am sure she will one day."

"I cannot allow such a meeting to happen."

"Well, I certainly can't make it happen, either. And as a foreigner she has no means of making such a thing happen." Yuri thought of all Cameron had done during her time in Russia. That young woman could make anything happen, but no need to reveal that to this man.

"You can tell this woman that Semyon—"

"Comrade, may I ask why you kept his given name? The secret would have been easier kept with a completely new name."

"He knew his name, Doctor, when he came to us. We would have changed it, but he clung to it, and we did not want to traumatize him further by forcing such a change." Again the man's eyes softened, as they seemed wont to do when his son was mentioned.

"So, you were going to say about him. . . ?" Yuri nudged the conversation back.

"Tell the boy's . . . relatives that he is healthy. You will have no difficulty in finding out, so I will tell you he is a political officer in the Red Army. He is very intelligent and talented and has functioned as an important artist and photographer for the Party."

A political officer, Yuri thought dismally. He had to be a member of the Party. That was not good. "Is he married? Does he have children?" Yuri asked so as not to think of what was just revealed.

"Not yet. He is very devoted to his work, but he is a handsome lad, and I am sure when the time is right he will find a nice girl to settle down with. More reason not to have his future spoiled by his past."

Devoted to his work . . . the work of the Party. Cameron wasn't going to enjoy hearing that. "Do you have a recent photograph I might pass on?"

Tveritinov visibly tensed, with defensiveness, Yuri was certain.

Then he relaxed, at least as much as he'd done during the entire conversation. "This might be possible," he finally acquiesced. "But I must know that there will be no attempt to contact my son. None! Do you hear? I will come down on you, or anyone who tries, with the full force of my office, which is not far removed from the force of Stalin himself. I am quite serious."

"I understand." And he did, only too well.

"You and anyone involved in this matter are safe now. I give my word. No repercussions will be felt from this conversation. That will change in an instant if any attempt to contact Semyon is made."

Cameron was not going to like that, either. But certainly what Yuri was about to report to her had to be more than she truly ever expected to learn. And if there was a photograph to give to her mother? That was far more than anything Yuri ever hoped to deliver.

Two days after the meeting with Tveritinov, a packet, delivered by special courier, arrived at Yuri's office. Inside was the promised photograph. With the help of Sophia, who knew of a friend of Cameron's in the American embassy, he made arrangements to get this material out of the country. He hoped it would be enough for Cameron and her mother. He knew not what else he could do.

43

V-E DAY! Blair looked around the huge Beverly Hills Presbyterian church that her parents attended. She had never seen it so full. Every pew was packed shoulder-to-shoulder; the balcony was overflowing; people were even standing in the aisles—and on a Tuesday evening! But that amazed her no less than being here herself, wedged between her mother and sister, with her father on her mother's other side. She could not remember the last time she'd been to church with her father.

But this was a day when even nominals found within themselves a sure belief in God.

The war in Europe was finally over. The entire world was rejoicing. In Los Angeles, as in other places, the celebrating would no doubt go on for days. Everyone knew, of course, it wasn't truly over. The Japanese still had to be beat. That knowledge contributed to the melancholy Blair felt when everyone around her was rejoicing. She was just a bit angry that anyone was rejoicing at all when the worst devils were still standing. She would not feel truly at peace until they were smashed.

It wasn't a very Christian attitude, especially to have in church.

She prayed every day to have a forgiving heart. Maybe when Gary was with her again, she'd find a way to do so. She had been home only a few days. It would probably take time. *Give me time, God. I will try to do better.*

There was so much to cope with these days that forgiving an enemy that, in Blair's mind, hardly deserved forgiveness was just one item on a long list of emotional demands. But she was glad to be home, no question about that. She thought back to how excited—and a little anxious—she'd been over the prospect of returning home. She'd had plenty of time to dream and fret in the weeks following her rescue from the POW camp. These she had spent in American military camps, which seemed like country clubs compared to Santo Tomas, as she waited for an available home-bound ship. Finally she boarded a freighter headed for the West Coast.

The State Department had sent word to all families of rescued internees informing them that they were safe. In turn, Blair had received a telegram from her mother, assuring her the family would be anxiously awaiting her homecoming. That had helped to allay some of her fears, though nothing had been mentioned about her father. She knew she had changed much, but what if he hadn't? Was she strong enough to face his rejection? Briefly she had considered staying with Gary's parents. He'd suggested it when she had voiced worry over her father's reception. But she decided her mother would be needlessly hurt, and it would only postpone any attempt to heal her relationship with her parents.

Many times she had bemoaned the fact that Gary could not be with her to offer support. They had been separated again shortly after the liberation of Manila. She was sent to a camp for refugees on Leyte to await transport home and would have protested their separation far more vigorously had she known it would take so long before a ship could be spared from war activities. She would have insisted on staying in Manila, where Gary would be hospitalized. But the idea of *home* had lured her away. Despite the fears and uncertainty home held, it had been beckoning her for so long over the last three years that it was a hard siren to resist. And Gary had encouraged her to go because he knew home was the one place where she could gain her health, her vigor, and her emotional well-being.

In the meantime he had been hospitalized for the wound in his leg, which apparently was worse than he'd thought. Part of a bone had been shattered by the bullet, and for a time amputation was considered. Blair still did not know his prognosis. Mail from the Pacific continued to be agonizingly slow.

Blair now stood with the congregation as the pastor offered the final prayer of thanksgiving. She stole a glance at her mother, who was looking at her, as well. They smiled at each other, and Blair felt warm all over at her mother's look of love and acceptance. Her mother put an arm around Blair's thin shoulders and drew her near. This was why home had lured her so; this was what she had been seeking, needing. Even her reunion with Gary had not filled this need, this deep craving for the compassion of her mother. Had it been only a few years ago that she had rebelled so vigorously against her parents? What a fool she had been!

As if to make up for the past, she laid her head on her mother's shoulder. The hurdles of home didn't seem so insurmountable after all.

Cecilia had planned a special family meal for after the service. It was late, but they'd had only a light snack before the service, so everyone was hungry. A ham had been roasting in the oven for several hours, its savory fragrance filling the house. Blair volunteered to peel potatoes and was standing at the sink doing so while Cecilia cleaned and cut up green beans. Jackie was holding that baby of hers, trying to keep her entertained.

"We have cherry pie and ice cream for dessert," Cecilia said. "I am not going to worry about rationing tonight."

"But there's still a war on," said Blair a touch defensively.

"Oh, we'll whip the Japanese in no time now," Cecilia replied airily.

"You don't know what vicious devils they are," Blair rasped with bitterness. "The fighting on Luzon, even after they knew they were doomed, was probably the bloodiest of the war."

"Well . . . ah . . . yes . . ." stammered Cecilia.

Blair realized then how harsh her words had been, hardly pleasant kitchen chatter. Three years of living like an animal had definitely dulled her social manners. But the last person in the world she wanted to alienate was her mother, so she went on, "Do you remember, Mom, when I didn't know how to peel a potato?"

"Nor would you step into a kitchen to learn," mused Cecilia, seemingly relieved for a new topic of conversation. "Where did you learn this in the Philippines? In a POW camp?"

"I wasn't in the camp the entire time," said Blair. Since coming home she had talked very little about her experience. She hadn't wanted to even think about it. One of the nurses at the refugee camp had suggested it might be good for her healing if she did talk about it. Perhaps if she began with only the lighter aspects, it wouldn't hurt so much. "I have learned to cook a lot of things. Perhaps tomorrow I can whip up a batch of rat stew with bananas and breadfruit. It's very tasty if the rat isn't too old. I can do a hundred things with bananas. And rice—no, I'll be happy if I never see another grain of rice again."

"I will make sure we have no rice, dear." Cecilia smiled.

"But you better not let me cook on a stove, because I still don't know how. I can do wonders over a campfire, though." Blair began chopping the peeled potatoes and scooping them into the pan her mother had provided. She started taking it to the stove, but Jackie stopped her as she put Emi down.

"I can do that," Jackie offered.

"I was joking about the stove," Blair answered dryly.

"Well, yes, but I can still help out. I feel funny just standing here while everyone else is busy." Just then Emi flung open her favorite cupboard and was noisily emptying it of its contents. "Emi!" Jackie looked at her daughter and then at the pan.

"Don't worry. I've got it, Jackie."

"Unless you'd like to keep an eye on Emi . . ." suggested Jackie before taking a look at Blair and stopping short.

Blair felt the color drain from her face. She hadn't been able to even *look* at Emi in the four days since her homecoming. Surely Jackie must have noticed. If so, she was being horribly insensitive now.

"I'll do the potatoes," Blair said firmly.

A stainless steel lid clattered to the floor, and Emi giggled. Apparently liking the sound, she reached for another lid.

"Emi, no!" Jackie scooped the child up into her arms and slipped her into the highchair.

Having been deprived of her amusement, Emi began to wail in protest. Jackie grabbed a box of crackers and put a few on the highchair tray. The little imp proceeded to take one in her fat fist, obviously in protest, and crumble it, scattering it all over the floor.

"No! No!" scolded Jackie. Then she cast a wan look at Blair. "She can be a spoiled brat at times. I can see why you don't want to play with her."

"Can you?"

"Well, you're probably like Cameron. She was afraid of Emi at first because she didn't know anything about babies. A two-and-a-half-year-old can be far more intimidating than an infant."

Blair said nothing, concentrating her attention on the pan of potatoes. Best to leave Jackie to her safe interpretation of the matter.

"That's it, isn't it?" pressed Jackie, an edge to her tone that now made clear she had indeed taken note of Blair's less than warm attitude toward her child.

"I don't want to talk about it," Blair replied, giving the potatoes such a hard stir that water sloshed out onto the stove. Apparently her earlier attempt to relate the lighter side of her experiences had failed. Talking about any aspect of her ordeal had quickly conjured unwanted images of suffering and loss.

"You've all but ignored Emi since you've been home," Jackie said.

"Jacqueline, dear," said Cecilia, "perhaps you ought to take Emi out to the garden for a few minutes. That would calm her I am sure."

"But, Mom, we all have to live together in this house," persisted Jackie. "I want us to get along."

"Give your sister time, Jacqueline."

"Time? Oh, dear me, it can't be—is it—?"

It seemed Jackie had been oblivious after all to the real reasons for Blair's struggles regarding Emi, or maybe she just hadn't wanted to believe such a thing of her own sister. Perhaps it *was* time to get it out in the open.

"Do you expect me to welcome a little Jap with open arms?" blurted Blair. She'd thought Jackie had more sense. "Do you expect me to look fondly upon the enemy and the woman who collaborated with them? In most of the world, you would have had your head shaved and been paraded like a criminal through the streets for being a traitor."

"Blair!" Cecilia tried to intercede.

"No, Mom!" Blair rushed on, unable now to control the flood of emotions once they had been forced out. "She said we had to live together; well, did she expect it would be nothing for me to have to wake every morning to ... to ... that—" She twisted her gaze toward the highchair. "Did she think I was just uncomfortable around children in general? Did she think I would have no feelings at all about living with a Jap and a traitor?"

"Don't call me that!" Jackie cried, tears streaking her face. "My husband was an American. He died for his country! Don't you ever speak of him or his child in that way!"

Blair swallowed hard, but no tears filled her eyes. Though she knew her words had been cruel and harsh and she wanted to apologize, she could not find enough regret within herself to do it. So she turned and fled the kitchen.

Perhaps if the garden could calm a child, it would have the same effect on her. So she headed toward her mother's rose garden and sat down on the bench provided there. She noted the garden was smaller than in the past. A vegetable garden had been added adjacent to the roses.

A warm breeze greeted her, while overhead the night sky was crisp and clear and illuminated by a nearly full moon. Blair shivered. After long exposure to the stifling heat of the Philippines, she felt chilled in the temperate warmth of Los Angeles. If she had more flesh on her bones, perhaps she wouldn't feel the chill, but even after three months of freedom she'd gained little weight. Despite all her dreams of food during the days of starvation in the jungle and in the prison camp, she found that she could eat little of the bounty set before her now. Back at the refugee camp the doctor had finally concluded she had an intestinal parasite, for which she was now being treated.

Food! What a thing to be thinking about! She thought she'd ceased to be so shallow. She truly did not want to focus so much on herself, her physical ailments, her emotional aches, but they were all still bubbling close to the surface. No one here understood. How could they? They believed they had made personal sacrifices during the war by giving up new clothes, a little sugar, a gallon of gasoline. They simply could not conceive of true starvation, of torture, of watching friends die daily. Of—

Don't, Blair! she admonished herself. It doesn't help to torture yourself.

She heard a footfall on the garden path. Please, don't be Jackie! Then she berated herself. Jackie wasn't the enemy. She hadn't slept with the enemy, not really.

Nevertheless, she was relieved when her mother came into view.

"May I sit?" Cecilia asked.

Blair scooted over. "I hate myself for what I said," she offered peremptorily.

"For a time I felt as you do about the Japanese," said Cecilia, "but because of Jackie I was forced to amend those feelings. I had to make a very conscious effort to differentiate between the enemy and the loyal Japanese in this country." A gaze full of sympathy swept over her daughter. "I know you have far more right to your feelings. They hurt you terribly, didn't they?"

"Mom, I don't want to think about it," pleaded Blair. "Maybe it will all go away then, and I can be normal again."

"Or it will just eat away at you like that bug in your bowels is doing. I'm no expert, but ignoring the kind of pain you must be feeling doesn't seem the best way to heal it."

"Mom, if I told you . . ." She closed her eyes and sucked in a shuddering breath. "It's too awful. I tried to make light of it in the kitchen. I thought that would help, but it always ends up in pain. Here's one example: in the camp we had to bow in respect to the guards, and according to their custom, they always bowed back. One day a group of nurses decided to get back at a particularly cruel guard. Rather than going together and receiving one bow from the guard as they usually did, this time they went by one at a time, with just a few moments in between, so the guard bowed once and just as he straightened, he'd have to bow again. This went on for about a dozen times in quick succession. I was watching. It was so funny. The man was honor bound to respond to each bow, and thus he bobbed up and down like a yo-yo. When the camp was liberated, this guard was captured, and as he was dragged out, hundreds of voices cried, 'Kill him! Kill him!' They would have done it themselves if they'd had weapons."

Cecilia nodded, compassion in her gaze. "Do you think I might feel differently toward you if you shared your experiences?"

"Maybe. Mom, I was yelling 'Kill him,' too." There was a great battle within her, a reticence to talk but a great need to do so, as well. There were at least two aspects of her experience she knew she had to share, especially with her mother. She made herself continue. "Mom, I haven't told you or anyone this, but I became a Christian in the Philippines."

"Blair, that pleases me so!"

"I didn't want to admit it because I am ashamed of some things

I had to do to survive. I put in danger some good people who helped me. I often had to lie to protect me and others. I stole food to stay alive. But mostly I am ashamed that I cannot shake the hate I feel for my enemies. I fight it all the time, but it is there. I can't look at a Jap face without revulsion. I want to flee from those faces because in the jungle a Jap face meant death. I flinch because after I was captured it meant torture or some kind of suffering. Mom, I love God. I know He alone sustained me the last three years. The least I can do for Him is to love my enemies. But I can't find the strength inside to do it."

"Give yourself time, Blair, darling. I believe God will do the same. You know what they say about time healing all wounds. I don't think that is in the Bible, but I think God understands the truth of it." Cecilia put a motherly arm once more around Blair. When Blair shivered slightly, Cecilia rubbed Blair's arm. "You've got goose bumps."

"Often it got to over a hundred degrees on the islands. I guess getting used to freezing Los Angeles will take time, too." Blair tried to smile. "Thanks, Mom. I have needed you more than I ever thought I could."

"Oh, my dear, dear Blair! Lean on me now as much as you wish. I want to be here for you. I know I never was the kind of mother you longed for, but—"

"No, Mom. I was never the kind of daughter you deserved."

"Well, we have both changed, I hope. I believe."

Those words prompted Blair to reveal her deepest pain. "Mom, when I was captured . . . I was pregnant. Gary and I were going . . . to have . . . a baby." She had to stop as emotion finally rose up in her. Cecilia squeezed her tighter. "I was captured and th-they tortured me, and I . . . l-lost him . . . the baby. I named him Edward . . . he was a perfect little boy, only t-too premature to live. . . ." The moment it was out, sobs choked Blair.

Cecilia wrapped her in both arms, one hand soothingly massaging her back. "There, there." Cecilia said nothing else, and Blair was thankful for her mother's sensitivity in knowing there were few words to assuage such a loss.

Later, after a quiet but relatively peaceful meal, Blair was in her room getting ready for bed when a soft knock came at the door.

"Come in," she said. She was seated at the dressing table

brushing her hair, which now was short and lanky and brittle. The nurses said improved nutrition would bring back its past luster. But the state of her hair paled in importance when Jackie poked her head into the room.

"Can I talk to you for a minute?"

"Sure." Blair tried to sound welcoming but knew she fell short.

Jackie came in and sat on the bed as Blair turned in her chair to face her.

Jackie took a breath, then spoke. "I don't want you to take what I have to say in the wrong way. But I think what I am planning will be best for us both. I just spoke to my in-laws, and I am going to go stay with them for a while—"

"In a concentration camp?" It rather startled Blair that anyone would choose to do such a thing.

"It wouldn't be the first time," Jackie replied, with perhaps a hint of a sharp edge to her voice. "But no. They are out of the camp. Dad has set them up in one of his rentals—"

"Dad?" The world had changed! Blair had not talked politics with her father or anyone in the States, but she would have wagered a pot roast—no small wager for her!—that he, of all people, would be the last to support Jackie's Jap relatives.

"Yes, as amazing as it sounds," replied Jackie. "I doubt he has any more fondness in his heart for the Japanese than you do, but he does have a little soft spot in his heart for his granddaughter. When my in-laws were released from the camp, he wanted to ensure Emi had a decent place to go when she visited them. Anyway, they have a spare room—"

"I don't want you to do this for me."

"It's for both of us. Well, maybe mostly for you. Mom said you needed time—"

"What else did Mom say?" For some reason Blair felt strange about Jackie knowing the things she had shared with her mother.

"Just that you needed time, and I thought this would be the best way. Please don't feel bad about it. It is for the best. Emi's other grandparents have been grieving, too, and it will do them good to have Emi around."

Blair knew she should offer sympathy to her sister for her husband's death. She knew it but could not force out the words.

"I feel so bad . . ." was all Blair could manage. Perhaps it would cover all that was left unsaid.

"Don't, Blair, please." Jackie jumped up, strode to the dressing table, knelt down, and took her sister's hands into hers. "We have been through a terrible war, and we have to heal. But no matter what has happened, we will always be sisters, and I love you. Let's just keep remembering that."

"I love you, too, Jackie." She truly meant it. When she looked at her sister now, it was as if nothing had happened. All she had to do was work on keeping other faces with slanted eyes from interfering.

"Besides," Jackie added in a pointed attempt to end lightly, "Cameron will be home soon, and I don't think Dad will be able to handle having us all at home at once."

44

KEAGAN PUT DOWN the telephone receiver. The world seemed to be tipped on its end. He didn't know what to make of it. First, a few months earlier there had been word of his Japanese son-in-law receiving a Distinguished Service Cross, one of the highest military medals for bravery. This had started the shaking of his world, the upsetting of his set of mind. Cecilia had always said Sam was a good boy, an honorable boy. Keagan hadn't wanted to believe it, not of a Jap. He supposed he had needed the weight of the military's citation to convince him.

Now this!

He stared at the phone, wondering if he had imagined that call from his friend in the State Department. But he hadn't. He wondered why his daughter had said nothing of these things. But since coming home, Blair had not talked much about the Philippines, not to him anyway.

He pushed his chair back from his desk, rose, and strode purposefully from his study.

"Cecilia!" he called as he came near the kitchen. She wasn't there. He looked into her solarium, but she wasn't there, either. As he was about to turn, he glanced out the window and caught a glimpse of her straw hat in the garden. He exited the room by the French doors and hurried to where she was weeding her vegetables.

"Cecilia, why don't you leave that for the gardener?" he said. "That's what I pay the man good money for."

"I find it relaxing," she said, tossing a handful of the intruding vegetation into a small pile by her side.

"I have just received the most extraordinary telephone call."

"Really?" She brushed dirt from her gloves and started to rise.

"Has Blair told you anything about her experiences in the Philippines?" Keagan asked as he gave her a hand up.

"Only a very little. I'm afraid it is too harrowing for her to talk of it." Cecilia peered at him in an odd manner. He had the feeling she knew more than she was saying.

"You remember William Frawley from the State Department?" She nodded vaguely, and he went on, "He just called to offer his compliments to our family for our daughter's extraordinary behavior. Apparently she was some kind of agent in the Manila underground. For several months she passed important information to the guerrillas, of which Gary was one. In fact Frawley had some high regard for *him*, as well. But as for Blair, she was captured and tortured—tortured, Cecilia! I can hardly fathom that. And even more amazing, she never revealed anything to the Japs. Our Blair!"

"Poor thing," murmured Cecilia.

"Of course what she suffered is terrible, but quite heroic, as well. Blair!"

Cecilia removed her gloves and stuffed them into the pocket of her garden apron, then she laid a hand on her husband's arm. "It saddens me, Keagan, that this amazes you so."

"Come on, Cecilia! You can't tell me you always thought Blair would be a hero one day." His tone challenged her to be honest.

She gave a shrug, conceding, "To be fair, I should have said it saddens me that we both should be surprised by such news. Maybe that was Blair's problem—we never believed enough in her."

"Well, she gave us good cause to doubt her. Don't forget all her shenanigans over the years, culminating in that sham of a marriage." Keagan still smarted over that and the fact that he'd made a fool of himself by walking her down the aisle. No, it wasn't easy for him to make a one-hundred-and-eighty-degree turn and now think of his once no-account daughter as a heroine.

"The marriage was no sham, Keagan. It was real."

"That's not the point." He eyed his wife dubiously. "Why the emphasis on that, Cecilia? Because they got back together on the islands? Do you fear I'll believe my daughter was living in sin?"

"You might."

"Well, I'll allow that the marriage *was* legal and them getting back together was on the up-and-up." He thought then of something else Frawley had said. "She made the greatest sacrifice of all." But when Keagan questioned the man about this, he had become reticent, saying only that he may have said too much, that the details were for Blair to disclose. Now Keagan focused his most penetrating gaze on his wife. "What more is there about this, Cecilia?"

"I don't know if I should say. . . ."

"I have the means to find out on my own," he responded, a firm statement with just a hint of a threat to it.

"I suppose you deserve to know."

"Confound it! You better believe I deserve to know! I am the father, the head of this house. I will not have secrets kept from me." He felt shaken inside as he spoke, but having to declare his authority seemed, more than anything, to actually lessen it. He knew there were secrets. There must be, for no one in this family ever confided anything of a personal nature to him.

As he ranted, Cecilia spoke quietly. "Come, Keagan, let's walk a bit." She gave a quick glance toward the house.

He hated walks in the garden, and she knew it, but perhaps she just wanted to be sure no one happened upon them as they talked. This must be quite a revelation she planned to make. But he followed her some ways along the path that divided the rose garden from the so-called victory garden. Soon there would be no need of this patch of eatables, but he suspected Cecilia would keep it regardless, because she seemed quite pleased with vegetable cultivation if one could judge by how often she bent his ear with reports on the garden's progress.

"Keagan," Cecilia finally began, "if you ever mention any of this to Blair, will you promise to do so with the greatest of delicacy?"

He rolled his eyes. "I am not a bull in a china shop." But her incisive gaze impelled him to add, "Well, not always. Okay, I promise to use discretion. Now, what is it?"

"Blair was expecting a child when the Japs—the Japanese—tortured her." Her lip trembled as she added, "She lost the baby."

"Dear God in heaven! No!"

"He was two months premature—"

"He?"

"Yes, it was a boy. She named him Edward. He is buried in Manila."

"A baby . . ." he breathed. "'The greatest sacrifice of all . . .'"

Another grandchild. A boy.

Oh, little Emi Colleen was sweet enough. He had to give her that much. And one couldn't be in close contact for long with the pretty, precocious child and not feel tenderness toward her. But a *grandson*. And not half-Jap but all American. He remembered when Jackie was born and how crestfallen he'd been because it was another girl. In addition to that, Cecilia had had some complications that made it impossible for them to have any more children. The doctor had comforted him by reminding him that with three daughters he'd be sure to have a few grandsons. It hadn't seemed like much consolation then, but as he grew older, he had looked forward to that more than he would admit to anyone.

Suddenly that dream was robbed from him before he'd even had a chance to appreciate it. Though it was selfish of him, he grieved as much for himself as he did for Blair. And feeling this loss in a personal way, he commiserated deeply with her and the sacrifice she had made.

He gaped at Cecilia, at a rare loss for words. "What should I do?" he asked plaintively.

She wrapped her slim fingers around his big fleshy paw. Her touch was cool and reassuring. "Go to her, Keagan. Tell her how proud you are of her."

"What about the . . . baby?"

"I'm not sure what you should say about that or if you should say anything. Why don't you just see what happens?"

"You trust me not to bungle the job?"

"Implicitly."

"Why?"

"Dear Keagan, I have seldom heard you ask so many questions of me in the span of so few minutes. Perhaps that's why. You are able, even willing, to reveal a little vulnerability, and that should surely make you aware of the same in another. Go to your daughter. She needs you. She needs to hear this from you."

A few minutes later as Keagan was striding up the stairs to Blair's room, he began to feel a little foolish. Cecilia had said Blair needed him, but how was that possible? All alone she'd survived jungles, disease, vicious enemies, starvation, and the deaths of many others besides her child. She couldn't possibly need him. Besides, there was certainly no love lost between them. She might think his overture too late.

But before he could work all this out in his mind, he suddenly was at her door. Only one thing was clear to him as he stood poised to take a very difficult step. He'd made peace, of sorts at least, with Jackie and Cameron. Blair was the only one left.

"May as well make a clean sweep of it, man," he muttered to himself. "Won't kill you."

He clapped his fist firmly against the door.

Blair was crying again. She missed Gary so much. She also missed Claudette and Meg, the only true girl friends she'd ever had. And in a rather perverted way, she even missed the Philippines. Oh, she had hated the place while there, despising the heat and the humidity and the bugs and the mud, thinking always of home as some kind of true paradise. But what she missed was not the stifling heat, the wretched jungle, or the lack of comforts. In the Philippines, she now realized, she'd had a sense of purpose. At first it had been just to find Gary and God, then later, mere survival, and then the purpose of winning the war. Her life had been full there, even if at times it was full of fear.

Here she was so empty of purpose. And that, no doubt, was why she so missed her husband and friends, why her deep pining often left her in tears. Her mother suggested she become involved in church activities or even in the war effort by selling war bonds or volunteering for the Red Cross. She felt as if her life were on hold, that she couldn't start something new, not until she could start over with Gary.

She was glad of the knock on the door even if the firmness of it indicated it was someone other than her mother. Her father? Well, even a browbeating from him would be better than sitting here feeling so empty and sorry for herself.

"Just a minute," she said. Giving a glance into the dressing table mirror, she freshened her lipstick so it might detract from her reddened eyes. Then she went to the door.

Her father stood there with an odd look about him. His fiery hair, dulled only a little with gray, was in disarray, as if he'd run his hand through it and not bothered to smooth it over. Most disconcerting, however, were his eyes; they were not flashing green sparks as they usually did around her. They had a subdued look, like an emerald under a shroud. Panic seized her. Something was wrong. Gary was dead!

"What's wrong?" she asked in a strangled voice.

"Nothing." His brow creased, perplexed. "Might I speak to you a moment?"

His tone was formal, but then, when had they ever been anything more to each other? There was, however, no hint of impending disaster in his tone.

Her insides calmed. "Of course, Dad." Now she only wondered what he wanted, wearing such a peculiar expression. She opened the door wide and offered him the dressing table chair while she sat on the edge of the bed.

He cast a gaze around the room as if he were uncomfortable or stalling for time. Neither one would surprise her. What he said next did surprise her but mostly because of the melancholy tone it held.

"This room hasn't changed much from when you were a teenager," he mused.

"I suppose it hasn't."

Her parents had let her and her sisters decorate their own rooms when they turned sixteen, and the rooms now reflected their personalities. Jackie's was soft and lacy and pink; Cameron's was brown, austere, and functional—though Blair had secretly always believed this represented more what Cameron wanted to be rather than who she really was. Blair's was white and sleek. The walls, the carpet, the curtains, the bedspread, the lampshades were all pure white. But perhaps that also was more of what she wanted than a true insight into reality. But the choice of white had been a form of rebellion, as well. Her parents had bemoaned the impracticality of it, but since they had promised she could have what she wanted, they'd conceded. They also hadn't approved of her plastering those pristine white walls with photos of her movie star idols. Those faces still stared down on her. When she was young, they had seemed so mature, and she desired more than anything to be all grown-up like them. Now those faces—Ronald Colman, Clark Gable, Spencer Tracy, Norma Shearer, Katharine Hepburn, Carole Lombard— seemed so young and pure, while she felt aged, though she was probably younger than any of them had been when they'd posed for those pictures.

Suddenly she realized her mind had wandered and her father was sitting there staring at her.

"I-I'm sorry, Dad," she stammered, her face heating up. "Wh-what were you saying?"

"You've been through a lot lately, haven't you, Blair?" Was that compassion in his voice?

Not knowing how to respond to that she answered, "I lose my concentration easily."

"You haven't talked to us about what happened in the Philippines."

"It's hard. I'd rather forget."

"I can understand that." He then sucked in a breath as if trying to gain momentum to continue. "Well, I may as well tell you, I just received a call from a friend of mine in the State Department. He was very impressed with your deportment in the islands and wanted to tell me so."

"Really?" She didn't know what surprised her more, that someone in the State Department knew about her, or that her father was mentioning it to her in a tone of voice that was as close to supportive as she had ever known him to be.

"He indicated your actions were . . . well . . . even heroic."

She laughed dryly. "Oh, Dad. You certainly don't believe that!"

"I do, Blair," he replied with great earnestness.

She fairly goggled at him. Goodness! He was sincere! She wasn't about to bask in that sincerity, though, or even let down her guard. He'd soon find a way to undercut whatever praise he might dole out.

"Dad, believe me, I did nothing that I didn't have to do in order to survive."

"You didn't have to work in the underground. You could have hid out in some safe place."

"It was survival, not nobility. That's all I can say."

"I don't believe you sacrificed your child for mere survival."

She gasped. "Mom told you?"

"I'm sorry if that broke a trust, but I'm your father. I have a—" He broke off, his green eyes taking on yet another unlikely expression—were they actually conflicted? He cleared his throat and began again as if changing tactic. "I wanted to know, that's all."

He'd been about to say he had a right to know, of that she was certain because that would have been so much more like him. Yet he'd softened it rather than make a demand of her. She felt as if she were talking to a stranger.

She looked away from him, hating the tears that now burned in her eyes. "Well, you especially can see why I wouldn't want to tell anyone. It was foolish, wasn't it, putting my child in danger like that in the first place?" She'd fought this battle within herself many times, sometimes winning, sometimes fairly successful in convincing herself she'd done the only thing she could do. Sometimes.

She'd intentionally verbalized that inner conflict in order to second-guess her father, who she was certain must think her actions had been selfish and foolish, just as one would expect from her.

"I don't think that at all," he said.

She felt the foundations of all she thought she understood tremble with his words.

"I think you made the most difficult decision of your life, stacking two lives against the lives of dozens of others, perhaps the war effort itself."

"I thought for certain I would die, too," she murmured shakily. "That's what should have happened. It would have been easier then."

"Dear God!" he muttered.

For a brief moment her eyes flickered toward him. He met her gaze, and what she saw in his eyes she couldn't even identify because she'd never before seen such an expression on him. Was it compassion? Was it sympathy? Was it . . . Oh, Lord, can it be so? Have you answered the prayers of a child? Of a girl who hung photos of strangers on her walls to admire when her true hero had always been out of her grasp?

Was that look in her father's eyes truly love?

"Can you forgive me, Dad?" she begged, tears now flowing unchecked from her eyes. "He was your grandson."

"You don't need to be forgiven for anything." He moved in his chair, almost as if he were going to rise, but he was hesitant. "Blair, I am so proud of you!"

"Are you, Daddy?"

Now he lurched to his feet. She saw how awkward this was for him, so she slid from the bed to meet him halfway. She put her arms around him first, with only a small fear that he might still reject her. But he lifted his own big arms and clasped them around her. Yes, awkwardly, stiff and uncertain. But as she cried in her father's arms, she was beyond criticizing his fumbling effort.

45

A LIGHT BREEZE wafted over the patio, carrying with it the sweet fragrance of Mother's roses. Jackie realized this was the first outdoor gathering here since Father's fiftieth birthday party over four years ago. Cecilia had wanted to gather in the parlor, worried that the August heat would be too much. It was warm, ninety degrees today, but all three sisters had opted for the outdoors, and that was a far too united front for Cecilia to fight.

"You know, Gary, we can always use someone of your caliber at the paper," Keagan said. "There are many positions there that don't require you to be a journalist."

"Thank you, sir. I will consider it," Gary replied. He had been home only three days, but he had already won the heart of Jackie's father.

"Dad, Gary has received his pay retroactive from the start of the war," said Blair. "And they have credited him with the official rank of captain from the fall of Bataan. He's received twelve thousand dollars. So he can take some time to decide what he wants to do."

Jackie had not seen Blair so bright and animated in months. Her husband was home safe and sound—well, mostly sound. His wounded leg was stiff, and he would probably walk with a limp for the remainder of his life. But that had not dulled the joy of their reunion.

Keagan sat on the wrought-iron patio chair surveying his daughter and son-in-law. Jackie wondered what he was thinking. Was it "Here is the son I always wanted"?

"I would recommend you invest your money for a nest egg and go to work as soon as you are physically able," Keagan was advising. "With the glut of returning veterans, finding work will not be easy in the coming months. However, I, for one, plan to do all I can for our veterans."

"What is going to happen to all the women now in the work force, Dad?" Cameron asked. There was the unmistakable note of challenge in her tone.

"They must step aside for the veterans," Keagan replied unequivocally.

Jackie braced herself for a debate.

"I support the veterans, too." Cameron's glance at Gary looked a bit uncomfortable, however that didn't deter her from adding, "But now that Pandora has been let out of her box, it won't be so easy to stuff her back in."

"A woman's place is in the home," rejoined Keagan. "Always has been and always will be. They did their part for the war effort, and I commend them, but that's the end of it. Veterans should be allowed back into their old jobs."

"You are forgetting one thing," put in Gary. "They may not want to go back to their old jobs. They have just had the adventure of their lives, and though most are sick of war and killing, they still may not be ready to go back to the sedate ways of the past."

As the conversation droned on, Jackie's thoughts inadvertently drifted, and she could not keep from thinking of the soldiers who would not come home. Her heart ached as if the wound of Sam's death had been inflicted only yesterday. Jackie wondered if her desire to be out of doors today was her way of trying to conjure up happier times. Four years ago there had been no war; life had been simpler, even carefree. At least for her. Cameron and Blair had endured their struggles even then. Regardless, Jackie now discerned a certain futility in the attempt to travel back in time. It would take more than that to obscure the gaping wound in her heart.

This should be a happy day. The war in Europe was over, and the fighting with Japan soon would be. More than that, Cameron was home again. Jackie had always appreciated having her big sister around, and the present tensions with Blair only reinforced that.

As if things weren't difficult enough with Blair, Jackie was faced today with another sad complication to their relationship. It was painful to watch Blair and Gary, seated close and clinging to each other as if afraid to let go, focusing eyes filled with love on each other. Jackie's throat clotted with unshed agony. She forced back the tears until she thought she would choke because she could not—she would not!—reveal any sign of her deep envy of them. She hated herself for it. What kind of low creature was she to feel this way? Blair and Gary, of all people, deserved the happiness they had now.

"No, I'm not ready to work for a private enterprise just yet," Gary was saying. "My leg may make me unfit for active service in the Army, but there are other options to consider in the military."

"The State Department has approached him," said Blair, beaming with pride.

"Yes, I know," said Keagan. "Undersecretary William Frawley, correct?"

"Then you spoke to him about this?" Gary seemed taken aback by this revelation and not exactly thrilled.

Keagan smiled, obviously pleased that his son-in-law was too proud to accept help from his wife's father. "Honestly, I didn't. But Frawley is a friend of mine, and he mentioned to me how impressed he was with you and that such a position was a possibility."

"Well . . . uh . . . I'm flattered." Heat rose on Gary's neck, noticeable even under his deep tan. He glanced at Blair, who grinned at him and snuggled closer.

Jackie was happy for them. She was. But how would it have been if Sam had come home? He was a hero, too, with medals and everything! Would their dreams have come true? Would the world have welcomed him with such open arms?

No, Jackie! Don't!

Cecilia, who had remained quiet during the conversation but as pleased as any mother would be to have all her children together and safe again, started to rise.

"I best check on dinner," she said.

Jackie jumped up. "Let me, Mom." She was halfway to the French doors before her mother could respond. "And I'll get more lemonade if anyone is interested."

Several voices affirmed this to be a marvelous idea. Jackie hurried into the house before the voices had died down. She had made her escape none too soon, as a sob broke through her lips long before she made it into the kitchen. Leaning against a kitchen counter, she tried to choke back the stream of emotion but was unsuccessful. She pounded her fist on the countertop.

"Ouch!" said a new voice. "I'm glad that's not me."

Jackie spun around. For a brief, awful moment she'd thought the voice was Blair's. There were times when the sisters, as different as they were in personality, could sound disconcertingly alike.

"Jackie, you're crying!" Cameron said. She strode to her side and laid a hand on her shoulder.

"I'm a horrible, horrible person!" Jackie sobbed. "Jealousy and envy are like a poison in me." Sniffing noisily, she groped in her pockets for a handkerchief but found none. "Crumb! My nose is running."

Cameron fumbled through a couple of drawers until she produced a linen table napkin and thrust it at her sister. "Mom can wash it later, and no one will be the wiser."

Jackie's lips twitched in a smile as she took the napkin and used it as a handkerchief. "Thank you. Mom won't be happy about it, but . . ." A new rush of tears assailed her. She blew her nose.

Cameron replaced her hand comfortingly on Jackie's shoulder. "What's wrong, sis?"

"Isn't it obvious? Couldn't everyone tell? Don't they all know now what a terrible person I am?"

"No one noticed anything. I just came to help out. Guess you're a better actress than Blair." She rubbed Jackie's back. "We all should have been more sensitive to how hard it would be for you to be around Blair and Gary—that's it, isn't it?"

"I don't want that! I don't want people to be on eggshells because of me," Jackie said, part imploring, part demanding. "Yes, it tears me up to see sweethearts reunite, to watch happy couples and families together. I want to crumble inside no matter who it is. They all have a right to their happiness, my sister especially. Should she and Gary ignore each other because of me?"

"Well, that is kind of silly to expect, I suppose. But you couldn't bring Emi today because of Blair, so maybe there's a fairness about it," reasoned Cameron, not without some irony.

"I haven't kept Emi away from Blair completely in the last three months. But today was a dinner honoring Gary's return, and I didn't want to distract from that. And I wasn't sure if he would have the same reaction to Emi as Blair did. Maybe I was protecting myself a little, too." She let out a sharp sigh and walked to the icebox. "Lot of good that did. This bout of envy surprised even me." She flung open the door and took out the pitcher of lemonade and a bowl of lemons. Balancing these precariously, she turned.

Cameron quickly relieved her of the bowl of lemons. "I know why no one seemed to notice your emotions just now." Cameron found a knife, plucked a lemon from the bowl, and started to slice it.

"Use the cutting board," Jackie admonished. "Mom will have a fit if she finds cut marks on the countertop."

Cameron gave a wan smile. "Unlike Blair, my time away hasn't taught me any domestic skills." She grabbed a cutting board and began slicing. "Anyway, Jackie, I think we have come to expect a lot of you. You have always been the steady one, the responsible one. We must have believed you would deal with your grief in the first six months and then be your usual stable self. How very stupid of us!"

"Oh, it's my fault, as well." Jackie put the cut lemon wedges back into the bowl. "I guess I tend to put up a front. If my faith in God is strong, then shouldn't I be able to deal with this, to give it to Him and walk in peace?"

"That's a lot of pressure to be under."

"I was thinking out on the patio that my pain still feels so fresh sometimes, like it's been just hours not months. It must be because I am not letting God heal me."

"Is there some kind of time limit on God's healing?"

Jackie shrugged. "I hope not. Oh, Cameron! I miss Sam so much! I don't think that empty place in me will ever go away. I may grieve for a long time yet. But I don't want to be bitter and envious of the happiness of others. I just don't believe that's part of grief, but I don't know how to get rid of it."

"Maybe you're confusing sadness with jealousy?" Cameron finished the lemons, then began looking through cupboards for a tray. "You look at a happy couple and naturally feel sad because you've lost that. It's not really jealousy or envy or even bitterness, unless you let it be."

"Do you think so? I truly don't want it to become that."

"Where are the trays?" Cameron asked, finally frustrated with her search.

Jackie went right to the place. A little smile played upon her lips as she opened the cupboard that was Emi's favorite one to empty out and play with all the lids and trays it contained.

"I have no right to be envious of anyone," she mused aloud. "God has given me the most amazing gift in Emi. I'll always have part of Sam to love and hold close to me."

Forgetting about the kitchen preparations, Cameron turned to her sister and offered a loving embrace. Jackie felt Cameron tremble with emotion and felt the moisture of her sister's tears against her own cheek. Jackie cried once again, but this time the tears were devoid of bitterness. God had truly given her so much!

"Thank you, Cameron! I do feel better." She sniffed and reached for the napkin. Noting that Cameron was none too dry, she offered, "Want to borrow this?"

"I'm okay." Cameron dragged a sleeve across her nose, then smiled sheepishly. "I've spent too much time in Army camps. Let me see that napkin."

When they had repaired their faces and put the now well-used napkin into the wash, they returned their attention to the dinner. Jackie opened the oven, drew out the roast, and basted it. Cameron wiped the lemon juice from the cutting board and put it back where she had found it.

"Jackie, can I ask you something?" There was an unusual reticence in Cameron's tone. Jackie nodded and her sister went on. "This is probably the worst timing, but I've put it off all week since I've been home, thinking I'd do it while everyone was together rather than telling it a half-dozen times. What you've been going through and what you said about this being Gary's dinner—"

"That wasn't entirely so," Jackie put in quickly. "It's your welcome home dinner, too."

"That's okay, then. But there's still you." Cameron wrung the dishcloth in her hands. This was odd behavior indeed for her!

"Whatever you have to say or do is your right," Jackie insisted. "I don't want special consideration. And that probably wouldn't even be good for me. I need to be part of the fabric of life. I think God uses that to heal."

"You mean that?"

"Yes, I do!"

Cameron licked her lips, the cloth now wound tightly around

her left hand. "I was going to make an announcement tonight."

"Please, go ahead and do it."

"I'd like to tell you now, before the others. Perhaps you can be my 'test subject.' If you don't consider me a complete lunatic, perhaps it will be okay with the others, as well."

"I've never known you to care so much about what others think."

"I guess I've hidden it well, but I did care, especially about what my family thought. And this . . . well, it's touchy."

"Now I'm dying of curiosity."

Cameron smiled mysteriously. "Well, here goes . . . When I was in Germany I . . . uh . . . well . . . I got married!"

Jackie screeched merrily, then flung her arms around Cameron. She stopped short and stood back. "To him, right? To your Russian doctor?"

"I'm not that fickle. Yes, of course!" She tried to muster up a droll tone but was grinning too broadly to make it work.

"But how? Where is he? What—?"

"I suppose that's where the lunacy comes in. I found him in Germany quite miraculously. I knew there was little hope of us being together for very long, and I . . . wanted to be his wife." Her brow furrowed slightly.

"But couldn't he escape from Russia? People have done that. Maybe it would have been easier in Germany."

"We thought of all that and decided it was too risky. Our country made certain agreements with the Soviet Union so that our government, or any Western government, could not give him asylum." She let the cloth slip from her hand as a rare helplessness stole over her. "Did we do the right thing? We thought so at the time. But I have questioned it a million times since. Not our marriage, but his not escaping. We didn't want to live as fugitives, as displaced people. I guess we had too much hope. Now I wish I could grasp back just a fraction of that hope."

"Can't you get back into Russia?"

"Dad told me he is trying. I keep thinking that the camaraderie of victory between our two countries will open things up. But the way the Soviets have imposed themselves on Germany worries me. Perhaps things will settle down yet."

"And in the meantime you must miss your Alex as I do Sam."

"Jackie, there's little comparison. But thank you for sympathizing. I'm so glad I shared this with you first."

Jackie slipped an arm around her sister's waist. "I am so happy for you. I know God will work it out." She smiled wryly. "But you always said you weren't the marrying kind."

"Love has a way of turning our lives upside down."

Jackie nodded, and the more solemn side of those words was not lost on either woman.

46

THE CLICKETY-CLACK of typewriters, the ringing of telephones, the buzz of a dozen conversations—these had to be among the best sounds in the world. Cameron would never tire of them, nor of the movement of her own fingers flying across the keys of her type-writer, her thoughts running almost as quickly as she put on paper her account of a bungled jewelry shop robbery in which the propri-etor had been killed. It wasn't all that long ago when she had hun-gered for stories like this while watching them fall into Shanahan's lap. Now, though, a mere robbery-homicide seemed rather tame stuff.

She wondered if her father had had any luck yet with her Soviet travel documents. She inquired of him daily about this and was told only yesterday in no uncertain terms, "I will tell you when it hap-pens!" He had glared at her, finally pushed beyond his limit. "Don't annoy me again with this."

Of course she wasn't going to be cowed. She had a feeling that if she didn't nag him about it, he would conveniently let it slide. He hadn't been thrilled to learn of her marriage.

"I thought you'd finally gotten some sense," he'd railed. "Now you do something stupid like this. Will none of my daughters ever have normal weddings?"

She would get back to Russia. If her father refused to cooperate, she was fairly sure Max Arnett would send her. She would give her father a few more months before taking matters into her own hands.

"Cameron," called one of her colleagues, "there's a courier at reception for you."

She arched a brow. "A courier from where?"

"I don't know," the fellow replied impatiently. "Go and find out for yourself. I'm not a message boy."

At the receptionist's desk a young man was waiting. He wasn't wearing the uniform of a postman or of Western Union but rather a plain gray suit.

At her curious look, he responded, "I'm with the State Department, miss. Douglas Conner."

"I'm Cameron Hayes. I thought there was some kind of delivery."

"Yes, there is." He held out a large brown envelope. It was carefully sealed. "Bob Wood and I attended college together. He sent this to me here in L.A. because it seemed quite important that you were to receive this without it going through the usual channels."

"Goodness! Sounds ominous." She laughed as lightly as she could, but her heart had started thudding at a rapid pace.

He smiled knowingly and winked. He obviously conjectured that this was some lover's correspondence from Wood. To her, that was almost as bad as his thinking she and Wood were exchanging spy secrets. But she did nothing to dispel that assumption.

She took the envelope. "Thank you very much."

"I'm happy to do it. I told Bob I would do this any time in the future should need arise."

"That's very kind of you."

"This is apt to be the most excitement I get working out here in Los Angeles."

After he strode away, Cameron stared at the envelope. The receptionist, headphones clamped to her ears and hand poised over the switchboard, looked up with interest. Cameron shrugged as if this were an everyday occurrence, then returned to her desk. Still, she was reluctant to open the packet. It could be anything and not necessarily something bad. As far as she knew Bob was still in Moscow. He knew nothing about Alex, but was it possible he had news of him?

She knew her speculations were ridiculous when all she had to do was break the seal and see for herself. She finally did so, her heart still making an awful racket against the wall of her chest.

Two envelopes fell out—one letter sized, the other somewhat larger. Neither was marked in any way. Also, there was a sheet of embassy stationery with a note.

Cameron,
These were passed on to me in a covert manner by a young woman. I had every reason to believe she was not attempting to pass sensitive material out of the country via the diplomatic pouch but rather items more of a personal nature. I miss the interest you added to my sojourn here!
Know that I am ever at your service!
Robert Wood

Under his name he included instructions for future communications. Cameron then picked up the larger of the two envelopes and slipped a letter opener under the flap. There was neither salutation nor closing name on the single page inside, but she recognized the handwriting as Sophia's.

Good friend,
I first must say I miss so much your company. I know you must feel bad because of the suddenness of your departure, but please don't, as I understand how these things are. Before you left you were searching for a special book, one that your mother had once enjoyed. I am happy to say the book has been found. That is to say, we know the title, but for reasons too complex to go into in a letter, we cannot approach the bookseller in order to make a purchase in case that might be premature. It may be best for you to purchase the book yourself should you return, though I cannot guarantee this would be possible even then. I will, however, try to make sure the book remains in stock and does not get lost again. Be assured that the book is in good condition. You will find a photograph enclosed, which I daresay probably negates all the secrecy of this letter, but we could think of no other way to get it to you. I must trust this is a safe route.
This seems such a short letter when there is so much I would like to share with you, such as how joyous we are that the war is over. But some things have not changed. My hope and my faith keep me, as I hope they keep you. I am always your friend.

Cameron smiled at the surge of joy the letter gave her. How she missed Sophia's gentle friendship! But that joy was tarnished a bit as she realized that Sophia, and no doubt her father, had kept up the search for Semyon at great personal risk to themselves. It worried her that they had placed themselves in jeopardy. Yet they had found him! That surely was what the "book" reference was all about. Cameron had not forgotten how to read between the lines. They had found him, alive and well, but had not approached him, which under the circumstances was probably a good thing. Why scare the man, or raise his hopes, when there was no telling how long it would take for her to actually meet him. She would not even entertain the notion that it would not happen eventually, because she was certain she would be returning to Russia. Sophia and Dr. Fedorcenko would make every effort to keep tabs on the fellow so that when Cameron did return she might be able to go right to him.

Now she looked closely at the photograph. Her heart clutched in her chest as she realized she was looking at her brother. No more the cherubic face of a sweet child. This was a man near her own age. He wore a Red Army uniform, but a small smile came to Cameron's lips as she noted those "Shirley Temple" curls of the child now stuffed under the soldier's cap. Hints of Yakov Luban were still there among the chiseled, handsome features of the adult Semyon. Yet Cameron was pleased to see hints of her mother, as well. His eyes, their shape and a certain depth, were definitely Cecilia's. Cameron didn't know why that should please her, but it did. There was a certain sternness in that countenance, as well. Perhaps he was merely trying to be a proper soldier, yet mingled as it was with a hint of pride, perhaps even hauteur, she wasn't certain. She had the almost surreal sensation of wanting to reach into that photo and pull the man out, to know him. Who was this man, her brother? She wanted intensely to know.

That thought forced another question to her mind. Should she tell her mother? Would hearing he had been found and seeing his present image only make the impossibility of them meeting that much harder on her? But she answered that quickly. If she herself had found Semyon, there would have been little chance of her mother seeing him face-to-face, even if her mother somehow went to Russia. Just learning that Semyon was alive and well was as much as Cecilia could have hoped for. At least Cameron could do that much for her mother.

Only then did the full reality of the message of the letter dawn on her. Her half brother was indeed alive! There was a chance, if not for Cecilia, for Cameron to meet the man—the little curly-topped child with the impish, slightly spoiled smirk on his round face. Another reason to get to Russia.

Now she picked up the second letter and sliced it with the opener, withdrawing handwritten sheets from it. Again there was no salutation or closing name. She was reminded of the letters her mother had received from Yakov. Would Russia ever be free of its paranoia?

But as she read the first line her heart clenched as all the failings of Soviet rule hit her in an eminently personal way.

Dearest,

Though I dare not write your name or mine, not an hour passes that my thoughts are not full of you. When I learned a communication was going to you, I sat down immediately to write this. Endless were the things I wanted to tell you, yet time, as always, was working against us, and I had to jot this quickly. Now that I know a route exists for some exchanging of information, I will start immediately to write you a proper letter. I should have thought of it (the route) myself, but I was never as practical a person as you, my love, or apparently as some of our friends. At least this will serve to assure you I am well. I still marvel I made it through the war unscathed. Not so for so many others.

I wonder, are you home, doing the things you love? I know it is as hard for you as it is for me for us to be parted, but I hope you have your work to fill your life and give you purpose. I have mine, as well, but we both know work is just that, a filler, when our souls long for the true nutrient of each other. I've questioned a hundred times if we did the right thing in parting without taking the risks that were before us. But I have never once questioned the wisdom of our joining. You were so right when you talked of the power it holds. Power in ways we cannot even imagine, but surely power enough to bring us together soon.

ALL MY LOVE!

Cameron felt tears sting her eyes, but realizing where she was, she held them back. Johnny Shanahan always told her newspapermen did not cry. Not that she hadn't broken that rule many times since he'd informed her of it. She thought maybe even he had cried once or twice. She looked at Alex's letter, tracing her finger gently over the ink of his handwriting. It gave her a sense of connection to him, not only the words, but the fact that he'd touched the pages and formed the words in his nearly indiscernible doctor's scrawl.

And why hadn't *she* thought of using Bob Wood as a conduit for communication? Her mind was no doubt too clouded with missing Alex, but she, or Alex, would surely have thought of it eventually. Now that it had been opened, she wasted no more time with her morose musings. Quickly she yanked from her typewriter the sheet with the robbery article—plenty of time for that later—and slipped in a clean page. She hoped Alex didn't mind the seeming impersonal use of a typewriter, but he would know that for her it was a very personal way of communicating. Besides, she thought much better with her fingers poised over a keyboard. She began:

Dearest Alex,

Immediately noting her error, she pulled out the page and inserted a fresh one.

Dearest,

How ecstatic I was to receive your letter! It gave me such a connection to you. Not as good as the real you but better than nothing and truly the best gift I have received in a long time. . . .

She went on for several pages, single spaced. She'd no idea there was so much in her to tell him. She only stopped when Harry Landis came by and inquired about the robbery article, which was slated for the front page of the morning edition, deadline in an hour.

Cameron thought again of the fate of her mother's communications with Yakov Luban. As she prayed that she and Alex did not fall victim to the same fate, she felt an odd confidence. They would not lose each other. The strength of the bonds between them was too strong.

———

Jackie had planned to come to her parents' home for dinner on Thursday, August 9, and despite the recent news decided to keep the appointment. Three days previously America had dropped an atom bomb on the city of Hiroshima in Japan. That had been an awful time at the Okuda home. Mrs. Okuda was so upset, she had taken to her bed for an entire day. The bombing was merely the culmination of a terrible year for them. First Sam's death, then the news that Toshio had been sent to Leavenworth Prison for resisting the draft. Then the massive fire bombing of Tokyo back in March, which had hit the Okudas harder than the Hiroshima bombing because they had family in Tokyo.

Now this.

"Do they plan to wipe Japan off the face of the earth?" Mr. Okuda had lamented.

When Jackie told her mother-in-law she would cancel her dinner engagement, Mrs. Okuda, who had finally risen from her bed and was trying to function again, said, "You must get away from this melancholy house for a while, both you and Emi."

Would it be any better in Beverly Hills? Jackie hadn't brought Emi to her grandparents' in some time and wasn't sure how Blair would respond. But upon their arrival, Cecilia took possession of Emi before Blair even came downstairs.

"Let me take this little sweetheart out to see my garden. She can help me pick radishes for our salad," Cecilia said, sweeping the child into her arms and hurrying away.

Cameron was in the parlor listening to the radio, which she switched off as soon as she saw her sister arrive. Jackie had the distinct impression her sister was trying to protect her.

"I've already heard about the second bombing," Jackie said.

"Dumb of me to think you might not have heard," said Cameron. "How are your in-laws holding up?"

"They have friends who have relatives in both Hiroshima and Nagasaki. Their own family comes from the Tokyo area. It's all very devastating for them."

The newspaper had indicated today that finally reports of the toll of the first bomb had come to light. Apparently the cloud of dust over Hiroshima had been so thick immediately afterward that photo reconnaissance had been unsuccessful in determining the extent of the damage. Today, however, the Japanese government reported that sixty percent of the city had been destroyed, and more than half of its population had been killed or injured. A similar toll was expected from today's bombing of Nagasaki. As horrible as that was, more people were probably lost in Tokyo during the incendiary bombing raids on that city in March.

"I was in Berlin and Dresden after the war," said Cameron, "where the destruction was tremendous, both cities nearly reduced to rubble. But this is unimaginable, not so much in numbers of dead and the breadth of desolation, but in the fact that it was accomplished using one plane to drop a single bomb."

"What have we done, Cameron?" Jackie dropped onto the sofa, feeling drained all over again.

She heard a sound at the parlor archway and turned her head to see Blair. She smiled as warmly as she could. Could Blair sense how hard Jackie tried to smooth the tensions that lurked close to the surface between them?

"I'm so glad you came," Blair said to Jackie, with just as warm a smile on her face. Blair was trying, also, to keep the peace.

"Where's Gary?" Jackie asked.

"He'll be here for dinner. He's out checking on an ad for an apartment for us."

"You're moving?"

"We don't want to stay with Mom and Dad forever." Blair shrugged. "It's not as horrible as I feared it might be, but Gary and I have lived with other people for so long that we are ready to be alone for a change." Blair sat on the sofa beside Jackie. "Were you talking about the news when I came in?"

"Yes," sighed Jackie, "but I wouldn't mind a change of subject."

"I have never been fond of discussing the news, and I'm still not," Blair said with a small hint of her old petulance. "But first, Jackie, I want you to know how sorry I am about what has happened. I know I'm not responsible for it, but it does break my heart that so many have died."

She seemed to just come short of saying, "Even if they are Japs." But she didn't say it, and for that Jackie was grateful. Blair had seemed sincere in her sentiment, and that should be enough.

"Thank you, Blair," Jackie responded simply. "Now surely we can talk about many other things." Jackie wished she could have followed her own statement with another topic, but her mind was blank, unable to conjure up anything trivial.

Cameron had been standing by the radio. She shifted uncomfortably. Two long minutes of silence passed before she spoke. "I guess we just don't have it in us yet to discuss the new styles or the price of milk. We have all been through so much. They talk about how the advent of atomic energy will change the world, but that has nothing on how a war can change three sisters."

Cameron strode to the sofa and eased herself between her sisters. She put an arm around each one and drew them close to her. "We'll never be the same," she murmured.

"Growing up," Blair said, "I always wished we could be closer. The only thing we seemed to have in common was our conflict with Dad. I always wanted real friends, but for some dumb reason I pushed away the two people who could have been my best friends. So what I'm saying is that maybe change is good. I feel closer to you now than I ever did before."

Jackie wasn't certain if those words were directed specifically at Cameron, but she wanted to believe that even with the tensions between them, she and Blair could be friends. Still, she could not take the risk and say the words. Instead, she just reached across Cameron's lap and grasped Blair's hand. Blair glanced at Jackie, but the smile she wore was tentative, as was the return grasp of her hand.

"We are now sisters by more than blood," said Cameron.

"Yes," said Jackie, trying hard to hold that truth near. No matter what traumas each of them had experienced, they now had something they had never had before—a common faith in God, a three-fold cord that made them stronger together than they had ever been as individuals. And the faith of Jackie's heart gave her assurance that the Great Physician would indeed heal all the gaping wounds of war.

Don't Miss

Homeward My Heart

Watch for this compelling book four in the
DAUGHTERS OF FORTUNE series!
Coming in the Spring of 2005

Danger and intrigue, courage and faith explode in a powerful climax, bringing the Hayes family saga to a stunning close.

The "war to end all wars" is over, and Cameron, in Nuremburg, Germany, is covering the war-crimes trial and celebrating her one-year anniversary—alone! Alex, now a well-respected doctor and war hero, is still not allowed to leave Russia. The past continues to haunt them and threatens to keep them apart—for how long?

Blair and Gary are in Washington, D. C., where Gary's position in the state department requires Blair's hostessing political dignitaries. They are happy, except for one thing. . . .

Jackie is in the U. S., struggling to cope with widowhood as a single mother to little Emi. Her daughter gives her joy and purpose, but Jackie is lonely without Sam and still feels the fallout of prejudice for having married a Japanese American. She fights resentment and works hard to maintain her Christian testimony.

Keagan Hayes has mellowed, and his marriage is better than it has ever been, but he suspects his wife is hiding something. Will Cecilia's secret tear down all they have built together over the years?